OF MOONS AND MONSTERS

BOOK ONE

WILLOW HADLEY

Edited by Taryn Gilliland
Cover Design by Psycat Studio

 Created with Vellum

This one's for me.

CHAPTER ONE

ISLA

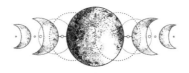

"COME ON, ISLA. PLEASE!"

I narrow my eyes and continue searching through the racks. Out of the hundreds of gowns Madame Deverell keeps in stock, one of these has to be perfect for our newest client.

"Please," my best friend Alistair whines again. "I'm begging you!"

My eyes catch on the gown I've been searching for, and a triumphant grin breaks out across my face. Lace, ruffles, beading, *floral accents*—this gown literally has it all, easily making it one of the gaudiest monstrosities I've ever had the misfortune of seeing. But this client is so goddamn extra she'll probably throw her money at Madame just for the chance to wear it.

Alistair steps in front of me, blocking the doorway of the storeroom. He clasps his hands together under his chin and sticks his bottom lip out in a ridiculous pout.

"Seriously, Al? You know Madame will kill me if she sees you back here or thinks I'm slacking off."

"That ancient hussy? Nah, you know she loves me." Al laughs and waves his hand dismissively. When he sees the unamused look on my face, he gives me an impish grin. "I'll leave if you just say yes!"

I purse my lips, fully prepared to tell him to fuck off. As if she was summoned by the simple mention of her name, Madame Deverell glides into the room with a haughty expression fixed upon her stunning face.

"Did I hear someone call me ancient?"

She tilts her head in a way that's almost predatory, her piercing blue eyes traveling over Alistair before turning to me. Her presence alone usually makes me feel anxious, but it's so much worse when she focuses all of her attention on me. Madame is one of the oldest, most powerful vampires I've ever met. I'm terrified of her, but I'm still constantly hoping to impress her.

The downside to having a best friend who's half-demon is being surrounded by supernatural creatures almost daily. It's a never-ending game of cat-and-mouse where I spend pretty much every minute of my life wondering if I'm about to be killed because someone's hungry or bored.

On the other hand, I met Madame because of Alistair. I've been working as her assistant for three years. Madame Deverell has been a fashion designer for something like two centuries. She changes her name and design style every few decades, of course. Her current fixation is on wedding gowns. While I'm not the biggest fan of some of her designs, she's brilliant at what she does and people love her work. It's amazing to watch these insane brides weep and bawl over these dresses, all while Madame sits back and spouts some bullshit about true love and charges tens of thousands of dollars.

Working for Madame also means I make enough money that I'll never have to worry about living on the streets or going hungry ever again.

"Of course not, Madame." I lower my gaze and nod my head respectfully. I hold up the dress for her approval and quickly add, "Alistair was just leaving."

Her eyes rove over the gown and she grins in wicked

delight. "Oh, *Gwyneth*! Yes, that's perfect. Why didn't I think of that? You certainly have a gift for reading people, Isla." Madame names all of her designs after her former victims. Sometimes I can't help wondering if there will ever be a gown called *Isla*. If there is, *god* I hope it doesn't have ruffles.

She takes the dress from me and spins around, gracefully sashaying back through the doorway of the storeroom. I quickly move to follow her, but I halt when she pauses to glance over her shoulder at me with a coy smile on her ruby-red lips. "Alistair can stay, so long as he makes himself useful."

Al punches the air triumphantly, and I grit my teeth at him in warning as I follow Madame. Al is usually pretty helpful with just about anything, so long as he has supervision and explicit directions. Still, he's lucky she's in a good mood.

The main floor of the shop is busy. There's a flurry of excitement while hopeful brides browse through the few selections Madame currently has shown on the floor. Tatiana, a pretty siren girl with rose-gold hair, stands in front of a full-length mirror with a client while she helps the bride-to-be choose a veil to go with her just-bought gown. Amber, the only other girl working today, stands behind the register while she assists another customer. Amber smiles lovingly at Madame as she passes before glaring at me.

Amber is Madame's lover this season, and she's human like I am. The difference is, I have never and will never hook up with my boss. Amber might be hoping she'll eventually be turned into a vampire, but I'm perfectly content with my mortality. Besides, it's much more likely that Amber won't live past the next few months. I fully expect for a new design in Madame's spring collection next year to bear the name *Amber*. It'll probably be some huge, puffy explosion of taffeta.

Alistair and I enter the private room where the newest bride-to-be is waiting with her entourage. Madame Deverell holds *Gwyneth* up with a flourish, and everyone in the room gasps.

"Oh my god," the bride exclaims, clapping her hands. "It's perfect! It's exactly what I imagined!"

Alistair gives me a cheeky smile, and I refrain from stomping on his foot with the heel of my Manolos. He finds the brides and wedding dresses just as obnoxious as I do, but these people are paying a lot of money. We need to look pretty and serene and supportive.

Everyone's attention is focused on the dress, thankfully. Well, *almost* everyone's attention. Two of the girls in the bridal party are staring at Madame with rosy cheeks, shy smiles, and heart-filled eyes. I totally get it. Madame is seriously gorgeous. Milky white skin, disarming blue eyes, sleek, white blonde hair cascading down her back, long legs, and a model-esque physique.

Alistair is pretty good-looking too, like most supernaturals. He's tall and lean with smooth skin, a permanently mischievous smile, and gorgeous, forest-green eyes. His messy black hair is shorter on the sides and longer on the top, so it's always falling into his eyes and giving him a boy-ish look, despite him being in his mid-twenties. But even he doesn't hold a candle to Madame when he's in the same room as her.

"So you're definitely going tonight, right?" Alistair whispers while everyone's distracted.

I roll my eyes and sigh quietly. "Why would I want to go to that? Unseelie parties are the fucking worst."

"Bryson will be there," he says.

At the mention of my douchebag werewolf ex-boyfriend, I narrow my eyes and scoff. "*Hard* no."

Madame beckons me to follow her into the fitting room so we can help the bride into the dress. For several minutes, I assist in pinning, buttoning, and lacing the bride into the mountain of fabric. Madame and I gush over how beautiful the girl is, and how well the gown fits her figure. As ostentatious as the dress is, it honestly looks pretty damn good on our client.

The moment we rejoin the bridal party, and the bride sees her reflection in the mirror, she bursts into tears. I wait a few seconds to make sure they're the *good* kind of tears, and Madame and I share a smug look. That's sixty-five grand in Madame's pocket, and a nice commission check for me.

Alistair and I help the bride choose her veil while Madame handles the payment with the bride's mother. The whole process takes a little over an hour, and I'm left in the fitting room to clean up with Al while we await the next appointment.

"Way to upsell her with that tiara." I quirk a smile at my best friend.

He flutters his eyelashes and smirks. "What can I say? Women find me charming."

I laugh and don't bother disagreeing with him. Alistair *is* charming. It's just that sometimes, that charm gets him into a lot of trouble.

"So, is there seriously nothing I can bribe you with so you'll go to this party tonight?"

"Alistair." I groan. I can't believe he's bringing it up again. I'm really not into parties in general, and being around so many supernaturals at the same time makes me super anxious. Especially when they're inebriated. If Bryson's going to be there with his stupid mate, I want to be as far away as possible. "Why do you want to go so badly? There will be other parties."

He doesn't answer right away, pretending to be wholly focused on stacking the boxes of shoes we let the bride try on. Finally, he glances up at me with a shy smile and admits, "Because Thaddeus will be there."

My eyes widen in disbelief, and an incredulous laugh escapes my throat. "No. Absolutely not! He was so awful to you! Why would you want to go anywhere near that dickhead?"

Thaddeus is another powerful vampire here in New York,

though he's nowhere near as old or as wealthy as Madame Deverell. He and Alistair dated on and off for about a year. Thaddeus was never faithful, and he constantly belittled my best friend. He loved to call Alistair a *half-breed*, as if Al had any say in his parentage.

"I know." Al's eyes darken for a split second. He shakes it off and gives me a goofy half-smile. "I promise I don't want him back. I just want to make him jealous. He called me last week and said he missed me, and I lied and said I'd moved on."

This already sounds like a terrible idea. I pinch the bridge of my nose and sigh exaggeratedly. "Can't you find a pixie to be your escort? Or like, literally anyone you're attracted to who might convincingly make him jealous?"

"Who says I don't find you attractive?" He smirks, his eyes roaming up and down my body in an obvious manner. When I make a gagging sound and flip him off, he chuckles. "I never totally understood why, but Thaddeus has always been super jealous of you. I think it's just because he's a controlling jerk who never wanted me to spend time with anyone but him."

There's never been anything romantic between Alistair and me. Sure, we may have fooled around when we were teenagers, but only because we were lonely and curious. He and I have known each other since we were young and were placed in the same toxic, abusive foster home. We've been homeless together, we've done shameful things to survive and protect one another, and we've seen each other at our darkest. Alistair is the only family I have, and I love him like he's half of my soul. The fact that Thaddeus was jealous of our friendship makes me furious.

And suddenly, I want to go to this party more than anything. Screw the fact that my ex will be there sucking face with some trampy fox-shifter. I never liked Thaddeus, and if I can spend one evening pissing him off, I'm game.

"Alright, fine. I'll go."

"Yes!" Alistair exclaims gleefully and pulls me into a hug. "God, I fucking love you, and I owe you so much for this."

We jump apart when Madame pokes her head in the door a few seconds later. Neither of us says a word as she stares at us with her dazzling, predatory gaze. Eventually, her mouth turns up into a terrifying grin and she steps fully into the room.

"I couldn't help but overhear your conversation, darlings. And I have to agree. I've never liked that little snake, Thaddeus. If you plan on making him jealous, Isla, you should let me dress you."

While I may not be totally, *completely* sold on many of the wedding gowns I help swindle people into buying, I'm still an absolute slave to fashion. And Madame Deverell knows it.

CHAPTER TWO
ISLA

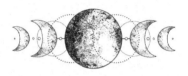

ANOTHER VACANT-EYED HUMAN GIRL OFFERS ME A GLASS OF faery wine, and I decline for what feels like the hundredth time. I sigh when she walks away to offer glasses to the other party guests. We've only been here for half an hour, and I'm already kicking myself for giving into Al's whining and pleading.

The last time I drank faery wine, I blacked out for two days. Faery wine tastes incredible, and it takes away all of your fear and inhibitions so you feel like you can do or say anything. It's crazy addictive for humans, which is why the Unseelie Lord throwing this party has so many human servants. It makes me feel extra prickly and uncomfortable every time I come into contact with one of them.

"Here," Alistair says as he hands me a glass of something bubbly. When I raise my eyebrows in question, he grins. "It's just regular champagne. You need to relax, Isla."

I take a sip and ignore his comment, letting my eyes wander around the room at all of the supernaturals present. I'm an idiot for agreeing to come here just to make some vampire prick jealous. I really want to leave, but we haven't even caught a glimpse of Thaddeus yet.

"Come on." Al wraps his arm around my waist, rubbing his hand over my lower back in a way that would probably appear intimate to anyone else. He looks down at me with one of his signature mischievous smiles and says, "Let's go and mingle. You look so fucking stunning tonight, I'm sure we'll make more than just Thaddeus jealous."

I do look pretty damn good, if I don't say so myself. The dress Madame lent to me is a long, silky, blood-red gown with an indecently low neckline and a slit that goes almost all the way up my thigh. The material clings to every one of my curves in the most delicious way, and my strappy heels add several inches to my height and make my legs look miles long. My dark brown hair cascades down my back and over my shoulders in perfect waves, and my eye makeup is dark and dramatic.

At that moment, a fae male walks by and slows his steps as his eyes run over me appreciatively. A smug smile forms on my lips, and I lean into Al's touch as he places a feather-light kiss against my shoulder. The fae male makes a growling sound and throws his drink back completely before snatching a new glass from the closest server.

Seeing the male's reaction makes a tiny thrill rush through my body, and I laugh when Alistair begins leading me through the house. After things ended with Bryson, I promised myself I'd never get romantically involved with another supernatural. But maybe I should rethink the idea of getting *physically* involved with any. It feels good to know some of the beings here find me attractive. It makes me feel powerful, even though I'm by far one of the weakest creatures here.

Alistair and I make our way around the party, talking to anyone we vaguely recognize and introducing ourselves to strangers who don't look too intimidating. People usually love Al the moment they meet him, which is why he's always been so welcomed into the supernatural community. I'm nowhere near as outgoing as my best friend, but I still make an effort to mingle. A few supernaturals are impressed when they hear I work for Madame Deverell, but most of them mostly just seem amused to see another human girl trying to insert herself into their world. Throughout the evening, I continue to receive heated glances from various male creatures. I'm tempted to take one of them home with me tonight.

"Are you sure Thaddeus was supposed to be here? It's getting pretty late," I say to Alistair a few hours later, glancing at an ornate grandfather clock in the corner of the room we're currently occupying. It's well after midnight. Thaddeus may be an arrogant bastard, but even he's not normally this late to such exclusive events.

The party has transformed from a formal, somewhat stuffy affair into something dark and chaotic. Expensive and timeless pieces of art and furniture are broken and scattered throughout the lavish apartment, groups of supernaturals watch on and laugh as humans make fools of themselves after drinking too much faery wine, and there are people having sex literally fucking *everywhere*. Unseelie parties are usually all the same.

"I know." Alistair sighs, squeezing my hip affectionately. "I'm seriously pretty pissed about it. I've been so focused on keeping an eye out for him that I haven't even given a second look to anyone here. And we've been getting a ton of attention, so it's a fucking waste."

I gently grab his chin and force him to meet my eyes. With a sympathetic smile, I brush my fingers over his jaw. "You never know. I'm sure you've left quite an impression on some of the people here, and you'll probably run into them again. Do you want to just call it an early night?"

He nods hesitantly, shifting his gaze away from mine. "Yeah, but let's introduce ourselves to Lord Rian first."

It doesn't take us long to find the host of the party, Lord Rian of the Unseelie Court. We've seen him several times throughout the evening, but we've kept our distance until now.

Meeting powerful and influential supernaturals like him can be extremely intimidating, and oftentimes dangerous.

Lord Rian is holding court in his library, surrounded by various supernaturals tittering and fluttering their eyelashes at him. He stands tall, with a smirk on his handsome face and a drink in his hand. His eyes land on us the second Al and I enter the room, and nervous butterflies erupt in my stomach.

The fae Lord brushes off the female who was hanging on his shoulder and begins walking toward us. Alistair's arm tightens around my waist, so I know he's probably freaking out just as much as I am. Have we accidentally offended the Lord before we even managed to introduce ourselves?

"Finally," the fae Lord says when he reaches us. His voice is deep and seductive, and his citrine eyes flit back and forth between me and Alistair as his feral smile widens. "I've been waiting for the two of you to approach me all night."

Alarm bells go off in my head, but I make sure to keep my expression composed. However, Lord Rian's words seem to have the opposite effect on my best friend. I watch as Alistair's gaze becomes heated, and he bites his lip before looking up at the much taller male in front of us.

"Our apologies, milord. We would have come to find you much earlier if we'd known you were interested."

Lord Rian's eyes flash with wicked delight at Alistair's boldness. He chuckles deeply and holds his hand out. "Call me Rian, please. What's your name, little demon?"

"Alistair."

I nearly groan when my best friend willingly gives his name without a thought and shakes hands with the Unseelie Lord. It's practically the first rule of dealing with the fae. Don't give your true name without asking for something in return unless you're looking to be tricked or bewitched.

I hold my tongue because I'm only a human in the presence of a powerful, immortal creature, and Lord Rian hasn't addressed me directly. When he turns his gaze on me a moment later, my cheeks flush of their own accord. I'm ridiculously anxious and wondering how the hell we managed to snag his attention. I've made sure to keep Alistair by my side all night, and I haven't let him get into any mischief like he might usually do otherwise.

"Your pet is absolutely divine," Rian purrs seductively. He brings his hand up and caresses my cheek softly, letting the back of his fingers trail down my jaw and along my collarbone. As nervous as I am, his touch makes me shiver as my skin tingles pleasantly and my nipples harden in arousal.

"Isla is my best friend. *Not* my pet." Alistair's voice hardens slightly, losing all trace of flirtation as he pulls me into his side possessively. He can't stand hearing other supernaturals refer to me as a pet, and he's quick to become angry and defensive whenever it happens. It doesn't bother me nearly as much, but I still appreciate Alistair always standing up for me and insisting I'm his equal.

But *god*, I wish I could hit him right now. He probably just offended our host, *and* he gave my fucking name away for free!

Lord Rian blinks, appearing both confused and intrigued. His smile only grows wider though, if possible, and he holds his hand out for me the same way he did for Alistair. "I'm sorry. It was rude of me to make any assumptions. I hope you'll forgive me, Isla."

"Of course." I cautiously place my hand in his. My skin tingles again, and Rian suddenly looks a lot more appealing than he already did. I force a smile onto my face. "It's a pleasure to meet you, Lord Rian."

"Just Rian, if you don't mind." He keeps his eyes locked on mine as he brings my hand up to his mouth. He softly brushes his lips over my knuckles, and I shiver in pleasure at the intimacy of the gesture. This guy is *good*.

"We were just leaving, actually," I blurt out. I feel breathless, and I'm almost positive he's using some kind of magic on us right now. The last thing I need is to get swept up in some fae Lord's mischievous game.

Alistair's entire body stiffens, and his arm tightens around my waist. At the same moment, Rian's eyes widen and he looks genuinely alarmed. The fae lord squeezes my hand gently and steps the tiniest bit closer to us.

"Leaving? But it's still so early! Surely I can convince you to stay?" His voice sounds aloof and almost playful, but there's something in his expression that makes it seem as though he's actually panicking at the idea of us leaving.

"Isla hates parties," Alistair says. I purse my lips when he meets my eyes, and he gives me one of his most charming smiles. "But I'm sure we can stay for just a little while longer?"

It's true that I'm not the biggest fan of parties, and especially supernatural parties. I don't mind smaller, more intimate gatherings, but I'd almost always rather stay home reading a book or watching Netflix if I can get away with it. Still, it's just like Al to paint me as the controlling villain here, even though he literally just agreed to leave early not ten minutes ago. I make a face at him, silently telling him he owes me. In response, Al sticks his bottom lip out at me in an exaggerated pout and gives me the most ridiculous puppy-dog eyes. I know he only wants to stay because he wants to hook up with Rian, but he could at least be a little more subtle.

"We can stay," I finally say to our host. I should probably figure out a way to back off soon though so that Alistair can have him to himself. Then again, Rian is showing a suspicious amount of interest in *both* of us, so maybe I'll stick around for a bit longer.

Rian's entire face lights up. He looks so young and happy, but I know it's entirely possible he's centuries older than us. He grabs Alistair's free hand and continues holding mine as he begins walking backwards, pulling us with him.

"Wonderful." He practically growls, his eyes flitting back and forth between me and Alistair. For the first time since

Rian approached us, I realize how many people are watching us. I feel my face warm up at all of the attention, and my heart beats just a little faster as Rian leads us to an armchair in the corner of the library.

He sits down gracefully, simultaneously pulling me and Alistair onto his lap. When a few other supernaturals step closer and surround us, Rian's eyes turn feral and he shows his sharp, fae teeth as he growls at them. We're given plenty of space after that, but there are still dozens of eyes watching us from afar.

I'm too slow to mask the shock on my face. The intimidating fae lord wraps his arm around my waist and leans forward to place a kiss on my shoulder. He grins up at me, his expression a weird mix between excitement and uncertainty.

"Don't be afraid, little human. I can see you're the cautious one in this relationship, but I promise there's no need to worry while you're here." He glances away quickly to nod his head at a nearby server, and then turns back toward me with a wicked smile. "Have you tried the faery wine?"

"She doesn't drink it," Alistair answers for me, stealing Rian's attention. "If you don't mind my asking, why were you waiting for us to approach you? There are a lot of guests here tonight, and I'm sure plenty of people have been dying to meet you. You haven't been in the city very long, if I remember correctly?"

Alistair has been staring at Rian with major freaking heart eyes for a solid five minutes, and I worry he's already stuck in whatever spell or charm the fae Lord is trying to weave. I'm immensely relieved to hear that my best friend still has some sense about him, and that he's at least slightly suspicious of Rian's motives too.

Rian's mouth curves into a roguish smirk, and he pulls Alistair closer to his chest while he slowly rubs his other hand over my hip. "Because the two of you are the prettiest things I've seen since I came to New York. I arrogantly assumed you'd introduce yourselves to me much earlier in the night like everyone else has. When that didn't happen, I came to wait in the library since I noticed you perusing my collection of books a few times throughout the evening."

Fae can't lie, technically, though they usually try to get around that by speaking vaguely and prettily. Rian's bluntness is seriously throwing me for a fucking loop, and I don't know whether to be flattered or more worried than I was already.

It's pretty obvious Alistair is thrilled. He wraps his arm around Rian's neck and leans close so that their lips are almost touching. "Impossible. You must have looked in a mirror at some point, my Lord."

I watch in amazement as Rian's face reddens, all the way from his cheeks to the tips of his pointed ears. His lips part slightly, and his eyelids droop as he stares back at Alistair. I've never seen any supernatural look so flustered. Not even Al. I smile to myself and decide maybe this strange, fae Lord is being genuine after all. When a server walks over with a tray of normal champagne instead of faery wine, I happily accept a glass.

Rian clears his throat and grabs two more glasses, one for him and one for Al. With a smile that's almost shy, he glances between us as he raises his glass to his lips. "So, how long have the two of you been together?"

"We're not together. Not like that." I giggle with a slight shake of my head.

Alistair throws his entire drink back, and responds candidly, "Isla and I grew up together. We were placed in the same human foster home when we were young, and we've stuck together ever since."

"How old are you?" Rian asks in a stunned whisper.

Seeing the fae Lord become so unnerved and act so strangely is giving me a crazy weird confidence boost. He's clearly attracted to me *and* Alistair, and Alistair's into him too. I can't deny Rian is insanely hot, even by supernatural standards. He's tall and muscular with broad shoulders, and his chest is hard and sculpted. I can easily imagine how toned he is under his clothing, just from sitting so close to him like this. His citrine eyes are ridiculously pretty, and his golden hair is styled to look just the perfect amount of messy.

It's almost definitely a stupid decision on my part, but I decide to play along with whatever game Rian is playing. I lean closer to him the same way Al did, and I run my hand through his hair when I answer his question. "We're both twenty-four, but I'm a few months older than Al."

"So young," he whispers again, a bit of a growl in his voice. His gaze lands on my wrist as I thread my fingers through his hair, and he lets go of my hip to grab my hand instead. He brushes his thumb over the tiny brand there and frowns. "What is this?"

I look down at Madame Deverell's initials that were carved into my skin with a spell three years ago and shrug. "It's an insurance policy, of sorts. My boss is a vampire, and this is supposed to protect me from being bitten by any other vamps as long as I'm under contract."

"I see," Rian says. But he looks pissed as he continues staring at my wrist for a few moments. He doesn't say anything more about it, turning to face Alistair instead. "And you, little demon? Are you under contract with anyone?"

Alistair shakes his head. "No. Sometimes I help Isla at her job, but only when Madame Deverell is in a good mood. She's a fashion designer, and she's super picky and anal about everything. That's why she likes Isla so much. They're both control freaks."

Rian laughs in surprise, and I give my best friend a fake-offended look. "Hey, don't pretend you don't love me for it too."

"Of course I do, darling." Alistair places his hand on the back of my head and strokes my hair affectionately. He uses his other hand to cup Rian's cheek and keeps his eyes on the

WILLOW HADLEY

fae male while he speaks. "Now, I think Rian here is very selfish for wanting both of us, Isla. But I'm willing to share him with you, if you're up for it."

Before Rian is given a chance to acknowledge that, Alistair kisses him. And he doesn't just give him a little peck either. He kisses him passionately, intimately, *possessively*. He puts his hands all over Rian, and Rian responds by growling into Al's mouth and pulling both of us closer. My legs are twined with Al's, with how close the three of us are, and the slit on my dress has ridden up so my entire leg is bare and on display. I can feel Rian's dick harden against my ass while his hand wanders up and down my side, and his fingers trail along the bare skin of my thigh.

Watching Rian and Alistair kiss while having them so impossibly close to me is a major turn on. It's extremely tempting to accept Al's proposal to share Rian for the night, so I wait patiently for my turn to kiss the Unseelie Lord.

Feeling brazen, I grind my hips against Rian's hard length and lean forward to run my tongue along the ridge of his pointed ear. Rian squeezes me tightly and growls as he finally pulls away from Al, and he stares at me with lust-filled eyes.

"Fuck," he breathes huskily just before he kisses my neck, and I gasp in pleasure as my eyes flutter shut. I'm far from being innocent or virginal, but this is one of the most erotic moments I've ever experienced. It almost makes it better that we're in a room surrounded by strangers and acquaintances. Bryson rarely ever even held my hand in public, let alone kissed me.

As Rian continues to lavish my neck with kisses, I tilt my head back and open my eyes to see just how many people are actually paying attention to us. I meet Alistair's gaze first, and he smiles mischievously. I can't help smiling back. I'm not sexually or romantically interested in my best friend at all, but it might be kind of fun to share a guy between the two of us. Just this once.

I gasp when Rian's teeth graze my skin where my neck meets my shoulder, and he pulls away with a deep chuckle. My eyes roam around the library, taking in all the guests lingering nearby. There are plenty of supernaturals watching us enviously, and even more watching us for their own entertainment. I see a few groups and couples hooking up throughout the room, and more than one male with his hand down his pants while he watches the display between me, Alistair, and Rian.

"I know you're both very young," Rian purrs. "But I'm assuming you're aware some supernaturals have soul mates?"

Before I can turn back around to face him, curious as to why he would bring up soul mates at a time like this, I catch sight of the one person I've been dreading running into all night.

Bryson is standing only a few yards away from us with *Amelia*—his chosen mate.

My entire body tenses, and suddenly all I can focus on is the newly mated couple. Bryson and I dated for over a year, and I naively assumed someday he would choose *me* to be his mate. Unlike other supernaturals, like fae or witches, it's much more common for shifters to form mating bonds simply because they get to choose who they pair with.

I loved Bryson so much, and I thought we were happy together. I was completely blindsided when he broke up with me a couple of months ago, and absolutely fucking devastated when he chose Amelia to be his lifelong mate just a few short weeks later. I can't even blame Amelia, as much as I'd like to. She could be the nicest person for all I know, but to her and the rest of the shifter community, I'm just another dumb human trying to fit into a world where I don't belong.

Bryson and Amelia are making out heavily, and he has her pinned against a bookcase. Rian says something to me, but my ears are fucking ringing. Bryson would never have touched me like that in public, and I finally realize it's because he was ashamed of me. Why is he even here? This apartment is fucking huge, and there's no way Bryson didn't see me when he walked into the room.

I cry out when there's a sudden, sharp pain in my hand, and I look down in shock to find that my champagne glass has shattered into several pieces.

"Are you okay, love?" Rian's voice is full of concern, and he cradles my hand in his while he waves over one of his servants.

Someone rushes over to pick up the pieces of glass that have fallen to the floor, and I realize I'm bleeding all over Rian. Tears of shame and embarrassment prick at my eyes. I can't bring myself to speak or look up at him.

Alistair gently takes my hand from Rian and touches his fingertip to my injury. Through blurry eyes, I watch him bring his finger to his lips where he licks a drop of my blood. Just a few moments later, I feel Alistair's magic embrace me while the cuts on my hand heal.

"He's so not worth it, Isla. And god, you're so much hotter than she is," Alistair whispers.

"I know," I tell him, even though I'm not sure how much I believe him right now. I force myself to meet Rian's eyes, and my heart clenches when I see the distraught expression on his face. "I'm sorry for ruining the moment. I just need to excuse myself for a bit, if you don't mind."

Rian doesn't protest when I climb off of his lap. I keep my head high and my expression composed as I walk out of the library, and I even manage to keep myself from glancing at Bryson and Amelia.

CHAPTER THREE
ISLA

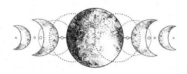

THE APARTMENT IS ABSOLUTE MADNESS. THERE'S MAGIC, mischief, and debauchery everywhere I turn while I look for somewhere quiet to hide. I just need a few minutes alone to brood and compose myself after seeing Bryson and Amelia together. I come across a balcony door and peer around cautiously. The curtains are shredded in some places, and they're partially torn down from their hangings. Nobody's nearby, and I don't see anyone when I glance outside. I quietly slip out and shut the door behind me, exhaling heavily when I'm finally alone and away from the ruckus of the party.

The autumn air is chilly, but it feels nice against my skin. I close my eyes and lean my head back against the glass of the balcony door, relishing in the cool breeze and the sounds of the never-sleeping city. After several minutes, I open my eyes to take in the absolutely stunning view and all the flashing lights. Alistair and I live in a cute two-bedroom in Chelsea, and while it's super nice—way nicer than anything either of us could have ever imagined when we were growing up—it totally doesn't compare to Rian's fancy Upper East Side apartment.

Feeling a bit calmer now, though not any less embarrassed or pathetic, I sigh and mumble to myself. "You're such an idiot..."

"I hope you're not talking about me."

I jump in surprise at the voice and whip my head up, looking frantically around the balcony until my eyes land on a guy. It's no wonder I didn't see him at first. He's sitting on the railing of the balcony, off to the side where there's not very much light, with his feet hanging over the edge.

"I'm sorry." I clear my throat. "I didn't realize anyone else was out here."

"I figured as much," he says. He has a slight accent, like he might be French or Dutch, but it's difficult to tell. That's usually the case with supernaturals, especially the older and more traveled they are.

He stretches his arms above his head and turns like he's going to get down. Instead, he stands up, balancing on the railing as he takes long, dramatic strides across it until he reaches my side of the balcony. There's more light here, and I can see his features much more clearly as he gives me this smug little smile and jumps down so he's only a few feet in front of me.

"Fae parties are the absolute worst, right? I still can't decide if I hate Seelie or Unseelie parties more."

I can't help smiling at the stranger before me. Now that I can see him better, it's obvious he's a witch. He's tall and thin with messy, coppery-red hair, dark eyes, and thick eyebrows. He's wearing a vintage black suit and jacket buttoned up haphazardly. He's barefoot and wearing a god-awful amount of jewelry—tons of layered necklaces, stacked bracelets, rings covering his fingers, and several earrings dangling from both ears. He's cute, and a little arrogant. Most witches I've met are incredibly blunt, and I always find that so refreshing.

"Unseelie are worse," I say. "They start off all prim and proper, and slowly throughout the night, they unravel into chaos and complete fuckery. At least with Seelie, they start off acting like savages. There are less surprises that way."

"I suppose you're right." The witch grins. He looks me up and down quickly, though not in a vulgar way. "So, human girl. Did you come here hoping to convince someone to turn you immortal?"

He doesn't sound rude or judgmental, but I still bristle at the question. "I have no desire to become immortal, thank you."

"Is that so?" His grin widens as he crosses his arms. "So what, then? Just realized how incredibly stupid and dangerous it is to hang around supernaturals? You should go back to your monotonous human life and pretend to be ignorant while you still have the chance."

"It's a bit late for that." I chuckle. Something about his presence and the directness of his words makes me feel at ease. In the back of my mind, I know that's probably not a good thing, but I still find myself relaxing and letting my guard down. "Why are you hiding out here, anyway?"

He tilts his head and holds his pinky out to me. "Secret for a secret? I'll tell you, but only if you tell me why you're hiding out here first."

Even more of my usual anxiety slips away. This is how things are supposed to be done in the supernatural world, and I'm relieved this guy is following the rules. I twine my pinky with his, and a tiny jolt of electricity shoots up my arm. I honestly don't think much of it, since he's a witch and I always expect supernaturals to use their magic around me.

The witch drops my hand like he's been burned and narrows his eyes, looking me up and down like he's truly seeing me for the first time. I wait for him to explain himself, but after a few moments, he smiles at me like nothing happened. "Well?"

My cheeks flush, slightly from embarrassment, and also from the dismissal of his reaction to touching me. But I technically made a deal, and talking to this witch is still better than going back inside to face Bryson or getting wrapped up in the intensity of Lord Rian again.

"I'm here with my best friend tonight because he wanted to make his ex jealous," I start, and then I bite my lip and sigh as I roll my eyes. "But my ex-boyfriend is here tonight too, and I didn't realize how painful it would be to run into him, and to see him with his mate."

"Ah, I see."

There's a surprising amount of sympathy in his voice, and his eyes soften as he blinks down at me. I exhale, and before I've really thought it through, I begin ranting and unleashing all the things I've kept bottled up in regards to Bryson and our relationship.

"He's such a fucking douche, it makes me want to scream. I can't believe I wasted so much time on him, you know? We dated for over a year, and I did *everything* for him. Everything he asked, and everything I could think to make him happy. And I never asked for a damn thing in return. After all that time together, he chose someone else to be his mate. He broke up with me by saying he was ready to settle down and choose a life partner, and *god*, I thought he was proposing! When I said that, he actually fucking laughed. He said he couldn't believe I ever thought he'd settle down with a human."

Tears form in the corners of my eyes. I look up and quickly try to blink them away, but a few still manage to leak out. The witch steps closer and brushes his thumbs over my cheeks, wiping the tears away. I'm totally mortified when I meet his eyes, but he simply opens his arms and offers me a hug without saying a word.

I feel awkward about it at first, but I still step forward into his embrace. He wraps his arms around me tightly, and I suddenly feel so warm and cared for. I know that's probably because he's using some kind of witchy magic on me, but I'm past the point of caring right now.

"Your ex is a shifter, I take it?" he asks. When I nod, he scoffs. "Shifters are even worse than fae. Trust me, you dodged a bullet with that one."

An unladylike snort escapes my throat, and I tilt my head up to smile at him in surprise. "You're probably right."

"I usually am." He smirks, swaying us back and forth gently. "I'm Matthieu."

"Isla," I say. We stand together like that in a comfortable silence until I remember our deal. I clear my throat and say, "Your turn. What are you doing at an Unseelie party, and why are you hiding?"

Matthieu doesn't answer right away. He continues to stare down at me like he's trying to work out a puzzle. I'm starting to feel kind of self-conscious about our entire interaction when he finally smirks. "Lord Rian and I are very old friends, and he asked me to be here tonight."

I pull back a little, but he keeps his arms around me. I look him over again, smiling at his odd appearance. "I can see that, actually. Both of you are a bit strange."

His eyes crinkle and he barks out a loud, boisterous laugh. "I'm almost afraid to ask what's given you that impression."

I giggle, but I don't bother explaining myself. I'm not sure I'd even be able to put it into words, anyway. It's just that I have such a weird feeling around Matthieu and Rian, and both of them seem surprisingly genuine. That's not something I ever experience with supernaturals, aside from Alistair.

"If you're such good friends with Lord Rian, why aren't you inside causing mischief with him right now?" I ask teasingly.

Matthieu's expression sobers, and he bows his head and smiles shyly. He still hasn't let go of me. "Did you know that fae and witches have mates too? It's different for us than it is for shifters. Instead of choosing our mate, our mate is chosen for us. It can take centuries to find that person, and many of us never find them at all."

I'm honestly taken aback by the turn in conversation, and my throat suddenly feels dry. "Yes, I knew that."

He raises one of his hands and messes his hair up even more, and the nervous smile on his face makes him look ridiculously young and vulnerable. "It's a long story as to why, but Rian and I are meant to share a mate. I haven't seen the idiot in a few years, but we had a dream recently that our mate was in New York. Rian has been blowing my phone up all night because he's certain they're here tonight."

I take a step back from him and look over my shoulder at the balcony door. "Seriously? You're hiding out here when you're possibly, like, two seconds away from meeting your soulmate?"

"Hey, that's a lot of pressure." When I turn back around to face him, Matthieu is legitimately pouting. "Besides, I worried our mate might feel overwhelmed or ambushed. You met Rian, didn't you? He can be a bit intense."

"A bit?" I snicker. And then I realize what he's actually telling me, and my heart jumps into my throat. Rian was saying something about mates before I caught sight of Bryson and ran away, and he was so forward with me and Alistair. I widen my eyes at Matthieu, feeling anxious and panicked and hopeful all at once. "You don't think it's me, do you?"

Matthieu opens his mouth like he's going to say something, but he just stares at me silently with wide eyes. Eventually, he clears his throat. "You might not feel it since you're human, but there's something between us. I'm not sure if it's a mate bond or not."

"Okay." I nod my head and swallow a few times, feeling equal parts disappointed and relieved.

I don't want to be someone's mate. After the way things ended with Bryson, I seriously can't imagine tying myself to anyone so permanently like that. And getting involved with *any* supernatural again would just end in disaster for me. At the same time, I do feel a weird pull towards Matthieu even though I know almost nothing about him. There's an idiotic part of me that feels heartbroken to hear it might not be because of a mate bond. I totally blame Matthieu's witchy magic and all the champagne I've had to drink.

"Okay?" Matthieu echoes me with a slightly incredulous laugh.

I cross my arms and narrow my eyes at him. "What am I supposed to say to that, exactly? I'm still kind of processing here. At least now I know why you and Rian seem so weird."

His eyes light up with amusement, and he bites his lip to hide his grin. "I'm sorry. You're absolutely right. I really don't know what I expected you to say. I'm not even sure what to think, to be honest."

Before he gives me a chance to respond, he steps closer to me and grabs my hand. I feel that tiny, electric zap travel up my arm again, but Matthieu doesn't let go this time. We hold eye contact, and his mouth slowly turns up in a sweet, joyous smile.

"I think I like you though. I'm excited to figure out this bond between us, whatever it is. Is it safe for me to assume you had a similar experience with Rian earlier?"

"Not exactly." I giggle nervously. I drop my gaze from his and peer over my shoulder at the balcony door. "My best friend and I were making out with him before I was distracted by my ex and came out here to hide."

Even when Matthieu was holding me, I didn't feel the desire to stick my tongue down his throat. And he hasn't been flirting with me at all. I honestly assumed Rian had been using some kind of lust-spell earlier to make me feel so open to his advances. It's possible that just had more to do with whatever bond is between us, if it's true he and Matthieu are meant to share a mate.

"Really?" Matthieu grins broadly, looking positively delighted by my admission. "I suppose I shouldn't be surprised. That sounds just like Rian, the old bastard."

Now that I think about it, what about Alistair? Is it possible he's their mate? Or does he at least have some weird bond with these guys the same way I supposedly do? I honestly don't know how he'd feel about that—if he'd be excited or wary, or *what*. I'm not even entirely sure I believe everything Matthieu's told me. I've been around the supernatural world long enough that I'm not very shocked by magic or things like mate bonds anymore, but I'm not a totally gullible idiot either.

"I think I need to find my friend." I take a cautious step backwards, away from Matthieu.

He blinks like I've confused him. But then he seems to realize the direction my thoughts have taken, because his entire expression lights up. "I think I'd like to meet your friend too."

"Um..." How do I tell him I want to talk to Alistair alone first, without offending him or hurting his feelings? Matthieu and Rian have been sweet and kind to me, and they seem excited at the possibility of meeting their mate. It just feels like there's a lot happening all at once.

The balcony door crashes open, and Rian steps out with a panicked look on his face. He doesn't see me right away, as I'm standing behind the door and partially hidden by the darkness. "Matthieu, thank god. I've been looking for you for ages. This is an absolute disaster!"

Matthieu smirks at me and then tilts his head at Rian. "Hello, old friend. What sort of disaster are we talking about here?"

"Our mates, of course!" Rian growls and tugs at his hair dramatically. "Everything was going so well, and they're both absolutely precious. But then one of them cut her hand and ran away, and the other one got into a fight with a werewolf. I have no idea what the fuck is going on or how I'm supposed to keep track of them."

My mind goes a bit fuzzy for a moment at hearing him

refer to me and Alistair as his mates. Until I realize what he just said about Al, and I step forward where he can see me and widen my eyes in alarm.

"Al got into a fight? Is he okay?"

"Isla!" Rian gapes at me and shakes his head incredulously. "Have you been out here with Matthieu this whole time?"

He turns and gives Matthieu this completely ridiculous look of betrayal, and Matthieu laughs. "Don't get upset at me. She found me on her own."

I grab Rian's hand, hoping he'll focus on me instead of whatever petty jealousy he's feeling. "Please, where's Al?"

Rian's entire demeanor softens, and he threads our fingers together. "He's okay. I left him in my bedroom and asked him to wait there for me. He said the werewolf was your ex-boyfriend?"

My face heats up, and I grimace as I lower my gaze. That's just like something Alistair would do—get into a fight on my behalf when I'm not there to cool him down or talk him out of it. A tiny, vindictive part of me hopes he got Bryson good, but the logical part of my brain knows he's totally not worth the effort or the drama. I hate that I'm the cause of such a scene at a party like this.

"I'm sorry," I mumble quietly.

"No, no," Rian says softly. He pulls me a little closer, hesitantly, and brings his other hand up to tenderly stroke my hair. "You have nothing to be sorry for. I'll make sure the shifter is black-listed in the fae community after tonight. I'm just so relieved you're okay."

Matthieu steps closer and bends down slightly so we're more eye-level. He's still smiling, but there's no trace of the arrogance he was showing when Rian first stepped outside. "Is your friend a human like you are?"

Being so close to Rian and Matthieu at the same time is incredibly nerve-racking. It's like my body feels comfortable and relaxed, and I'm still crazy attracted to Rian. But my brain is telling me not to trust these feelings, that these males are dangerous and powerful, and I have no business getting involved with them. Besides, this mate thing is totally confusing and overwhelming. The more I think about it, the more anxious I feel. God, I just need to get out of here and talk to Al!

"Alistair is half-human, half-demon. We're not really sure what kind of demon his father was."

Rian smiles at Matthieu as he continues to hold me. "I'd say quite a powerful demon, just from the short time I've spent with him. He has healing magic, and he can summon fire."

"Impressive," Matthieu hums thoughtfully.

Rian's eyes heat up, and a deep growl escapes his throat. "Just wait until you see him. God, wait until you see them *together.*"

Matthieu chuckles and grins mischievously at me. My emotions are completely at war. I can't decide if I'm more turned on at Rian's seductive voice and flattering comments, or if I'm just straight up fucking embarrassed.

"I'm not entirely sure Isla's my mate," Matthieu says, shrugging apologetically.

"What?" Rian scoffs. His eyes scan over me from head to toe, and his expression is so loving when he meets my eyes again. "How is that possible? Just looking at her is making me feel insane."

I pull away from him. He sounds so sure, but how can you even tell someone's your mate or not? It's too much for me to understand or try to deal with right now.

"Listen, I just…" I back away slowly and hold my hands up. "I really need to find Alistair. Maybe we can talk about this all later when I'm sober. It's just a lot to take in."

Both males look extremely guilty, and Rian runs his hand through his golden hair as he clears his throat. "Right, yes. That's completely understandable. My bedroom is down the hallway right past the library, last door on the left. You're both free to sleep there tonight if you'd like, and I promise not to bother you again until you're ready to talk."

That's actually an incredibly sweet offer. Butterflies are writhing nervously in my stomach, but I offer Lord Rian a grateful smile as I turn to make my way back inside.

Matthieu jumps forward and stops me, cupping my face between his hands. He grins down at me and asks, "Promise not to sneak out or disappear without saying goodbye?"

I'm not stupid enough to make a promise to a witch, even if he seems sweet and says we share a connection. I raise my eyebrows at him defiantly. "I'm not very hard to find."

I leave them on the balcony, and I force myself not to look back over my shoulder as I make my way through the apartment. In the short time I spent outside, the party has become even more chaotic. Someone's turned on some modern music, and it's so fucking loud that the bass is making the floor and all the furniture shake. People are dancing and grinding everywhere, and the unmistakable scent of sex, alcohol, and magic is lingering in every room.

I step carefully over a broken vase and grimace at a couple of goblins who are having sex on the floor a few feet away. After passing several more similar obstacles, I finally reach the hallway just past the library.

There are a couple of people standing and talking in the hallway, but it's not crowded like the rest of the apartment is. I breathe a sigh of relief as I walk toward the door Rian said was his. Hopefully Al really is okay, and we can have a long chat about everything that's happened tonight.

When I'm only a few feet away from the bedroom door, someone grabs my hair and jerks me backwards. I screech in surprise and trip over my heels, and the person continues dragging me. When they pull me through another doorway, I grab the door frame and try to kick at them even though I can't even see my attacker.

There's a grunt of pain when one of my heels makes contact, but the person just jerks me roughly by my hair and yanks me the rest of the way into the room. I fall onto the floor as they slam the door. I'm in a lot of fucking pain, but I'm way too terrified to focus on that as I scramble backwards and look up to see who grabbed me.

A gasp escapes my lips when my eyes fall on my worthless ex-boyfriend. "Bryson?"

CHAPTER FOUR
ISLA

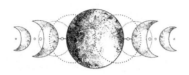

Bryson stares down at me, his teeth bared and his eyes full of rage. There are bright, red claw marks marring his face, all the way from his left eye down to his chin. He's shaking in anger, and my heart feels like it's going to beat out of my chest. I've never felt afraid of Bryson before. I loved him. Never in a million years did I ever think he'd hurt me or look at me with so much hatred.

"What are you doing, Bryson?" I ask, hating the terrified whimper in my voice.

"You have her now, so make sure your little half-breed fuck boy never comes anywhere near me or my mate ever again. Got it?"

His eyes never leave me, so it takes me a second to realize he's speaking to someone else. I turn my head slowly and find Thaddeus sitting behind a large, mahogany desk with his feet propped up. There's a cruel smirk on his face as he gazes down at me, and fear quickly takes hold of me. Two other vampires are standing behind him, but I don't recognize either of them.

Thaddeus was young when he was turned—only twenty-one years old. He's tall, thin, pale, and blond, and he has the distinct appearance of a pretentious trust-fund kid despite being more than a century old. I've never liked the creep, but I can see why Al might have originally been attracted to him.

"Alistair won't bother you again, mutt." Thaddeus waves his hand dismissively.

Bryson growls once, walks out of the room, and slams the door behind him. I'm left alone with the vampires. I have no idea what's going on right now, but it can't be anything good. My heart is beating so loudly and erratically that I can barely hear anything else as I slowly shuffle backwards and force myself to stand up.

There's an agonizing pain when I try to stand on my left foot, so I balance on my right and force myself to keep my eyes trained on Thaddeus. After meeting Rian, I seriously forgot the whole point of coming here tonight was so Al could make his ex-boyfriend jealous and prove he'd moved on from their relationship.

"What do you want?" I grit my teeth. I hope I look angry and not just scared.

Thaddeus doesn't answer me. He just continues staring at me coldly, like a predator watches its prey. I decide to try to make a break for the door. There's a chance he's just fucking with me and won't even stop me from leaving. If he's being serious right now, I can maybe call out for help. I don't think most supernaturals here would pay me any mind, but I'm positive Rian and Matthieu would be pretty pissed to discover I was hurt and being kept locked in an office.

Just as my hand touches the doorknob and I turn it to let myself out, one of the vampires I don't know appears beside me and grips my wrist as he pulls me away. I fight to pull my hand away from him, but he only tightens his hold and drags me back across the room.

Thaddeus moves lightning quick, appearing right in front of me. "There's no way you're getting out of here until I'm done with you."

"Then what the fuck do you want?" I scream angrily. "Is this about Alistair? Fucking Christ. You don't really think he'll take you back after you've treated me like this, do you?"

"Alistair is mine, regardless of what he may believe." Thaddeus curls his lips, revealing his sharp canine teeth. "He's been under your influence for too long. He's young and impressionable, and he hasn't yet learned how our world works. I watched him make a spectacle of himself earlier, throwing himself at the Unseelie Lord with you. It was absolutely disgusting. I'll be sure to apologize to Lord Rian as soon as we're done here."

I widen my eyes in disbelief and laugh incredulously. "You're insane! Rian wanted us. He's going to fucking kill you, you blood-sucking psycho!"

Thaddeus ignores me completely, flicking his gaze over my shoulder to the vampire who grabbed my wrist a moment ago. "Drain her. Hopefully her blood is sweeter than her mouth."

I'm given no time to react before the vampire yanks my hair back and buries his teeth in my neck. It's fucking excruciating, and I scream and kick in pain. The vampire covers my mouth with one of his large hands and digs his teeth in deeper as he drinks from me.

In all the time I've known Al and been around other supernaturals, I've never been bitten by a vampire. I've heard that it can feel amazing—better than an orgasm, even—*if* the vampire makes it feel that way. It quickly becomes evident that this vampire has no intention of dragging this out or making it pleasurable. Everything hurts, and my neck is burning. Tears stream down my face as I continue to try and fight, though my efforts prove to be futile.

When there's a sudden burning on my wrist, the vampire lets go of me without warning. He hisses in pain and clumsily steps back, and I turn around to watch him through blurry, tear-filled eyes. He blinks at me, and then, like something out of a horror movie, blood starts pouring out of him. His mouth, nose, eyes, fucking *everywhere*. He doesn't even scream. He just makes these awful choking sounds and pats his hands all over his face like that's going to help stop the bleeding.

I don't wait around. While Thaddeus and his other vampy sidekick are distracted, I run across the room and yank the door open. I only make it a few feet into the hallway before someone grabs me again and pulls me back into the office.

"What have you done?" Thaddeus pins me to the wall with his hand around my throat. I claw at his hand as I gasp for breath, and he grabs my wrist. When his gaze focuses on Madame Deverell's brand, he growls in frustration. "Deverell put a protection spell on you?"

Honestly, I kind of thought the protection spell was for show more than anything. But from the corner of my eye, I see the vamp who bit me lying in a heap on the floor surrounded by blood. With way more confidence than I'm feeling, I sneer at Thaddeus.

"She did. And you'll all die if you try to kill me or hurt me again."

Thaddeus bares his teeth and squeezes my neck a bit tighter, but then he drops me onto the ground. I bring my trembling hand up to my throat, coughing and gasping for breath, and watch as he steps away and straightens his suit jacket. A tiny thread of hope blooms in my chest. I don't think Thaddeus will kill me if he's the least bit uncertain about Madame Deverell's protection charm. But I can't imagine he'll let me go after what's just happened either. If I can just get out of this room—if I can find Alistair, Matthieu, or Rian —I know I'll be okay.

"Get rid of her. I need to speak with the Unseelie Lord."

My breath falters at his words, and I turn my head to look at the other vampire in the room. He's been silent until now, and hasn't moved an inch from his original spot behind the desk. At Thaddeus's order, the vampire male raises his eyebrows and scoffs.

"I'm not dying for this. Deverell is known to be extremely protective of her pets. I sincerely doubt the girl is lying about the consequences of breaking her spell."

Thaddeus is clearly pissed at his crony's straight up refusal to follow his bidding. He's starting to lose his cool a bit, which makes me think the vampire prick is actually panicking right now. He smooths his hair down and spits venomously over his shoulder as he makes his way from the room, "I don't care how you do it. Just get rid of her. Take her to Giovanni if you must."

He slips out the door, leaving me alone with the disobedient vampire. He sighs loudly and rolls his eyes as he mutters, "No way is this worth it just to sleep with some little half-demon hybrid."

When his gaze turns toward me, I start crying. I'm terrified and pretty badly hurt, and he's literally my last chance at finding a way out of this. Maybe if I beg, he'll take me to Lord Rian. Hopefully he's too scared of Madame to listen to Thaddeus.

"Please," I cry, not caring how pitiful I look or sound.

"This isn't personal, human girl." He slowly walks over to where I'm huddled on the ground and bends down in front of me. His eyes sweep over my form quickly, and he shrugs. "You're pretty enough, so I'm sure someone else will make you a pet."

I open my mouth to plead with him again. It occurs to me that I should tell him I'm Rian's mate. Even if it's not true, it might get me out of this. But his vampiric reflexes are too quick, and I'm unable to speak a word before he grabs my face between his hands and forces me to stare into his eyes. Most supernaturals can use some level of compulsion. It's usually easy enough to fight against, but in my weakened state, I only last a few seconds before my eyelids flutter closed and I fall into a deep sleep.

The muffled sound of weeping wakes me up.
My head is absolutely killing me. It feels ten thousand
times worse than my worst hangover, and I groan as I fight to
open my eyes. As I slowly become more aware, I realize I'm
lying on a cold, hard surface. Panic immediately sets my heart
racing, and I blink rapidly while I try to figure out where I am.

It's dark enough that it takes me a moment to make out
the shape of a person sitting just a few feet away from me. I
tense up and try to scoot backwards, but my movements are
slow and sluggish and everything hurts so badly. It's not until
my back presses against cold, metal bars that I realize I'm in a
fucking cage, and the person next to me is crying.

"Hello?" I whisper, but my throat is dry and my voice
cracks.

They don't answer. They just continue weeping quietly,
curled into a ball in the corner opposite from me. I decide
they're not an immediate threat for the time being, and I force
myself to move into a sitting position so I can take stock of my
injuries and try to get a better look around.

I'm still wearing the red evening gown I borrowed from
Madame, but it's wrinkled and stained with blood in some
places. It's also probably the least practical thing I could
possibly be wearing in a situation like this. I'm barely covered,
and it's absolutely freezing in here. I'm also still wearing the
Rene Caovilla sandals I'd been drooling over before Lord
Rian's party, and even though this is so not the time, I whine
in dismay when I see one of the heels is broken. I'm pretty
sure my left ankle is broken too, or at least badly sprained, and
I wince as I pull the shoes off my feet. As much as it pains part
of me to let them go, I know I've got a way better chance of
getting out of this if I can actually run.

There are a couple of dim light bulbs flickering high up in
the ceiling, and they only give off barely enough light to see

by. I can't tell how big the room we're in is, or if there are any people or creatures outside of the cage, but I move around to familiarize myself with my surroundings as much as I possibly can. The cage is probably ten feet long and ten feet wide, but it's not tall enough for me to stand up. When I sit up on my knees, I still have to bend over slightly in order to fit in the space.

There isn't any food or water in our cage, and there also isn't any piss or shit on the concrete floor. It actually smells surprisingly clean in here, wherever I am, which leads me to believe my cell-mate hasn't been here much longer than I have. They've been sitting and crying since I woke up, and after checking my surroundings as much as I'm able to, I decide to try and talk to them again.

"Hey," I hiss quietly. I clear my throat a few times and move closer, cautiously reaching out to poke their shoulder when they don't respond.

They jump like I've startled them and finally lift their head. I meet the eyes of a scared young girl with light blonde hair. She's dressed much more practically than I am, in jeans and a dark sweatshirt, with the hood pulled up to hide her hair. She stares at me with her lips trembling while tears continue streaming down her face.

"Do you know where we are?" I ask since she's clearly not going to start a conversation. She shakes her head but still doesn't speak. Growing a little frustrated, I sigh angrily. "Well, do you at least know why we're here?"

"No," she whimpers. "I just woke up a little while before you did. I met this guy who said he could help me, but—but then I..."

She trails off and cries harder. I'm terrified and trying really hard to hold it together. Part of me wants to shake this girl and demand she tell me every detail she possibly can about this place or anyone she interacted with in order to end up here. But she's clearly losing her shit, so I sigh in defeat and rub my hand up and down her arm to try and sooth her.

"It'll be okay," I lie.

I scoot even closer to her and wrap my arms around her tiny frame, hoping to give her some kind of comfort. She hugs me back and cries more openly. We stay like that for a long time before she eventually falls asleep.

CHAPTER FIVE
ISLA

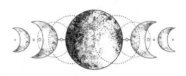

"ARE YOU GOING TO BE GOOD TODAY, OR ARE WE GOING TO have to restrain you again while we shove this down your throat?"

I sneer and flip the guard off, not bothering to give him a verbal answer. Fucking asshole. He watches me for a few more seconds before shaking his head and mumbling something under his breath, and quickly opens the tiny slot of our cage to slip in our daily meals. I laugh when I notice the trembling in his hands, and that scares him enough that he almost drops the tray. He slams the slot closed and glares at me, but he doesn't say anything else before moving onto the next cage.

I wait until he's a few cages down before crawling forward to grab our food. I lift the lid on one of the bowls and frown angrily when I find a decent-sized portion of rice, chicken, and green beans. It honestly infuriates me that they feed us well when our living conditions are otherwise fucking unbearable.

I've been here for four days now. Four long, cold, miserably agonizing days. The first two days, I refused to eat because I figured they probably drugged the food. But yesterday, Giovanni—the demon in charge of this disgusting operation—ordered the guards to hold me down and force me to eat. They kept me restrained for most of the day just to make sure I wouldn't purposely throw it all up.

The food isn't drugged. Giovanni just wants to keep us all healthy enough that he'll actually be able to profit off of us.

"Here." I sigh as I crawl to the other end of the cage and offer Sadie her meal. Since my first night here, she hasn't improved much. She spends most of her time either crying or sleeping. I've hardly gotten any information out of her. All I know is that she's nineteen, and she was ignorant of the supernatural world before she tried to make some kind of ominous deal with a warlock.

She sniffles and reaches out to take her plate. "Is it safe?"

I bite my tongue before I say something mean and unnecessary. I know she's having a hard time coping, but it's difficult to feel sorry for her when she's not making any effort to escape. The reason the guards are all wary of me is because I stabbed one of them with the heel of one of my Rene Caovilla sandals the first time they opened the slot of our cage. I actually got ahold of his keys too before Giovanni came over and put a sleeping charm on me.

"Yes," I say through gritted teeth. Sadie's eaten her meals every day we've been here. And yesterday she sat in the corner and cried, never once attempting to help me when they held me down and forced the food down my throat.

While Sadie hasn't been the greatest moral support in this situation, I've luckily been able to befriend the selkies locked in the cage next to us. There are four of them, though only one of them speaks English. Because of them, I've learned that Giovanni deals in human and supernatural creature trafficking. Humans aren't very popular and don't sell as often since they're so common and are already usually pretty gullible when any kind of magic is involved.

Case in point: all of the guards here are human. Not one

of them is under any sort of spell, other than the promise of a large paycheck and the hope of eventual immortality.

Female creatures like selkies, pixies, mermaids, and nymphs are most in demand with Giovanni's usual clients. But there are all sorts of creatures locked in cages in the warehouse here, many I've never seen before—gargoyles, trolls, satyrs, and even one lone wendigo kept in a cage a little further away from everyone else.

I settle into my corner, opposite from Sadie, and nibble at my food. My thoughts inevitably turn to Alistair whenever it's quiet and I'm idle like this. If he knew where I was, he'd have figured out a way to get me out of here by now. So he either has no idea, which means Thaddeus, his lackey, and Bryson have managed to keep their mouths shut about my disappearance. Or something bad has happened to Al too.

My heart aches whenever I start thinking like that, and I just hope and pray that Rian and Matthieu might have been right about some of that mate stuff and they're looking out for him.

Much later, I'm feeling restless. I make sure to stretch and exercise as much as I can in the tiny space. My ankle is still injured, but I've almost gotten used to the constant dull ache so long as I don't move it around too much. My neck where I was bitten is sore, and I'm sure there's some bruising there. Mostly, I just feel really gross. I haven't bathed since I've been here, and my skin is crawling. It doesn't help that I still have blood caked to my dress and skin, and my hair is completely matted. Giovanni has brownies clean our cages each night, but they're not permitted to use their magic directly on us.

I crack my neck and look around the large warehouse-like room we're being kept in. Most creatures appear to be sleeping, or they're pacing their cages. The selkies next to us are asleep too. One of them is reaching her hand through the bars to touch the canister of water that's connected to all of our cages. There's a tiny faucet outside each cage you have to reach through the bars to access, and it only ever gives you a small amount of water to drink at a time—never enough to bathe with, and never enough to sate the water-based creatures here.

The lights begin to flicker on and off, and a loud clanking sound reverberates through the room. Guards begin walking around, tapping against the bars of the cages and yelling at creatures to wake up. I sit up straight, fully alert now. My heart races faster in panic while I helplessly wait to see what's happening.

"What's going on?" Sadie asks groggily.

I shush her and keep my eyes trained on the door the guards use to come in and out. The room is slowly filling with the low, hushed voices and cries of supernaturals. After several tense minutes, Giovanni appears in the doorway. He glances once around the large room, and holds the door open wide as a line of people file in.

"I think he's bringing buyers in to look at us," I say quietly, holding my arms around myself to try and keep myself from shaking in anger and fear.

Sadie begins sobbing loudly and obnoxiously. I grind my teeth and force myself not to look at her. I know this probably makes me a terrible person, but I seriously can't deal with her right now. I need to look out for myself first, to do whatever it takes to survive. I just don't know which outcome is worse—being bought by somebody who will potentially hurt and abuse me, or staying here to live in a cage like an animal? And if I'm not bought, how long will Giovanni realistically keep me around?

I've been in some pretty messed up situations before with Alistair. I've been in numerous foster homes with sick, twisted individuals. I've been homeless, and I've had to lie, cheat, and steal in order to survive. I've hurt people before. But this situation really fucking takes the cake.

Only the worst type of people would pay money for a

person like this. I'll do whatever I need to stay alive and get back home to Alistair, but just the thought of being bought— the thought of becoming someone's fucking property—makes bile rise up in the back of my throat.

Most of the buyers are human, which doesn't surprise me. Wealthy, middle-aged business men in expensive suits walk around and ogle at all the supernatural creatures. Just like the selkies told me, the more feminine appearing creatures draw the most spectators. Three men almost immediately crowd around the selkies' cage. When the selkies hiss and show their sharp, needle-like teeth, that only seems to excite the potential buyers.

"Fucking pigs," I spit angrily. Nobody's looked at me or Sadie yet. I know it's smarter to keep my mouth shut. But god, I'm furious.

One of the men glances over and blanches when he catches sight of me. "Jesus, they're selling humans too?"

Giovanni walks up behind them, followed by a guy wearing a long, brown wool robe. He kind of looks like a monk, except he has long, braided hair and a bushy gray beard. One of the men beside the selkies' cage crosses his arms and scoffs at Giovanni. "You never said you sold human girls. I'm not sure I'm okay with that."

Right, he's a *real* stand-up guy. Even though he clearly has a hard-on for an imprisoned, defenseless selkie who he'll probably buy for hundreds of thousands of dollars. Sick fuck.

Giovanni gives the man a dismissive glance and shrugs. "Some of our clients are a bit skittish of supernaturals."

He beckons the creepy-monk dude closer, gesturing at our cage. The monk guy looks first at the selkies and visibly flinches before focusing his attention on me and Sadie. He frowns when he sees Sadie curled up and crying, but I meet his gaze dead-on and glare daggers at him. When he smiles at me, I curl my lip in disgust.

He points at me and says something in a foreign language.

Giovanni sighs and bends down slightly, settling his cold black eyes on me. "He wants me to let you out, human. Behave yourself."

I scoff and narrow my eyes. "You're fucking stupid if you think I'm going to make this easy for you."

Giovanni tenses and grits his teeth, and he says something in the same foreign language the monk spoke. Monk Guy chuckles and bends down so he's more level with me, and he grins broadly when he speaks again. Giovanni sighs in defeat at whatever was just said, and he moves to open our cage.

The door swings open, and I hold my breath for a few seconds while I gather my courage. *This guy wants to buy me.* There's no other reason they'd be opening the cage. Two of the businessmen who were eyeing the selkies are watching on in interest, and they stand silently just a few feet behind Giovanni and my potential new owner.

I crawl out slowly and cautiously, and I shakily pull myself into a standing position once I'm out. I balance most of my weight on my right foot, but my knees still buckle since I haven't been able to stand up for several days.

Even though I'm scared, and I'm weak enough that I need to lean against the cage in order to stand, I give Monk Guy the haughtiest expression I can muster. He speaks rapidly with Giovanni while he looks me over. To keep myself distracted, I try to decipher what language they're speaking. I'm certainly not an expert. I can only speak English, and I only took, like, one year of Spanish in high school before I dropped out. But I think he's maybe speaking Russian or some other Slavic dialect.

Monk Guy steps forward and picks up a lock of my hair, still speaking words I don't understand. I'm so startled by the sudden closeness of him that I panic and act without really thinking it through. I bring my hand up and punch him right across his cheek, hard enough that he stumbles backwards and almost loses his balance.

One of the guards runs over and slaps these heavy, primitive-looking handcuffs around my wrists so quickly I barely have time to blink. I'm terrified I'm going to be hurt or punished, or even killed, but Monk Guy just starts laughing wildly.

"Dokonalá," he chuckles as he clasps his hands together in front of him.

Giovanni snorts at me and raises a dark eyebrow. "Well, the crazy bastard thinks you're perfect. I'm not one to judge a man's taste, so it looks like you'll be heading off world. Good fucking riddance, if you ask me."

Off world? My heart drops into my stomach, and my mouth falls open in shock. He can't be serious, can he? I've never heard of anyone actually traveling between worlds and realms, though I've heard stories of those places existing. But if I get stuck somewhere that far—not even on the same fucking world as Alistair—there's no way in hell my best friend will ever find me. No matter how long he searches or who he has helping him.

I'm so shocked that I don't even notice the stupid guard putting cuffs around my ankles right away, but I let out a sharp hiss of pain when I feel the rusted metal press against my injured ankle.

Giovanni and the creepy monk exchange a few more words, and they exchange payment. That's when I seriously lose my shit. I kick and scream and fight and plead, but it doesn't help whatsoever.

I've been bought and paid for. Any sliver of hope I had left of finding my way back home to my best friend and the life we'd built together shatters into a million pieces.

He bought Sadie too.

I was kind of surprised, to be quite honest. The Monk—

his name is Amias, but I'm pretending I didn't understand him when he spent a good five minutes gesturing to himself while repeating the name over and over—didn't really show much interest in Sadie when we were at the warehouse. But here she is, crying and clinging to me and asking where we're going. She's not restrained like I am, and I'm pretty fucking irritated about that.

We've just come through a portal, and I'm scared and nauseous and totally disoriented from the sensation of traveling through realms. Amias is chattering a mile a fucking minute like he expects us to suddenly understand every word he says as he leads us down a hallway of some sort.

"Oh god, I think I'm going to throw up," Sadie cries. She leans most of her weight on me and almost causes me to fall, and I roughly push her away. I don't even bother saying a word to her. I just keep hobbling after Amias while I try not to think about where he's taking us or what's about to happen to me.

Amias smiles at us over his shoulder and opens a large, wooden door. Two other bearded men appear behind him, both wearing the same ugly robe as Amias. They're clearly excited to see us, whispering and laughing with Amias as they look Sadie and I over with interest.

A loud, booming voice calls out from inside the room, and Amias tugs on the lead attached to my shackles. I know I don't actually have a choice, but I keep my feet planted and refuse to budge just to be difficult. The new monks widen their eyes at me and quickly lead Sadie into the room ahead of us, and Amias tugs on my lead a little more frantically.

He says something to me in a pleading tone, but I just growl at him. I figure whoever's waiting in that room for us is my *real* owner. Amias must just be the unlucky delivery guy. I refuse to submit to these people, whoever they are.

I don't even know where I am. I'm pretty sure Amias is human, and I have no clue why he'd specifically want human girls from an entirely different realm. For all I know, I'm being led into some kind of prehistoric, sacrificial ceremony. I have to force myself not to think about it, not really. Otherwise, I'll probably break down completely.

Footsteps echo through the room and into the hallway where I'm standing. The person stops just outside the door where I can just barely see their shadow. Amias bows his head and says something in his complicated language, tugs half-heartedly on the lead and points at me, demonstrating that I'm the one who's being difficult.

A tall, broad man steps into the hallway and glares down at me. I blink in shock for a quick second before I remember to school my features into an angry, annoyed expression. This man has a beard like the monk-guys too, but his is much shorter and better groomed. He's also younger-looking, though probably in his late-forties or early-fifties. He's wearing an elaborate military uniform with dozens of medals, and there's an actual sword attached to his belt. He's beyond intimidating, and my throat goes totally dry the longer I stare at him.

His icy blue eyes travel from the lead in Amias' hand to the restraints on my wrists and ankles, to my bare feet and the torn, ragged gown clinging to my frame. When he finally meets my eyes, I refuse to blink or show that I'm scared at all.

A grin breaks out across his face and he barks out a laugh. He slaps Amias on the shoulder good-naturedly and takes the lead from him, and then he turns and walks into the room while dragging me behind him. I fight a little at first, but he's much more aggressive than Amias was.

Once inside, it takes me several seconds to realize I'm in some sort of throne room. The space is huge with marble floors, high ceilings and ornate chandeliers hanging down. Beautiful lamps line the walls and give off plenty of light— there are windows high up on the wall, but it appears to be dark outside. Across the room, there's a dais with four large thrones. Only one is occupied by an older woman who's glaring down at everyone with pursed lips.

In front of the dais, Sadie stands with four other human girls. They're all crying and looking around in confusion, and a few men in those monk-robes are trying to settle them down. There's also another guy wearing a military uniform. He doesn't have nearly as many medals as the guy dragging me does. Even though he has a beard like all the other males present, he can't be more than twenty years old. He's standing slightly apart from everyone else with a distraught expression on his face.

I'm pulled over to stand beside the other girls. When the younger military guy sees me, pure rage flashes in his eyes and he storms over to stand in front of me. He begins yelling at the older military guy—who I assume is the one in charge—and points at my restraints. The older man grunts and waves a hand dismissively, but that only seems to anger the younger man further.

Truthfully, I don't think I've ever been more terrified in my life. I have no information about my whereabouts or why I'm here, and I can't understand the language being spoken around me. I'm trying my best to appear calm, stoic, and inconvenienced more than anything. But I'm not sure how much longer I can hold up before I start bawling like the rest of these girls.

When the younger military guy steps in front of me and starts trying to undo the archaic handcuffs around my wrists, hope begins to blossom in my chest. He's the only person in the room who looks angry. I just hope he's angry on my behalf.

The older, more intimidating man smacks his hands away and shakes his head, and then he points at Amias. Another of the monk-guys snickers quietly, and I realize they're talking about the swollen, black eye I gave my buyer. It's actually kind of ridiculous that they're that concerned about me, or that they consider me threatening at all. I'm clearly outnumbered and at a total disadvantage in every way possible. Even if the restraints were taken off, where am I going to go?

"Slabá," the older military guy shouts as he points at one of the crying girls. He shakes his head like he's disappointed and paces back and forth in front of us. He points at the girl beside the first one and grunts, "žalostná!"

He repeats the two words, pointing at each scared, confused girl. I'm growing angrier and angrier as he does. These girls were stolen and sold, just like I was. They don't know what's going on anymore than I do. I don't know what he's saying for sure, but his tone makes it pretty obvious he's not complimenting them.

He comes to stand in front of me again, a cruel smile on his face as he chuckles. He says something to me, or maybe to the rest of the room. But I'm not even trying to listen or pay attention anymore. My ears are ringing, and it's suddenly hard to breathe. Because I've just realized how completely, stupidly idiotic I am.

I've made myself stand out in a group full of girls who are here for reasons that can't be good.

Things happen quickly after that. The frowning woman steps down from her throne and gathers the other girls together, and she leads them from the room. I'm left alone with the monks and the two military-clad men while they yell over one another.

Eventually, I'm roughly led through a different door from the one I originally came through. I don't try to fight it this time. I'm so numb and frightened that I barely notice my surroundings, and when I'm led outside, I hardly react when I'm hit with a blast of freezing air.

Wherever I am, it's snowing here. My bare feet leave tiny prints in the untouched snow as I'm forced to walk down a long, paved pathway lined with hundreds of tiny lights. A sled being pulled by two large elks is waiting for us. The sled is packed with all sorts of crates and boxes tied with colorful ribbons. Amongst these gifts, there's a small, empty cage with the door swinging open. It's just big enough for me to fit in.

I almost want to laugh at the bizarre scene unfolding in front of me. What kind of fucked up Christmas do these people celebrate where it's acceptable for Santa to deliver a slave along with the rest of your gifts?

The older military guy shouts something at the monks, and everything's a bit chaotic for a moment. I swallow back the bile rising up in my throat and force myself to look up instead of at the sled or any of the people around me. It's too dark and cloudy to see much of anything. I can barely even see the nearly-full moon peeking through.

Someone pushes me forward and shoves me into the cage, and a scratchy, wool blanket is tossed in with me before the door is shut and locked. I keep still and quiet, even when a cover is thrown over the entire cage, blanketing me in total darkness.

I don't let myself cry until I feel the sled moving.

CHAPTER SIX

ISLA

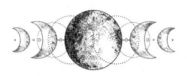

I'm going to freeze to death.

My teeth are chattering so loudly I can't hear the driver singing anymore. Maybe it's a blessing, because the guy cannot hold a tune to save his life. I chuckle humorlessly to myself and pull my scratchy blanket more tightly around my body, tucking my feet in as much as I can. I can't feel my fingers, and it's difficult to hold the blanket up. The fact that I'm trembling violently from head to toe doesn't help much either.

When we first departed, I actually felt stifled and over-heated despite the fact it had been snowing outside. The cage felt too small, the blanket too thick and coarse. The cover over the cage allows barely any air to drift through, and that made me feel extremely claustrophobic.

But now we've been traveling for hours. At least. And the longer we travel, the colder I feel. I have no way to know for sure how long the sled has been moving, encapsulated in dark-ness like I am. It feels like days. I know that's probably not logical, considering we haven't stopped once yet. Surely the elk things pulling the sled will need a break at some point.

When my eyes start to drift shut, I shake my head and slap

my cheeks. I'm so cold that falling asleep could literally be a death sentence. As much as I hate myself for thinking it, I hope we don't have much further to go. I cried for a long, long time when the sled first departed. And I've had a long time to think. No matter what happens to me, no matter where I end up, I don't want to die.

It's likely I'll never get back home or see Alistair again, but he would be so disappointed in me if I just gave up. And I know he won't give up looking for me, not ever.

The sled begins to slow. At first I think I'm just imagining it, but sure enough, we come to a complete stop. It almost feels jarring after the bumpy swaying of the ride the entire way here. I pull my blanket to my body as tightly as I can and clamp my teeth together, trying my best to stop the chattering and trembling so I can hear what's happening outside.

The elk make some grunting noises, and the driver with the terrible singing voice says something softly to them. After a few minutes of hearing nothing else, I start to think we are just stopping for a break. My breath hitches at the thought of being stuck in this cage for several more hours, slowly freezing to death.

A man's voice suddenly calls out, and my heart jumps as hope blossoms in my chest. He could be a rapist or a murderer, but right now, I don't even fucking care. I just hope he takes me somewhere warm.

The driver greets him, and the men talk in friendly tones for a minute. I hear their feet crunching against the snow as they walk around the sled, and the new voice laughs happily. Even though I can't understand the words they're speaking, it's pretty obvious this guy is receiving the gifts piled upon the sled. I let out short, panicked breaths, waiting for him to reach my cage. Hope and fear are at war within me at the prospect of his reaction to seeing me.

Their footsteps stop right beside me, and I hold my breath. The driver chuckles and taps against the cage before pulling the cover off with one swift movement. I'm momentarily blinded at the sudden, bright sunlight. Tears form in my eyes and I blink rapidly, holding the blanket over my face to give myself time to adjust after being stuck in the dark for so long.

The new voice makes a sound like he's startled or dumb-struck, and his tone completely changes. He begins growling and shouting, and he literally rips the door of the cage off its hinges and tosses it behind him. I still can't see him clearly, and he sounds so furious that I cry out in surprise.

When he reaches his hands into the cage and roughly grabs my arms, I don't even think. I act totally on instinct, kicking and screaming and slapping his hands away. I even manage to bite his hand before he grunts in pain and steps back away from the cage.

Tears stream down my face from the stress and fear and uncertainty of my situation. I blink and squint into the bright sunlight so I can attempt to see him. I'm ready to plead with him any way I can, if only he'll let me out of this awful cage. I'm terrified he's going to keep me locked in here if he thinks I'm dangerous or acted too much like an animal.

As my vision returns, I find a guy close to my age staring back at me. He has messy, dark brown hair and a full beard, and he's kneeling on the ground in the snow as he watches me with sad green eyes. He reaches his hand toward me, slower this time, and says something to me that I don't understand.

My teeth chatter together, and my voice is raspy when I try to speak. "P-please…"

He flinches, and rips his jacket off. It's thick and lined with fur, and it looks *so warm*. I vaguely recognize that he's only wearing a thin black shirt underneath, but I'm way more focused on the jacket. He holds it open and stretches his arms toward me, and he says something that sounds soft and coaxing.

I still hesitate, But the promise of some sort of warmth is way too tempting. All my idiotic pride and confidence I've been projecting over the past few days has disappeared. I slowly climb out of my cage, stumbling over my feet, and nearly slip on the icy ground. The guy stays totally still and lets me come to him. When I reach him and touch my fingertips to the fur lining of the coat, he moves so fast he's almost a blur. He swaddles me in the coat and pulls me against his chest, lifting me up from the ground and cradling me in his arms like a baby. He even takes a second to tuck my feet under his shirt, even though he hisses against the cold when my frozen toes touch his warm skin.

I'm so grateful for his kindness and the warmth, even if it's temporary. I'm still confused, but I can't help snuggling against him and burying my face in his neck. He stands up slowly, carrying me carefully like I'm the most fragile thing in the world. I feel him watching me, so I look up. He lets out a shaky breath when our eyes meet, and I feel his body tremble the slightest bit. The moment he looks up at the other man, pure rage and hatred flash in his expressive green eyes.

I'd almost forgotten about the sled-driver Monk. The guy holding me looks over at him and says something, a deep growl in his voice. The driver shakes his head and holds his hands up, and he says something in return like he's trying to defend himself. My—rescuer? New owner? —growls again, even more ferociously as he bares his teeth.

I'm fairly certain this guy is some kind of shifter. I've been around enough shifters to recognize their body language and mannerisms—especially those who fit under the predator category.

The driver's eyes widen, and his face pales. Whatever this shifter guy said to him clearly scared the absolute shit out of him because he doesn't waste another second before cutting one of the elk loose and jumping on the animal's back like a fucking horse. He kicks the animal's side, and they take off. Shifter Guy and I watch him flee down a path through the forest until he's no longer in view.

I'm not sure what's going to happen now, but I take the opportunity to look around. We're completely surrounded by woods, and I can see snowy mountaintops peeking above the tall tree line. Behind us, there's a large cabin with smoke billowing from a chimney. There's a large front porch wrapping around it, and a wooden shed off to the side.

Shifter Guy murmurs something quietly and tucks my feet under his shirt more securely as he turns toward the cabin. I whimper without meaning to, and he squeezes me a bit tighter. It's almost comforting.

After he steps inside, he kicks the door shut behind us. I lift my head to look around, but he doesn't pause or hover near the doorway long enough for me to see much more than a large, open room with wood floors and rustic furniture. He quickly stomps across the room and uses his foot to push a large, cozy-looking armchair closer to the blazing fireplace.

He mumbles under his breath the whole time. Since he's speaking the same language as the Monks and the military guys, I can't understand him. Still, listening to his voice is soothing. He gently sets me down in the armchair, and I watch him intently as he tosses more logs onto the fire.

My breath catches when he takes his shirt off. Under normal circumstances, I'd probably appreciate the view—the guy's got abs for days, huge, muscly biceps, and a delicious little happy trail leading down to the waistband of his pants.

Unfortunately, these *aren't* normal circumstances. Seeing him undress without warning seriously freaks me out. It's certainly crossed my mind that I might be sold to somebody as a sex slave. Just because this guy acted surprised and angry to see me, and he's treated me kindly so far, that doesn't automatically mean he doesn't have messed up intentions.

When he sees the alarmed expression on my face, he quickly shakes his head and speaks rapidly. I sit there, totally tense, and wait to see what he's going to do next. I mean, it's not like I can run away at this point. I can't trust anybody on this realm, or even understand them, and I wouldn't last long at all if I somehow managed to get outside and hide in the woods.

He runs his hands through his hair, and gives me a super guilty look as he reaches down to lift me up. Just like outside, he moves too fast for me to really process. I hardly have time to blink before I find myself sitting curled up in his lap with his jacket wrapped around both of us.

I try to push myself away from him at first, but he makes these soft shushing sounds and hugs me tightly. I realize I'm still shivering when he rubs his hands up and down my back and arms, though nowhere near as much as I was when I was stuck in the cage. I let myself relax then, just a little. His body heat will warm me up much faster than just sitting beside the fire alone.

He takes one of my hands between his much larger ones, rubbing it roughly in order to warm up my frozen fingers. It hurts a little, but I know it's probably necessary. I don't know much about frostbite, but I have to assume that regaining feeling in my frozen fingers is a good thing. He spends several minutes on my right hand before moving on to my left. While he works, I keep my eyes on his face. This guy is totally saving my life right now. The longer we sit here like this, the more I feel myself relaxing and warming up to him.

Eventually he looks up, never stopping his ministrations to my hand, and smiles timidly when our eyes meet. "Reule."

At first I assume he's saying something else in his native language that I can't understand, and I smile back awkwardly at him. He drops my hand, clears his throat and taps his fingers against his chest.

"Reule," he says again.

I realize he's telling me his name, and I smile for real. He stares at my mouth for a quick second, and meets my eyes with a hopeful expression on his face. I'm not going to be an asshole like I was to Amias and pretend I don't understand.

Reule is the first person who's shown me any real compassion since I was kidnapped from Rian's party. Well, there was that younger military guy who tried to take my shackles off, but he didn't really try *that* hard to help me.

"Reule," I repeat his name softly. My throat is still a little raspy, but Reule doesn't seem to mind. He grins at the sound of my voice, and I bring my right hand up and touch my fingertips to my chest so I can tell him my name too. "Isla."

"Isla," he repeats my name with a slight growl and the hint of an accent. But god, it feels so good to be called by my name after so many days of being treated like an animal or a possession.

Tears form in my eyes, and I quickly bury my face in his neck. I'm a little embarrassed I'm reacting so strongly to hearing him use my name. But he just hugs me tightly to his chest, encasing me in warmth.

I know he won't understand me, but I can't help saying the words, anyway. I nuzzle his neck and whisper, "Thank you, Reule." Hopefully he'll be able to pick up on my tone well enough to figure out what I'm telling him.

His arms tighten around my frame, pressing me more firmly against him. He inhales sharply, almost hissing like he's in pain. I go completely stiff and lift my head to stare at him in shock when I feel his hard cock digging into my ass.

Reule cringes when he meets my eyes, immediately averting his gaze as he stands up and gently positions me back in the chair by myself. His cheeks have turned bright and rosy. He's clearly embarrassed by his reaction.

And that honestly makes me feel like a million times better. I don't know what kind of world I'm in, or what the culture is like. I mean, these people are obviously okay with slave trading and human trafficking. I know I'm incredibly lucky to have ended up with someone who seems kind and decent. I truly don't think Reule is going to take advantage of me. I can't really blame the guy for getting a hard-on. We're both half naked, and I've been sitting in his lap, pressed up against him for at least half an hour.

On the other hand, I'm pretty fucking horrified. I haven't bathed in almost a week, and I'm totally covered in grime. There's still dried blood caked to my neck and shoulder, and I don't even want to think about what my hair looks like. I must look and smell awful, especially to a shifter with enhanced senses.

Reule stares down at me apologetically, biting his lip while he tugs at his hair. I don't really know what to do or say. We don't speak the same language, and I'm afraid if I smile or try to play it off, he might take that as an invitation for something. After a few awkward moments, he turns around and opens a large wooden chest beside the fireplace. He picks up a huge, fluffy white blanket and brings it over to me.

He mumbles something softly in his deep, growly voice and kneels down in front of me. He's tall enough that we're pretty much eye-level like this. There's something really sweet about the gesture. I let him help me adjust the coat I've been using so that I'm actually wearing it, and he tucks the fluffy white blanket around me until I'm completely covered up to my chin. I'm not sure what kind of fabric this blanket is made of, but it's warmer and softer than anything I've ever felt before.

I sink back into the cozy armchair and smile gratefully at him, and he gives me a nervous smile in return. He makes some sort of hand gesture at me that I think is supposed to mean 'stay,' and leaves me beside the fire to make his way across the room. I'm not able to see him anymore, even when I try to look over my shoulder. But I hear what sounds like cupboards opening and closing, as well as dishes clinking together.

A short while later, Reule returns carrying a bowl of something steaming. It smells delicious, and my stomach rumbles loudly. I ate back at Giovanni's warehouse not long before

Amias and the other buyers showed up, but that feels like ages ago. I don't think even one full day has passed since then, but it's hard to tell what day or time it is. Plus, I don't even know if days last the same amount of time here as they do at home.

Reule kneels down in front of me again, showing me the bowl of soup before lifting a spoonful into his own mouth. I furrow my eyebrows in confusion and watch him lift another spoonful and offer it to me. A grin spreads across my face when I realize he's trying to show me that the food is safe to eat. I can't believe how thoughtful he's being. It almost makes me want to cry again.

No way am I going to let him feed me though. I'm totally grateful for the gesture, but I refuse to let a sweet, hot guy spoon-feed me like a freaking baby, no matter how messed up of a situation I'm in. I wiggle around to get my arms free from my blanket cocoon and shakily reach out to take the bowl and spoon from him.

Reule snorts softly in amusement and sets the bowl down on the floor beside him. He looks around the room thought-fully for a moment, and then he stands up and moves behind my chair. He comes back a few seconds later with a tall, wooden stool. I'm assuming he grabbed it from the kitchen, but it's the perfect height for me to eat the soup from without having to leave the comfy armchair beside the fire.

I scoot forward a little and finally take the spoon from Reule after he sets the soup down in front of me. My hand is still shaking like crazy. I hadn't realized how weak I still am, and I can feel Reule gazing down at me in concern. But I'm determined to at least feed myself, and I manage to take a bite.

The soup is pretty good. It's some kind of broth, but it's savory and filling. I'm probably the worst cook ever. Alistair and I eat out nearly every night back home, I'm ashamed to say. So, even though I can't identify the flavor, I'm pretty impressed that Reule made this for me. I mean, he could have made it from a can, but I certainly wouldn't know the difference.

After I've taken a few bites, Reule sighs in defeat and I look up to offer him a smile. He rocks back and forth on his feet in front of me for a moment, and points between himself and the front door while he says something in his deep, growly voice.

I wish I could tell him I appreciate everything he's done— even the simple act of letting me know he's going to step outside. But I just smile shyly and nod, continuing to eat my soup with shaky hands.

Reule picks up his discarded shirt from the floor and slips it back over his head. I can't help feeling a little disappointed, even though this is so not the time to be having those kinds of thoughts. Once his sexy chest and abs are covered up again, he walks over to a small closet by the front door and pulls out another thick coat, just like the one he gave me. He glances over at me one last time, and then he walks outside.

The house instantly feels quieter and so much more intimidating somehow. I eat a few more bites and glance around the room anxiously, and I can't help casting my eyes at the front door every few seconds to check if Reule is coming back in.

I know he's not holding me prisoner. It's pretty obvious I was dumped on this guy's doorstep without his knowledge or consent. I wish I knew why, but it's not like I can ask. Even though it seems like I've been given to Reule as some kind of messed up gift, and I'm fairly certain the guy is some kind of scary type of shifter, I haven't gotten any bad vibes from him. After being around supernaturals most of my life, I can usually read people pretty well.

But still, I'd be stupid not to look around while I'm alone. What if Reule secretly has a bunch of little slave girls hidden somewhere? I really doubt it, but you never know. At the very least, maybe I'll find a clue to help me figure out where the hell I even am.

I carefully push the stool with my soup bowl away so I have enough room to stand up. My legs are stiff and sore—which probably has more to do with being stuck in cramped cages the past few days than with nearly freezing to death—so I stretch for a few seconds and wrap the fuzzy white blanket around myself as I slowly pad across the room. My ankle twinges painfully everytime I bear any weight on it, but I'll just have to wait a little longer to try and find a wrap or something to help it heal the way it needs to.

The room I'm in is large and open with high ceilings, and the floors and walls are wood. There's no TV or anything, but there are two large, cozy-looking tan couches and a coffee table close to the fireplace. Behind this little sitting area, there's a long, wooden dining table and chairs. Further back in the room, there's a loft with a wooden ladder leading up to it. The place honestly looks like something out of a *Log Cabin Homes* magazine. It's clean and tidy and cozy, but there's nothing personal anywhere. No art, no photos, and no trinkets. There are a few cabinets and another chest like the one Reule pulled the blanket from, but I decide not to snoop through those until I've checked out the rest of the house.

I find myself in the kitchen next. It's huge, with tons of counter space and this giant, very old-fashioned looking oven. I wouldn't even know how to begin to use that thing. A quick glance through the cabinets shows lots of dishes, pots, and pans, but no food. When I look around for a fridge, it dawns on me that I haven't seen anything electric since I've been here. The lights in the living room area are these weird looking lantern things, but there are so many windows letting in light that I hadn't thought to really inspect them.

Oh, god. Did I end up somewhere that doesn't have electricity *at all?* I'm extremely stupid for not having considered it before. But I mean, why else would they have needed to travel by fucking *sled* if they didn't have cars or planes or anything?

Feeling completely horrified at my new theory, I wrap the

fluffy blanket more securely around myself and shuffle out of the kitchen. I figure Reule keeps his food in a separate pantry or something, but I'll just have to investigate that later. There's a long hallway between the kitchen and living area with three doors on each side and one at the end.

The first two doors open up into bedrooms. They're similar in size and have the same rustic style like the rest of the house I've seen. There's also a little bit more personality in these rooms. There are photos on the walls and clothes scattered across both floors, at least. For the first time, it occurs to me that other people might live here with Reule. The thought makes me feel beyond anxious. Was I supposed to be a gift for someone else, and just got lucky that Reule was the one who happened to be home instead? I force myself not to think about it anymore, otherwise I'll just end up driving myself crazy.

The next door I open leads to a bathroom, and I almost burst into tears on the spot. They may not have electricity here, but at least there's actual plumbing. I think I might literally die if I could never take a real shower again. This bathroom is giant too, with a walk-in shower, a huge copper tub, and three sinks with a beautiful mirror hanging above them. I'm super tempted to strip off my disgusting scrap of dress and hop into the shower now. But I want to finish snooping through the house while Reule is still outside, and I'm certain he'll let me take a shower later if I ask.

I quickly check out the next few rooms. I find two more bedrooms, an office with, like, a million books I'm dying to look at, and a room twice as big as all the others that's filled with crates and boxes. The boxes are suspiciously similar to the ones that had been loaded onto the sled with me, so I decide to take a closer look.

To my surprise, the first few crates I manage to pry open are filled with bolts of fabric. I really want to look through them more carefully, because the patterns and colors are absolutely gorgeous. But I'm afraid I'm going to get the fabric dirty, so I refrain from touching them as much as possible. Another crate holds nothing but small wooden boxes filled with all sorts of gemstones and different pieces of jewelry.

After I discover another crate filled with shoes, I stand back and survey the room with my eyebrows furrowed. Why would anyone keep all this stuff locked away? It's a fucking travesty, honestly, because just the few things I've found are stunning. Does Reule sell these items somewhere? Do they belong to a woman who lives here, or used to live here?

As weird as it is, I haven't seen anything that might suggest Reule is a bad person—or anyone else who lives here, for that matter. Granted, there's still a lot to look through. But I feel okay. I feel as safe and as comfortable as I can, given the situation. I decide to go back to the front room to check if Reule's still outside. If I don't see him, or if he looks too busy, I'll just take a shower while I wait for him to finish with whatever he's doing.

There's a large window in the front of the house beside the door. The first thing I notice when I peek outside is that it's still snowing. Even though I'm pretty warm here in the cabin now, I automatically snuggle into my blanket. I step a little closer to the window and see that Reule is standing by the sled.

It looks like he's let the elk loose, and he makes a shooing motion at the animal before bending down to lift one of the crates. When he turns toward the house, I quickly kneel down low so he doesn't catch me creepily watching him. He carries it over to the front porch and sets it down, along with all the other crates and boxes that were on the sled. Earlier, I didn't really care to know what was inside any of them. But now I'm super curious. I wonder if he'll let me look inside once he brings them all in.

Reule walks back over to the sled, and I slowly sit up a little higher on my knees to see him better. He circles the sled for a moment, pausing once to shoo the elk away again. After he walks all the way around the sled to the back of it, he stops and puts his hands in his hair. He's still for so long, and I find myself practically pressing my face to the window to see what he's doing. He's not that far from the front door, but it's sort of difficult to see much with the falling snow.

Without warning, Reule lets out this loud, terrifying roar that causes the window to shake. I gasp quietly and lean back, and I watch in total shock as he lifts the metal cage he found me in and tears the thing apart with his bare hands. When it's broken into several pieces, he throws it to the ground with another sorrowful roar.

I should probably be terrified that Reule has that kind of strength. I'd already guessed that he's some kind of shifter, and I knew he was strong from the way he tore the cage door off earlier. But what he just did is a whole new level of crazy enhanced strength.

I'm not afraid though. Reule is clearly upset about the cage and the way that I ended up here, and I feel my heart softening toward him. Whatever happens to me after this, it's obvious he's not going to hurt me. Not on purpose, at least.

"Isla?" Reule calls out my name breathlessly as he suddenly bursts through the door.

I jump in alarm and blink up at him. I don't realize I'm crying until Reule crouches down in front of me and brushes my tears away with his thumbs. I take a shaky breath, trying to keep more tears from falling, but I feel like I'm about two seconds away from a breakdown.

Reule stares at me pleadingly, and he starts mumbling words so I fast I can't even attempt to make them out. I think he must have seen me crying through the window, and he probably assumes I'm crying because he scared me.

"I'm okay." I shake my head, but I'm crying harder now. I know Reule won't be able to understand me, especially not when I'm sobbing in front of him like this. So I throw my arms around his neck and hug him tightly.

He seems surprised at first, but he doesn't hesitate to wrap his arms around my waist. He's so warm and sweet, and he holds me while I cry and grieve over everything I've been through the past few days. It seems surreal to think about how I ended up here, and I'm not sure I'll ever really understand why.

CHAPTER SEVEN

ISLA

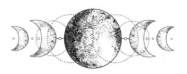

I CRY FOR SO LONG, I'M SURPRISED I HAVE ANY TEARS LEFT. I
know I'm just exhausted, but I thought I'd gotten my breakdown out of the way earlier when I was first put into the cage
on the sled. Apparently not. Reule has been incredibly sweet
and patient. I must be such a burden to him, but he hasn't
made me feel that way.

When I finally manage to calm down, I slowly pull away
from Reule's embrace with a slight grimace. I'm kind of
embarrassed after making such a scene. I wish so badly I could
just talk to him. I want to explain myself and tell him where
I'm from, and I want to ask him where we are and who he is
and about ten million other questions.

Reule cups my cheek with his hand and tilts my face up to
meet his eyes. He looks so sad and desperate and hopeful, all
at the same time. "Statečná."

He repeats the word a few more times, and I feel myself
blushing. I have no clue what the word means, but he makes it
sound like a compliment. I'm not sure I've ever held a guy's
complete attention like this, or had anyone look at me the way
he is. It's crazy intense.

I can't help letting my eyes wander over Reule's face. I've

never been a fan of facial hair on guys, but the beard suits him really well. He's incredibly handsome in a rugged sort of way, and his damned expressive eyes kind of make me feel like jelly. I think I might want to get to know him.

As soon as the thought crosses my mind, I mentally slap myself and quickly stand up. Reule stands up with me, looking totally alarmed, but I don't let myself make eye contact with him while I gather my wits. Seriously, what am I thinking? I don't know anything about this guy. Just because he's kind of cute, has a crazy-hot body, has been incredibly kind and has offered me pretty much the only scrap of safety and comfort I've felt since getting into this whole mess, that does *not* mean I need to start fucking idolizing him. Is it still considered Stockholm Syndrome if he's not technically my kidnapper or keeping me prisoner?

"Isla?" Reule says my name quietly. When I look up, he's biting his lip with this adorably vulnerable expression on his face.

I let myself relax. Reule is literally my only ally in this world right now, and my only chance at surviving for the time being. I'm beyond lucky I somehow ended up here with him when things could have gone so much worse for me.

"I'm sorry." I know he won't understand, but I say the words anyway and offer him a shy smile. I'm not sure what else to say or do, since we can't exactly have a conversation. I glance awkwardly around the room before pointing questioningly toward the hallway. I figure this is as good a time as any to ask about using that fancy bathroom.

He looks where I'm pointing and gestures toward the hallway as well, but it's clear he has no idea what I'm trying to ask or show him. I feel kind of weird leading him through his own house, especially because I'm making it pretty obvious I've already had a look around. But he doesn't seem perturbed as he follows me down the long hallway.

I stop outside the strangely-luxe bathroom that doesn't fit

in with the rest of the rustic-styled house. I raise my eyebrows at him and push the door open, pointing first at myself and then at the large copper tub.

Reule grimaces and slaps his forehead, groaning something under his breath. It's kind of adorable, and not the reaction I expected at all. When he darts into the bathroom before me and turns on the faucets in the tub, I have to stifle a giggle. Once the water is running, Reule turns around and starts rummaging in a little closet I hadn't noticed tucked into the corner of the room. He pulls out a large, fluffy towel and sets it on a little ledge behind the tub.

I don't think I've ever been more excited to take a bath, and I have a huge grin on my face as I step into the bathroom. At least until I look to my right and catch sight of my reflection for the first time since I was kidnapped from Rian's party.

"Oh, god!" I gasp in horror, throwing my hands up to cover my mouth. I knew I probably looked bad based on how dirty and grimy I've been feeling the past week, but I look *so much worse* than I expected. My skin is literally layered with dirt and sweat, my makeup from the party has smeared all over my fucking face so it looks like I have two black eyes and have been playing in a chimney, and the dried blood caked to my neck, shoulder, hair and chest makes me look like some kind of wild animal. Or worse, like a super fucked up-looking extra from *The Walking Dead*.

"My hair, oh my fucking *god!*" Tears form in my eyes and I swear I'm about to have another hysterical breakdown in about two seconds. My hair is so matted and hanging in *clumps* around my face. I don't see how I'm ever going to fix it. Oh god, I'm going to have to shave it off!

Reule interrupts my freak-out by putting his hands on my shoulders and spinning me around so I'm no longer facing the mirror. He shakes his head at me and says something in his dumb fucking language *that I can't understand.*

"Look at this!" I yell hysterically, grabbing two handfuls of my hair and shaking it at him. "I'm never gonna get this shit untangled!"

He purses his lips at me, and I instantly regret taking my frustration out on him. It's not his fault. I can't help feeling a bit fearful too, since I honestly have no idea how he's going to react to being yelled at.

"Isla." He sighs. My heart does this erratic little somersault at hearing him say my name. He shakes his head and smooths his hands down over my hair.

I expect him to say something else, even if I won't know *what* he's saying. But a surprised little yelp escapes my throat as he suddenly picks me up like I weigh nothing and sets me down closer to the tub, much further away from the vanity mirror.

Reule checks the temperature of the water filling the tub and gives me a little lopsided smile over his shoulder. I take a deep, calming breath and force myself to give him a shaky smile in return. When he stands up again, he makes a hand motion at me to stay put, and walks out of the bathroom.

Once I'm alone, I close my eyes and take another deep breath while I remind myself that things could be so much worse for me right now. I tilt my head back and slowly open my eyes, staring up through the skylight in the ceiling. All I see is white. I'm fairly certain it's still snowing outside, but the lavish bathroom is flooded with light, and it's starting to feel warm and steamy in here from the tub filling up.

Reule returns a few minutes later with his arms full. I watch curiously as he sets several bottles on the ledge next to the towel, along with a couple of fancy looking sponges. He picks up one of the bottles and glances at me from the corner of his eye, and proceeds to dump nearly the entire thing into the bathtub. Almost immediately, the bath fills with bubbles and a delightful floral scent permeates the air.

He lines the other bottles up neatly and points to them one by one, ticking them off on his fingers, and points at my hair. I step closer to him, hoping he's showing me products that will untangle my mess of hair. I blink up at him with wide eyes, and a slight blush forms on his cheeks. He clears his throat, growling a bit, and points to the last two bottles on the shelf as he awkwardly motions to my body. Lastly, he sets a toothbrush and a little bottle of what I'm assuming is toothpaste beside the sink. He points at it and mimes brushing his teeth like I might not realize what it's for. It's honestly really cute to watch.

"Thank you," I whisper. I wish I could express just how much I really do appreciate everything he's doing. Most guys would never put forth this much effort, and Reule doesn't even know me.

Reule nods, so maybe he does understand what I want to tell him. He threads his fingers through his short hair and gives me one last bashful smile, and exits the bathroom and shuts the door behind himself.

I FEEL AMAZING.

Seriously though, after soaking for over an hour and scrubbing every last bit of filth from my skin, I feel like a totally new person. Plus, whatever kind of shampoo Reule gave me worked wonders on my hair. I keep running my fingers through the long, dark strands just because I can.

I stand in front of the large vanity mirror and admire my reflection while I towel-dry my hair and body. The tub is still draining behind me for the second time. I had to drain and refill it once already after the water turned black from how disgusting I was.

To my pleasant surprise, I discovered that the last bottle Reule set on the ledge for me was lotion instead of soap. It smells like honey and vanilla, and I slather every inch of my smooth skin with the stuff—*thank god for laser hair removal!* A small part of me feels kind of bad for using so much of the products and water, but well...Reule gave them to me, didn't he?

Once I feel sufficiently pampered and my spirits have been lifted significantly, I wrap myself up in the fluffy towel and open the door to the bathroom. Steam billows out into the hallway as I peek my head out, and I don't see Reule right away.

"Reule?" I call his name softly. If he's a shifter like I think he is, he's bound to hear me if he's somewhere in the house. I'm just not sure if I should check the bedrooms or go back into the living room area to find him. I'd rather not drip water all over the place if I don't have to.

He steps out of the office with a book in his hands and goes totally still when he sees me. His eyes slowly travel up my form, his cheeks reddening with every passing second. My body tingles pleasantly at the attention, even though I know it's a bad idea to entertain the thought. I didn't want to get involved with any more supernatural creatures before I ended up in this mess—and especially not with any shifters.

But this is the first time Reule's seen me not looking like a nightmare, and I feel pretty fucking smug about it. I give him a coy smile when he finally meets my eyes, and I watch as his pupils dilate and his nostrils flare. Yep, definitely some kind of shifter.

"I feel so much better after that, you have no idea! Thank you!" I say it just to break the silence, but I think he'll basically understand the sentiment I'm trying to express.

He shakes his head slightly and mumbles something to me before darting into the next room over from the office. I follow him and stand in the doorway because I'm nosy and want to see what he's doing. He rummages through a dresser drawer, presumably looking for something for me to wear. It's so freaking sweet of him, and I sigh happily as I look around the room.

When I explored the house earlier, I only had a quick peek into the bedrooms. There's a king-sized bed taking up most of the space with beautifully intricate vines, leaves, and flowers carved into the wooden headboard. There are two matching side tables, both of them holding small lamps and tall stacks of books. Besides the dresser that Reule is looking through, there's also a large wardrobe and a cozy-looking leather arm chair under the window. On the wall opposite the bed, there's a fireplace that's quite a bit smaller than the one in the living room—I noticed there's one in each of the bedrooms—and it appears Reule has already lit a fire in here.

There are a couple of paintings pinned to the walls, but otherwise the walls are mostly bare. However, I nearly gasp in awe and delight when I look up at the ceiling to find the most gorgeous painting of the night sky, mapped out with unfamiliar constellations. Reule clears his throat, and I turn my head to find him holding a shirt and a pair of socks for me. He mumbles something to me with an apologetic expression on his face.

I take the clothes he's offering and smile gratefully, running my fingers over the fabric. The shirt is a muted gray color with long sleeves, and it's made of this incredibly soft material I've never felt before. If these are the only clothes he can find that might fit me, then it's probably safe to assume there aren't any females living here. I kind of hate myself for feeling relieved about that. But at the same time, this naughty, slutty, *obnoxious* part of my brain is telling me to drop the towel and get dressed right here in front of Reule while he's watching me.

With a tight smile, I spin around to make my way back to the bathroom to change, and I wonder again what the actual hell is wrong with me. I throw the clothes on quickly once I have some privacy. The shirt is pretty big on me, falling off one shoulder and hitting me mid-thigh. I have to roll the sleeves up a bit, but all in all, it's soft and comfy and about a million times better than my ragged evening dress. The cream-colored socks are warm and plush, and they're about knee-high on me.

Reule is still waiting in the bedroom—likely *his* bedroom. His eyes go straight to the small amount of skin on my thighs visible between the shirt and the socks, and he actually groans. It's extremely satisfying, but I pretend to be oblivious.

I'm not really sure what happens next. I've eaten, bathed, and I'm not in critical danger of getting hypothermia anymore. Am I just supposed to follow Reule around and wait to see what he's going to do with me? My smile slowly falters as my anxiety rises again. And then my heart practically leaps out of my chest when Reule steps in front of me and places his fingers on my chin, tilting my head to the side.

When his thumb brushes over my throat where I was bitten by Thaddeus's lackey, I let out a small gasp of pain. The area's still a little sore and bruised, but it seems to be healing okay. Normally, vampires can heal their victims' bites with their saliva to stop excessive bleeding when they're just trying to feed rather than kill. My bite has had to heal naturally, and I'm sure it hasn't helped that I haven't been able to clean it until now.

Reule grunts quietly, clearly displeased. But I checked the wound in the bathroom, and I'm confident enough that the wound is healing properly. It doesn't look puffy or infected, at least. He picks me up without warning and sits me on the edge of the bed so my feet are dangling over the side. I barely have time to blink before I find him kneeling on the floor in front of me, and my cheeks flush. My hormones are already on over-drive for some ungodly reason, so seeing him like this is sending all sorts of naughty, unwanted thoughts straight to my brain.

His hand grips my left ankle gently, and I cry out before I manage to bite my tongue and slap my hand over my mouth. Reule frowns up at me, mumbling something softly that I'm sure is an apology. With the tenderest touch possible, he slowly pulls the sock down my left leg and off of my foot. He touches different parts of my ankle, and I hiss quietly every time I feel a twinge of pain. I know he's not trying to hurt me, and it seems like he might know a little something about healing. I'm impressed he even noticed I was injured since I was trying to hide it, and he's spent much of our time together holding me or carrying me around.

After several minutes of testing the injury, he sighs and sits back on his heels. He stares up at me sadly, and I wonder what he'd say to me right now if he could. Instead of speaking, he lets out a short breath and stands up, motioning for me to stay put as he makes his way out of the room.

He returns quickly, holding all sorts of supplies in his hands. First, he hangs an old-fashioned-looking tea kettle on a little hook over the fire, and sets a mug on top of the dresser. I'm feeling like a pretty useless damsel in distress when he kneels in front of me again.

My whole life, I've always taken care of myself and Alistair. I'm not used to being helped so much, or of even needing this much help with anything. Being in this situation is terrifying and bizarre, but something about Reule makes me feel so…safe. There's something nice about being coddled like this. It's like I can set all of my worries aside for a little bit while he takes charge.

Reule holds up a bottle and pours out this weird-looking green paste into his hand. He flicks his gaze up to meet my eyes and gives me a rueful smile, and begins rubbing the pasty stuff all over my ankle. I grit my teeth and try not to move or react. It hurts a little, but mostly it feels super tingly—like that feeling you get when your foot falls asleep. Once most of my foot and ankle is covered in the stuff, Reule wraps a white bandage all around the area.

As soon as he's finished, he carefully helps me pull my sock back on. And then he freaking kisses the top of my foot and grins up at me. It might actually be the most adorable thing ever, and I'm fucking *swooning* over this guy. I can't help giggling, and he seems extra pleased about that.

I want to talk to him so fucking badly. Even if I have to mime my way through the whole conversation, I decide to give it a try. I awkwardly motion around the room and point at him. "Is this your room?"

He nods, and I smile as I point at the starry mural on the ceiling. "Did you paint that? It's beautiful."

Reule looks up and chuckles, shaking his head slightly. "Audun…" he trails off, saying something else in his language. I try to focus on the words he says, and I perk up when I realize *Audun* might be someone's name.

"Audun?" I repeat and point out into the hallway. I'm still curious and beyond anxious to find out who else lives here.

Reule's eyes light up, and he grins, nodding excitedly. He finally stands up and walks over to one of the bedside tables, rummaging in the drawer for a moment before sitting beside me on the bed. For a second, all I can focus on are the few inches of space he's left between us. But when he holds a photograph up in front of me, my interest is piqued and I lean in to get a closer look.

I have to blink a few times to comprehend what I'm looking at. It's an old-looking black and white photo of four guys in military uniforms. But the picture is actually moving, like they do in the *Harry Potter* movies. I've spent a lot of time around magic, but it seems like a really bizarre thing to find here. Especially so casually, just shoved in Reule's side drawer like it was. And in a place where they don't have cars or electricity, for fuck's sake.

"Já," Reule points to himself and then the first guy on the left in the photo. I peer closer and smile when I recognize him, appearing just a bit younger with a shorter beard and a stony expression. He points to each of the other guys one by one, from left to right, giving me their names as he does so. "Cae-lan, Audun, Maalik."

The three of them look to be the same age as Reule, and they all have short, tidy beards. It's difficult to make out distinct features because of the quality of the photo. Caelan is the tallest, Maalik is the burliest, and Audun is the only one who's smiling.

"Cute," I murmur quietly, tapping my fingers against my lips. I'm really confused about the military uniforms they're wearing in the photo, and I wonder yet again who the hell Reule is and why I was sent here. I glance sideways to meet his eyes and smile nervously, pointing at the photo and motioning toward the hallway and around the rest of the house. "They live here with you?"

He nods again. I'm glad he understands what I'm trying to ask, even if he can't tell me anything in detail. I wonder where these guys are right now and when they'll be back. Will they be as welcoming as Reule has been? Will they be angry I'm here, or will they be cruel? Somehow, I doubt it. If they're friends with Reule and they're anything like him at all, I imagine they're probably pretty decent. Even if they dislike me or they're annoyed at my presence, I don't feel fearful over my life at the thought of them coming home. Not like I did earlier.

Reule seems pretty happy, and I think it's because we're slowly figuring out a way to communicate with each other. He grins at me, and reaches behind us to grab a couple of books from the bedside table. He opens one of them up and sets it across our laps, and my eyes widen in amazement when I find myself staring down at a map.

He's speaking and pointing to a northern region of the map, and I get that he's probably showing me where we are. But for once, I'm not trying to keep up with what he's saying to me. My eyes rove over the pages, taking in this unfamiliar world. It's like looking at a map in the front of a fictional fantasy book, and I really can't make sense of it. But there's only one reason he'd be showing me a map right now. He's trying to figure out where I'm from.

Hope slowly blossoms in my chest. I thought for sure there'd never be any way I'd find my way back home. *To Alistair.* But Reule has a lot of books, and there's clearly magic in this world. I motion frantically at him, trying to mime drawing with a pencil.

Reule furrows his eyebrows and tilts his head at me. But then his eyes widen and he smiles. He quickly stands up, holding one finger up to show me he'll be right back. My heart pounds anxiously, so I focus on the map Reule was showing me to distract myself while I wait.

The area he'd pointed to appears to be primarily mountainous, and the borders of the region take up much of the land in the North. I suppose that might explain why it's so cold here. There are a couple of other regions with lines drawn to show their borders, and most of them are smaller than the one we're in. I wonder if this is just one continent, or if this map shows the entirety of the realm.

I bring the book closer to my face when I notice a few tiny scribbles above the mountains in the northernmost area of this region. The scribbles don't look like the rest of the writing on the map, and I realize it's a drawing of four tiny dragon-looking creatures. I hum curiously and squint as I try to make it out better. Is this what Reule can shift into? It's convenient that there are four of them drawn here, and Reule has three other roommates.

Upon closer inspection, I realize there are little dragon-like scribbles in certain areas of the other marked regions too. I'm so intrigued, my nose practically pressed against the page of the book to look closer at the impractically small words and drawings, that I don't notice Reule walk back into the room until he says my name.

I blink up at him, debating whether or not to ask about my

theory. When I see the sketchbook and pencils in his hands, I decide to leave it for later. I grin excitedly and thank him, setting the map book aside so I can take the supplies from him. The sketchbook is gorgeous, with thick pages and a leather binding. I wonder idly if he took it from Audun's room. He did suggest that Audun was the one who painted the constellations on his ceiling.

He doesn't sit back down next to me right away. Instead, he pulls the tea kettle off the fire and pours the contents into the mug he brought in earlier. I watch him for a moment before I begin making a rough sketch of a map of my world. I'm not the greatest at geography—I never finished school past tenth grade, and I've always been more interested in art and literature than anything else—but I do my best to make it look as accurate as possible. I even draw rivers and mountains in areas I'm positive there are some, and I draw a little star over New York City.

Reule slowly sits down next to me on the bed again, his eyes bright and full of curiosity as he looks over the map I've drawn. I point at New York and then myself. "That's where I'm from."

He doesn't respond verbally, but he holds his hand out to take the sketchbook from me. At the same time, he hands me the steaming mug. I take it carefully and raise my eyebrows at him, and he points at my ankle and then the mug. He kind of grimaces and says something in his language, and makes this goofy-as-hell hand signal while he closes his eyes and fake snores.

I burst into giggles. He just looks so cute and funny, but I get what he's trying to say. I'm incredibly grateful he's giving me a warning because I probably would have freaked out a little if I started feeling drowsy after drinking this without any sort of heads up. When I take my first sip, I realize with a start that I trust Reule. My stomach flutters nervously at the revelation, but I keep drinking the tea. It certainly tastes medicinal, so hopefully my ankle will be healed in no time.

Reule looks down at my map and rubs his hand over his jaw thoughtfully. After studying it quietly for a few moments, he picks up one of the other books he grabbed and flips through it. I catch a glimpse of several other maps. If I wasn't so worried about potentially finding a way home, I'd probably be itching to look through it more carefully. I didn't realize how many realms there were, or that traveling through realms was so common.

For a long while, Reule and I sit in silence while he compares my map to the ones in his book, and I sip my tea. The longer he looks, the less hopeful I feel. But it means a lot to me that he's even trying to help me by figuring it out. By the time he reaches the end of the book, a remorseful look on his face, I've finished off the tea he made for me.

"It's okay." I sigh and lean against him, rubbing my cheek against his arm affectionately before smiling sadly up at him. "I appreciate everything you've done for me."

He keeps his eyes on mine as he slowly closes the book and sets it aside. He hesitantly wraps his arm around my shoulders, and when I snuggle closer, he pulls me fully into his lap and hugs me tightly. My heart beats a little faster, from excitement and anxiety. I'm all-too-aware that I'm not wearing any underwear, and I know I smell way better than I did earlier when he was holding me. It would be super easy to give into this weird, exaggerated lust I feel for the guy right now.

But Reule doesn't get handsy or make any moves at all. He's a total gentleman and a sweetheart, just like he's been from the first moment I met him. He simply holds me and offers me comfort, and I relax against him. Eventually, my eyelids begin to droop, and I feel extra peaceful and sleepy.

Reule says something to me that sounds like a question, and I smile when I feel his chest reverberate from his growly voice. I blink up at him, and he smiles softly as he brings a hand up to brush a strand of my hair behind my ear. He points behind him at the pillows on the bed.

I know I need to sleep. I've lost track of how many hours have passed since I left Giovanni's warehouse. Even when I was locked up there, I didn't sleep well. But I still want to talk to Reule, at least for a little while longer. Who knows what's going to happen tomorrow, or where I'll end up next? I grab the first book he showed me with the map of this realm, and I open it up while he watches me curiously.

Once I find the right page, I point to those little dragon things and then at him. "Is that what you are?"

Reule appears totally dumbfounded. His mouth parts slightly, and he glances back and forth between me and the map. A grin slowly spreads across my face and I laugh, "It is, isn't it?" I point at the drawing with more confidence.

"Ano," he says, clearing his throat and nodding. With a shy smile, he hugs me tighter and chuckles as he says something else in his language.

Feeling pretty proud of myself for guessing correctly, even though I'm still not totally clear what he is *exactly*, I reach around him to grab the photograph of Reule and his room-mates. I point at the other guys and the map drawing, asking the same question. "Are they shifters like that too?"

Reule nods again, staring fondly at the photograph. Something else occurs to me. Clearly, there aren't any females living here, and I don't see a mate rune on Reule's wrist. Mating for shifters might work differently here, so that doesn't necessarily mean anything. But still, my curiosity gets the best of me.

I point at Reule and the other guys in the photo. Wiggling my eyebrows, I ask, "Are you guys together?" Reule frowns, not understanding my question. So I wiggle my eyebrows more suggestively and touch the tips of my index fingers together in a lewd gesture while I smirk.

The look on Reule's face when he finally realizes what I'm asking is priceless. He makes a noise somewhere between a snort and a growl and covers my hands with one of his. He tries to give me a stern look, but I notice his mouth twitching in amusement when he tells me in a firm voice, *"Ne!"*

My entire body shakes from giggling so hard. He chuckles along with me after a few seconds. There's something really sweet about laughing together and sharing a moment like this. After we settle down, Reule holds the photo up again and points to Audun, Maalik, and Caelan. He smiles affectionately and mumbles something softly under his breath as he gently brushes his fingers along my jaw.

Butterflies flutter in my stomach. I know I'm going to end up meeting them soon. A yawn escapes me, interrupting my anxious thoughts, and Reule hums softly as he lifts me up. Just a few seconds later, I find myself being tucked into the bed while Reule fluffs the pillows.

Part of me wants to fight to stay awake, just a little longer. But as soon as I rest my head on the soft, squishy pillows and curl up under the warm, fluffy blankets, I fall fast asleep.

CHAPTER EIGHT

ISLA

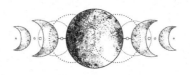

IT'S DARK WHEN I WAKE UP.

My eyes open slowly, and I panic when I can't remember where I am. I sit up so fast I make myself dizzy, and I glance frantically around the room while I try to remember what happened to me. I try to keep my breathing calm and even, but tears stream down my face. My gaze finally lands on the fireplace in front of the bed, and I rub my teary eyes as memories rush back to me. I'm at Reule's cabin in the middle of freaking nowhere in an unfamiliar world.

The fire has mostly died out, just a few embers emitting a tiny bit of light throughout the room. It's much chillier in here now, and I shiver as I wrap myself snugly in the blankets. I go still when I notice Reule sitting in the leather arm chair in the corner, a book open in his lap and his head propped up on his hand. He must have fallen asleep reading.

"Reule?" I call his name quietly.

He jolts up with a start and clears his throat, saying my name in a gruff, sleepy voice.

I whimper in response. I can't stop crying, and I don't understand why. I must have had a nightmare that woke me up, and I just don't remember. I'm sure my brain is still catching up and processing everything that's happened to me, but I still feel like a needy crybaby.

Reule crouches beside the bed and cradles my face in his hands, speaking in hushed tones. When I still can't seem to calm down, he sits down on the edge of the bed and pulls me into his lap. I seem to be finding myself in this position a lot, but I'm not about to complain. Reule is sweet and muscly and strong. If he's willing to offer me comfort while I'm on the brink of losing my shit, I'm going to take it.

He rocks me back and forth in his arms, still whispering and shushing me softly. I cry and cry, and even though he can't understand a word I'm saying, I unleash everything I've been trying not to feel the past several days.

"I can't believe this happened to me. Everything was fine. Al and I were *fine*. We were just having some fun at a party! I never thought his ex was that much of a jealous psycho that he'd actually try to kill me, or do something like this to me! And Bryson..." I sob even harder, curling my fingers against Reule's hard chest. He rubs his hand consolingly over my back and encourages me to continue. "I thought Bryson loved me. Just because we broke up and he picked someone else, I didn't think that would just erase everything we had together. I never thought he'd hurt me or want to see me dead. What did I do to deserve this? It's not fucking fair."

Reule mumbles something into my hair, and I lift my head to meet his eyes. "What am I going to do without Alistair? We've always had each other to rely on, and I don't think..." My lips tremble and another strangled sob escapes my throat. "I can't do this without him! I don't even know where I am, and you've been perfectly wonderful, but oh god, I'm never going to see my best friend again."

Alistair must be worried sick about me. I know if he'd disappeared like this, I would have gone fucking mad looking for him or trying to figure out what happened. But then my darker thoughts creep in and remind me that Thaddeus could have done something to Al too. How do I even know he's safe? What if he's in a worse situation than I am? Not knowing anything is killing me. I just hope and pray that Rian and Matthieu weren't full of shit like most supernaturals are. If Alistair is their mate like they said, I hope they're treating him well and taking care of him. I have to just keep telling myself that's the case, otherwise I'll never be able get through this with my sanity intact.

"What's going to happen to me?" I whine pitifully. "You weren't expecting me to show up here, and I can't just let you keep taking care of me like this. I can't just *live* here, mooching off of your kindness. And what happens when your friends come home? Was I sent here to, like, be your guys' pet? I don't understand."

Reule doesn't say anything. He just listens to me the best he can, and he offers me physical comfort by holding me close. He threads one of his hands through my long hair, and leans down to press a soft kiss to my forehead. Heat rises to my cheeks, and I'm glad it's too dark for him to see me blushing. I'm not sure I've ever felt more cherished, but that could be because I'm desperate for any kind of connection right now.

When he moves to stand up, I whine and hold onto him tighter. "Please, stay with me..."

He whispers something, squeezes my hand, and does that thing where he moves away really fast so he's nothing but a blur to me. I relax slightly when I realize he's just adding a few more logs to the fire, and I'm immensely relieved when he returns to the bed right after he's finished.

Rather than sitting on the edge like he was before, Reule pulls the covers back and slips in beside me. His movements seem hesitant at first, but I have no problem snuggling up to him. I rest my head in the crook of his neck and shoulder and keep my hands pressed against his hard chest, and he holds me close with both his arms wrapped around me. His beard is kind of scratchy, but it doesn't bother me as much as I thought it would.

We lie in silence for a few minutes, the only sounds coming from our soft breaths and the crackling of the fire. Reule is so warm and comfy, and I can feel myself slowly drifting back to sleep.

"If I'd met you back home somehow," I whisper to him. "I'd be so into you, it's not even funny. You'd probably be such a good boyfriend."

Reule hums in response. As much as I'd love to talk to him, it's kind of nice being able to say whatever I want without having to feel embarrassed.

WHEN I WAKE UP THE NEXT MORNING, I FEEL SO MUCH MORE rested and peaceful. Reule is still wrapped around me, only now I'm facing away from him with my back pressed against his chest. His large hand is splayed across my stomach, and I'm so ridiculously comfy that I'm hesitant to move and wake him up.

Sunlight is streaming in through the window, but it's not blinding. I wonder if it's still snowing out, or if it's pretty much always snowing here. The room is freezing too, like it was last night, so I assume the fire died out again. When I exhale, I can see my breath. That convinces me that I'm definitely better off staying snuggled up in bed with Reule.

A tiny smile forms on my face, and I softly brush my fingers over his arm. After spending so much time crying and freaking out yesterday, I've decided I'm going to try and make the best of my situation. I have no control over where I am or how I got here, and the fact is, I may never get back home. It's heartbreaking to admit that to myself, but I'm strong and I can adapt. Reule has more than proved he's pretty much the universe's biggest sweetheart, and I really do trust him to make sure I'm safe. Even if that means staying here with him and his friends.

Reule growls quietly, interrupting my thoughts. I turn my head slightly to see if he's awake or not, and he buries his face in my neck and nuzzles me gently. His beard tickles, and a quiet giggle slips out of my mouth.

I expect him to pull away, and to say good morning in his language or something. Instead, he pulls me closer so that our bodies are pressed together, and his hand rubs over my stomach as his fingers brush against the underside of my breasts. A delicious tingle runs through my whole body as I flush from head to toe. When Reule growls again and I feel his breath against the back of my neck, my nipples harden and my toes curl.

When I push my hips back, I'm not disappointed to find his hard cock digging into my ass. I let out a short breath that's almost a moan and move my hips again, encouraging him to take things further. I'm practically dizzy with lust, but I'm too nervous to initiate anything first. Reule and I don't really know each other, and I haven't been with anyone since Bryson.

But still, why shouldn't I sleep with Reule? He's fucking hot, and he's taken such good care of me since I wound up here. It's obvious there's chemistry between us, even if we can't communicate with words. And besides, Reule has literally seen me at my worst, and he still found me attractive. The language barrier is enough of an obstacle. I decide there's no need to be shy with him.

He pulls his hand away from my stomach, and I start to protest. But he pushes my hair back and begins lavishing my neck with open-mouthed kisses. His hand returns to the front of my chest where he lightly begins kneading my breasts over the shirt I'm wearing.

His mouth feels *so good*, and I need more. My nerves are quickly starting to dissipate as I become more turned on, so I let a long moan escape my mouth to let Reule know I'm enjoying what he's doing. He bites down on my neck lightly as he growls for the third time, and I place my hand over his. I guide his hand down my body to where the shirt stops just past my hips.

Reule pauses for a moment, his fingers hesitantly brushing under the hem. I'm not wearing any panties or *anything*, and I whine impatiently for Reule to just fucking touch me already! Slowly, so slowly, his hand slides over my hip and down to my pussy. The moment his fingers caress my clit, I moan his name and his entire chest rumbles with an animalistic roar.

He pulls away immediately, scooting backwards so there's a few inches of space between us. I furrow my eyebrows in confusion and roll over to face him. I find him biting his lip with the guiltiest expression ever while he grips his hair between his fingers.

My eyes soften as I scoot closer, and I rub my hand over his bicep consolingly. I figure he must feel bad because I can't verbally consent, or that he's afraid he's taking advantage of me. He's been such a gentleman about everything else that I wouldn't be surprised.

"It's okay," I whisper quietly. I trail my fingers over his chest, down to the hem of his shirt so I can slip my hands underneath to feel those wonderful, yummy abs. "I want you, Reule."

He still doesn't move, but I watch as his pupils dilate in that feral way that shifters' usually do when sex is involved. It's even more validation for me that he *does* want me, and all sorts of naughty scenarios race through my mind. What will it be like with him? Will it be rough and dirty? Or is he going to be soft and slow, the way he's been with me when it comes to everything else?

I slip my hand under the waistband of his soft, linen pajama pants and wrap my fingers around his huge, throbbing cock. His eyes close as he inhales sharply, and a whining growl gets caught in his throat. I gasp in amazement and excitement, slowly running my hand up and down his length as I press myself as close to him as possible in this position. God, I'm so fucking wet and so ready for him to fuck me. If he doesn't make a move in the next few seconds, I swear I'm going to just crawl on top of him and take control myself.

Reule grabs my wrist and pulls my hand away, and he finally opens his eyes as he shakes his head at me sternly. "Ne, Isla."

For a moment, I go still because I'm so shocked. Never in my life have I ever been rejected *while I'm in bed with a guy*. Did I read him completely wrong? I mean, he was *just* kissing my neck and fondling my tits a minute ago! What the fuck happened?

I'm so confused and mortified and ashamed. All those emotions hit me at once, and embarrassing tears prick at my eyes. I pull away from Reule, moving to the opposite side of the bed from him, and turn around to face the other way. I don't even have the luxury of leaving or storming out of here angrily. I'm stuck here in this stupid fucking cabin with him.

Reule sighs, and I feel him get up from the bed. I don't turn around, but I hear him putting logs on the fire again. I expect him to get in the bed again, to try and talk or apologize, but instead I hear his feet pad softly against the wooden floor as he walks out of the room.

The tears I was fighting fall freely, and I sniffle pitifully as I wipe them away with the sleeve of my borrowed shirt. I'm stupid to feel so upset and offended, but I can't help it. I feel connected to Reule, even though I know I shouldn't. I try to remind myself of everything I told myself yesterday. Getting involved with supernaturals is always a bad idea, but especially in a situation like this where I'm totally reliant on Reule.

I think the worst part is that I still feel incredibly horny. As mad and embarrassed as I am by Reule's rejection, I know I'd totally fuck him if he came back in here and changed his mind.

I've been sulking in bed alone for about fifteen minutes when Reule finally returns. Even though it's his room, he knocks on the door and calls my name softly. I don't turn around, choosing instead to glare at the window.

Reule sighs loudly and walks around to my side of the bed. When I still refuse to look at him, he sets a tray on the bedside table and crouches down on the floor so he's eye-level with me. He says my name and something else that sounds remorseful, but I still don't meet his gaze until he makes a truly pitiful whining sound.

His forest green eyes are full of guilt and regret, and I feel my heart stutter. I'm honestly being such a brat to him, and it's really not fair at all. Reule doesn't have to sleep with me if he doesn't want to, and who am I to get mad about that? He's already gone above and beyond to help me and make me comfortable, despite the circumstances.

For all I know, he has a mate or a partner somewhere. I also need to remind myself that I'm in a completely different world than the one I'm used to, and I don't know anything about the customs here. Maybe Reule is religious, or maybe there are laws against humans being with whatever type of shifter he is. I'm sure he would explain things to me if he were able to.

"I'm sorry," I mumble. I'm still too embarrassed to look at him for more than a few seconds, so I avert my eyes quickly.

Reule turns and grabs the tray, and my curiosity gets the best of me. I sit up to see what it is, and I swear I almost laugh. The guy will snuggle with me and bring me breakfast in bed, but he won't sleep with me? If I wasn't convinced before that I'm in a different realm, I certainly am now.

He seems extra shy around me as he sets the tray over my lap. There's a bowl of something that looks like porridge or grits, a glass of some sort of purple drink, and a smaller bowl full of unfamiliar berries. I give him a small smile in thanks and take a sip of the drink. It's sweet and refreshing, but I'm at a loss when I try to guess the flavor.

"Are you not going to eat?" I ask when Reule sits on the bed in front of me. I don't really expect him to answer, and he just tilts his head at me in confusion. I feel sort of weird with him just sitting there watching me eat, especially when things are still so awkward between us. But it's his room, and he was nice enough to make breakfast for me.

The porridge is okay, and I make sure to eat every bite. I don't want to offend Reule and make him think I don't like his cooking, and I also don't know what's going to happen today. Who knows when I'll get another chance to eat? When I move on to the berries, my eyes widen the moment I pop one of them into my mouth.

"Ooh," I gasp in delight. I've never tasted anything like these. There's so much flavor in just one little berry, somehow tasting both incredibly sweet and just a little bit tart. I look closer at the bowl full of them. They sort of look like black-berries or raspberries, but the shape is slightly off and they're all different shades of purple. My thoughts turn dark for a moment, and I wonder if maybe they're poison.

Reule grins and says something that sounds like a question, picks a berry from the bowl and pops it into his mouth. I feel terrible for thinking he'd feed me something poisoned, and I smile back at him shyly. We share the rest of the berries in a much more comfortable silence than before, and I quickly finish off the drink as well.

As soon as I'm finished with my breakfast, Reule moves the tray and sets it on the floor beside the bed. I feel nervous and uncertain about how the rest of the day will play out, but I watch Reule with interest as he crawls to the other side of the bed and grabs some of the books from the bedside table.

First, he opens the map book from last night to the page he'd originally shown me, and sets the moving photograph of him and his friends in their uniforms on top of the page. Reule appears slightly nervous, and I raise my eyebrows as he points to the photograph, the tiny dragon-things scribbled onto the map, and finally opens another book.

On the page, there's a colored illustration of a creature I've never seen before. It's large and grotesque, appearing to be a mix between a dragon and a leopard. Its body is covered in scales, and it has the legs and head of a large cat, impossibly sharp teeth and claws, and demon-esque horns protruding from its head. It also has wings that are almost as large as its body with sharp spikes on the tips, as well as spikes on the end of the beast's long, reptilian tail.

The illustration shows the creature foaming at the mouth, blood dripping from its teeth and claws. It's almost impossible to imagine a creature like this existing in real life, and even crazier to imagine sweet Reule shifting into something like this. But I know that's why he's showing this to me.

Reule's cheeks are red when I look up at him, and he won't meet my gaze. It's honestly heartbreaking that he's so ashamed, and I don't want him to start thinking I'm afraid of him. I reach forward and take his hand, threading our fingers together. He appears surprised when he looks up, and I give him a reassuring smile.

His eyebrows furrow, and he points at the illustration and then himself as he says something in his language like he's sure I must not be understanding.

I laugh and nod. "Yeah, I got that." I turn my head to the window and point outside. "You should just shift in front of me!" I make several more gestures, trying to get this point across.

Reule's jaw goes a bit slack as he stares at me in pure shock. I realize most people must react fearfully when they see him, and I think of the Monk-guy who dropped me off here and the way he took off running after Reule threatened him.

I squeal in surprise when Reule pulls me into his lap and

wraps his arms around me tightly. He mumbles something into my hair, and his voice is so full of emotion that I feel my heart drop into my stomach. I don't hesitate to hug him back. The awkwardness between us from earlier this morning has all but disappeared.

He pulls back slightly to rest his forehead against mine, and cups my face between his large, calloused hands. He keeps mumbling things I don't understand, repeating the word *'krásná'* several times. My heart races at the intimacy of the moment. God, I hope he didn't reject my advances earlier just because he worried I'd be afraid of the creature he shifts into!

When he sits up, he appears even more distressed than before. I thought he was happy that I seemed so accepting, so I'm more confused than ever. He won't stop staring at me either, his eyes traveling over my face in a way that makes me feel breathless.

"Reule," I whine pleadingly. I hold my hands up in an exaggerated shrug and shake my head, silently begging him to just try and explain what the hell is going on.

He bites his lip and grabs the book with the illustration again, flipping forward several pages before setting it in front of me. This time, the illustration shows three bright, full moons and a pack of the shifter-beasts underneath. They're chasing a woman, and the illustration depicts her screaming and crying, her expression full of unadulterated terror.

I admit, *this* illustration definitely gives me pause. I stare at it for several long moments, trying to figure out what exactly it means. Eventually, I give up and point to the three full moons, and I raise my eyebrows questioningly at Reule. Is it even possible for a world to have three moons like this? I'm fairly certain the moon back home controls the tides of our oceans, and I wonder what sorts of things would be affected by having three of them. Or does it even matter, since this is a different realm with totally different rules?

Reule nods and points up, like that'll help it all make more sense to me. But I just have to see it for myself, so I scoot off the bed and step over to the window. I don't particularly want to go outside in the cold yet, but I will if I have to.

It's not snowing anymore, but the ground outside Reule's window is completely blanketed in white. It's beautiful and untouched, and I spend a few seconds admiring it. Whenever it snows in New York, it never lasts long before it turns all gray and mushy. I remind myself to focus and look up at the sky, and I'm surprised to discover that I *can* actually see the faded shapes of two full moons.

I turn my head to look at Reule over my shoulder, and he gives me a tight smile as he nods. He points up again, toward the other side of the house, indicating the position of the third moon as he holds up the book and points to it once more.

"Úplněk Nestvůr ," he says mournfully.

"Okay," I say quietly. Even though I still don't know what he said, or what this all actually means. I slowly walk back over to the bed and sit down beside Reule, looking at the awful illustration of the shifters chasing the terrified woman.

Reule runs his fingers through his hair and breathes through his nose, clearly frustrated over our lack of communication. He meets my eyes, a silent apology written in his expression. He points at himself, the photo of his friends, and the shifters on the page. And then he hesitates just for a second before pointing at me, and finally pointing at the woman in the illustration.

My brain goes fuzzy while I piece everything together, and I gasp and clamp a hand over my mouth. Is he telling me that tonight, a night with *three* full moons, he and his friends are going to chase me down and kill me? Suddenly everything makes so much sense. I can't imagine that this triple full moon thing is that common of an occurrence, and all of the gifts on the sled must have been sent because of it. No wonder they put me in a cage like that. I was meant to be used as a sacrifice all along.

It's obvious Reule doesn't agree with this, that it never would have been his choice to have me brought here. That just makes it so much more heartbreaking, because I can't even blame him. If it's in his nature when he's shifted, I know he won't be able to control himself.

Still, I need to be sure. A few tears fall as I take a couple of gasping breaths. I have to trust that Reule will try and figure out a way around it. He's only telling me now so I'm prepared, and so that I know what he's doing if he takes insane measures to protect me from himself. I point desperately at the illustration of the crying woman and ask, "You guys are going to kill me?"

He looks distraught at my reaction, but I can tell he has no idea what I'm asking. I point at the shifters on the page and then the woman, and make a ridiculous growling sound as I act out gnashing my teeth together like an animal. I finish my stupid little game of charades by slicing my finger across my throat and pretending to be dead.

Reule stares at me like I'm insane, and rapidly shakes his head. "Ne, ne! Isla…" He trails off and says something else, but all I can focus on is the word *no* coming out of his mouth.

I nearly collapse in relief and widen my eyes at him incredulously. "No? Then what? What's going to happen tonight?"

He turns shy again, and his eyes flit down my body and stop on the bare skin of my thighs. He motions between the two of us, but he's *so* hesitant about it. He's really not very good at this charades thing, but after a few awkward moments on his part, I think I might understand what he's saying.

I feel stupid when I do it, but the gesture worked well enough last night when I asked Reule if he and his roommates were lovers. I point at the photograph of him and his friends, and then myself, and I make a gesture where I insert my index finger into the closed fist of my other hand. "The full moon is going to make you guys want to fuck me?"

Reule's face turns as bright as a tomato, and he covers my hands with his to stop me from making the gesture. But he nods once, and that's more than enough confirmation for me.

I snort in amusement and annoyance, and I smack his shoulder as I roll my eyes. Seriously, the guy made me think I was going to be eaten in some kind of sacrificial ceremony for monsters. I don't think I've ever been so relieved in my life.

Being ravished by four shifters may not be the most ideal situation to be in, but it's a hell of a lot better than being dead! I figure they'll probably have to be in their human forms for it to actually be possible, and I can see how awful things might have turned out if I'd been completely ignorant of everything when it happens. As long as I can meet Reule's friends before nightfall, when this whole ceremony is supposed to go down, I think I'll be okay. If everything is consensual, it might not actually be that bad.

I pull the book closer to me and flip forward a few pages until I come to another illustration. This one shows the same pack of shifters and the woman as before, only now the woman is standing in the center of the page while the shifters sit in a circle around her. There's a crown on her head.

The next page shows a close up drawing of her hand, and my breath hitches when I see the complicated rune mark etched into her skin.

"Oh..." I turn and look at Reule with wide eyes. He looks more apologetic than ever.

I'm an idiot for not understanding before, but now I know why he pushed me away earlier. After dating Bryson for over a year, I'm very familiar with the mating practices of shifters. Once a shifter chooses a mate, and they complete a mating bond during a full moon, they'll share a connection for the rest of their lives. A mate bond can be passionate and over-whelming, and shifters never separate once they're mated.

From the illustration in this book, it appears that it prob-ably works similarly for shifters here in this world. Only, Reule is a type of shifter I've never seen before, and I imagine three full moons will make the bond much more intense than anything I'm used to seeing from back home.

I rub my hands over my eyes and lie face down on the bed. I need a minute to freak out and wrap my brain around all of this. If I have it right, tonight during this triple-full-moon, Reule and his shifter friends will be compelled to ravage and mate with me, and then I'll be stuck here with them forever without any possibility of ever finding my way home.

Reule is sweet, and I really like him so far. But how can I begin to entertain the idea of spending the rest of my life with him? We don't even speak the same language! And as for Caelan, Maalik, and Audun, I haven't met them yet. What are they going to think of all this? Think of me?

I feel Reule place his hand on my back, and he says something quietly. I sit up and turn to face him, willing myself not to cry. It's not his fault or his choice. Honestly, he's just as much a victim in all of this as I am. I move closer and wrap my arms around him, hugging him tightly so he knows I don't blame him for anything.

He hasn't tossed me out or abandoned me. He's done everything possible to explain things to me, to help me understand. And I guarantee he only pushed me away when I wanted to have sex so I wouldn't resent him for it later.

Reule hugs me back, and I remind myself of everything I told myself when I woke up this morning. Things could be so much worse, and I'm strong enough to adapt. I can make the best of anything.

CHAPTER NINE
MAALIK

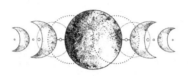

CAELAN RAMS HIS SHOULDER AGAINST MINE AS HE STORMS PAST, but I don't reprimand him for it. Not today.

We've been dismissed and given reprieve from our duties and responsibilities for the next week. Normally, I'd be ecstatic at the opportunity to spend this time with my brothers. We usually only get a few short days to spend together each month. But tonight is Guardians' Night, and in just a few hours, the Beasts' Full Moon will be shining down upon us. Already, I can feel Caelan and Audun withdrawing into themselves, and I know the four of us will probably isolate ourselves from one another through tonight and the next few days.

I watch my brothers walk ahead of me into the forest. Caelan shifts the moment we reach our usual clearing, but Audun glances back over his shoulder at me and raises his eyebrows in question.

"Go on ahead. I'll see you both at home." I wave my hand in dismissal, and he shifts a moment later. The two of them push up from the ground and take off into the air, and I keep my eyes trained on their beasts' forms until they're only a speck in the sky.

A melancholy sigh leaves my mouth, and I rub my hand

over my aching chest as I glare up at the three full moons. They're all visible now, since it's such a clear day, and they'll be much brighter in a few hours when the sun sets. The Beasts' Full Moon only presents itself once every forty years, and this is my and my brothers' third time experiencing it. It's the only time we're able to choose a wife, and to bond her to us. When darkness falls and my beast takes control of my thoughts and actions, I know I'm going to feel as though my soul is shattering and my heart is breaking.

The same thing has happened the past two Guardians' Nights we had this damned Beasts' Moon hanging over us. I have a feeling it will be even worse this time. The more time that passes without a wife, without a soulmate, the emptier and more feral I feel.

Caelan likes to blame me whenever he's in a surly mood, and whenever his loneliness starts to become too much to bear. But for years, the four of us have always been in agreement. The cons outweigh the pros when it comes to claiming a wife.

I sigh again and shift into my beast. As the leader of our family, I need to stay strong for my brothers' sake. I hope Reule is doing alright at home. He always takes my side in matters of importance, but he's much better at cheering our brothers up than I am.

Even though they had a head-start, I catch up to Audun and Caelan within minutes. Audun nips at my heels playfully, and I swat a paw at him in response. Caelan is entirely unamused. He growls at us and flies ahead so he doesn't need to be near us. My heart clenches, knowing he's in pain, and being unable to help.

The moment we reach home, I can tell something's amiss. I stand in the yard and sniff around anxiously, and Caelan and Audun peer up at me curiously in their human forms.

"What's the matter?" Audun asks, holding his hand up to keep the sun out of his eyes.

My beast's eyes catch on a glimmer in the snow, and I shift back and walk over to investigate. I pick up a piece of jagged metal and hold it up for my brothers to see. "I'm not sure." I grunt. "But I have a weird feeling. One of you go and grab Reule while I have a look around."

As soon as I say his name, Reule steps outside and walks toward us. He looks anxious and keeps tugging at his hair, and my body tenses as I go on high alert. A million scenarios race through my mind of what could have happened in our absence.

"What's wrong?" I ask with a growl.

Reule stops in front of us, out of breath with his hands on his hips. He refuses to meet my eyes as he looks between Caelan and Audun. "What's up, guys? How much time did the King give us off?"

Audun and Caelan exchange a look, and Audun shrugs. "A week. Same as last time."

"Brother." I snarl. I'm losing my patience quickly, and my panic is rising at the thought of my family being in some sort of trouble. I hold the piece of metal up and shake it toward Reule. "What's going on here? I can sense that something is off."

Reule's eyes flash with anger when he catches sight of the metal in my hands, and he snarls as he grabs it from me and throws it across the yard. My eyes widen in shock, and there's a moment of thick silence between all of us.

"Listen," Reule finally says. He tugs at his hair again and meets my eyes. "You know one of the Elders came yesterday to deliver more gifts from the King, right? Well, he brought a girl with him. King Janak gifted us a *wife*."

Caelan and Audun perk up at the same time I recoil. "No! Why would he do such a thing? We've told him time and time again how we feel about this matter."

"She agreed?" Audun asks hopefully. "She *wants* to be with us?"

I cut a glare at the youngest of my brothers before turning back to Reule. "Tell me you sent her back."

Reule shakes his head, his eyes slowly filling with rage and heartbreak. "She doesn't speak the same language as us. She's not even from this realm, and she had no idea what was going on when she got here. Maalik, they..." Reule bares his teeth and tugs on his hair more forcefully. "They had her in a cage."

Caelan and Audun snarl, and my eyes go to the spot Reule threw that jagged piece of metal he grabbed from me. My gaze darkens when I realize that must have been part of the cage he's referring to.

"Where is she now? Is she okay?" Caelan demands, glancing up toward the house as he takes a step forward.

Reule holds his hands up to stop him and nods. "She's fine. She was pretty hurt when she got here, and nearly frozen to death. The cage they had her in was so small, she could barely move around in it. She was wearing hardly any clothing, and they only gave her one blanket. I'm surprised she even survived the trip. You know it's probably an eight-hour journey by sled from the castle."

I brush past Reule and storm toward the house. Betrayal is heavy in my heart. I've always been loyal to my kingdom, and to my King. To learn that King Janak would allow a human being to be treated this way, that he would participate in human trafficking and send a scared, defenseless girl to a pack of monsters against her will...I feel as though I'm going to be sick.

When I step inside, I expect to be met with the sound of a weeping girl. But I have to blink several times in surprise as I take in the scene before me. The crates and gift boxes sent by the king are strewn all about the room, every one of them open with items spilling out. I don't think I've ever seen our living room in such a messy state, but I don't have time to think about that now.

My eyes land on a beautiful girl standing beside one of the

crates. She's holding a pile of fabric in her arms, and she's wearing an intricate crown on her head.

She appears surprised to see me standing in the doorway for a moment, but she gives me a shy smile and says my name like it's a question. "Maalik?"

My heart flips and my face warms at the sound of her voice. I hate myself for thinking it, but she's stunning. And she looks…happy. Reule said she'd been hurt and held in a cage like an animal, but *this* girl is so far from what I'd expected to find.

Caelan and Audun step in behind me and pause when they see her. Reule shoves past all three of us with an annoyed expression on his face and walks over to stand beside the girl. I glare at him and say, "She's not crying."

"Of course she's not. I've been taking care of her!" Reule rolls his eyes at me. He turns to smile at the girl and places his hand on her back, and my eyes narrow at the familiarity between them. "Guys, this is Isla. Isla, these are my brothers —Maalik, Caelan, and Audun."

He points us out as he says our names, and I feel myself growing more defensive and confused. "How did she already know my name when I walked in? I thought you said she couldn't speak our language."

Is this some kind of trick? Did the King send a girl here, pretending to be weak and defenseless so we'd take her in and grow attached to her?

"She doesn't." Reule bares his teeth at me, obviously growing frustrated. "But she's not stupid. I showed her your photograph so she'd know who you all were when you got home."

Caelan finally shuts the door behind us and furrows his eyebrows at Isla. "What the hell is she wearing?"

My eyes return to the girl and my face warms again as I take in her outfit. It looks like she's wearing one of Reule's shirts and a pair of his socks. *Nothing else!* Her thighs are bare where the shirt falls, and the shirt is thin enough to show the outline of her breasts and the peaks of her hardened nipples.

Reule shrugs defensively and brushes a strand of her dark hair over her shoulder. She looks nervous as her eyes move between me and my brothers. Reule gestures at the crown on her head and says, "She likes it. She wanted to see what was in the crates that were delivered, and she found it in one of them."

"Not the crown." Caelan laughs. He walks closer to Isla and Reule and smiles down at her, and gestures at the indecent outfit she's wearing. "The crown is cute, but I'm talking about *this*! Did you dress her, Reule?"

Caelan and Audun snicker at the look on Reule's face, but I don't find it very funny at all. Reule glares at our brothers and says, "I didn't have anything else that would fit her!"

"Sure, pervert." Caelan teases. His entire demeanor has changed since we left the castle a short while ago, and I know he's entertaining the thought of making Isla our wife. He bends down so he's eye-level with her and gives her a charming smile as he takes her hand. "It's very nice to meet you, Isla."

She giggles when he kisses her hand, and he looks extremely proud of himself. The sound of her laughter makes my heart race a little faster, and I realize with a bit of panic that the Beasts' Moon might already be affecting me. Just being in Isla's presence right now is dangerous, and if we spend much more time around her so close to nightfall, it might be too late to stop a bond being formed between us.

"Tell us everything," I growl at Reule. The sooner we get Isla out of here, the better. I can't very well kick her out in the snow with nowhere to go, and I need to know all the details of how she ended up here and what's happened since.

"Yes, but first…" Caelan stands up, still holding Isla's hand in his. I have to bite my tongue to keep myself from yelling at him to stop touching her. Cael grins and pats his stomach, and he mimes spooning something into his mouth. "Are you hungry, beautiful? Has Reule been feeding you?"

Reule crosses his arms petulantly. "Of course I have."

Caelan smirks in bemusement and asks, "What did you make, then?"

"She had soup yesterday, and I made oatmeal this morning."

"Good lord, tell me you're joking!" Caelan exclaims, making an exaggerated face of disgust. Reule makes a rude hand gesture, and Audun barks out a laugh at their antics. As anxious as I feel, I can't help cracking a smile too. Isla smiles back and forth between all of us, and then she giggles and says something incomprehensible to Caelan in her sweet, melodic voice.

His smile softens, and he gently pulls her toward the kitchen. She follows him, and I nearly have a heart attack when he picks her up and sets her on the counter.

"Are you insane?" I growl angrily. "She just met you, and we have no idea what this girl's been through! What if she didn't want you to touch her? You're going to give her the wrong idea, Caelan!"

He has the decency to look ashamed of himself, and he gives Isla an apologetic look before going to rifle through the pantry.

Reule shakes his head and leans against the counter opposite from Isla. "Don't worry. She's not shy about letting you know when she's annoyed with you."

Audun walks over and stands a few feet away from Isla, smiling at her shyly. Like me, he's never been as forward with women as our other brothers are.

"She's really pretty," he says. "Did the king really send her here to be our wife? I honestly can't imagine him doing something like that."

Reule nods, clenching his jaw angrily before he begins explaining. "Her cage was covered so I didn't see her right away, and the Elder was so damned smug when he revealed her to me. He said, and I quote, *'the King had something special sent for you, just in time for Guardians' Night! All the way from another realm, I heard!'* She was crying and trembling, and *god*...he actually expected me to be excited. To be grateful!"

I keep my eyes on Isla, feeling that awful betrayal burn in my chest again. There's no reason for an Elder to lie, not to us. I know the King would prefer for us to pick a wife, and we've argued about it countless times. But I never expected he'd go this far, or do something so insane, in order to make it happen.

"Once I had her out of the cage, I told him we would personally be hunting him down once you arrived back home. I promised to tear him to shreds, slowly. The man nearly pissed himself. He couldn't get away from me fast enough."

Caelan returns from the pantry and sets all sorts of ingredients on the counter next to the stove. "We can do that. Once she's our wife, we legally have the right to kill anyone who's harmed her in any way."

"We're not making her our wife." I sigh deeply and rub my temples. Before Caelan can argue with me, I narrow my eyes at Reule. "You said she was hurt?"

Reule glares back at me when he answers. "Yes. Her ankle was sprained, and I think she was bitten by a vampyre." He steps closer to her and delicately touches his fingers to her jaw, and she allows him to tilt her head to the side. "Look at these marks here. They're healing okay, I think. But when she arrived, she had dried blood caked all over here and in her hair."

My chest constricts, and I feel sick to my stomach. *A vampyre?* Audun leans closer to Isla and voices my thoughts, a slight growl in his voice. "Where the hell did she come from that she's seen a vampyre?"

"No idea." Reule shrugs. "She drew a map of her world for me, but I don't recognize it. I looked through the *Atlas of*

Known Realms, and I didn't see anything remotely similar. But I think she's familiar with shifters too, because she guessed what we are before I attempted to explain anything to her."

"How could she possibly have guessed that?" I growl, narrowing my eyes at her again. I just want to understand. Even if King Janak wanted us to find a wife this badly, why go to all the trouble of finding a girl from an entirely different realm unless he wanted to make sure she didn't know anything about us?

Isla meets my eyes and sits up straighter with a frown on her pouty lips. I realize it probably seems like I'm glaring at her, and my face heats up for the millionth time since I walked through the door. I quickly avert my gaze from hers.

"I don't know! I must have given something away, because she almost immediately pointed out the Guardian markings on the map of Briya once she noticed them. And when I showed her the illustrations in the *Book of Guardians* later, she didn't seem very surprised. Just curious, if anything."

Reule gazes at her with so much admiration and light in his eyes. He reaches out and tucks a strand of her dark hair behind her ear. When she smiles back at him, I know I need to speak up. Reule's been in her presence alone for too long that he's completely lost his mind to the Beasts' Moon already.

"Brother," I start with a remorseful sigh.

"She's clever, and she's so sweet and funny. The language barrier sucks, but it's easier to talk to her than you'd think." Reule cuts me off, his eyes turning more and more feral by the second. "I just know you guys are going to love her, and honestly, tell me she isn't the most beautiful woman you've ever seen in your life."

"Reule!" I put enough of a roar in my voice to make the window above the kitchen sink shake, and everybody gives me their attention. When Reule blinks at me, I hold my hands out in a disbelieving shrug. "What are you doing? You know we can't make her our wife. I can't believe you're even considering it! She can't consent!"

"We can *try* to explain things to her," Audun suggests unhelpfully. I glare at him and shake my head. We can't even talk to her. How could we possibly explain something so complicated?

Isla makes a humming sound and looks around at each of us, and then she focuses on Reule. "Beasts' Full Moon?" She has an accent and her pronunciation is off, but it's obvious what she's attempting to say. She says a few more words in her language, and looks around at us questioningly.

"Yes!" Reule nods vigorously, giving her the most pleading, pathetic look I've ever seen. "They think you don't understand, sweet girl."

She points to the crown on her head and looks at each of us like we're stupid. I exchange a glance with Audun, silently asking if he understands her, but he shakes his head and shrugs. Isla rolls her eyes and hops down from the counter.

Reule cringes and reaches for her, calling after her like he's reprimanding her. "Isla! Your ankle!"

She peers at him curiously over her shoulder, and he points exaggeratedly at her foot. She wiggles it a bit, holds her thumb up to him with a coy little smile on her face, and walks toward the hallway where our bedrooms are.

I feel like I'm in shock as I stare after her, and my heart does this ridiculous little somersault. Caelan nudges my elbow, a smug expression on his face. "Did you see that? You're standing here screaming and roaring like a lunatic, and she just rolled her eyes at us."

Isla returns a moment later with a few books in her hands, and she sets them on the counter where she was sitting. My brothers and I watch her curiously as she holds up the *Book of Guardians* and flips to a page depicting an illustration of a group of Guardians surrounding their chosen wife while they're in their beast forms.

First she points at the Guardians, and then around at each of us. I know Reule *said* she knew about our beast forms, but I've never met a single person who isn't terrified when they see us shift. Isla doesn't appear fazed in the slightest, and my heart races faster as I continue to watch her. Dear god, if this is how I feel after being around her for half an hour, no wonder Reule is unable to think clearly.

When she points at the Guardians' wife next, then to herself and the crown on her head, I inhale sharply and widen my eyes at her. My face suddenly feels like it's on fire, I'm blushing so hard. There's no way she realizes what she's insinuating, is there?

"What?" Audun coughs, and he stares at Isla in shock. "Is she...does she mean it?"

Reule bites his lip and looks at her like he's a second away from claiming her right here in front us. He taps his finger against the illustration of the Guardians' wife. "Is this why you're wearing a crown, Isla?"

I look closer and realize the woman in the illustration is wearing a crown too, and my stupid heart practically leaps out of my chest. Isla nods, touching her fingertips to the crown upon her head. She looks a little embarrassed, and I hate that I can't explain what her gesture truly means to us.

"Sure looks like she's consenting to me." Caelan gives me this self-assured smirk that would normally make me want to punch him in the mouth. But underneath his cockiness, I can tell he's genuinely delighted. It's been a long time since I've seen him so happy.

He's going to hate me for not allowing him and our brothers to claim Isla and bond her to them.

"You guys aren't thinking clearly." I growl in frustration. "This is a girl who was taken from her home and brought to a strange world where she doesn't know anyone or speak our language. You've known her for a *day*, Reule. It would be cruel and selfish for us to trap her here, unable to ever leave or find her way home. What does she actually know about Guardians, or the bond we would have to form with her?"

Reule and Audun look devastated at my words, and Caelan glares menacingly. They know I'm right, but Reule still rubs the back of his neck sheepishly and argues, "She knows it involves sex with the four of us, and she seemed to recognize the rune marks that occur with the bond when she saw a picture of them in the book."

My eyes seem to have a mind of their own, because my gaze drops to the smooth, tanned skin of Isla's thighs that's on display for us all to see. I wonder if her skin feels as soft as it looks, and I wonder what sort of sounds she might make if I were to brush my fingers underneath the hem of her shirt or kiss the sensitive skin of her inner thighs. I've always wanted to share a woman with my brothers. The magic of our nature makes it so that we have to share a wife, but we've never seriously considered claiming somebody before. All of us have had lovers and brief romances with women over the many years we've been alive, but most women are offended and scandalized at the mere idea of being shared between the four of us. Maybe things would be different with Isla...

No! I shake my head, desperately trying to rid myself of the thoughts. "Please, Reule. We've discussed this so many times, and nothing has changed. Look at the other Guardians' wives. They're all completely miserable. I don't want things to be like that for us, and Isla would resent us. Maybe she knows what a rune mark is, and maybe she's willing to be intimate with us. But how are you going to explain to her that being with us means becoming immortal? She'll never change or age, never grow old. We'll never be able to give her children. There's no way for us to know how she would feel about those things."

Every year, we're allowed to visit with the Guardians of the other Kingdoms in our realm. Nearly all of their wives are resentful and wretched. I'm sure they started out as nice girls, but time has turned them cruel and unhappy. In the Kingdom of Aequvir, the Guardians' wife shows obvious preference for the leader of their family and never gives her other husbands any sort of time or attention. And even worse, the wife of the Guardians in Kova is terrified of her husbands. It's common knowledge that she spends nearly every day locked in her own room, and she cries any time her husbands try to show her any affection.

The Guardians of Briya before us were unhappy too. From the stories we've heard, their wife was mostly content. But she never came to terms with the inability to have children.

Just thinking of winding up in a scenario like that, with a wife who hates and despises me and my brothers, honestly makes me feel sick. Audun, Caelan, and Reule are the most important part of my life, and they deserve all the love and happiness in the world. But our life is so strange and unconventional. How could we ask any woman to give up every aspect of her life just to be with us?

"We won't be like those other Guardians," Audun mumbles. "We can make Isla happy."

I take in the closeness between Reule and Isla, and I shake my head again. "She's already showing Reule favoritism."

Caelan snorts. "*You* might have something to worry about, but women find me charming. Just give me a day or two, and I guarantee I'll be her favorite."

Before I can point out that trying to become her favorite would literally only help my argument, he winks at Isla lasciviously. She giggles at him, and he grins triumphantly as he turns back around to focus on making dinner.

Audun appears a bit deflated, and Reule reaches around Isla to pat his shoulder consolingly. "Ignore Cael. You know he's an idiot. Isla's going to love you too. In fact, I think she's interested in art. She was really impressed by the mural on my ceiling, and the map she drew doesn't look half bad."

"Really? Can I see it?" Audun asks excitedly.

I rub my hands over my face and curse inwardly. All three of them are convinced we should make her our wife, and they're deluding themselves into thinking everything will be fun and easy. I knew they were lonely—I am too. But I didn't realize how badly all of them have been aching for a soulmate. I still know without a doubt that bonding Isla to us would be a terrible idea, but maybe if I can compromise with them…

First, I need to make them see that I'm looking out for Isla's best interest too.

"What if she already has a husband or a partner back home? What if she has a family? You're all being completely selfish right now. We should be talking about a way to help her find her way home. Not convincing ourselves to trap her here for the next thousand years or so."

Reule, Caelan, and Audun go silent and stare at Isla guiltily. Reule hesitates for a long moment, but eventually he sighs and admits, "She did mention a couple of names to me. I mean, I think they're names, but I wasn't sure how to ask."

Even though I know it's probably a good thing, and it looks like I might finally be getting through to Reule, I feel a sharp pain in my stomach at the thought of Isla being with somebody else. I know it's only because of that damned, cursed moon, but it's already starting to feel like she's ours.

"Well? What were the names?" I demand.

"Uh…Alistair?" Reule stumbles over the word that might be a name, and raises his eyebrows at Isla in question.

She'd been peeking over Caelan's shoulder to see what he's cooking, but she gasps and spins around to face Reule when he mentions the name. She repeats it excitedly. "Alistair?"

Judging by the looks on my brothers' faces, I think it's safe to say we all feel a mix of curiosity and despair. Reule holds his hands out like he's shrugging and asks, "Who is Alistair, Isla?"

Isla blinks at him, and her eyes fill with tears. I feel my

chest tighten, and Caelan makes a low whining sound beside me. She quickly wipes them away and begins speaking rapidly, and starts pointing between the four of us before clasping her hands together. She says something else we can't understand, her voice lowering and carrying a slight wobble, and touches her heart and clasps her hands together again.

Reule pulls Isla into a hug, and she wraps her arms around him. While he comforts her, Audun hums thoughtfully. "Her brother, then? Or maybe her friend? They're obviously very important to her."

"So she has a family," I say pointedly. "What were the other names she mentioned, Reule?"

He still has his arms around Isla when he peers down at her and asks, "Bryson?"

Isla reacts even more strongly to that name. Only, this time she pulls away with a disgusted look on her face. She shakes her head and angrily spits, "No!"

I think we're all a little shocked, and aren't really sure what to say or how to react. But Isla doesn't give any of us a chance to try before turning around and opening the sketchbook she set on the counter, quickly flipping to an empty page. Audun hovers over her shoulder and watches as she scribbles something furiously.

We wait anxiously until she's finished, and she holds the drawing up for us to see with an extremely pissed off expression on her face. The figures she's drawn are cute and almost childlike, but it's clear she does have some artistic talent like Reule guessed.

"Isla, Bryson..." She points to the first two figures in the drawing—a couple holding hands with little hearts above their heads. She takes her pencil and scribbles a jagged line between them and draws an arrow from Bryson to another couple that's holding hands much like the first one. Isla breathes angrily out of her nose and points to the new couple. "Bryson, *Amelia*."

"What?" Caelan scoffs. "He left her for some other girl? Was he blind?"

Audun takes the sketchbook from Isla and draws a big 'X' over both drawings of Bryson. He makes an exaggerated angry face at Isla and growls at the page. "Bryson's an ass, and we hate him!"

Isla laughs and smiles broadly at Audun. She says something to him in her sweet voice, and I know it doesn't matter that he can't understand a word she's saying. Reule was right about it not being so bad trying to find a way to communicate with her. And he was certainly right about her being sweet, funny, and clever too.

"We *can't* claim her as our wife," I sigh despairingly. "There are too many things that could go wrong, too many ways this could end up disastrous. And it would be so unfair to her. She has a family, and a whole life in a completely different world than ours. I'm not saying we need to kick her out, or anything like that. She can stay here with us while we try and figure out a way to get her home. I'll go and personally speak with King Janak first thing tomorrow."

Reule's face twists, and I can practically feel his pain like it's my own. "Maalik, I think it's too late for me. My beast has already claimed her, and I know this sounds insane, but...I think I love her."

My beast takes control for half a second, and a deep, satisfied growl fills my chest. It occurs to me that Reule might have slept with Isla before we arrived home. That could be how they formed a connection so quickly, and why a connection is forming so easily and naturally for me, Audun, and Caelan too.

I bite my tongue before I ask him whether he did or not, and take a deep breath to try and remain calm and rational. "We just need some distance." I glance anxiously out the window, trying to gauge how many hours we have left until nightfall. "It's probably too late to take her to Runa's now, but we'll lock her in the cabin while the four of us spend the night up in the mountains. If your beast tries to get to her, we'll hold you back."

"I won't!" Caelan snarls. "Why are you doing this, Mal? I've always wanted a wife, and Isla is perfect! If she's mad at us later for claiming her, then we'll do everything we can to make her happy and make this life worth it for her. Just because you're afraid she won't be able to love you, that's no reason to punish the rest of us."

His words hurt more than I'd like to admit, but I try not to let it show. Reule threads his fingers through his hair and tugs at the strands with a heartbroken expression on his face.

"I don't think I can let her go."

"We'll still care for her," I promise quietly. "And we'll try to help her find her family. We just won't make her our wife. I swear, the next Guardians' Night where a Beasts' Moon is present, we can truly choose a wife. I didn't realize how badly you all wanted one. We'll find someone just as perfect, someone who wants us and cares for us all equally."

The kitchen is quiet, and nobody argues further with me. I can feel my brothers withdrawing again, pulling away from me and from one another. My chest feels tight and heavy, and I don't know how to help them. All I know is that it wouldn't be right to claim Isla, to take her life and her choices from her for our own selfish needs.

I meet her eyes, and she frowns. She looks almost as heartbroken as my brothers do. Even though she doesn't speak a word of Briyan, something makes me think she understands much more of our conversation than I realized.

CHAPTER TEN

ISLA

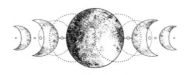

I DON'T THINK MAALIK LIKES ME VERY MUCH.

Caelan and Audun are being sweet, which is a relief, but I can't help glancing over at Maalik every few minutes. I know I'm being stupidly obvious about it too. I had no idea what to expect when Reule's friends came home, but I was still somehow thrown when they started arguing about me. I can only pick up on a few basic words thanks to Reule now, but it was pretty obvious their discussion revolved around me and this *Úplněk Nestvůr* thing.

From what I can gather, Reule wants me to be their mate and Maalik doesn't. I'm so confused, and I can't figure out what's going on. Is it going to happen, or isn't it? I feel so anxious, and I keep going back and forth between feeling relieved and feeling hurt. I know it's not the same thing, like, *at all*, but knowing Maalik doesn't want me makes me feel really shitty and reminds me of how I felt when Bryson chose Amelia to be his mate instead of me.

Reule made it seem like becoming their mate was inevitable. When he was showing me the book with the illustrations, he acted so guilty and distressed over trying to make me understand. I spent the entire morning and afternoon trying to come to terms with it, to convince myself it wouldn't be so bad. People end up in arranged marriages all the time, right? I told myself it would be like that.

I even put a fucking crown on my head to be cute and show that I'm trying to embrace my new life. If I don't have a choice in the matter, and the guys don't either, I figured I can be a good sport and try to do my best to get to know them. When I was with Bryson, I was an amazing girlfriend—even if the douchebag did take me for granted. I'm sure I can be a good mate to these guys too.

I'm honestly feeling pretty stupid about the crown now.

I know I should be more pissed at Reule. Either he exaggerated by making it seem like this mating thing was going to happen no matter what, or he's just nowhere near as determined as Maalik to keep it from happening. Plus, they asked about Alistair and Bryson. So that might mean they're still going to try and help me get back home, right?

Every time I look over at Reule, I feel butterflies in my stomach and a weird ache in my chest. I can't stop thinking about our almost-moment in bed this morning and every sweet little thing he's done for me since I ended up here. Would it be so bad to be his mate? He'd probably treat me like a queen. His friends are cute too, and I certainly wouldn't oppose to being the center of attention of four strong, sexy shifter men. Especially if they treat me as well as Reule has. Of all the things that could have happened to me after Thaddeus tried to have me killed, and then sold on the supernatural black market, getting stuck here with these guys isn't so bad at all.

God, what the fuck is wrong with me? I should be focused on getting back home. Not jumping into bed with four strangers, no matter how hot they are. I totally blame this Stockholm Syndrome thing. Or maybe these crazy moons are messing with my head.

As soon as the thought crosses my mind, I realize I might

be onto something. If these moons are powerful enough to force these guys into choosing a mate like that book suggests, it's pretty reasonable to think it might be affecting my judgment. Maybe it's affecting Reule's too, and that's why he was arguing in favor of mating with me instead of helping me get home.

My eyes move to the other side of the room where Maalik is standing beside the front door. He's hammering something into the wall on each side of it, and nervous butterflies writhe in my stomach as I watch him. I don't have a clue what he's doing, but his roommates are ignoring him. It's clear they're not very happy with him, but I think I may have judged him too harshly before. He's obviously in charge, and I'm sure there's a good reason for that.

"Isla," Caelan growls my name. It's a cute growl, and I turn around to face him with a smile.

"Caelan?" I sing his name back to him playfully and flutter my eyelashes. I probably shouldn't flirt with these guys until I know what's happening with this full moon stuff, but I can't help it. Caelan is ridiculously hot. He's tall and broad-shouldered, and he has this perfectly-tousled dirty blonde hair, very pretty hazel eyes, and a smirk that makes me want to do some extra naughty things with him. He has a beard too, like every male I've come across in this world, but it's short enough that it's more stubble than anything.

He looks exactly like the kind of guy I'd go for back home, which should probably be a red flag, but he's been so friendly to me since the moment he walked through the door. I'm pretty sure he was teasing Reule about his cooking earlier, and I'm excited to see what *he's* cooking for me now.

"Ochetnuj," he says, holding a spoon up to my mouth. He's asked me to taste every single thing he's made so far, and everything has been freaking delicious. There's some kind of meat dish cooling on top of the stove, along with some vegetables I've never seen before. I think there are still some potato-looking things in the oven too. He's obviously really talented in the kitchen, and I've never been so eager for a meal before.

I open my mouth without hesitation, and I don't miss the feral glimmer in his eyes when he puts the spoon in my mouth for me to taste his next dish. My eyes light up when I taste chocolate—or something that tastes extremely similar to chocolate, at least.

"Ooh, that's really good!" I exclaim. I hadn't realized he'd moved onto making dessert.

Before Reule, I've never had a man cook for me before, and I'm feeling awfully spoiled right now. It's making me feel even weirder about this mate thing, and it's like every kind gesture any of them makes gives me all sorts of butterflies and makes me think I *want* to be their mate. Which is stupid. I have to keep reminding myself that these moons are most likely screwing with my head.

Caelan chuckles and says something to Audun, and Audun looks up and gives me a charming half-smile before going back to his drawing. After the four of them finished their discussion, they all seemed a little irritable. But then Maalik walked away and started working on whatever the hell he's doing to the door, and Caelan focused on dinner. Reule picked me up and set me back on the counter, kissed my fore-head, and started carrying all of those crates down the hall-way. I assume he's putting them in that room filled with other boxes, but I'm still curious to know what all that stuff is for and why they keep it locked up like that.

Instead of helping Reule or one of the other guys, Audun hopped up on the counter with me and started drawing in the sketchbook I've been using. He's sitting about four feet away from me, and I can't see *what* he's drawing, but it's surprisingly nice having him nearby. Actually, both he and Caelan are amazing company. It's fun sitting here with them, even though we don't speak the same language. I was super nervous when they first got home, and it's definitely weird and jarring listening to them have a conversation while not really being able to understand or contribute. But so far, the guys have done their best to find ways to make me feel included. I wish I could tell them how much I appreciate that.

I watch Caelan pour the chocolatey mixture into a pan, and I turn to gaze at Audun. He's seriously freaking adorable, and I'm dying to see what he's drawing. If he painted that mural on Reule's ceiling, I know he's an amazing artist. He's concentrating so hard, biting his lip, with his dark, curly hair falling into his brown eyes. He has gorgeous, warm brown skin and long, elegant fingers. He has a beard too, but luckily it's just a *little* bit longer than Caelan's.

His eyes flick up and meet mine, and his face breaks out into a grin. Normally, I'd probably be embarrassed at being caught watching somebody so intently. But his smile is infectious, and I find myself smiling back easily.

"Isla," Caelan sings my name to me this time, drawing out the syllables like I did to him a few minutes ago. When I turn to face him, he hands me the bowl and spoon he'd just used to mix his dessert.

"Oh my god. You're letting me lick the spoon?" I ask tenderly, shaking my head. "Why can't the guys back home be like you? This is seriously the sweetest thing ever!"

Caelan doesn't bother trying to decipher my rambling. He just gives me a sexy little smirk, swipes a finger in the bowl, and sticks it in his mouth. Audun leans over and swipes a finger through it too, and I giggle at them before bringing the wooden spoon to my lips so I can enjoy my pre-dinner chocolate-batter snack.

Reule walks into the kitchen carrying two crates, and he says something to Caelan before setting them down. I peer into them, raising an eyebrow when I see a bunch of fruit on the top. Those crates look ridiculously heavy, and he's carrying them like it's nothing. I know he's a shifter with crazy

enhanced strength or whatever, but I can't help letting my eyes
wander up and down his body appreciatively.

He does a double take when he catches me checking out
his butt, and he snorts in amusement when I give him an innocent smile in return. I remind myself again of the moons and
the fact that becoming these guys' mate would *not* be a good
idea, and I turn my head to look over at Maalik again. He has
to have a plan or something, right? How many hours are even
left until the sun sets?

I'm a little surprised to find Maalik is only standing a few
feet away, and he's already watching me. When our eyes meet,
his face reddens and he nervously rubs the back of his neck.
He quickly looks away, and I allow myself to admire him for a
few seconds.

He's a bit shorter than the other guys, but he's much
broader in his chest and shoulders. He has striking, fiery red
hair that's just the slightest bit wavy, and a constellation of
freckles scattered across his face and the backs of his hands.
I'm more than a little curious to see if he has just as many
freckles covering the rest of his body. His beard is thicker and
fuller than Reule's, and his eyes are the most gorgeous
cerulean blue.

"Isla, ah…" He hesitantly meets my eyes again and
gestures awkwardly with his hands. I think he's trying to ask
me a question, but he's even worse at charades than Reule is.
Eventually he points at the door, so I figure he wants to show
me whatever he was building over there.

Reule and Caelan bare their teeth at him in annoyance,
and Maalik stands up straighter and schools his features. He
doesn't bother to berate them or defend himself, and it kind of
makes me respect him more. I feel badly that they're fighting
because of me, and I don't want to cause any problems if I
can help it. Not when they've been so nice and welcomed me
into their home under the circumstances.

I hop down from the counter so I can take my bowl to the

sink and wash my hands. If Maalik wants me to go look at the front door, I don't see why I shouldn't. Reule frowns at my feet and grunts under his breath when I jump down, and I smile to myself at his over-protectiveness. Seriously, my ankle doesn't hurt at all anymore. That weird green stuff he rubbed all over it and the tea I drank must have worked wonders.

After I set the mixing bowl and spoon in the sink, I pull my sleeves up and look around for anything that looks remotely like soap. There's a little dish with a lid sitting near the faucet that looks like it belongs in an old lady's house. Before I can check to see if that's where the soap is, Reule startles me by grabbing my wrist somewhat roughly.

"Reule?" I try to pull my hand away, but he doesn't let go. His pupils have dilated so much that I can barely see any green in his eyes, and his gaze is locked intently on Madame's brand on my wrist. I raise my eyebrows and tap my finger against the brand questioningly. "Is this what you're worried about?"

He blinks at me, his eyes slowly losing a bit of that feral glint. Instead of answering me, he calls Caelan over and holds my wrist up for him to see. I feel myself getting annoyed, but I hold still and let them gawk at the brand for a few moments.

Caelan seems worried, rather than angry like Reule does. Caelan asks me a question, but I just stare at him blankly since I can't understand a word he's saying. I'm not sure why they're freaking out about it so much. I'm a little surprised Reule didn't notice the brand before when he was so observant about everything else.

Reule loosens his grip and rubs his thumb over the brand, and he stares down at me with a heartbroken expression as he asks me a question too. The butterflies in my stomach go crazy over that, but then Maalik walks over holding the book with all the shifter illustrations Reule showed me. Maalik opens it up to the page with the mating rune marks, and then awkwardly gestures between the drawing and my wrist.

I furrow my eyebrows and shake my head. My brand is just Madame Deverell's initials, and I don't think it looks anything like a rune mark. But since their written language looks so different from mine, I can maybe see why they're concerned or confused over it. While I try to figure out the best way to explain the brand, I wonder if the spell is even active anymore. I mean, my contract has technically been broken, right? It's not like I can work for Madame *now*.

"Um…" I point to my neck at the bite marks that are still healing. Reule had pointed them out to his roommates earlier, and I'm pretty sure they'd even used the word 'vampire.' Only, they said it kind of weird so it sounded more like *vam-peer*. But still, I figure that means they're at least somewhat familiar with the creatures. I repeat the strange pronunciation of the word and hope I'm right. "Vampeer?"

Reule, Caelan, Maalik, and Audun give me their complete attention, and they look horrified at what I've just said. Audun gives me these sad-but-adorable puppy dog eyes and touches his canine teeth, and softly brushes his fingertips over the side of my neck as he repeats the word. "Vampeer?"

"Vam*pire*," I nod, pronouncing it the way I normally would.

Audun smiles a little, and points to the brand on my wrist to silently ask whether or not it came from a vampire too. I start to nod, and then change my mind and shake my head. I have no idea how to explain Madame to them, so I figure I'll just do my best to explain what happened with the vamp that bit me and died from it. I gesture to the sketchbook and pen that Audun left on the counter behind him, and he hands them to me without question.

The book is still open to his drawing, and my mouth drops in awe when I see that it's a drawing of *me*. It's an unfinished sketch of my face, but it's already so fucking good and I'm ridiculously flattered. He even drew the crown I'm wearing, and I grin broadly at him before I flip to a blank page. He smiles back bashfully.

I quickly scribble a little cartoon of a girl and a vampire on the page. I'm nowhere near as good as Audun is at drawing, but I'm not normally *this* terrible. I hope I get a chance to show him something better later, and I'd at least like to see more of his work if he'll let me.

"Isla, vampire." I point to the drawings. I feel kind of dumb demonstrating this way, but it worked well enough when I was trying to explain who Bryson is. I point to the vampire drawing and chomp my teeth together, tapping the side of my neck. All of the guys frown, and Caelan lets out a low, keening whine.

"This mark," I tap on my wrist and take a shaky breath. I've already cried about what happened, but I didn't realize it would still be so difficult to remember how terrifying and awful and painful it all was. I grimace at the cartoon I've drawn and point to the vampire, and then I slice my finger across my neck. Reule seems to understand what I mean right away, but I draw an 'X' over the vampire for the other guys just in case.

"It saved my life," I say quietly. After all the time I spent working with Madame Deverell, I never truly thought she cared for me. I was just useful to her. I'm sure the only reason she went to such lengths for a protection spell had more to do with her interests than mine, but I still hope someday I'll be able to thank her for it somehow.

All four men stare at me in horror, and Caelan pulls me into a hug. He wraps his arms around me protectively and kisses the top of my head, and Reule begins stroking his hand over my hair from behind me. I close my eyes and relish in their attention. Even if they don't know exactly what happened or why, it's incredibly sweet of them to offer me so much comfort. It feels like they really do care about me.

I've never felt that with anyone but Alistair. Maybe I

convinced myself I felt that with Bryson for a short time, but looking back now, it's obvious that I was just projecting a lot of my own desires onto him and our relationship. His feelings for me were never genuine. I was just so desperate for someone to love me and cherish me.

As I hug Caelan back and rub my cheek against his chest, I think I can definitely get used to this. Even if it's not with him, or with Reule, Audun, or Maalik, *this* is how I want to be treated. *This* is how I want to be loved.

"Ne," Caelan growls suddenly. I lift my head to look at him, only to see that he's baring his teeth angrily at Maalik. Reule's doing the same, and Audun jumps in by shouting something furiously at their red-haired roommate. Maalik is only able to get a couple of words out before the other men start yelling at him in outrage.

Poor Maalik glances at me for a quick second, and then he sets his jaw and crosses his arms in a defiant manner while he stares his roommates down. I have no fucking clue what this is all about, but Reule, Audun, and Caelan honestly look like a pack of angry puppies barking at their friend.

"Cut it out!" I pull away from Caelan and Reule, and spin around so I can face all four guys at once. I narrow my eyes and point at the three shouting idiots one at a time so they know I'm irritated with them. "What the hell are you all going on about? It's not like it's Maalik's fault I was bitten by a fucking vamp!"

They've all just reminded me how dramatic and short-tempered shifters can be, and I roll my eyes when the four of them just stand there staring at me like I'm the one who's insane. It's probably good timing because I'm getting way too comfortable with them way too quickly. *Stupid. Fucking. Moons.*

Maalik blinks his pretty blue eyes at me like I've stunned him, and his face reddens as he continues to stare. I wish I knew what he was thinking. Eventually he clears his throat and turns around, and he motions at me over his shoulder to follow him.

I ignore the other guys when they whine at me, and I follow Maalik over to the front door. I'm pretty curious to see what he was building while Caelan cooked dinner, and I wonder if it has anything to do with making sure the guys don't try to mate with me tonight.

On either side of the front door, there are these large, metal brackets hammered into the frame. There are three on each side, with about two feet between each of them with the highest brackets being about a foot above my head.

"Uh...?" I stare at them for a few seconds, and turn to look at Maalik quizzically.

He looks so uncomfortable, and he completely avoids my eyes as he gestures awkwardly to a few beams of wood lying propped against the wall. I hadn't noticed them before, and I watch as Maalik picks one up and fits it into the brackets so that it acts as a barricade on the door.

It takes me more than a few seconds to figure out what the hell he's showing me, and I feel my heart drop into my stomach and the blood drain from my face. I wrap my arms around myself and stare up at Maalik with wide eyes, shocked he would be so cruel to me. Even though the other three guys are clearly upset with him, I still thought for sure that Maalik was on my side.

"You're going to lock me outside?" I point to myself, and at the door and the window to the right of it. I hate how weak and terrified I sound, but I'm honestly panicking at the thought of being stuck in the cold again. I'm not sure I'll be able to survive it again, and certainly not overnight.

"Ne, Isla!" He exclaims, shaking his head frantically. My heart stutters a little, but I'm still too anxious and frightened to feel any kind of relief yet. Maalik flinches when he meets my eyes, and he seriously looks devastated. He says something else in his language and glances behind me a few times like he's waiting for one of the other guys to jump in, but the three of them remain surly and silent.

A frustrated growl leaves Maalik's throat. He points exaggeratedly at himself and his roommates and points outside. His gaze softens when he points at me, and he points at the floor and waves his hand to gesture around the house. "Isla, zůstaň."

Oh. I guess that makes a little more sense, but now I can't help staring at the beams of wood dubiously. They're thick, and they look really heavy. I watched Reule tear apart that metal cage like it was made of paper yesterday. There's no way in hell three hunks of wood are going to keep giant leopard-dragon shifters out, especially not when there are three full moons making them all feral and crazy. The illustrations in the book Reule showed me made it pretty clear the guys will literally hunt a mate down if that's what it takes.

"*This* is your plan?" I ask in disbelief. I raise my eyebrows at Maalik and shake my head. After all that arguing, I thought he'd have some fool-proof idea that would keep this mating thing from happening without question. I furrow my eyebrows and point at the front window. "Even if these pieces of wood somehow do *anything*, you guys can easily just break through the glass on all the windows!"

Audun and Caelan snicker from behind me, and Maalik's face reddens again. I'm honestly not trying to tease him. I'm legitimately concerned and confused.

Maalik grunts and mumbles something under his breath. Without meeting my eyes, he gestures for me to pick up one of the beams of wood to stick it in the brackets he made. I'm still extremely doubtful of this so-called plan, but I humor him anyway.

To my surprise, the beams are way heavier than they look. I have a pretty hard time lifting it, and I feel kind of embarrassed having the guys watch me struggle to fit it into the second-highest brackets. Even with a stool or something, there's no way I'll be able to lift one of these wooden beams any higher than this.

"Mal..." Reule sighs and says something else in a consoling tone. Maalik doesn't respond. He threads his fingers together and rests his hands on top of his head while he stares at the front door like he's trying to solve the world's hardest riddle.

I'M NOT SURE HOW LATE IT IS EXACTLY. IT'S STILL LIGHT outside, but I think the guys are getting ready to leave soon. Caelan and Audun are cleaning up from dinner while Reule stokes the fire in the living room. Maalik disappeared into one of the bedrooms. There's a tense, aggravated silence between everyone that's putting me on edge.

Dinner was really nice, and everything tasted delicious. I was so right about Caelan being an amazing cook. I tried my best to make sure he knew how impressed and thankful I was, and I think he understood.

Besides the food, just sitting with the four of them while we ate was fun. They had me sit at the head of the table, and I felt like their guest of honor. Or like I was a part of their family. The four of them had been so quiet and glum at first, so I started talking. I said any little thing that popped into my head. Even though none of them could understand a word I was saying, the guys gave me their rapt attention and smiled like I was the most entertaining thing they'd ever seen. At one point, Audun started trying to teach me some words in their language—the words for the dishes and utensils, all of the food we were eating, and even some of the furniture around the room. I know I was getting all of the pronunciations wrong, but he was so cute and encouraging about it. I'll have to write down everything I can remember later, so I don't forget.

I feel pretty useless as I stand around watching them clean up and prepare to leave for the evening. The mood in the house is drastically different now than it was while we ate dinner, and my heart feels heavier with every second that passes. I know it's at least partially the full moons and this bizarre world and situation making me feel so connected to the guys. But I really like them, and I really just...

I don't want them to go.

"Don't be fucking stupid, Isla," I mumble angrily to myself. It's not like I won't see them again. They're only leaving for tonight so they don't make me their mate. When they come back, things will be fine and normal. I can get to know them and still try to figure out a way to get back home to Alistair.

Reule steps in front of me. His expressive green eyes are full of hope and desire and heartbreak, and my heart skips a beat as he cups my face between his large, calloused hands and presses his forehead against mine. He whispers my name and says something else that makes me wish so desperately I could understand him.

I close my eyes and lean into his touch, and I allow myself to say exactly what I'm feeling even though the logical part of my brain knows it's ridiculous. "I don't want you guys to leave. I want to be with you."

"Reule!" Maalik growls as soon as he walks into the room. Reule reluctantly pulls away from me and turns to look at Maalik with the most disdainful expression I've ever seen anyone make. In any other situation, I'd probably find it pretty amusing.

Maalik ignores Reule and barks something loud enough to get Audun and Caelan's attention. They walk into the living room area with glum looks on their faces. All four men hover near the door for a couple of minutes, speaking in hushed tones to one another. When they turn to face me at the same moment, I know they're about to say goodbye.

"No!" I whine loudly. Panic is quickly rising in my chest at the thought of them leaving me, and I feel stupid tears prick at the corners of my eyes. I don't care if it's some sort of magic making me feel this way, and I don't care about the consequences. I give each of them a pleading look and beg, "Please, stay here with me."

Audun groans, and Reule tugs on his hair with a look of pure agony on his face. Caelan just growls and crosses his arms, but Maalik is the only one who responds to me.

"Isla." He sighs and takes a step closer to me. From his tone alone, I know he's not going to change his mind. I pout at him and only feel mildly satisfied when a blush forms on his cheeks. Maalik quickly walks into the kitchen and comes back with the sketchbook in his hands. He opens it to the page I used to draw a map of my world, and he meets my eyes with a determined expression on his face as he points first at me, and then at the star I drew over New York City.

The tiny part of my brain that's still thinking rationally feels grateful and excited over his gesture. I knew Maalik was probably worried about helping me get home, and this just proves it. But my emotions are too wild and muddled, and all I can focus on is that they're going to leave me.

I turn my head and raise my chin, refusing to look at him any longer. I don't care that I'm acting like a brat. He's made it clear he doesn't like me or want me the way that Reule, Caelan, and Audun do.

Maalik sighs again and says something to his roommates in an authoritative tone. Tears fill my eyes when I hear the front door open and a sudden burst of cold air causes goose bumps to form on my bare skin. I can't bring myself to watch them leave.

After a few moments, Maalik growls my name in that same bossy tone he just used on the other guys. I finally turn my head to glare at him, only to find him standing alone in the door frame. His cheeks are red, but his features remain emotionless otherwise as he points to those obnoxious wooden beams sitting next to the door.

I roll my eyes and force myself to walk over to him, and I nod my head in acknowledgment when he keeps pointing at the beams. He and I stare at each other wordlessly, and the butterflies in my stomach go crazy as I watch his pupils dilate.

Maalik shakes his head, killing the moment between us. My heart clenches painfully as he mumbles something quietly, and he steps outside and shuts the door behind him. I hold my breath, desperately trying to hold back my ridiculous tears while I listen for any sign that they're truly gone yet or not.

"Isla!" I jump at the gruff sound of Maalik's voice from the other side of the door. When he growls, I realize he's waiting for me to put the damned wooden beams up in the fucking brackets he spent so long fussing over.

"Okay, *Jesus*." I yell back, rolling my eyes hard even though he can't see me. I lug the heavy pieces of wood up and stick them in the two lower brackets.

I wait to see if he's going to say anything else or bark any more commands at me. When I'm only met with silence, panic replaces my annoyance and I quickly rush over to the window to peer outside.

Maalik, Audun, Reule, and Caelan are already gone.

CHAPTER ELEVEN
ISLA

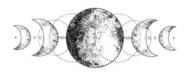

I CRY FOR ABOUT AN HOUR AFTER THE GUYS LEAVE ME ALONE at the cabin.

Like some pathetic-ass damsel in distress, I sit next to the front window wailing like a little bitch, hoping they'll come back and love me. The house feels so strange and terrifying without them here, and I've never felt lonelier in my entire life than I do now.

I finally snap out of it, thank god, and now I'm just pissed. Stupid Maalik thinks he's too good for me? That I'm not good enough to be their mate? What a fucking prick! Those guys would be lucky to have me, and I guarantee they'll never find a girl hotter or more amazing than me to be their mate. They have no idea what they're missing.

Since I have all the time in the world, assuming those jerks won't be back until morning, I decide to snoop through the house. Unlike last time I looked around, I'm not going to bother trying to be sneaky about it. They'll be able to smell me on everything anyways, so why try to hide it?

I start in the living room and kitchen, making sure to check every single drawer, chest, cabinet, and closet. My anger dissipates for a couple of minutes when I discover the pantry and freezer behind the kitchen. They're huge, and there's so much food that we could probably survive for months up here without ever having to leave the house. The pantry holds tons of jars and canisters with different ingredients, and even some things that look pre-prepared. It's probably ridiculous of me, but I really admire these men for being so organized and practical.

We probably could have been happy together. They could have cared for me and spoiled me, and I would have spoiled them right back. I would have done my best to learn their language, and they would have helped me find Alistair. And Al would have been so freaking happy for me. All I've ever wanted is a real family, and to be loved. Really, truly, loved.

Reule, Maalik, Audun, and Caelan clearly share a very close bond. I'm only just starting to discover how close they really are, and how special and important they are in this realm. I know I still have so much to learn about them, and even though I only spent a couple of hours with them, I just know in my heart that I could have fit perfectly into their family.

My hurt and anger return in full force. *They don't want me as a mate.*

Bryson was right. Who would want me as a mate? I'm nothing special. I never finished high school, and I'm not particularly skilled at anything. The only reason I landed the job as Madame Deverell's assistant was because of Alistair, and I wasn't gunning for immortality like most humans are. I know I'm attractive, but that doesn't mean much, does it? There are other pretty girls in my realm, and probably this one too.

Tears prick at my eyes again as I stomp down the hallway toward the bedrooms. It's just not fair, any of it. I step into Reule's room first, and I frown when I see the fireplace already lit. Maalik was the last one in the bedrooms before they all left. I thought he was in his room, or maybe the bathroom. But he must have come in here to light the fire, *assuming* I'd sleep in Reule's bed.

The rational part of my brain understands he probably did it to be sweet. I've spent the most time with Reule, so it makes sense for him to think I'd be most comfortable in his bedroom. But the totally irrational part of me is livid that Maalik would assume anything about me or think I'd ever show favoritism between the four of them. I can sleep wherever the hell I want! After Reule showed me that book and I came to terms with being their mate, I was ready to throw myself at all four of them, to let them pleasure me and ravage me. But they all fucking left me!

I angrily open the drawers of Reule's dresser and pull out all of his clothes, throwing them haphazardly all over the room. I do the same thing to the drawers of his nightstand, throwing out everything besides the photographs he has there. As soon as I'm finished going through his things, I jump onto his bed and roll around like a fucking animal. My scent is probably still lingering since I slept in here last night, but I want to make sure I mark every single inch of it. I'm going to make these men regret rejecting me. I'm going to make them want me so fucking badly, and make them wish they had taken me as a mate.

Audun's room is right next to Reule's, and I do the same thing there. I scatter his clothes and belongings everywhere, only taking care when I find a bunch of art supplies under his bed and a stash of letters and photographs in his nightstand. I push past the guilt and the tiny voice of reason in the back of my head, and I rub myself all over his bed too so he won't be able to smell anything but me.

Caelan's room is next, and then I find myself in Maalik's. I can tell it's his because it's the most plain. He doesn't have any photographs in his drawer the way the other guys do. Something about that makes my heart hurt, and I weep quietly while I stand in the middle of his room surrounded by the mess I've made.

I crawl onto Maalik's bed, still crying. It's all his fault, anyway. He's the one who told the other guys to leave. He told them I'm not good enough to be their mate, even though it was obvious Reule, Audun, and Caelan wanted me. I need to make him regret it most of all.

After I mark my scent all over Maalik's bed, I collapse back onto the pillows and let out a pitiful sob. When they left the cabin, where did they go? From the way it looked in that book, they'll become feral enough to hunt for a mate to claim tonight. Who's to say they won't find someone else while they're gone? What if they bring another girl back with them in the morning? What will happen to me then?

The thought of them claiming another girl makes me *furious*. I was sent here specifically for them, no matter how fucked up the circumstances were. I felt a connection with Reule almost right away, and I know I would have felt that with the other guys if I'd been able to spend a little more time with them. Why did they have to leave me?

I picture Maalik's cerulean blue eyes and the constellation of freckles scattered across his skin that I'd love to map out. He's quiet and strong, and so handsome. I pull my shirt up and trail my fingers across my stomach, imagining it's Maalik touching me instead. I rub my hands further up my body and let out a quiet moan when I squeeze my breasts. God, what I'd give to feel Maalik's large, rough hands on me instead.

I've had a threesome before. That was a few years ago, with a guy I dated briefly and another girl we both sort-of knew through a mutual friend. It was an okay experience, but certainly not spectacular enough to make me want to try group sex again. I've definitely never considered having a fucking *fivesome* with four guys, making me the center of attention. But now that the idea has been planted in my brain, it's nearly all I can think about.

How would it feel to have all of them at the same time? To have Caelan, Audun, Reule, and Maalik all touch me and pleasure me together? They're probably the hottest guys I've ever met. I wonder if they all have delicious muscles and abs like Reule does. But even if they don't, I know they all have to be ridiculously strong, and I'm sure they'd be able to toss me around easily.

"Fuck." I moan loudly as I continue to caress my body and brush my fingers teasingly over my clit. I'm so fucking wet, and I'm seriously going crazy with lust thinking about these four gorgeous men.

My body trembles in pleasure and my heart races faster as I continue to let out quiet, breathy moans. I use my left hand to knead my breast while my right hand teases my pussy. I tap my fingers against my clit until I'm practically aching to be fucked, and then I slide two fingers into my hot, wet cunt.

While I finger myself, I think about Reule, Caelan, Maalik, and Audun and all the things I want them to do to me. I imagine all of their mouths and hands on me, touching, licking, and kissing every inch of my body. And then I imagine them taking turns fucking me. Over and over until I've orgasmed so many times I pass out from the pleasure and over-stimulation.

I cum so hard that I practically see stars behind my eyes. My breathing is harsh and ragged, and I feel like a puddle of mush as I slowly come down from my high. When my heartbeat finally slows and settles, and the lust is no longer clouding my mind, I sit up on my elbows and glance around the room at the mess I've made of Maalik's things.

My cheeks heat up in shame and embarrassment. *Holy fucking shit.* I've gone batshit-fucking-crazy. What are the guys going to think when they come home and see what I did? How angry are they going to be? *Oh my god.*

I really hope it's these moons making me act like a fucking nutcase, and not just me losing my goddamn mind.

THE SUN SET A COUPLE OF HOURS AGO.

After my psychotic meltdown, I shamefully went back to the living room to wait for the guys to return. I considered trying to clean up and put their clothes away, but I'm worried being around their rooms and touching their stuff will send me into another temper tantrum. I'll have to apologize profusely in the morning, and I'll do my best to help them clean up.

Right now, I feel sad and lonely and so, so embarrassed. I feel too guilty to sleep in Reule's room again, even though the fire is lit in there. So I took all of the blankets out of the chest in the living room and set them up next to the fireplace in here. I did slip on a pair of sweatpants I found in the hallway too, as it was getting really chilly in the house. I have no clue who they belong to, considering there are several articles of clothing and little knick-knacks strewn about the hallway.

I'm warm and cozy, even if I am sad beyond belief. To distract myself from the ache in my chest and thoughts of the guys, I've been looking through the books Reule showed me. There aren't many other illustrations in that shifter book besides the ones I've already seen, and I can't read a word of it. I find my attention drawn more to the map book. There must be hundreds of maps in here, all of different worlds and realms I didn't even know existed. After looking through it for a couple of hours, my eyes are still glued to the pages as I take in every tiny detail.

Even though Reule made it clear he hadn't found anything remotely close to my world's map, I'm still confused and disappointed when I don't find anything that looks familiar. How can it not be in this book, when the people here obviously know my world exists? How else would they have found me and bought me from Giovanni's warehouse?

A loud, ferocious roar interrupts my thoughts, and I gasp as the windows in the kitchen and by the front door tremble. My heart flips over about a million times. That has to be one of the guys, right? Anyone else would probably be terrified from that sound, but I'm filled with hope as my stomach flutters in excitement. Are they on their way home?

Did Maalik change his mind? Are they coming back for me?

I have the overwhelming urge to go outside. It feels a little like a compulsion spell, but I quickly push that thought aside. What will it hurt if I go out, just in the front yard? Even if that roar did come from one of the guys, that doesn't necessarily mean they're on their way home. And if they are, and I stay inside like Maalik wanted me to, I still think there's no way those stupid wooden beams will stop them from getting in.

Besides, I want to see these moons for myself after the emotional evening I've had.

I pull out a coat and a pair of boots from the closet by the front door. The coat is so big I'm practically swimming in it, but it's warm and long enough to cover me all the way down to my calves. The boots are way too big, but I don't plan on wandering far.

Once I'm bundled up enough to brace the cold, I spend a couple of minutes struggling with those damned wooden beams. I grumble Maalik's name angrily under my breath, but the moment I have the door open, I'm filled with relief and excitement.

It's snowing out again, and I giggle madly as I waddle down the steps of the front porch into the yard. My feet sink into the fresh snow, and I clumsily stumble further away from the house. I only make it about a dozen yards before I have to stop and catch my breath, and I take a moment to look around.

The moons are bright enough that I can see everything clearly, all the way to the edge of the forest surrounding the cabin. It's a stunning winter wonderland here, and the fresh snow makes everything look gorgeous and magical.

I tilt my head back to get a good look at these moons I've been speculating so much about. I gasp and widen my eyes in awe as soon as I see them. Even though I expected it, it's still surreal to see three full moons shining down on me—one large, bright moon and two smaller yet equally bright moons on either side of it. Aside from the glittering moons, there are millions of stars shining in the sky too.

I've lived in New York my entire life where it's impossible to see any stars most nights. Tears form in my eyes as I stare up at the sky in this strange realm. I've never seen anything more beautiful.

Another savage roar breaks through the peaceful silence, and a chilly gust of wind makes me pull my borrowed coat tighter around myself. Something that sounds like thunder surrounds me, but when the wind becomes strong enough to nearly knock me off my feet, I realize the sound is actually coming from the beating of large, powerful wings.

I gasp when I see him. A huge, dragon-like beast slowly descends and lands with a crashing boom about a hundred feet from me. The force of his landing is enough to send snow flying up, and I lose my balance, falling backwards onto my butt.

The beast lets out a growl, but it's almost gentle-sounding compared to the roars I heard before. I refuse to blink, watching him in wonder as he slowly steps closer to me. He's *huge*—bigger than the cabin or any animal I've ever seen. His head resembles that of a large cat, with impossibly long whiskers and his lips pulled back from his sharp teeth. His fur is mostly white, shining like starlight under the moons, except for the black spots on his face, and black rosette marks on the fur of his chest. His ears are pinned back as he watches me, a quiet growl emitting from his throat that's making the ground vibrate.

On top of his head beside his furry, feline ears, he has two large, curled horns that resemble a ram's. He lowers his front legs so he's half-lying down in the snow, so I'm able to get a better look at his entire body. His front feet are furry and cat-like, with large deathly-sharp claws. Right around his ribcage, the fur on his body begins to transition into shining, white scales. The entire back half of his body is much more dragon-like, all the way to the long, reptilian tail with black spikes on the end just like I'd seen in Reule's book. His wings look nothing like I expected from the illustrations. They're not spiky or leathery at all—they're huge, and covered in shimmering silver feathers.

I'm shocked and wonderstruck as I continue to stare at him. I've been around supernaturals most of my life, but I've never come across or heard of anything like him. Is there even a name for what he is? I'm sure there must be, but I wouldn't be able to understand it in his language. The closest thing I can come up with is a chimera—the technical term for a creature that's derived from two or more types of animal.

He lets out a long whine, dropping down onto the ground as low as he can as he slowly shuffles closer to me. He's still towering over me, but I don't feel fearful at all. My heart and stomach flutter in excitement. I struggle to stand up, and I take a few steps closer to him until his head is right in front of me. He drops his head to the ground and breathes out of his nose, still making that rumbling sound in his throat.

I giggle when I realize he's purring, and I pat his muzzle as I grin up at him. His forest green eyes are watching me, unblinking. He's being so careful not to scare me, and I lean against him and continue petting him to let him know I'm not afraid.

"Reule?" I ask breathlessly.

He shifts, and I gasp when I find myself being held in Reule's strong arms as he gazes down at me. His eyes are bright and feral, his pupils almost completely dilated. He keeps one arm locked around my waist, holding me up effortlessly as he brings his other hand up to the back of my neck.

"Isla." He growls my name once before he kisses me.

Pleasure erupts over every inch of my skin, and my heart pounds furiously. I press my lips to his more firmly, desperately, and I curl my fingers against his chest. His mouth devours mine, and I welcome the heady feeling of being dominated by this powerful man.

When I hear another roar, and the ground trembles from the landing of another chimera beast, I pull away from Reule's kiss. He growls and bites my lip, making me gasp as I return my attention to him. He continues kissing me and whispers against my lips, "Caelan."

Part of me still wants to see the other guys in their shifted forms, but that will just have to wait until later. I'm more than happy to keep kissing Reule. I hope Caelan joins us, and I hope we can take things a bit further soon. I groan in anticipation and wrap my legs around Reule's waist, and he moves his hand to my ass to hold me up better.

Caelan appears beside us, his eyes just as feral as Reule's as he says something to his friend. Reule finally pulls his mouth away from me, only to grip my hair between his fingers as he forces me to turn my head toward Caelan. Caelan's lips crash against mine, and I moan in delight at the sensation of kissing these two sexy men one after the other. I'm at their fucking mercy, and I love it.

Reule begins walking toward the cabin, and Caelan stays right beside us with his hand softly caressing my leg. Neither of them has taken their eyes off of me, and I tremble from lust and excitement as we get closer and closer to the house. There's still no sign of the others, and I want all of them.

"What about Audun and Maalik?" I ask breathlessly as Reule steps through the doorway.

He grunts, and Caelan gives me a feral grin and nods his head as he says something in his strange language. They leave the front door open, so I hope that means the other guys will be here soon. Reule captures my lips again, fully distracting me. I smile into the kiss when I feel Caelan's hands at my back as he pulls my coat off.

"God, yes!" I exclaim, kicking my boots off and wiggling until Reule sets me down. I'm so fucking ready to move things along, and I want them to take their clothes off *now*.

Reule and Caelan watch me with heated eyes, but they seem a bit hesitant. If they feel even the least bit as crazy and lustful as I do, they're probably dying to touch me. Reule was gentle outside too before he shifted into his human form. I hadn't expected them to be of sound enough mind to worry about hurting me or forcing me into anything. It's the sweetest thing ever, and I feel my heart warming to them even more.

I'll just have to show them that I want them, and let them know I want them to do all the naughty things to me, even if I can't consent in their language. I give both men a cheeky smile and slip the shirt up over my head. Caelan and Reule growl, but I don't pause before tugging off my borrowed sweatpants and the socks I've been wearing.

Once I'm completely naked, I look up at the men through my eyelashes and stroke my fingers down my body seductively. My nipples are hard and my pussy is *aching*. All of my dirty, sexy fantasies are about to come true. I just need them to take off their clothes!

Their eyes take me in greedily, but neither of them moves until Audun steps through the door. His eyes nearly pop out of his head when he sees me, and he growls something that sounds like it might be a curse word.

Caelan moves first. He practically tears his clothes off of his body, walks over to me, and gives me a dominant kiss as soon as he's naked. Like Reule, he has delicious abs and v-lines leading down to a large, throbbing cock. His soft lips move from my mouth to my neck, and I moan when I feel my sensitive nipples rub against his chest and his cock press into my belly. I slide my hands up and down his chest and stomach, reaching down to tease his cock just a little until I feel someone step behind me and take my full breasts in their hands.

"Krásná," Reule whispers as he nibbles on my earlobe. He's said that to me before, but I'm too distracted by the feeling of his body and Caelan's against mine. I moan both their names, feeling needy as I wait for them to take control. I wonder which one of them will fuck me first.

Reule lifts me up, holding me with his hands under my thighs as he spreads my legs open. I blink in surprise and delight before I throw my head back against his shoulder in ecstasy when I feel a warm, hot mouth on my pussy. I tangle my fingers in Caelan's hair as he continues to eat me out, and I bring my other hand up to the back of Reule's neck as I turn my head to kiss him. I feel another mouth on my right nipple, and I open my eyes to find Audun standing beside us. I moan his name when our eyes meet, and he growls and starts rubbing his hands over my body while he continues to lavish attention on my breast. The heat of their mouths, hands, and bodies against mine clashes with the cool breeze still coming through the open doorway, and the sensation feels fucking incredible.

An orgasm is building up quickly. This feels a million times better than I imagined it would. But I'm still craving one more mouth, one more set of strong hands. Where on earth is Maalik?

Caelan thrusts two fingers into my pussy, pumping them in and out while he does something fucking magical to my clit with his lips and tongue. I moan and writhe in Reule's arms, and he and Audun growl something at me. God, I fucking wish so badly I could understand their dirty talk.

My orgasm hits and it's *so fucking good*. My entire body trembles, and my eyes roll to the back of my head as I relish in the pleasure these men are giving me. Caelan stands, and my eyes flutter open when he gives me a sloppy kiss. I can taste myself on him, and that only turns me on more. I moan at him and quiver in anticipation when he rubs the head of his cock against my clit. I'm still being held up by Reule, and I almost cum again just at the thought of being sandwiched between them while Caelan fucks me.

Just before Caelan enters me, I look up to see Maalik standing a few feet behind him. He's still fully clothed, but his eyes watch me intently as his nostrils flare and he clenches his fists at his sides. The stubborn jerk is *still* holding himself back. Obviously I'm getting what I want tonight, so he'd better suck it up and come over here to service me!

"Oh, fuck!" I moan loudly when Caelan slides his hard cock into me with one quick thrust. He grips my hips roughly as he pounds into me over and over. He's holding me tightly enough to leave bruises, and it hurts so fucking good. "God, Caelan baby! Fuck, you guys are all so fucking hot!"

Reule's fingers are digging into my thighs just as hard as Caelan's holding me, and he's growling like mad as he helps Caelan in lifting me up and slamming me back down onto his cock. When I peer to my right, I'm thrilled to see Audun stroking himself as he watches me hungrily. A second, mind-numbing orgasm hits me, and Caelan groans and bites my shoulder as he cums inside of me.

My entire body is limp, and every one of my nerve-endings feels like it's on fire in the most delicious way possible. Reule sets me down gently and supports my weight since my legs feel like freaking jelly. He whispers something and strokes my shoulders, but I have no idea if he's talking to me or not.

"Isla?" Caelan whispers my name like a question, his voice

still a bit ragged as he catches his breath. I open my eyes to find him staring at me worriedly with his pretty hazel eyes, and I smile at him to let him know I'm more than okay.

He grins in relief and says something that I'm sure would be totally sweet if I could understand him. He tenderly cups my face in his hands and presses his lips to mine, but this kiss is so much sweeter and gentler and more intimate than the erotic kisses we shared before. I didn't expect such an affectionate gesture after such wild sex, and it causes butterflies to erupt in my stomach. I've had my fair share of partners over the years, and nobody has ever looked at me or kissed me like Caelan is right now.

Maalik growls something loudly enough to capture all of our attention. When I look up at him, his eyebrows are furrowed angrily and he's holding his hands on top of his head like he's exasperated. But I don't miss the erection causing an impressive bulge in his pants. I can't help but feel hurt that he's still trying so hard to reject me. He's so against taking me as a mate, and I don't understand why!

Reule scoffs and says something in a sarcastic tone, and Audun chuckles under his breath. Maalik's eyes meet mine, and I realize he's not *angry*. I think he might be afraid.

I step away from Reule and Caelan on slightly shaky legs, and I stop in front of Maalik with a soft smile on my face. Never once do I break eye contact as I slide my hands up his chest. I need to show him that he shouldn't be afraid. I'll take care of him, of *all* of them.

He doesn't move or touch me, but he does let me take his shirt off and unbutton his pants. He lets out a harsh breath when I push his pants down, and his large, swollen cock springs free. He's much thicker than Reule and Caelan, and they're both incredibly impressive. I hum in satisfaction as I brush my thumb over the tip, rubbing a bead of precum all over the head.

Maalik growls and tenses up even more, and I look up at

him as I stroke my hand up and down his thick length. I have to stand up on my tippy toes to reach his mouth, and I kiss him gently and offer him a sweet smile. "Just relax, handsome. I know you want me as much as I want you, so stop pretending otherwise."

I know he can't understand what I'm saying, but the tone of my words seem to do the trick anyway. He shudders and brings his hands up to twine in my hair as he finally kisses me back. His lips are soft and sweet and so much better than I thought they'd be. The other three guys give us space, so I know they realize Maalik still needs to be won over a bit. After kissing for a few moments, I trail my lips down Maalik's chest. He's so strong and muscular, just like the other men. God, how did I get so fucking lucky?

"Isla," Maalik groans when I kneel in front of him. I blink up at him innocently, and stick my tongue out to give the tip of his cock a few teasing licks. He moans and grips my hair with one of his hands, but he lets me stay in control. I hum in approval and wrap my hand around the base of his cock, and take his entire length in my mouth until the tip hits the back of my throat.

I suck his cock for a few minutes, feeling encouraged by the moans of pleasure he's making. Eventually, I feel another pair of hands on my body, and I tremble in excitement. The way Caelan fucked me was hands down the best sex I've ever had in my life so far, and I just want *more!* I feel more hands in my hair, and another hand on my breast. The third set of hands I've been anticipating grabs my hips, and I squeal in surprise as I'm forced into a new position on my hands and knees.

Maalik kneels so I'm still able to suck his cock in this position. He's finally let go of his control, and he tugs my hair roughly as he thrusts his hips, eagerly fucking my mouth. At the same time, the guy who grabbed my hips suddenly thrusts his cock into my pussy with one smooth motion. I orgasm pretty much immediately at the rough and sudden movement.

I gag on Maalik's cock and tears form in my eyes, all while one of the other guys slams into my pussy from behind. Everything feels so goddamn good, I seriously never want this to end. I want them to just fuck me over and over and *over*. It almost makes it better that I can't see who's fucking me.

"Zlobivá holka," Reule growls as I feel a hand smack my ass. I cum again, so hard that my entire body trembles violently. I feel my pussy clench around Reule's cock, and he grunts and releases his load inside of me.

Maalik keeps fucking my mouth, faster and faster, until he holds my head down with his cock shoved all the way down my throat. I choke a little, and he groans as he finally reaches his orgasm too. My mouth is filled with his hot, salty cum and I feel some of it dribbling down my chin when I pull away to take a breath.

I lick my lips and rub the back of my hand over my chin, looking up to find Maalik watching me with the most love-struck, affectionate expression I've ever seen on anyone's face. I giggle, slightly breathless, and reach up to kiss the corner of his mouth. I turn around to face Reule, and I find him staring at me the same way. I quickly kiss him too before I look around for Audun.

Audun is sitting next to the fire, still leisurely stroking his cock. The poor baby obviously isn't as aggressive as Caelan or Reule, and I feel like he's been neglected. My body is deliciously sore, and I'm covered in sweat and *other fluids*, but I need to make sure Audun knows I want him just as much as the others. I need to claim all of them.

I crawl over to him, feeling sexy and confident and powerful. Audun gives me this absolutely devilish smile as he watches me with half-lidded eyes, and he pulls me into his lap as soon as I'm close enough. I wrap my arms around his neck and press my lips softly against his. I'm pleasantly surprised when he kisses me back fervently, despite the fact that I still taste like Maalik. He runs his hands up and down my sides and squeezes my ass, and I align the head of his cock with my pussy before sliding down until he's buried deep inside of me.

While I ride his cock, Audun goes back and forth between kneading my ass and playing with my breasts. He's fucking amazing with his mouth, and he keeps rolling my nipples between his thumb and forefinger. I kind of like that he's letting me take total control too, and soon enough I reach another fantastic orgasm.

After Audun cums inside of me, I collapse onto the blankets beside the fireplace. I'm so greedy to have more of my men, but I'm honestly pretty exhausted. I hum in satisfaction when Audun lies down beside me, and I stretch out languidly while I enjoy his closeness and the toasty warm fire behind us.

Maalik crawls over to us and hovers over me, his gorgeous body slick with sweat. He asks me a question that I don't understand, but I *do* feel his hard length brush against my thigh. I guess it's not really fair that he just got a blowjob when the other guys got so much more. My nipples harden and my heart flips excitedly at the promise of another orgasm, and I quickly wrap my legs around Maalik's waist and urge him to slide his cock into me.

He thrusts back and forth slowly, making sure to pull all the way out before sliding back in again. I wasn't expecting such an unhurried, intimate pace, and I keep my eyes glued to his as I gasp in pleasure at the overwhelming sensation. Maalik never looks away from me, but he does throw one of my legs up over his shoulder so he can bury his cock even deeper.

When I reach my final climax for the evening, I swear to god I see fucking stars. I've never felt so full and sated and relaxed in all my life. I'm hardly even aware when Maalik pulls out and peppers my face with kisses, and then he does the same thing to my wrist while he whispers something incomprehensible.

I'm so happy and *so sleepy* all of the sudden. I can't remember why I was so sad earlier, or what I was worried about. It all seems silly now as I snuggle up to the guy closest to me and nuzzle my cheek against his strong chest.

I know without a doubt that I'm their mate now. Caelan, Maalik, Audun, and Reule. I'm theirs, and they're mine.

CHAPTER TWELVE
REULE

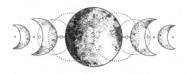

SOMETHING TICKLES MY NOSE, AND I SMILE WHEN I CATCH Isla's scent. I open my eyes slowly, my heart stuttering in my chest when I find my *wife* lying beside me. My head is pounding like I had too much to drink last night, but it's well worth it for waking up like this. I don't think anything in the universe could dampen my mood right now.

"Reule!" Maalik growls my name quietly as he kicks my foot.

I fight back a groan. Can't he just let me enjoy this for a little while? My eyes wander over Isla's form. She's lying between me and Audun with her face pressed against his chest. He's holding her close with his arm around her waist, and some of her hair has fallen over my face and shoulder.

My hand is resting delicately on her hip, and I rub my hand over her smooth skin. She's so *soft*, every inch of her. I don't want to wake her up, so I stop my movements before I get too carried away.

Maalik's scowling when I turn my head to face him. He's wearing a towel around his waist, and his hair is still wet while water drips down his torso and shoulders. Our brothers and Isla are still fast asleep, so I don't understand what would possess Mal to be up and about already. It looks like he relit the fire, so I'm grateful for that.

I stand up slowly, taking my time to stretch out my muscles. I'm still stark naked, and that reminds me of everything that happened last night. The most incredible night of my long, tedious life.

"What?" I hiss irritably when Mal continues to glower at me.

"Just come here," he says, baring his teeth.

I follow him through the living room and widen my eyes when he stops in front of my bedroom door. There are clothes and blankets and all sorts of random shit strewn about the hallway.

"What happened?" I whisper.

Maalik points into my bedroom, a stony expression on his face. "Isla tore our rooms apart. She must have done it after we left last night, but we were all too distracted to notice anything when we came back."

I peek my head into my bedroom. All of the drawers of the wardrobe and bedside tables are pulled open with items spilling out. Every article of clean clothing I own is scattered across the room and my bedsheets are rumpled and hanging over the edge. Even one of the curtains has been pulled down so that it's hanging askew in the window.

It looks like a damn lutin snuck in here to wreak havoc. I have to cover my mouth with my hand to hide my bemusement at my angry little kitten.

"She was so angry at us," Maalik growls. At first I assume he's pissed off, but when I turn to meet his eyes again, I realize he's terrified. "I don't think I can handle her being this angry at me. When she wakes up…"

He trails off, and I step around him to peer into my brothers' rooms. She didn't touch the office or the bedroom we've been using for storage—the bedroom that was always meant to be hers—but Caelan and Audun's rooms are just as messy as mine. I snort when I step in front of Maalik's room. The now-very-familiar scent of our wife's arousal is lingering heavily in the air here.

"She must have been *extra* angry with you, Mal." I chuckle.

Maalik grimaces. His face and ears are as red as his hair. "I know."

I look around quickly again to reassess the damage. "You're not upset at her, are you? She was probably affected by the Beasts' Moon, and she didn't want us to leave. It doesn't look like she broke anything."

"I know she was affected by the Beasts' Moon." Mal grunts angrily as he narrows his eyes at me. "That's what I'm trying to tell you. If she was pissed enough last night to do this, how's she going to feel when she wakes up with a clear head and realizes we took advantage of her? The last thing I wanted was to trap her here against her will, and Reule...we were so rough with her. Do you think we hurt her?"

The good mood I woke up in deflates, and my heart constricts painfully in my chest. *Did* we hurt her? I know we were rough last night, but she seemed to like it. We've always been told that claiming a wife can be brutal and traumatizing for the woman in certain circumstances, and that was another factor that always held us back from claiming somebody all these years. We may transform into huge, terrifying beasts, but my brothers and I are *not* monsters.

I know my beast was mostly in control of my thoughts and actions last night, but I still remember everything clearly. I remember trying to hold back, to let Isla set the pace. I may just be remembering incorrectly, or maybe I truly was lost to the fog of the Beasts' Moon, but I'm certain Isla enjoyed everything between us. She was beautiful and insatiable, and I'd like to believe we would have stopped if she'd protested or made it clear we were taking things too far.

Maalik does make another good point. How is she going

to feel when she wakes up and realizes she's stuck with us? She seemed okay yesterday when I tried explaining the Beasts' Moon to her. I mean, she was a little upset at first, but she seemed sort of resolved and certainly not unhappy by the time my brothers came home. She even put that silly crown on for us to show her acceptance of the bond.

Is it so wrong for me to be happy? I know Isla was brought here against her will, and I still want to help her find her family somehow. But...I love her, I think. She's funny, sweet and intelligent, and I've never felt such a strong connection with another woman before.

"We didn't hurt her," I say more confidently than I feel. I don't want to talk about how much we might have messed up, and how much Isla might hate us for claiming her. I quickly change the subject and hold my wrist up to show my rune mark. "Have you looked at your mark yet? Why do they look so different from the other Guardians'?"

The Guardians of the other kingdoms have small, simple rune marks that match the illustrations we've seen in books given to us by the Elders. But the matching marks on my, Isla's, and my brothers' wrists are much larger and more elaborate. Delicate lines form an intricate design that wraps all the way around my wrist and continues onto the back of my hand and down my fingers. It's beautiful, and my beast seems pleased with it, but it's so different from any rune mark I've ever seen that I can't help feeling a bit concerned.

"I don't know." Maalik grunts as he frowns down at his own wrist. "We'll have to ask King Janak about it. We need to speak with him as soon as possible. That's the other reason I woke you up."

"You want to leave now?" I ask in bewilderment. I turn my head to glance down the hallway to the living room where Isla, Caelan, and Audun are still asleep. "You don't want to wait until after she's awake?"

Maalik bares his teeth and snarls. "Have you already

forgotten that Janak had her delivered to us in a fucking cage? I need to know what he was thinking, and we need to find out where she came from and how she got here. I've already failed her by not keeping the three of you away last night, and for not being able to control myself. But I promised her I would help her find her family again."

He's right. Just thinking of finding Isla in that cage makes me want to tear someone apart, and King Janak owes us an explanation. As much as I want to stay home and spend every waking moment with our new wife, I agree that speaking with the king as soon as possible is of utmost importance. Anything we can find out about Isla will be helpful.

As I step into the bathroom, I turn to smile sadly at my eldest brother. "We didn't fail her, Mal. It's not our fault or yours. We knew how strong the Moons would be, and how much worse it gets each time. Just try to stay positive, alright? Isla's incredible, and we'll take good care of her."

"CAELAN!" MAALIK HISSES QUIETLY AS HE SHAKES OUR brother's shoulder. He's lying a few feet away from Isla and Audun, who are still snuggled up close to the fire.

I pick up one of the blankets on the floor and place it over them. Isla's breathing so deeply and peacefully, and I can't help but stroke my fingers through her long, dark hair. She's the most breathtaking woman I've ever seen, and I wish so badly I could be here when she wakes up. After last night, after claiming her and forming the bond, I want to talk to her and see her face and know she's at least a little happy to be with me.

Audun opens his eyes and bares his teeth at me, pulling Isla closer as he tucks her more securely under his chin and against his chest. I blink at him, and quickly stand up when I feel the insane urge to punch him and pull Isla away. There's an angry, burning feeling in my chest that's completely unfamiliar to me. My brothers and I have always known we'd share a wife, so I wasn't anticipating any jealousy between us.

"What?" Caelan finally groans in response to Mal's attempts to wake him. He rolls over and glares at us.

Maalik glances at Isla to make sure we haven't woken her, and he's careful to keep his voice low. "Reule and I are going to speak with the king. After Isla wakes up, make sure to feed her and help her get dressed. You and Audun need to take her into the village to see Runa so we can get her some real clothes. We'll meet you there if we don't make it back before you leave, alright?"

"Yeah, yeah." Caelan waves his hand dismissively at Maalik. He sits up and yawns, and when he sees Isla and Audun lying a few feet away, he quickly scoots closer and gets under the blanket with them. Isla is sandwiched between them, and Audun bares his teeth at Cael the same way he did to me. Caelan wisely ignores him and kisses the top of Isla's head before making himself comfortable.

Happiness mingles with my lingering jealousy. Isla sighs quietly in her sleep, and it makes me feel good to see that she looks so comfortable and cared for by my brothers. Still, I wish it were me holding her instead.

"One more thing." Maalik growls. "Isla, uh, had an accident last night that you guys will need to clean up. Do *not* make her feel bad about it or get angry with her, okay?"

Caelan turns his head and scrunches his face up at Maalik. "Did she piss on the floor or something?"

I snort in amusement, and I have to cover my mouth to keep myself from laughing out loud. The way she threw our things around and marked her scent in our beds was so...possessive and animalistic. "Not that we saw, but I wouldn't be surprised if you discover she did do something like that."

Mal gives me an unamused look. We mumble goodbye to our brothers and take our leave.

We don't waste any time. We shift into our beasts the moment we leave the house, and we fly straight to the castle without stopping. While it's normally an eight-hour journey by sled, it only takes about half an hour for us to make the trip.

Whenever we come to the castle, we normally stop to shift in the clearing in the woods behind the queen's gardens. Today, Maalik and I don't bother. We land right in the middle of the courtyard in our beast forms, and when most of the nearby Elders, servants, and courtiers scramble away in terror, I can't help roaring at them.

Maalik bares his teeth at me once in warning, and shifts into his human form. I follow his lead, but now that we're here, I'm furious on Isla's behalf. The way she was treated was disgusting, and I gaze murderously around the courtyard while I wonder who was involved. Who hurt her and put her in that cage? Whose idea was it to have her brought here and sent to us? Who knew what was happening to her and did nothing?

For all they know, we could have hurt her. We're lucky Isla is fearless. That she's sweet, smart, and accepting. If they'd sent any other girl to us, things could have been catastrophic. Now that I have a bit of distance from my beautiful new wife, I feel so guilty. Mal was right all along. It was selfish to claim her.

An Elder approaches us cautiously, stopping about ten feet away to bow low and respectfully. "Guardian Maalik, Guardian Reule, this is a pleasant surprise. What brings you here this morning?"

The man swallows audibly, and there's a bead of sweat on his forehead. He's clearly terrified, but for once, I don't care. I watch his gaze dart to our wrists, but our coat sleeves cover our fresh rune marks. My nostrils flare in anger. Did he hurt Isla? Is he responsible for what happened to her?

Maalik storms past the Elder, practically shoving him out of the way so the man stumbles over his own feet. "We're here to speak with King Janak. I suggest you fetch him for us, *quickly*."

A wicked grin forms on my face as I follow my eldest brother up the pathway leading to the throne room. Between the four of us, Maalik is always the one to keep a level head. I've never seen him disrespect an Elder or the king. Even though he's awful at sharing his feelings, it's obvious Maalik is just as smitten with Isla as the rest of us. He's ready to defend her honor no matter the consequences.

Prince Ilari and Princess Ozara are lounging up on the dais, but the throne room is otherwise empty. They're laughing until they see us, and Ilari nearly falls out of his seat from trying to sit up too quickly. Ozara remains in her relaxed pose, her calculating eyes watching our every move.

"Maalik, Reule!" Ilari stands up, grimacing when his voice cracks the slightest bit. I almost smile at that. He and his sister recently turned eighteen, and it's been quite a few years since I've heard his voice change.

"Where is your father?" Maalik asks, leaving no room for polite conversation.

Ozara tilts her head at us, resting her cheek on her hand lazily. She's wearing boys' clothing and has dark makeup smeared around her eyes. I've always had a soft spot for the princess, despite her being widely-disliked by the nobles. But the bored expression she's trying to project is seriously pissing me off to no end.

"Did you claim that girl last night?" she asks disdainfully.

I bare my teeth in anger and snarl loudly enough to frighten her. I feel a sick sense of satisfaction when she sits up straight, finally showing us the respect Maalik and I deserve. "Did *you* watch as she was shoved into a cage like an animal by people she doesn't know and can't understand? Did you think of her wellbeing for one second after that Elder left here with her in the back of his sled? She almost froze to death!"

Ozara's face crumples, and Ilari holds his hands up

defensively as he shakes his head frantically at us. "I tried to stop it, I swear! Father wouldn't even let me take off her shackles!"

Shackles? My fists clench, and I breathe angrily out of my nose while I desperately try to keep myself from shifting. Discovering that my poor, sweet kitten was restrained at any point makes me a thousand times more furious. I only know a little of what Isla's been through, and I'm amazed at her strength and bravery.

Maalik grips my shoulder hard in warning, and it helps to ground me. Ozara is weeping quietly with tears streaming down her face.

"Is she okay? I only saw her for a moment before she left, but the other girls stayed with me the past two nights. They were so frightened…"

"Other girls?" I ask in shock. Mal appears just as horror-stricken as I feel.

The twins glance at each other, and Ilari nods hesitantly. "Father had a bunch of girls brought here who were being held captive by demons in other realms. He planned on giving most of them jobs here in the castle so they could have a fresh start in Briya, but he wanted to choose one of them to be your mate."

Mate. My brothers and I hate that word. It sounds so primal and inhuman. That may be how most of the world sees us, but it's certainly not how we see ourselves. Isla is our *wife*, even if our claiming her and the bond we share with her are magical and unconventional.

My brain catches up with the rest of what Ilari just said about a half second before Maalik rasps, "Demons? Isla was being held captive by a demon?"

He and I stare at each other, and I know we're thinking the same thing. Vampyres and now demons? I'm still certain Isla is familiar with shifters too. There's no other explanation for why she seems unbothered by our nature. Whatever sort of world Isla came from, I swear to never let her fall into harm's way again.

"Isla? That's a pretty name." Ozara sniffles. "Where is she now?"

"She's at home with Audun and Caelan." I soften my voice. Ilari and Ozara are young, and it's not fair for us to place any blame with them for what's happened. At least they seem concerned about Isla and these other girls.

The door at the far end of the room crashes open, and we turn to watch as King Janak enters with two Elders on his heels. He's dressed in full military regalia with all of his medals proudly on display. He grins broadly as he approaches us.

We've always had an easy relationship with Janak. Unlike his father before him, who was King when we first became Guardians, Janak has never shown us any fear or hostility. My brothers and I have always been open and honest with him, and I know we all truly see Janak as our friend, not just our King.

That's why it hurts so much to realize he tricked us, that he went behind our back to set up this whole thing with Isla. He knew it was going to be impossible for us to resist her so close to Guardians' Night.

"Let me see your wrists, friends!" Janak says by way of greeting.

Maalik and I bristle, but the bond we share with our king and kingdom are strong enough to force us to follow his order. We pull our sleeves up, and I try to ignore the quiet gasp I hear from Ozara and the smug expression on Janak's face.

Amias, one of the Head Elders here in the castle, steps forward to get a better look at our marks. I pull my sleeve down abruptly and drop my hands to my sides, cutting a glare at these people I've always trusted so blindly.

"Janak," Maalik says in a clipped tone. His hand is trembling as he slowly pulls his sleeve down, and it quickly becomes evident to everyone in the room that Mal is about a second away from exploding.

"I'm sure you have many questions and concerns, my friends. We'll talk in my office in a moment." Janak gives us a placating smile. He turns his head toward the Elders and says, "But first, send out the announcement! We have so much to celebrate—Briya finally has a new Queen of Beasts!"

I lose it. I've been calm for way too long, and I won't go another second acting like everything that happened to Isla is okay. She never should have ended up here. We don't deserve her.

"Have you lost your mind?" I snarl ferociously, stepping closer so my face is only inches from Janak's. His eyes widen the slightest amount, but otherwise he shows no fear or outward reaction. "You've kidnapped girls and brought them here against their will to be slaves? And you threw Isla to us like a sheep to a pack of wolves. You nearly killed her by putting her in that cage! What kind of man treats another human being that way?"

"Reule," King Janak says my name firmly. "Calm down, my friend. I swear to explain everything to you."

"You're no friend of mine!" I snarl again. Maalik pulls me back, but he's still trembling and fighting his own anger.

"The girls will not be slaves, Guardian Reule." Amias bows his head, and he's careful to keep his eyes lowered submissively as he continues to speak. "All of them came from dark, evil worlds where they were being held prisoner by demons. We saved them. We brought them here to start a new life. They'll be tutored to help them learn our language, and they'll receive shelter and good-paying jobs."

"Isla, you said her name was?" King Janak asks. When Maalik nods stiffly, Janak grins and continues. "She was the strongest of the bunch, by far. A tiny, fearless thing covered in blood—most of which was not her own, mind you. These other girls came in here, crying and trembling, which was to be expected. Your girl walked in here with her head held high, taking in every detail of her surroundings. I have no doubt she would have tried to claw my eyes out if she hadn't been restrained."

A growl leaves my throat at the mention of her being restrained. But my heart stutters happily in my chest at hearing yet again how brave Isla is. It doesn't surprise me to hear she acted so courageously, and that she didn't show Janak or the rest of these people any weakness. I feel ridiculously pleased, and so proud of her.

"She punched me, you see." Amias smiles bashfully and points to his left eye. I hadn't noticed before, but his eye and cheek are swollen while the surrounding skin is bruised yellow and purple. It's a pretty impressive injury considering it's a couple of days old, and I have to fight a smile. "She was very argumentative with the demon holding her captive, though I can't tell you what she said. He told me, however, that he'd had problems with her. He actually warned me not to buy her because she'd killed one of her guards the first night she was brought there."

"How did she kill him?" Ozara asks curiously. She steps down from the dais to stand beside her father.

Instead of dismissing his daughter like he so often does, Janak grins maniacally. "She killed him with her shoe, if the demon scum is to be believed. It makes me think you might be onto something, daughter. After I speak with Maalik and Reule, you are free to pitch your idea of allowing women to train and fight in our military."

His words make me feel conflicted. On one hand, I'm ecstatic for Ozara. She's been arguing about this very thing with her father for years. On the other hand, I've always been taught that women and children are precious and need to be protected. Luckily, it's not my place to speak on these sorts of issues. Anyway, Maalik and I are here for Isla today.

Ozara beams excitedly at her father, and Janak motions

for Maalik and me to follow him across the vast throne room and into the main part of the castle. The hallways and rooms we pass through are bustling with servants, and all of them bow their heads at the three of us. Maalik and I catch several whispers of *'Guardians' Night'* and *'Beasts' Moon.'*

Once we reach his office, Janak locks the door behind us to ensure we won't be disturbed. I collapse into one of the armchairs beside the fireplace, but Maalik paces back and forth beside the window looking out into the gardens. It's a clear day, and the fresh snow from last night is making everything gleam and sparkle.

Janak opens the hidden liquor cabinet he keeps behind one of his bookshelves, and he pours each of us a glass of whiskey. I'm still angry with him, but I take the glass and toss it back. The liquor burns the back of my throat, but it's a welcome distraction from my scattered thoughts.

"You must know bringing those girls here was in their best interest. The places they came from, and the situations they would have ended up in...I'm sure you can imagine how bad it could have been for any of them." Janak takes a seat across from me, taking a sip of his drink while his eyes travel between me and Maalik.

Maalik turns with his arms crossed and glares down at our king. "Let's cut the shit. You didn't have your Elders go looking for girls to rescue. You had them search for a girl you could force into becoming our wife. The others who ended up here are just extra collateral."

Janak grimaces and holds his hands up defensively. "Okay, yes. But how many times have we discussed this? It's important for the four of you to claim a mate. You refused to choose a girl yourselves, so what was I supposed to do?"

I lean forward with my elbows on my knees, and place my head in my hands. I feel sad and dejected, angry and hurt, and so guilty because all I want right now is to go back home and be with Isla. She's probably only thinking of how badly she wants to go home. "We didn't want a wife. You know that."

Before Isla, I was just as determined as Maalik not to take a wife. He tried reminding me of all the reasons it wouldn't be a good idea. Most of the Guardians in the other kingdoms have wives who are absolutely miserable. The Guardians of Briya before us had the shortest lifespan of any Guardians ever recorded. All because their wife was so unhappy she took her own life, and they couldn't go on living without her.

When that Elder showed up with Isla, I was a goner as soon as I looked into her honey-brown eyes. I know it's mostly because I was already susceptible to form a bond, since it was so close to Guardians' Night and the Beasts' Full Moon. But taking care of her when she was cold and hurt made me feel more special and important than I've ever felt in my life. While communicating with her is frustrating, she's surprisingly funny, and it's amazing trying to decipher what's going through her head at any given moment.

"You may not have wanted one, but you needed one." Janak slams his glass down on the small table beside his chair. "The older you get, the more feral you'll become if you don't have a mate to keep you grounded. To keep you human. The two of you, Audun, and Caelan are my oldest friends, and I hate seeing you pull away from people as the years pass. Don't even try to tell me you're not lonely, living so far up that mountain away from everyone. You need a girl to warm your beds, and to give you something to live for. I'm not arrogant enough to believe that your loyalty to me and my family will always be enough."

I lift my head slowly and meet his eyes. There's so much I want to say, but I'm at a loss of where to start. And what's the point of arguing? We've already claimed Isla. It's not like we can undo it.

"Why put her in a cage though?" Maalik asks quietly. "If her world was as bad as you say, and she'd already been through so much, why treat her like an animal and offer her to us like that?"

"She bit me when I opened the cage." I shake my head. "She was terrified, Janak."

"Listen, I'm sorry," Janak says guiltily. "You have to understand, I've thought a lot about this, and about your situation. What do the other Guardians' mates all have in common? They are weak, submissive women. They're not suited for the life you lead. You need a woman who's strong, determined, and brave. *But*, your beasts are attracted to those who need protection, right? Isla was only here very briefly before I had her sent to you. It was my decision not to have her wounds dressed or have her cleaned up. I was assured she wasn't hurt badly, and I thought you'd be more likely to take her in and form a bond with her if she was still in the same state we found her."

"I get it. I truly do," Mal says. He finally takes the seat beside me, and it's impossible to read his expression as he stares at Janak. "But you need to understand that you've broken our trust. You planned this behind our backs, and you've put us in an unfair situation. Isla is a sweet girl, but she still has a family she's worried about."

"Does she?" Janak asks with his eyebrows raised.

"Her brother, Alistair." I don't bother telling him we're not entirely sure what his relationship to Isla is. But he's obviously important to her.

"I'm sorry to hear that." Janak frowns, sounding sincere. "I'll see about sending a few Elders back to her home-world to dig around. But please believe me when I say that world is a lost cause. It's on the list of Forbidden Realms. It's completely overrun with demons and every dark creature you can imagine."

My heart drops into my stomach. I was afraid that might be the case, especially since I wasn't able to match her hand-drawn map to one in the *Atlas of Known Realms*. At least Janak will have people looking for Alistair. If we can reunite Isla with her family, maybe there's a chance she might somehow learn to love us.

"You swear to keep us in the loop this time?" Maalik growls. "The moment you hear anything about her brother, good or bad, you need to let us know immediately."

"I swear it. And I swear to earn back your trust too, friends." King Janak leans forward and shakes Maalik's hand. He gives us both a half-smile and asks, "So? How was the claiming? Was it as brutal as you'd feared? You know I won't judge you."

Maalik's cheeks redden, and I chuckle at his embarrassment. I shake my head and answer candidly, "No, not at all. I mean, we were rough, but it was almost like our beasts let her be in charge. I guess I can't speak for my brothers, but the whole time, I just wanted to please her and make sure she was enjoying herself."

Janak grins like the cat that got the cream. "And you, Mal? Did you enjoy claiming your wife?"

"Yes," Maalik growls, baring his teeth. His entire face is red, and I snort at him good-naturedly. There's no way we'll get him to admit anything else in regards to his feelings.

"It appears she is a true Queen of Beasts, then." Janak chuckles. "I know you're not a fan of the title, but the people of Briya love it. They'll be mad with excitement when they learn about Isla."

We discuss the best way to announce to our people and the rest of the realm that we have indeed finally claimed a wife. I still feel a bit guilty and nervous after our conversation and everything I've learned, but I can't help being filled with giddy anticipation at the prospect of introducing Isla as ours at court.

Before we leave, I ask Janak to give us any books about Guardians and Briya that have illustrations I can show to Isla.

CHAPTER THIRTEEN
ISLA

I sigh in content at the quiet, gentle male voices around me. I'm so warm and comfortable and *happy*. I don't think I've ever woken up feeling so happy before.

The sound of a door clicking shut startles me, and my eyes shoot open. Memories from last night come rushing back, and my body tenses up as I realize I'm lying squished between two hard, male bodies. And we're all still very, very naked.

"Isla?" Caelan's gruff, sleepy voice whispers my name from behind me, and Audun pulls away slightly so he can look down and meet my eyes.

When Audun smiles, looking shy and happy and so fucking sweet, my heart does about a million somersaults. My thoughts and feelings are all over the place, and it doesn't help at all that my head is pounding like I drank a fuck-ton of faery wine last night.

"Um, good morning." I mumble quietly, lowering my eyes because I can't deal with Audun looking at me like that.

Caelan says something and kisses the top of my head, but I have no clue if he's talking to me or Audun. Their bodies are pressed against mine, and it feels good, but I'm way too overwhelmed to focus or appreciate it. The guys must realize I'm uncomfortable because they scoot a couple of inches away. They're still close, and I can feel their eyes watching me with concern, but the tiny bit of distance makes me feel just a little less tense.

I raise my hand to brush some of my hair out of my face, cringing when I realize I'm shaking. The last thing I want to do is make the guys worry or feel bad, but I just...I need a minute to process. When I look up to try and meet Audun's eyes again, my gaze catches on my wrist instead and I stop breathing.

The mate rune on my wrist is bold and fresh and way too fucking real. I nearly lose it. It's just too much. Everything is too much. Tears prick at my eyes, and I quickly sit up. The blanket slips down so that my chest is exposed, but I can't find it in myself to care. Audun and Caelan have already seen every part of my body, anyway.

"I just, uh..." I stand up, looking around frantically as I grab the first articles of clothing I see. I slip into a pair of ill-fitting pants, two mismatching socks, an oversized sweater, and throw open the closet beside the front door and grab a thick coat while I step into a pair of men's winter boots.

When my hand touches the knob of the front door, I glance over my shoulder to find Caelan and Audun watching me with wide, heartbroken eyes. Guilt squirms in my belly, but I seriously just need some fresh air and a minute alone or I'm going to freak out. I hold my hand out toward them with my pointer finger up, hoping they understand the gesture that I'll be back in a minute. I open my mouth to tell them just that, but it's not like they'll know what I'm saying. So I open the door and step outside, and quickly close it behind me.

The cold air takes my breath away, a welcome distraction. I wrap the coat tighter about myself before stepping into the snow-covered front yard. Everything is white and bright and so pretty, and I keep my eyes on the snowy tree line as I take clumsy steps further away from the cabin.

I stop to catch my breath when I'm a few dozen yards away from the door, and I look around slowly. It's really gorgeous here, though I imagine not many people live nearby. And it's so quiet. All I hear is the soft rustling of the wind in the trees and the idyllic chirping of birds. I've never spent much time outside of New York, and I've never been anywhere so mountainous or rural before. It's not bad, but it's definitely strange. I guess I'll need to get used to it.

"Okay," I mumble to myself. I pull my sleeve up and gaze down at the rune mark on my wrist. Last night really happened, and I have four fucking mates now. I dreamed about seeing a rune mark on my wrist when I was dating Bryson, but I never in a million years thought it would happen after he broke up with me. I almost want to laugh at the irony of my situation, and I brush my fingers over the mark as nervous laughter bubbles up in my throat.

It's pretty and intricate, more so than any mate runes I've seen on shifters back home, and my skin tingles pleasantly as I stroke my finger along the lines of the design. I'm surprised to discover Madame's protection brand is nowhere to be seen. My skin is smooth and unblemished where it used to be.

I don't blame Caelan, Audun, Reule, or Maalik. Reule warned me this was going to happen, and Maalik did his best to stop it. I'm sure they were affected by those stupid moons even more than I was, and *I* acted like a fucking lunatic. Just thinking about my behavior last night makes me cringe. I can remember every detail, but it's like I had no control over my actions.

The sex was amazing though. I already wanted to sleep with Reule, but holy shit those guys are so hot and they seriously know what they're doing. My body still aches pretty much everywhere, but it's the best kind of ache. If I hadn't been so mind-fucked by those crazy moons, I know there's no way I would have been as bold or as confident as I was with them.

A coughing sound interrupts my thoughts, and I turn my head to find Audun standing on the front porch watching me. He's fully clothed, wearing a thick jacket and a hat on his head. When he sees me looking back at him, he awkwardly raises a hand and waves at me before shoving his hands into his pockets.

My heart melts a little, and I wave back shyly before turning around. It's really cute that he came out here to keep an eye on me, while still being sure to give me some space. It makes me feel cared for, and maybe it's just this fresh, new mate bond making me feel extra sweet toward the guys, but I don't feel that upset about being here with them. A big part of me feels excited.

Honestly, I think the fact that I feel more excited than upset is freaking me out more than anything. I barely know these guys, and I don't know a goddamn thing about this world. I pace back and forth in the snow agitatedly and grumble to myself. How the hell did I end up becoming mates with four sexy, chimera shifter guys? Why was I brought here for this? I'm still convinced that Reule and the others had no idea, and had absolutely no part in bringing me here.

I can't change what happened. The only thing I can control is how I handle my circumstances now. And until they give me reason to do otherwise, I'll try to get to know these guys. It's not fair to me or them not to give this relationship a chance. Judging by the way Audun and Caelan were cuddling with me this morning, I have to assume they feel the same way.

But...Alistair.

I close my eyes and pinch the bridge of my nose. I know I'm stuck here officially because of this bond. But how can I just...not think about Al? I feel sick not knowing if he's okay, and I hate that he's probably worrying about me too. I paid our rent for the next six months, and there's plenty of money in our joint account that he should be totally fine getting by for a while. But Al is sensitive, easily distracted, and he's even more easily manipulated. I'm holding onto a tiny thread of hope that Rian and Matthieu are his mates and care enough about that sort of thing to look after him. But I don't think I'll ever feel totally content until I know without any doubt that my best friend is okay.

As for everything else in my old life, like my job with Madame Deverell and my stupid dream of getting my GED so I could take some classes at one of the many design schools in New York, well...if I've learned anything in my fucked-up twenty-four years of life, it's that nothing ever goes the way you plan.

Audun's still watching me from the porch, but he quickly averts his eyes and pretends to be interested in his feet when I look up this time. I bite my lip to keep from smiling. He's seriously way too cute.

Maalik seemed really serious about helping me get home last night. I wonder if he and the others would still help me find Alistair? They've been so nice, and they've all been great about making me feel comfortable since I ended up here. Figuring out how to talk to these guys is difficult, but I'll do my best to let them know I'm all in with them, so long as they treat me well and help me find Al.

I spend a few more minutes pacing and gathering my courage to go back into the house. Just because I've decided I'm going to try to make the best of things here, that doesn't mean I'm suddenly comfortable with these guys. They're still strangers, no matter how much I like them already. Plus, I'm humiliated about the way I acted last night. Like some crazed, slutty nutcase. I also haven't forgotten the mess I made of their things.

Audun looks up when I start walking back toward the

cabin. He stays where he is as I slowly and clumsily approach, a nervous expression on his face. I feel bad that I probably freaked him out or worried him, and my heart beats anxiously as I get closer and closer.

"Hi," I say quietly when I reach the steps of the front porch. I look up at Audun through my eyelashes, feeling shy but also trying to look cute.

The corner of his mouth turns up, hinting at the slightest of smiles. "Ahoj."

I wish I could explain myself. I wish even more I could ask him what he's thinking and how he feels about all of this. But since I can't, I take the few steps up onto the porch and stop in front of him. We're close, only a couple of inches apart, and I tilt my head back a little to meet his eyes. Audun is only a few inches taller than I am, barely taller than Maalik, and his build is slimmer than the other guys'.

He asks me a question and hesitantly brings his hand up to brush a loose strand of my hair behind my ear. The gesture makes me smile, and I lean against him a little more confidently. The hat he's wearing is one of those dorky lumberjack-looking hats with flaps over the ears, and I playfully tug on it as I continue to grin up at my new beau.

His eyes spark with hope and surprise. I quickly stand up on my tiptoes and lightly peck him on the lips. "You're super adorable, Audun."

For a moment, he stares at me with his mouth slightly open like he's completely awestruck. And then he smiles so brilliantly it takes my breath away, and he raises his hand again to brush his fingers over my cheek. He leans down slowly, like he's waiting to see if I'll pull away, and he slants his mouth over mine.

It's such a sweet kiss, and butterflies flutter like mad in my stomach. After a minute, Audun pulls away and wraps his arms around me to pull me close. I wrap my arms around him and rest my head against his chest. He mumbles something quietly while he kisses the top of my head, and I can't stop the ridiculous grin from spreading across my face. Just being held like this by him is almost sweeter than the kiss, and I'm already glad I decided to give this whole polyandry mate thing a chance.

My stomach rumbles, totally killing the moment, and Audun pulls away again with a quiet chuckle. He turns around and opens the front door, gesturing for me to go inside first. I stomp my feet a few times on the porch, attempting to shake most of the snow from my borrowed boots, and step inside with another smile directed at Audun.

It's so much warmer inside the cabin, and my eyes scan the front room curiously. I'm still nervous, but now that I'm not having a total meltdown, I'm able to focus a little more and take in the atmosphere. There are clothes and blankets scattered all over the living room floor, and it hardcore smells like sex in here. If I can smell it, then the guys definitely can, and my face warms up at the thought of everything we did together last night.

Caelan calls out to us across the room, and I look up to see him standing by the stove in the kitchen. Audun answers him, places his hand on my lower back, and gently pushes me through the house. When we pass by the hallway, I turn my head away and force myself not to look at the mess spilling from the guys' bedrooms. I am so not ready to deal with that yet.

Once we reach the kitchen, Caelan turns around to face us. He looks sad and nervous as his eyes sweep over me, and the butterflies go crazy in my stomach again. He's wearing sweatpants low on his hips, and he's not wearing a shirt. His yummy abs are on full display and he looks so damn good. I'm stuck between staring at him lustfully while thinking about last night, and feeling so freaking anxious about my brand new relationship with him and wondering how I'm supposed to act.

Audun mumbles something and rubs my shoulders lightly as he kisses the top of my head. Caelan doesn't spare him a glance, keeping his eyes on me instead, and his entire face lights up at Audun's words.

"Krásná dívka," Caelan says. He steps forward and cups my face between his hands, leans down, and kisses me passionately.

"Oh," I gasp when he pulls away. I bring my fingers to my lips and stare up at him dazedly, and a nervous giggle escapes my throat. He's a crazy good kisser, and he's just so fucking hot. Guys who look like him back home would usually act aloof and uninterested after hooking up. But he's being so affectionate and giving me his full attention, and it's honestly kind of intoxicating.

Caelan keeps his hands on my face, and he softly strokes his thumbs over my cheeks as he smiles down at me and says something in his language. I desperately wish I could understand, and I feel like an idiot as I stare at him cluelessly. When my stomach growls again, his grin widens and his nose scrunches up adorably.

A delicious scent hits my nose, and I realize Caelan is in the middle of cooking breakfast. I smile at him thankfully as Audun leads me over to the dining room table and pulls a chair out for me to sit. Instead of sitting down with me, Audun begins picking up the blankets on the floor of the living room. I go to get up so I can help him, but he moves crazy fast like Reule's done in front of me a few times, and he puts his hands on my shoulders to keep me in my seat.

"Zůstaň," Audun says quietly. I purse my lips at him, but he just gives me a crooked smile before leaving me at the table while he cleans up the mess by himself.

I feel a little guilty sitting down while the guys cook and clean, but it's also really nice to be spoiled. I wonder if they're just as nervous as I am. They seem happy, and that makes me feel better about everything. I stroke the mate rune on my wrist absentmindedly while my gaze travels back and forth between the two of them.

Eventually, Caelan calls Audun back into the kitchen. They carry several dishes over to the table and set them in front of me. Everything looks and smells delicious. My eyes practically bug out of my skull as I take in the mouth-watering sight of pastries, fruit, eggs, something that looks like bacon, and a tall stack of pancakes. I've been super relieved to find that most of the food in this world is generally familiar to me.

"Thank you, Caelan." I don't waste any time filling my plate.

Caelan seems extra pleased, and he scoots his chair close to me before filling his own plate. When Audun does the same thing, I glance around the cabin and voice the question I've been wondering since I came back inside after my freak-out.

"Where are Reule and Maalik?"

Audun and Caelan glance at each other over my head, and then Caelan says something to me in his complicated language. When it becomes clear that I have no idea what he's saying, he starts gesturing to the top of his head and repeating the words, "Král Janak."

I think that might be a name, but I don't understand what Caelan's gesturing means. If Reule and Maalik went to talk to this person, I hope it was for a good reason. I feel kind of sad and weird not seeing them this morning. I know it wasn't really our choice, but I still hope they're not very angry or upset about having me as a mate. It's going to be a strange adjustment for all of us, and I just want them to be as open to this as Caelan and Audun seem to be.

While the three of us eat, Caelan and Audun converse back and forth quietly. Even though I can't contribute, Caelan plays footsies with me under the table and Audun keeps reaching over to rub my back or touch my hair while giving me bashful smiles.

By the time we're finished with breakfast, most of the food is gone and I'm sufficiently stuffed. I want to ask what we're doing for the rest of the day, or if the guys already have a plan. But since I can't, I patiently wait to follow their lead.

Audun gets up first and begins clearing the table. I stand up too, but I hover and wait to see if he'll let me help clean this time. Before I get an answer, Caelan steps up behind me and rubs his hands up and down my arms as he turns me around and directs me toward the hallway.

I cringe when I see my mess, and I try to plant my feet and refuse to budge. Caelan snorts at the action and picks me up effortlessly while he continues walking until we're in the middle of the hallway. When he sets me down again, I bite my lip and glance up at him to gauge his expression. I feel awful about going through their things and throwing their clothes around, and I'm terrified they're going to be angry at me for it.

Caelan rests one hand on his hip and uses the other to rub his chin thoughtfully while he glances around the hallway and inside each bedroom. He hums and furrows his eyebrows, and my heart pounds wildly the entire time I watch him.

He looks at me, and I see the slightest smirk form on his face. I realize he's laughing at me, and he finds the entire thing amusing. I groan and cover my face with my hands, but I can't help laughing a little because I'm so freaking relieved despite the embarrassment I feel.

"I'm sorry, Caelan. I don't know what I was thinking last night."

Caelan chuckles and gently grabs my wrists, pulling my hands away from my face. He smiles at me and gives me another one of his amazing, passionate kisses.

When he starts picking up the clothes in the hallway, I bend down to help him and follow him into his room. We quickly fold all of his clothes and put them away, along with all of the knickknacks I'd thrown about. I feel myself blushing when we make the bed together. Caelan doesn't say anything, but he has a telling smirk on his face the whole time that has me rolling my eyes.

It's the same way in Reule's and Audun's rooms. We quietly and efficiently tidy everything up, and Caelan doesn't make me feel bad about what I did. He continues to give me teasing glances every now and then, but I pretend I don't notice.

When we make it to Maalik's room, Caelan pauses in the doorway and goes totally still. My face is fucking on fire as I realize he can probably smell what I did in here when I was angry at them. I glance up at his face to see his reaction, and I huff when I see that the jackass is grinning with an amused twinkle in his eye.

I brush past him roughly and begin picking up the clothes. Caelan snickers and quickly joins me in helping clean up. Since Maalik has fewer personal belongings than the other guys, it takes almost no time at all. I try not to meet Caelan's eyes when I step over to make the bed, but I can feel his teasing eyes on me.

"Hmm..." He steps around to the other side of the bed and makes a show of fluffing the pillows. I still don't look at him, but he starts making loud, obnoxious sniffing noises.

"Seriously?" I whine as I finally look up at him. He has the biggest fucking grin on his face, *ever*, and it's so fucking annoying and embarrassing and *cute* that he's teasing me like this. "Would you cut it out already?"

Caelan bites his lip and *innocently* straightens the blankets on his side. He only lasts about two seconds before I see his nose twitch again, and he starts laughing quietly under his breath.

"Ugh!" I pick up one of Maalik's pillows and throw it at

Caelan, feeling way too pleased with myself when it hits him in the face.

He stares at me like he's stunned, then he grins mischievously and jumps over the fucking bed so he's on my side. I barely have time to blink before he grabs me and jumps onto the bed with me in his arms, and I squeal as he starts thrashing and rolling around with me all over the blankets. Now both our scents are going to be all over Maalik's bed, and the whole thing is so stupid and funny that I lose my breath from laughing so hard.

Audun's voice catches our attention from the doorway, and Caelan and I look up to see him watching us with a soft smile on his face. Caelan chuckles and responds back to him, and Audun walks into the bedroom.

To my absolute delight, he crawls onto the bed on my other side so I'm sandwiched between them. Kind of like I was when I woke up this morning. I blush at the unbidden thought. Luckily, I'm distracted when Audun starts rolling around like he's trying to mark his scent on Maalik's bed too.

"Poor Maalik." I giggle.

Caelan snorts in amusement and picks up my hand, threading our fingers together. He holds our hands up a bit higher and tugs the sleeve of my shirt down so my rune mark is visible. His fingers trail over the mark, and a low purring sound emits from his throat. I turn my head to smile shyly at him. His expression is warm and affectionate as he brings my wrist to his mouth and places a kiss to the mark.

I really like him and Audun so much already, and it's easy to be with them and play around even though we're not able to talk. Whenever Maalik and Reule get home, I'll try to talk to them again about Alistair. But right now, I feel happy and hopeful that things are going to be okay. Ending up here with these guys is totally not the worst thing that could have happened to me, by far.

I bring Caelan's hand to my lips and kiss his mate rune,

and I turn my head to face Audun as I do the same to his mark. Both men seem overjoyed at the action, and they snuggle me close.

They make me feel absolutely precious and cared for, and I think I might almost feel a little bit lucky to have ended up here.

CHAPTER FOURTEEN
AUDUN

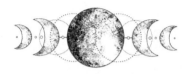

"She's taking forever in there." Caelan whines.

I roll my eyes and walk past him to my bedroom, my arms full of items I collected from the storage room. "Maybe she's never seen a shower before. Just leave her alone, Cael."

Caelan groans and rests his forehead against the bathroom door. Isla has been in the shower for a long time, but I don't want to bother her or make her feel rushed. I step into my room and drop everything onto my bed, quickly taking stock of what I grabbed and trying to remember what else we might have packed away that Isla can use immediately.

The room at the end of the hall was always meant to belong to our wife. When we didn't claim one during our first Guardians' Night together, it quickly became a room we use for storage. Over the years, we collected every sort of gift imaginable a woman might like, hoping to someday present all of them to our chosen wife.

Forty years later, the next time the Beasts' Full Moon came around during Guardians' Night, we didn't claim a wife on purpose. Somehow, the gifts kept piling up. Every year, people send us things for the woman who's supposed to keep us grounded. The woman who's supposed to keep us human.

The room is packed, and I don't recall even a fraction of the items stored there.

"Do you really think she's never seen a shower?" Caelan leans against my doorframe and crosses his arms, a thoughtful expression on his face. "I'm not so sure. She's at least somewhat familiar with magic, and she didn't have any trouble getting it to work properly."

I shrug when I can't think of anything else to say. Truthfully, I'm really interested in learning more about the world Isla's from. Whenever my brothers and I travel off-world, it's always for work and usually to hunt and kill demons. We've seen some interesting things, but there's never been a time where I've been able to just explore and enjoy seeing a world outside of my own.

"Think these will fit her?" I change the subject and point to the small pair of boots on the bed. I grabbed two other pairs just in case, but I think Isla will like these best. They're a pretty tawny color, and they're lined with rabbit fur so they'll be extra soft and warm.

Caelan walks over to join me beside the bed. "If they don't, we have something like two hundred other pairs of shoes stashed away in that room."

He picks up the gloves and scarf I grabbed too, looking them over appraisingly. There are a lot of accessories hidden away in the crates and boxes in the bedroom, but we don't have any actual clothes. There are thousands of bolts of different fabrics, but we chose to never have anything made. We weren't sure what our wife might like, as fashions and trends are constantly changing, and we never wanted to presume what size she might wear.

I never imagined our wife would come to us without any belongings of her own to start with. Honestly, I'd given up on the idea that we might ever have a wife at all. I don't want to mess this up, and I want Isla to have everything she could ever dream of. I feel terrible that she'll have to borrow my clothes for one more day until we can take her to some of the shops in the closest village.

Caelan turns to me with a grin, still holding the gloves and scarf I picked to help keep her warm. "I can't wait until she realizes everything in that room is hers. And I'm going to buy anything she sees that she wants in the village today."

The sound of the bathroom door opening has us both spinning around enthusiastically. I hear Isla's feet pad softly against the hardwood floor, and she peeks her head into my room and gives us a dazzling smile.

She says something that sounds like gibberish in her sweet voice and steps further into my room. My face feels warm as I take her in. She's wearing a towel wrapped around her body, and so much of her smooth, tanned skin is visible as water droplets drip down her arms and legs tantalizingly. I've never seen a woman more beautiful than Isla, and I can't believe she's ours.

Isla speaks again, and there's an obvious teasing lilt in her voice even though we can't understand what she's saying. I pull my eyes away from where the towel hits her thighs, feeling guilty when I see the smirk on her face.

I want her so badly. I want to worship her body and make sure she knows how much I appreciate her. I want her to know how happy I am to have her here. But when she woke up between Caelan and me this morning, she was so upset and anxious. When she went outside to clear her head, my brother and I agreed we should take things slow with her. She's barely had time to get to know us, and the language barrier doesn't make anything easier.

Besides, it's not like it was her choice to come here. She didn't choose us. My brothers and I feel guilty about that, but I can't help also feeling lucky to have her and so excited to get to know her. I'll do anything to make her happy. I want her to like us, and I pray she doesn't end up resenting us like Maalik's afraid might happen.

"Oh, shit." Caelan grunts. He steps closer to her and brushes his fingers over her shoulder. I'm annoyed at first, thinking he's going back on our agreement to go slow with Isla. I tense up when I see the horrified look on his face, and I quickly step closer to her to see what he's looking at.

I inhale a sharp breath when I see a large bruise and bite marks marring her shoulder. They were obviously caused by one of us last night. Maalik was right. We were too rough with her. Isla furrows her eyebrows and turns her head to see what Caelan's fussing over. I bite my lip, bracing myself for her reaction. I just know she's going to pull away from us again, and I don't know if I can handle it. Things have been amazing all morning since breakfast.

She snorts and rolls her eyes, catching Caelan and I off guard. She shakes her head as she touches the marks on her shoulder, and gives us a salacious little grin as she suddenly drops her towel.

If my face was warm before, it's on fire now. I can't help letting my eyes sweep over her body, and I nearly groan when I see that her nipples are hard. She brushes her still-wet hair over her shoulder, completely unbothered that she's standing naked in front of us.

She turns slightly, angling her body so we have a better view as she points out several fingerprint-sized bruises around her hips and thighs.

"Isla," I gasp in horror. I reach a shaky hand toward her, my fingertips hovering near the bruises on her hips. I'm terrified to touch her. I don't deserve to touch her. I can't believe we hurt her so badly.

A soft, light-hearted laugh leaves her mouth, and I find myself gaping at her in surprise. She grins back and forth between me and Caelan like she's amused at this entire situation, and she closes her eyes and sighs in content while she makes this weird little hand gesture. Her middle, ring, and pinky fingers are sticking up while she makes a circle with her thumb and pointer finger.

"Is she saying she likes it?" Caelan asks, running his fingers through his hair roughly. I nod slowly, feeling a weird mix of relief, confusion, and arousal. My brother curses and steps away, glancing at Isla once more over his shoulder before he leaves the room. "I need to take a cold shower, or else I'm going to claim her right here in front of you, Audun."

Isla pouts at him as he retreats from my bedroom, and she turns to focus her mesmerizing honey-brown eyes on me. I swallow thickly, suddenly terrified to be alone with her. She's still standing here naked, and she's so incredibly tempting. But I don't want to freak her out again, and I don't want her to feel obligated to be physical with any of us just because of the claiming last night.

"I, uh…" I frantically look around the room and dart over to my bed to pick up the tawny-colored boots. "I have shoes for you."

She giggles, and I feel like an idiot. It might actually be a blessing that she can't understand my words. If she could, there would be no way I'd ever manage to win her heart or affection. She picks up the towel she dropped, and I try not to frown as she wraps it around her body.

Isla walks across the room and joins me beside the bed, and she smiles at the boots and the other stuff I brought from the storage room. She points at herself, raises her eyebrows and asks, "Me?"

I nod and bite my lip anxiously. Several seconds later, I realize I still need to find her some actual clothes, and I begin digging through my wardrobe. Everything is folded neatly, so I quickly find an old pair of pants that are a little too small for me and one of my warmest shirts and sweaters. I feel weird giving her a pair of my underwear, but I know she doesn't have anything else yet. I bashfully hold everything out to her, and she gives me the sweetest, warmest smile in return.

Before she can drop her towel again or tempt me any further, I quickly step out into the hallway and wait for her to get dressed.

A SHORT WHILE LATER, THE THREE OF US LEAVE THE CABIN AND begin our trek down to the village. It's about a half hour walk, and I'm worried Isla will get too cold or over-tired. We have no idea what the terrain was like where she lived before, so I'm not sure if she's used to the elevation up here in the mountains. It's pretty obvious she's not used to snow. She looks like a newborn calf every time she steps foot in it.

"Maybe I should just carry her," I say to Caelan when Isla falls down for the second time.

My brother laughs and grins down at our wife fondly as he helps her up. "She looks so happy though. Besides, she's going to have to get used to the snow sooner or later."

She does look happy, and her excitement is contagious. Once she realized we were leaving the house, she lit up and started babbling away in her confusing language. I'm certain she's wondering where we're going, but I have no idea how to begin explaining. Cael just talks to her normally like he would anyone else, even though she can't understand a word he says. Reule seems to know how to communicate with her the best so far, but I'm sure that's only because Isla's spent the most time with him.

I've never been great with words. Even if Isla could under-stand me, I have no idea how I would explain who Runa is to us or that we're going to the village I grew up in before I became a Guardian. It's always bittersweet visiting my child-hood home, even while it's comforting knowing that my old family is close by in case they ever need anything.

When Isla falls down again, giggling the entire time, I give Caelan a look. He smiles at her and chuckles. "On second thought, it will probably take us all day to get to the village at this pace."

I crouch down in front of Isla and awkwardly gesture for her to climb onto my back. I would cradle her to my chest, but I'm worried that might seem too forward. I'm still not even sure if I should be touching her much at all until she's more comfortable with us.

Isla climbs onto my back without any hesitation and leans forward to kiss my cheek. I'm grinning like an idiot as I stand up and settle my hands under her knees to keep her stable. When I catch Caelan's eye, I expect him to tease me, but he's grinning just as widely as I am. I think this might be the happiest I've ever seen my brother.

"She's incredible, isn't she?" Caelan walks beside me, reaching out to stroke Isla's hair.

Her arms are wrapped around my neck and her legs are around my waist, and I'm warm all over from feeling her body against mine. I nod in agreement. "We're really lucky. I thought she'd be angry or distant with us. Do you think she feels the effects from the bond the same way we do?"

Cael hums thoughtfully. "I think so. She definitely felt it last night, right? I want to make her happy more than anything in the world, and I know you and our brothers feel the same. I'm sure Isla feels that about us too, at least a little."

Part of me is glad for it, but mostly I hope Isla might someday fall in love with us because of *us* and not just the magic bonding us together.

As if he can read my mind, Caelan grins at me again and says, "Don't get me wrong, we're still incredibly lucky. If she's feeling the slightest effects from the bond, that means she's *accepted* the bond. I'm sure that's why some of the Guardians in other kingdoms have so many issues with their wives— because their wives never fully accepted them or the bond, and they continue to fight against it. Isla may have been brought here against her will, but she's embracing us and our world. Our wife is an amazingly strong woman."

I ponder over my brother's words and realize he's right. Hearing stories about some of the other Guardians' wives has always been the biggest reason we've held back from claiming a wife for ourselves. In our closest neighboring kingdoms, they have a sort of lottery system where a girl is chosen from a drawing and given to the Guardians on Guardians' Night when the Beasts' Moon is present. It's easy to understand why any of those girls would fight against such a bond. Even the Guardians of Briya before us had issues with their wife, and she came to them willingly.

Knowing that Isla has accepted us and that she's willing to give us a chance makes my heart swell. Like Caelan said, I'll do whatever it takes to make her happy. I'm sure Mal already has a plan to track down Isla's brother Alistair, but I make a mental note to bring the matter up with my brothers again later.

We're quiet the rest of the walk, presumably lost in our own thoughts. Isla looks around curiously the entire time, even though there's not much to see besides trees and snow. When we catch the first glimpses of the village, she perks up and points at a few buildings as she babbles in my ear.

The paths are much easier to walk here, so I carefully let her down and take her hand instead. I'm nervous and giddy to introduce Isla to my family. I wonder what they'll think of her. But more importantly, I wonder what she'll think of them.

"Not much further, beautiful." Caelan takes Isla's other hand and continues walking toward the main road of the village.

There are only a few people out and about, and they don't pay us any mind at first. Sometimes it can be awkward dealing with the public, even here where I grew up. People call us gods and they show us respect, but they're always nervous and wary around us. We make them uncomfortable.

Isla points to a storefront window and I focus my attention on her and the present. When I turn to give the store a second look, I'm surprised to see that there are decorations covering the entire front of the shop and hanging in the window. The display shows three full moons, four beasts, and a girl wearing a crown.

"Did you know they celebrated Guardians' Night here?" Caelan asks.

I shake my head slowly and look around the street. Every storefront seems to be decorated similarly, and there are lights and ribbons hanging above us covering the main streets of the village. I knew Guardians' Night was considered an official holiday, but we've never visited any towns during it. For the years the Beasts' Moon was present, we stayed holed up at home the entire week, feeling miserable and lonely. Every other year on Guardians' Night, we were required to attend court at the castle, or to visit some of the other kingdoms and the Guardians there.

"Interesting," Caelan says quietly as we continue on our way. Runa and her family live in one of the largest houses on the main street. The closer we get to the center of town, the more people we see. Isla looks curious and excited.

When a young couple and their child step out of one of the shops and move to walk around us, Isla calls out to them. "Hello!"

I'm surprised at her boldness and impressed that she's already trying to learn our language, even if she's only using simple words like hello. Mostly, I'm nervous that she's drawn any attention to us. I sort of hoped we'd be able to slip in and out of the village without making a scene.

The man and woman look up to return the greeting, and their faces fill with shock when they recognize me and Caelan. I smile at them awkwardly, and I nearly groan when they bow to us.

"Guardians, good morning! My sincerest apologies. My

wife and I didn't realize it was you at first," the man says anxiously. He keeps his eyes down to avoid looking directly at us. The woman is trying to get her daughter to bow to us as well, but the child stares up at us obliviously with wide blue eyes.

"That's perfectly alright," Caelan says in a friendly tone. "We were trying to be a bit incognito this morning, but our wife apparently had other plans."

The man and woman look up at Isla at the same moment, and their expressions light up with understanding. The woman gasps and brings her hand to her chest. "You've finally chosen a mate? Oh my goodness, congratulations!"

I frown at that word—*mate*. My brothers and I can't stand that word, but it's the word they teach in school when children first learn about Guardians. It's the word used in all the texts that have ever been written about us, in reference to the woman we share a soulmate bond with.

"Yes, thank you," Caelan replies proudly. He brings Isla's hand up to his lips and kisses her knuckles. "We're taking Isla to visit Audun's nieces."

"Oh, Miss Runa is going to be so happy!" the woman exclaims. She grins exuberantly at Isla and asks, "Which village are you from, milady? I'm sure ours isn't as grand as you're used to, but I can assure you that you'll be most welcomed here!"

Isla has been watching this entire exchange closely. She appears happy but confused, and she glances at me after the young woman addresses her. I nervously clear my throat and say, "Isla isn't from Briya, and she doesn't know our language yet."

If the couple is confused by the fact that Isla's not from our kingdom at all, they don't voice their questions. They simply smile at her joyously, and the man picks up his daughter and rests her on his hip. The child can't be more than three or four years old, and she keeps her gaze locked on Isla while ignoring me and Caelan entirely.

"Sweetheart, this is Isla—Briya's Queen of Beasts. Isn't she beautiful?" the man asks his daughter.

"A real queen?" The little girl's eyes light up in excitement.

I flush at the title given to Isla. I knew it would happen, and I know it's not an insult. But I think I might hate the title 'Queen of Beasts' even more than I hate the word 'mate.'

"We really must be going. We don't want to keep Runa waiting, and we have a few errands to run before Reule and Maalik join us." Caelan speaks in a way that's friendly while still showing his authority—something I've still never been able to master even after almost a century.

The couple congratulates us again, and we continue on our way down the street. More and more people are out and about, now that it's getting close to lunch time. Isla looks more intrigued and curious than ever, and I find myself admiring her so much more. Anyone else in her situation would be angry or terrified.

We manage to make it to Runa's house without running into anyone else, and my heart beats erratically as we walk up the front steps. Caelan knocks loudly on the door, and we wait in silence for someone to answer. Caelan knows how nervous I am. He knows how strange it is for me to come back here, and how it gets worse as more time passes.

I grew up in this house with my parents and my twin sister, Niani. My father was the mayor, and we were the wealthiest family in the village. I had a happy childhood, and my parents were supportive of my silly dreams to travel and pursue art once I finished school. Of all my brothers, I was certainly the luckiest with my home-life before I became a Guardian.

When my first shift happened, everyone here in the village was shocked—my parents most of all. I'd never thought much of Guardians, and I'd never shown any signs of magic my entire life before my fifteenth birthday. Despite the shock, my parents were still supportive and encouraging. They treated Maalik, Caelan, and Reule like family and they always made it known that the four of us would have a home here.

That's why we built our cabin so close to my childhood home in the first place. My brothers didn't have the same support I'd been blessed with growing up. Even after my parents died, my sister and her children have kept the house and have stayed close with us. In return, my brothers and I have helped them in any ways we've been able to all these years.

Runa is my sister's granddaughter, and she lives here now with her daughter Marieke and Marieke's son Naren. Runa's parents died a few years ago, and her other children have all moved out. I know my brothers come to see her occasionally on their days off, but it's been several months since I've seen Runa. She knows how we've always felt about claiming a wife, so I can't imagine what she's going to think of Isla and how she ended up here.

But if there's anyone who will be able to comfort Isla the way a mother would, it's Runa. Runa and Marieke will also be much more helpful at helping Isla choose clothing than me or my brothers would be.

Marieke answers the door, and her eyes widen as her gaze darts between me, Caelan, and Isla. "What are you guys doing here? I thought you didn't go out during the week of Guardians' Night."

Naren pushes past his mother and darts out the front door, throwing himself at my legs. "Uncle Audun!"

I pick up the toddler and grin, despite all my nerves and insecurities that Isla may not like my family, or that my family may not approve of the way we claimed our wife.

"Good morning, Marieke." Caelan throws his arm around Isla's shoulders and gives my great-great niece a charming smile. "We'd like to introduce you to our wife."

CHAPTER FIFTEEN
ISLA

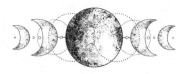

THE GIRL WHO ANSWERS THE DOOR IS STUNNING.

While her eyes move back and forth between me, Audun, and Caelan, and she asks them a question, I look her over critically. Her skin is dark and smooth, her wavy black hair cascades down to her waist, and her eyes shine like sapphires.

I'm trying to figure out who she is to Audun and Caelan and understand why they brought me here to see her. When we first left the house, I was excited to be given the chance to see more of this world. The guys have all been insanely sweet to me, but I worried they might try to keep me isolated and cooped up in that cabin. In my experience, shifters are extremely territorial and jealous.

The walk down the mountain seemed to take forever, but it was nice being able to relax and take in the picturesque scenery while Audun carried me. And the town here is so cute! All the shops and cobbled streets look like something out of a storybook, and seeing all the decorations celebrating the guys was eye-opening. They're clearly very important in this world, and I want to know them so much more now than I did before.

Now that I'm standing in front of this gorgeous girl, I feel prickly and self-conscious. She obviously knows them well if they're coming to her house, and *she* can speak to them. She certainly knows them better than I do, and something about that really pisses me off. I don't care how I ended up here or why. Audun and Caelan are mine, and I refuse to let any other hussies touch them ever again. No matter what sort of history my men might have with anyone.

When a child rushes outside and attaches himself to Audun's legs, I feel my heart drop into my stomach. I'm barely aware of Caelan wrapping his arm around my shoulders as I look at the little boy and the absolute joy on Audun's face. The toddler looks exactly like Audun, except for his sapphire blue eyes.

"You have a kid?" I ask. I'm jealous and hurt and freaking the hell out, even though I know logically I have no right to be. When Audun looks up to meet my eyes, I frown and point between him, the girl, and the little boy in his arms. "Did you bring me here to introduce me to your son and your baby-mama? Oh, god. I really don't know if I'm ready for this. Being mated to four hot guys, sure, I can handle that. But a kid?"

Audun stares at me like a deer in headlights, and he's just so damn adorable that I can't be mad at him. As much as I really don't like kids, seeing him hold his son is probably one of the cutest things ever.

I sigh and stand up straight as I face Audun's baby-mama. She's staring at me with her eyebrows raised, but she doesn't seem unfriendly or hostile. I know she can't understand what I'm saying, but I need her to understand that things between her and Audun are over now for good. I pull up my sleeve and point to my mate rune, and I point to Audun's wrist while I gesture between us.

"Audun is with me now, okay? I don't care what sort of history the two of you have. I'm not gonna try to take your kid or become his step-mother or anything. But Audun is *mine*." I point to Audun several times before tapping my chest. I feel like a freaking caveman, but I just don't know how else to get my point across.

Caelan snorts loudly and squeezes my shoulders. He can make fun of me all he wants, but I'm going to take this mate thing seriously. They might be cool with sharing me among each other, but I'm not okay with sharing.

The girl at the door giggles and says something to Audun. I'm offended for a half second until she faces me with a friendly grin and opens the door wide enough to let us into the house. Caelan pushes me forward gently, and I walk through the doorway with my head held high even though I'm incredibly anxious.

Audun is still carrying the little boy, and he gives me a shy smile when I glance over my shoulder. Caelan looks way too amused for this situation, which somehow doesn't surprise me. He seems amused by almost everything I say and do, so I try not to pay him any mind. The house is lovely, and I'm slightly distracted as I walk through the foyer behind Audun's baby mama. It looks like I've stepped into a fancy European story-book cottage, with wooden rafters on the ceilings and the most charming paintings and decorations leading into a large, open kitchen and dining area.

There's a woman standing at the sink, facing away from us. I can't see her face, but she's wearing a long, black skirt with embroidered folk-art looking flowers in bright red, orange, blue, and white. She's wearing a long-sleeved white shirt with a red vest over it, and a black scarf tied over her shoulders and head. I blink at her outfit a few times, and dart a quick glance back at the guys and the girl that answered the door. They're dressed totally normal—the girl is wearing a long, modest blue dress, but it still looks like something I'd see back home, and the guys are wearing plain black trousers, long shirts and jackets.

"Kdo přišel?" the woman asks over her shoulder without looking up from her task.

"Ahoj, Runa." Caelan grins at the woman as he rubs his hand across my lower back.

She drops something in the sink and spins around to stare at us in shock. She has the same gorgeous skin tone as Audun and the toddler, but her eyes are the same captivating blue color as the girl's. She looks to be middle-aged, maybe in her forties or early fifties. I find myself growing more confused by the second, but the woman's face immediately breaks out in a bright smile.

She exclaims happily and rushes over to pull Audun into a hug. He looks a little embarrassed, but he hugs her back after setting the child down. She hugs Caelan too after stepping away from Audun, and then she stands in front of me and grabs both my hands.

The woman who looks an awful lot like Audun, and who I'm starting to suspect might be a relative, continues to smile at me with genuine warmth as she asks a question. Caelan steps closer, wrapping his arm around my waist in a way that's slightly possessive, and he answers, "Naše žena, Isla."

Naše žena. I've heard him say that a few times now. He said it outside just a few minutes ago, and he said it to the couple we met in the street on our way here. He also mumbled it multiple times when we were snuggling in bed earlier while he and Audun kissed the mate rune on my wrists over and over.

I wonder if the words mean mate—*their mate.* The thought makes my mouth curve up into the stupidest, most idiotic smile ever. I really hope I'm right because just the thought of them introducing me to people as their mate already, without even really knowing me yet, makes me so incredibly happy.

The woman exclaims once more, and hugs me the same way she did Audun and Caelan. When she pulls away a few moments later, she begins speaking at me rapidly and excitedly, but Audun quickly cuts her off with an apologetic grimace.

The girl from the front door laughs and says something else to the middle-aged woman, and I watch as her expression slowly transitions into something between confusion and amusement. The girl laughs again and steps in front of me as she gestures to herself, the woman, and then the little boy that's hiding behind her legs.

"Marieke, Runa, Naren."

I'd already guessed Runa's name because of how Caelan greeted her, but I'm glad to finally know Marieke's and her son's names. Caelan and Audun look rightly chastised when Runa realizes I was never introduced properly. She gestures toward the dining room table and continues speaking hurriedly.

Caelan directs me to sit at a long, wooden table. He pulls my chair out like a perfect gentleman, and he and Audun sit on either side of me. Everyone is being super nice, but I can't help feeling nervous while I wait to see what's happening. I hate that I can't understand what everyone is saying around me, and I hate that all I can do is sit patiently.

I trust Audun and Caelan, as stupid as that might make me. Maybe it's this mate bond I share with them now, but I've always been pretty good at judging people. I don't think either of them would purposely put me in a dangerous or uncomfortable situation. At least without a good reason.

"Oh," I blurt out in surprise when Naren suddenly climbs into my lap. Marieke is busy in the kitchen, and Caelan and Audun smile encouragingly when I glance at them for help. I pat the kid's back awkwardly as he settles in my lap, and I try to smile when he starts blabbering on in their language that I don't understand.

Caelan and Audun answer Naren, and they even laugh a few times at whatever the toddler is saying. Naren keeps looking at me and trying to talk to me, and he's seriously an adorable kid. But I just…really don't like kids, and never have. They're loud and fussy and usually smell weird. It doesn't help that I spent so many years in foster care with Alistair suckered into babysitting tons of younger children, and being around kids now always makes me dredge up uncomfortable memories.

The guys keep giving me these weird, unreadable side glances, and it's making me freak out the longer I hold Naren in my lap. I'm trying to keep it cool, but I've just realized that I'm their fucking mate and they're probably expecting me to pop out a bunch of kids. Sooner rather than later, I'm sure.

When I was dating Bryson, we talked about having kids. But the conversations were always super vague that I didn't worry much. Every shifter I've ever known is extremely territorial, and they love big families. I just hoped that having kids would be something I could put off, and that hopefully I'd come around to the idea of being a mother when I was older. Even now, the idea still really doesn't appeal to me. And I'm not a weak-minded girl trying to impress a dumbass wolf shifter anymore.

I got my last depo shot a few weeks ago, so I won't have to worry about getting pregnant for a couple of months at least. I just hope that in that time, I can figure out how to tell my new mates I'm just not ready to have kids. There has to be some form of birth control in this world, right? The four of them have been incredibly sweet to me, so I really hope they're understanding about this.

Naren gets down from my lap when Marieke finally joins us at the table, carrying a large tray with a tea set. Neither of the guys move to help her when she pours each of them a cup. It seems a little weird and insulting to me, but I follow their lead and remain still and silent as she pours a cup for me too. When she's finished, she bows deeply and says something in a reverent tone.

The guys mumble something that I hope means thank

you, but they both look slightly uncomfortable when I raise my eyebrows at them. I thank Marieke in English, since I have no idea how to say it in whatever language they speak here. She appears pleased, and she takes a seat across from me at the table as she pours her own cup.

Caelan and Audun take a sip of their tea at the same time, and I slowly lift my cup to my lips as I subtly glance around the table for some sugar or honey. It doesn't look like there is any, unfortunately. The tea is extremely strong and bitter, and I set my cup down in relief when Runa walks up behind me.

"Podívej se na tohle," she says as she sets a large book, a pen, and some paper in front of me.

She nods encouragingly when I hesitate to open the book, so I quickly open the front cover and gasp in surprise. It's not a book—it's a photo album! The photo taking up the entire first page is similar to the photos I found in guys' rooms. It looks old, all black and white, but the people in the photo are moving. Even though I've seen this trick already and I know that magic clearly exists in the world, it's still crazy bizarre to see a family waving at me from a photograph.

There's a man, a woman, and two young children staring at me from the photograph. They all look so happy and friendly, and I'm already smiling when Audun scoots close and points at the little boy in the photo.

"Já," he says. He points at the little girl next and says, "Niani, má sestra."

The words sound similar enough to '*my sister*' that I feel confident in my assumption that this is an old photo of Audun with his family. If Runa has this photo album, she's obviously a relative too. Marieke probably is as well, so I feel a little embarrassed for my rant outside on the front steps.

"Matka a otec," he continues, pointing to the couple I'm assuming to be his parents in the photo.

I grin as I look closer at the photo, and I turn my head to smile at Audun. "You were so adorable!"

Runa makes a shooing motion at Caelan, and he grunts before standing up and giving her his seat. I almost laugh as she scoots in close beside me, but she has a serious expression on her face as she begins drawing something on the blank paper.

First, she draws two stick figures at the top of the page—she obviously doesn't share Audun's skill in art—and then she draws a line between them, and a line down from that leading to two more stick figures. She points to each stick figure, verbally labeling them for me as Audun, his parents, and his sister.

When she begins drawing more lines and stick figures beside and under Niani, it quickly becomes evident she's drawing a family tree. The room is eerily silent as understanding slowly dawns on me. Runa draws four more generations under Niani, ending with Naren all the way down at the bottom.

There are no names beside or under Audun's, and I hold my breath as I count the names and deduce that Runa is Niani's granddaughter. Making her Audun's great niece.

"You're immortal?" I feel stupid when I ask Audun the question, knowing he won't understand my words. He looks so heartbroken and guilty, and I can't stand seeing that expression on his face.

Caelan kneels down on the floor beside me, in between my seat and Audun's. He takes my hand in his and kisses the back of my knuckles, and he gives me the same guilty look as Audun as he answers, "ano."

I know that means *yes*, so they must understand my question after all. I meet Caelan's pretty hazel eyes and ask, just to be sure, "Reule and Maalik?"

He nods, and hesitates for a moment before pulling my sleeve up just enough to show a bit of my mate rune. He points to the mark, then at me, and whispers, "a ty."

I react without thinking, pulling my hand away from his in

shock as I stare down at him with wide eyes. I'm not unfamiliar with immortal beings, but I never considered for a second that the guys might be immortal. Shifters in my world are mortal.

Clearly, these guys aren't normal fucking shifters, and I'm an idiot for comparing them to Bryson or anything else from my world. Things are different here, and I need to remember that. Still, even if I'd suspected they might be immortal, I never in a million years would have guessed that becoming their mate would change me.

Audun and Caelan whisper my name, sounding completely pitiful and remorseful. I ignore them and stare down at Audun's family photo without really seeing it. I seriously fucking hate that I'm stuck in front of people right now. I don't want to seem rude, but I really wish I was alone to process this right now.

I take a deep breath and exhale slowly. *I'm immortal. I'm going to live forever.*

A nearly hysterical laugh bubbles up in my chest, and I have to cover my mouth so I don't look like a crazy person. Less than a week ago, I arrogantly told Matthieu I was perfectly content with my mortality at Lord Rian's party. This must be some form of fucked up karma.

Caelan and Audun speak in hushed tones with Runa, but it's all background noise to me while I take another calming breath and attempt to think things through logically. I don't feel any different, but it doesn't make sense for Caelan to lie to me.

It's not like I haven't thought about what it would be like to be immortal. About a year and a half ago, Alistair started showing signs of immortality once his magic finally started balancing out. We never found any concrete proof if he was or wasn't, but it became a pretty sore subject between us. The only way it would have been possible for me to become immortal back home would have been to become a vampire.

Madame Deverell might have agreed to change me if I'd asked, but there are always so many stipulations and crazy loopholes vampires write up in contracts when they change someone.

Long story short, I would have most likely ended up becoming her slave for a century or two, and I'd be a literal fucking monster that needs to drink blood to survive. I just wasn't willing to do that, not even for Al. Fae can make someone immortal too, but only if that person is their soulmate. It's almost unheard of, so I never considered that as an option.

I never truly thought about what it would be like to become immortal without physically changing. I'm not really upset at learning this side effect of being mated to Audun, Caelan, Maalik, and Reule. I'm just shocked.

When I glance sideways, I find Caelan and Audun staring at me openly. They're talking to Runa, but they're still giving me their full attention. My heart practically melts when I see they still look so worried and distraught.

Not for the first time, I feel incredibly lucky to have somehow ended up with them. Anything could have happened to me when I wound up in Giovanni's warehouse, but instead I ended up here with the four sweetest men I've ever met in my life. A smile slowly forms on my face the more I think about it.

They didn't pick me as a mate, but I ended up here at just the right time under circumstances out of their control. They've treated me so well and have been so kind to me every moment I've spent with them. I mean, *god*, the very first thing they decided to do after making me their mate was introduce me to their family. They brought me to this town, held my hands in public, and have introduced me as their mate to every single person we've come into contact with so far.

Bryson only ever showed me affection in private, and he never introduced me to his family. I met some of his pack by accident, and looking back, he always acted so ashamed of me. Caelan, Audun, Reule, and Maalik hardly know a thing about me, but they've made it glaringly obvious that they're proud to be with me.

Caelan's no longer kneeling beside me. Now he's standing behind my chair, almost hovering over me as he converses with Runa and Audun. I'm sure they're talking about me, but I don't really mind. Any time I've asked the guys a question, they've done their best to answer me despite our language barrier. I know they probably had no idea how to bring the immortality issue up. The fact that they even found a way to tell me, with Runa's help, honestly makes me like them so much more. They chose to tell me this, even though they didn't know how I'd react.

I turn in my chair and stand up, and I smile shyly at Audun and Caelan when they stop talking. I lean down and kiss Audun first, smiling wider when he gasps quietly against my lips, and I turn and stand on my tiptoes to kiss Caelan.

Caelan blinks at me in shock. He wraps one arm around my waist and places his other hand on the back of my head as he pulls me into a deep, passionate kiss. He doesn't seem to care that we're standing in front of Audun, Runa, Marieke, and Naren, and I laugh breathlessly when he pulls away.

He grins like I've just made him the happiest man in the world and says something I wish more than anything I could understand. Audun stands up and gives me an equally breath-taking smile, and he hugs me so I'm squished between the two of them.

They kiss and nuzzle the top of my head. I glance up to find Runa and Marieke smiling at the three of us, and that makes me feel even happier.

I sigh blissfully and look up at the two men showering me with affection. "I swear I'm gonna end up falling in love with you guys."

CHAPTER SIXTEEN

CAELAN

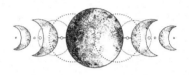

When Isla pulls her hand away from mine, I feel like my heart is going to shatter into a million pieces. Audun whispers her name at the same time I do, but she ignores us both. I curl my hand into a fist, forcing myself not to reach out to her again, and I watch helplessly as she stares down at Runa's family photo album with a blank expression on her face.

"She really doesn't know anything about Guardians," Runa mutters in quiet disbelief.

"Nothing," Audun practically growls. "We told you she's not from our world. We can't even speak to her. How were we supposed to tell her about any of this?"

He's clearly distraught, and I don't blame him. I stand up on shaky legs and remind myself that Isla pulled away from us this morning too. When she first woke up, she needed a minute to herself. I was worried and heartbroken then too, assuming she regretted the claiming and all that happened between us. But everything was fine afterwards. More than fine.

I hope this situation is the same. The language barrier between us hasn't bothered me much before this. Obviously, I wish it was easier to communicate with her. I would be more than happy to tell Isla anything she wants to know. But I'm confident we'll be able to get to know her perfectly well without having to speak the same language. She's smart and confident, and I love trying to figure out what's going through her mind and watching her piece things together.

"I'm sure King Janak has a perfectly valid explanation for bringing her here the way he did." Runa doesn't sound like she entirely believes that, but it would be borderline treasonous to say that Janak was in the wrong. Even if that's what we all truly think.

"Yes, well, that's why Mal and Reule went to speak with him first thing this morning," I say. We were just telling Runa and Marieke about how Isla came to be our wife and what a surprise it was.

My brothers and I have stayed close with Audun's old family. They've always been such kind people. My parents died shortly after I became a Guardian, and I had no siblings or other extended family, so it was nice to have Audun's parents to lean on back when we were young and new to being immortal beasts.

We've always been just a bit closer to Runa. She's feisty and open-minded, and she's one of the only people I've ever met during my long existence I can share my true thoughts and feelings with. Reule and I come here far more often than our other brothers just to talk to her.

"She would have found out eventually that she's immortal like the rest of you are, and it's probably better that it happened now," Runa says.

"I just don't want her to hate us," Audun mumbles. His eyes are still locked on Isla. Neither of us have looked away from her for a second since she realized what Runa was showing her.

"Maalik was worried about claiming her before figuring

out a way to tell her these things," I admit. "She still doesn't know that we can't have children."

Not that she looked very comfortable holding Naren. I was nervous at first, that she might fawn all over the child once she realized he was Audun's nephew rather than his son. Most women I know seem to catch baby fever quiet easily once they reach a certain age, but it was pretty amusing and relieving to see her stare at me and Audun like she was silently screaming for help when the kid climbed into her lap.

Still, that doesn't mean Isla never wants kids. We'll need to tell her very soon that unfortunately, that's just not a possibility with us.

"From what you said, there wasn't much you could have done." Runa reaches up to pat my arm consolingly. "Reule had already started to bond with her when the three of you arrived home, and you only spent a few measly hours in her company before the moons caused you to shift. Besides, if you brought her here, the results likely would have been the same. Only, the four of you would have terrified the townspeople with your beasts' forms in the process."

I chuckle humorlessly and nod in agreement. That had been my argument when Maalik started insisting we bring Isla here after dinner last night. Luckily, I convinced him it was a terrible idea.

Isla glances sideways at me and Audun, and my heart stutters in my chest. She goes right back to staring at the photograph of Audun with his parents and sister though. Audun makes a low whining sound and slumps his shoulders a bit.

"Just give her some time," Marieke says. "If I suddenly found out I was immortal, I'd be hysterical. And I've known about Guardians all my life."

Marieke has been quieter than usual since we showed up. I think she's a little nervous around us so close to Guardians' Night. Besides, Isla yelled at her the moment they met. I'm sure she's trying to be submissive so she doesn't accidentally offend our wife again.

The thought makes me smile. I honestly can't wait to tell Reule about how Isla immediately became possessive of Audun when she saw Marieke and Naren. It was almost funnier than seeing the aftermath of her temper tantrum in our bedrooms this morning.

I open my mouth to thank Marieke and Runa for being so patient and understanding, but Isla stands up with a shy smile on her face, and all of my words escape me. I watch in amazement as she leans over and presses her lips to Audun's.

After, I find her standing in front of me, and she stands up on her tiptoes to kiss me too. I'm too stunned to react for a moment. When I finally regain my sense and my heart feels like it's going to explode from happiness and absolute relief, I pull her close and kiss her like she means everything to me.

Because she does. I think I love her, and I don't give a shit that I've only known her for one day.

I've always wanted a wife, ever since I first became a Guardian. Maalik and Reule had already been Guardians for a few years when I first shifted and became one of them. The three of us used to talk for ages about what attributes we should look for in a wife, and all the features we found attractive in women. Audun was so young and innocent when he finally joined our family, and it didn't seem right to choose a wife when he was still practically a child. He was only sixteen during our first Guardians' Night with the Beasts' Moon present.

Things changed after that. Somehow, I was the only one of my brothers who actually wanted a wife. The rest of them decided it was too risky, that it would turn out too badly no matter who we chose. I've been angry at them for so long for making that choice. For nearly a century, I've been desperately lonely and in want of someone to love, to cherish, to protect, to spoil, and to confide in. I'm not sure my brothers even know how low I've gotten, or how I spend my days off drinking myself into a stupor. I used to distract myself by sleeping with any woman who would have me, just so I could pretend for a little while that I wasn't so damn lonely. Isla is the best surprise I could have ever imagined. To be honest, I probably would have been happy with any wife. But Isla is more perfect than any woman I could ever have dreamt of. She's sweet, funny, smart, and so beautiful it makes my chest ache. Every moment in her presence has been fun and exciting, and I can't wait to spend the rest of my existence getting to know her.

"I'm going to spend every day for the rest of forever trying to make you happy, my love." I don't care that Isla can't understand my words. She laughs quietly and smiles up at me like she's just as overjoyed as I am in this moment.

Audun comes up behind her and hugs her so that she's pressed between us. Isla looks even more pleased, if possible. It's not really appropriate to show this much affection in public, but I couldn't care less right now.

Isla smiles up at both of us and says something in her mother tongue. I grin in response, even though I have no clue what she's saying. Audun nuzzles the top of her head again and says, "I can't believe she's accepted us. Just...every time she learns something new, she accepts us so easily."

"I told you she's a strong woman," I say proudly.

Marieke sighs dreamily from her seat at the table. "It's like you were meant to be together." She's always been a romantic at heart, but even more so since she married her childhood sweetheart. Her husband is in the Briyan army, and he's away for work more often than not.

Isla pushes away from me and Audun, and she takes her seat at the table again. I watch curiously, and still a bit nervously, as she flips over the paper with Audun's family tree and begins writing something.

When she's finished, she points to herself and the paper

while looking back and forth between me and Audun. I lean over to take a look before he can, and I smile when I see she's drawn twenty-four tally marks.

"I think she's telling us how old she is," I say to Audun. I'm honestly pretty relieved to discover she's not younger. Time works relatively the same in most worlds, and seeing confirmation that Isla is twenty-four lets us know that years last roughly the same amount of time in her old world as they do here.

Even though I'm sure she can guess Audun's age roughly based on the family tree, I still draw ninety-six tally marks and point to him, and then add six more and point to myself. Isla nods in understanding and flips the paper back over again.

She gestures to the entirety of the family tree and points at me with her eyebrows raised in question. I smile sadly and cover the majority of the drawing, until only the figures representing Audun and his parents are showing. Isla seems to realize I'm letting her know that I have no living family left, and she gives me a sympathetic look as she places her hand over mine.

Audun, Marieke, and Runa are speaking quietly again, but their voices are purely background noise to me. I stare down at Isla in absolute wonder, feeling surer with every passing second that I really am falling in love with her. She understood what I was telling her immediately—no words were needed at all.

"Maalik? Reule?" She asks in a soft voice. I know they won't mind if I tell her anything about them or their pasts, so I shake my head sadly. Unlike me and Audun, Reule didn't have a good upbringing. Maalik didn't know his family at all.

I clear my throat and gesture to the family tree the same way Isla did, and raise my eyebrows at her. She hasn't mentioned anyone other than Alistair or her ex-lover. But still, I'll take any opportunity I can to learn more about this incredible woman.

Isla lowers her eyes and shakes her head quickly. I'd suspected as much, but my heart still aches for her at hearing she doesn't have a family. I lean forward and wrap my arms around her small frame, nuzzling the top of her head affectionately.

"You have us now, Isla."

"HAVE FUN, AND PROMISE TO VISIT AGAIN SOON!" RUNA SAYS warmly as we pull our coats on by the front door.

I can tell Isla's curious about where we're going now, but I'm excited to be able to surprise her this time. Even though she doesn't really need the help, I step forward to finish buttoning up her thick, winter coat and adjust her scarf.

"Thank you, Runa." Audun ruffles Naren's hair, making the child laugh and hide behind Runa's legs. "We'll be sure to bring Reule and Maalik with us next time."

"Do you know which shop you'd like to visit first?" Marieke asks as she finishes tying her boots.

After we finished our tea and Isla spent a little while longer looking through Runa's photo album, we asked Marieke if she would be interested in accompanying us to take Isla shopping. My brothers and I come down to the village often enough, but Marieke knows the shops and current fashions much better than we do. We also thought Isla might feel a little more comfortable shopping with another girl rather than with just us.

Marieke is positively beaming from excitement. I'm glad to see she's taken to Isla so quickly. Runa agreed to stay home and watch Naren so Marieke would be able to come with us.

Isla giggles at me when I finish the last button on her coat. I smirk down at her just as Audun answers Marieke's question, "We should probably start with undergarments."

I snort in shock, not having expected him to say that. I

know he probably didn't mean anything by it—Isla does liter-ally need to start from scratch with everything—but I'm stilldefinitely going to make fun of him.

"Wow, Audun. I didn't realize you were just as perverted

He glares daggers at me as he shoves his stupid-looking hatonto his head and takes a step closer to the door. "Shut up,Cael. You know she needs stuff, and it makes the most sense to

I throw my arm around Isla's shoulders and go to open thefront door. As I turn the handle, I look back at Audun with anasinine smile and wink. "Never said I was complaining,

The last thing I'm expecting when I finally open Runa'sfront door and step out onto the porch with Isla is the deaf-ening sound of cheering and applause. I nearly stumble insurprise and blink several times as I slowly take in the crowdedstreet in front of Runa's house. In the short hour we've spenthere, the main street of the village has become crowded withvendors and food carts, and it looks like nearly every singleresident of the village is here to celebrate.

Audun looks even more dumbstruck than I do as he stum-bles out behind us. Marieke closes the door behind herselfand laughs merrily when she sees the crowd. "Wow, wordcertainly travels quickly! The festival wasn't supposed to startuntil later this evening!"

A smile slowly forms across my face. I've vastly underesti-mated the people of Briya, it seems. I suppose I knew therewould be some speculation once people realized we'd finallytaken a wife, but I had no idea everyone would be this excited.

"Me?" Isla taps her chest and grins as she peers up anddown the crowded street.

She's so damn confident and completely adorable. Shelooks excited at the prospect of being the center of attention.

Any other person would be confused or terrified to deal with something like this in a world where they don't even know the language.

"Yes," I say. I pull her even closer to me and proudly lead her down the steps of the porch and into the street. "They're celebrating you, beautiful."

"We only spoke to that one couple on the way here," Audun mutters in disbelief. Marieke laughs from beside him, staying a few steps behind us.

People bow in respect and congratulate us as we walk by. Some of the elder people in the crowd even weep with joy. Nobody touches us, and they give us plenty of room to walk. Isla smiles and says hello to every person she sees. I doubt anyone realizes it's one of the only Briyan words she knows, and it brings me so much joy to see her interacting with people and to see them look at her with so much admiration.

Marieke gives us directions to the first shop, which isn't far from her house. It takes forever to get there with all the people and commotion in the streets though, even though they're moving out of our way. A few people are brave enough to approach us, and some of them offer flowers to Isla. There are only a few types of flowers in bloom since it's winter, but Isla accepts them all with a grateful smile. Audun offers to carry them for her once she has enough to make a bouquet.

Everyone is careful to keep their eyes averted submissively. Even though it's clear the people from this village are ecstatic for us, and elated to have a Queen of Beasts to worship along-side us, they're still anxious and wary in our presence. I wonder if Isla notices or not.

When we finally reach the first shop, I take a quick look around for any sign of Mal or Reule. I thought they'd have met up with us by now, especially considering how much time we spent having breakfast and cleaning the house before leaving and how much time we spent at Runa's. I'm sure Isla is wondering where they are too. She's asked about them a few times. As much as I joked around with my brothers that I was going to be Isla's favorite, it's a relief to know she's still thinking of them while she's spending time with me and Audun.

The shop is vacant of any customers when we enter. I quickly look over the shelves and racks around the small shop, and Audun makes a choking sound behind me. I didn't realize Marieke was bringing us to a shop that *only* sold undergarments. Hell, I didn't know shops like these even existed these days—at least not here in Briya where people are typically more conservative than in other kingdoms. It's a bit of a slap to the face to realize just how out of touch with the world I've become.

Isla pulls away from me. For a moment, I panic, thinking she's going to be angry or embarrassed that we brought her to a place like this. Instead, she turns and glances between me and Audun with a saucy little smile on her face as she laughs and says something in her melodious voice.

She's teasing us and calling us perverts. I just know it.

A curvy blonde woman comes out from a back room behind the register and calls out, "Happy Guardians' Day! Everything today is—oh!"

She stops speaking once she's close enough to recognize us. The look of panic on her face is something I've grown used to over the years. When people aren't expecting to see us in public, they tend to show their fear a little more noticeably. Most days, this sort of thing would bother me immensely. After all, we've dedicated our immortal lives to protecting the people of Briya from evil they can't even fathom. They may worship us and call us gods, and I know in the back of my mind they're grateful to have us. But I always feel like such a monster when I see people react fearfully to me and my brothers. As though we would ever hurt the people we live to protect.

Today, it doesn't bother me at all. Isla knows what we are and she even saw Reule in his beast form. He said that she showed no fear at the sight of his beast, and never once has she looked at any of us like we're monsters.

"Hello!" Marieke greets the shopkeeper when Audun and I stay silent. "Guardian Audun and Guardian Caelan were hoping to buy their wife some new undergarments today."

"Ah, yes, of course!" the girl exclaims, her voice raising a few octaves. Her gaze moves to a sign above the register before she quickly turns to face us once more. When I realize she's blushing, I curiously look up at the advertisement.

A surprised laugh escapes me before I can help myself. How the hell did I not notice this sign when we first walked in? It's several feet long and depicts a graphic illustration of four beasts salivating over a scantily-clad woman. The advertisement reads: *"Wear something that will make your man act like a beast in the bedroom. Buy-One-Get-One 50% off during Guardians' Week Only!"*

"This is very awkward." Audun groans. I feel a little bad for my youngest brother. He's always been so easily embarrassed. I know the only reason he wasn't shy with Isla last night was because of the Beasts' Moon.

On the other hand, this is pure gold. I wish Reule were here right now—he'd agree with me wholeheartedly.

"Does the discount still apply to us?" I grin at the embarrassed shopkeeper.

She ignores my question and bows deeply to Isla. "Do you know what size you wear, milady? If you're not sure, I would be more than happy to measure you."

Isla tilts her head at the girl. I'm sure she finds it strange that people are addressing her so formally, and I'd love to know what exactly is going through her head. After staring at the shopkeeper, she shrugs and walks over to one of the displays. The brassiere she picks up is black and lacey with all kinds of straps.

I'm suddenly a million times more interested in this shopping trip than I was already.

The shopkeeper furrows her eyebrows when Isla begins speaking to her. Before Audun or I can do so, Marieke steps in and explains, "Lady Isla is new to Briya and she doesn't know our language yet. She would be grateful if you could take her measurements and pick out a few things in her size. I'm afraid she's actually starting from scratch with her wardrobe."

"Absolutely!" Intrigue replaces the girl's embarrassed expression as she meets Isla's eyes for the first time. She smiles broadly as she pulls a measuring tape from the front pocket of her apron and holds it up for Isla to see. "Are you able to translate for her, Miss Marieke?"

Isla's eyes light up when she sees the measuring tape, and she starts unbuttoning her coat. Audun groans and asks in a pleading voice, "You have a dressing room, right?"

He's probably worried that Isla's going to fully undress right here in the middle of the shop. For all we know, that's a normal and acceptable thing to do wherever she's from. I wouldn't mind at all, but a dressing room would probably be best to spare Audun and the shopkeeper the embarrassment.

Marieke gives me a look when I grab a few items I very much want to see Isla try on.

"Just remember we have other shops to visit after this. We can't spend all day here!"

A FEW HOURS LATER, THERE'S STILL NO SIGN OF REULE OR Mal. I'm starting to think Janak might have roped them into work, which is honestly really shitty. We only get a couple of days off together every month, and Guardians' Week is the only real holiday we get. With Isla here, our time together at home is even more precious.

"What's the matter? You're having fun, aren't you?"

I turn to face Marieke and smile. "Of course! I'm just wondering where my idiotic brothers are. I thought they'd meet us before we even left your house."

My arms are full of bags and boxes from shopping with Isla. We bought more than she really needs, considering we plan to have her clothing custom-made in the future, but spoiling her felt even better than I expected it would. She became so much more animated while shopping than I've seen so far, and it quickly became apparent that she loves fashion.

All the shopkeepers we visited today adored her, and they all sounded so genuine when they congratulated us. Despite the fact that Isla knows only a few basic words in Briyan, everyone she's met today has said she's charming, sweet, and absolutely beautiful.

The streets are more crowded now than they were earlier, and people have become braver the longer we've stayed in the village. More and more people have approached Isla—to welcome her to Briya, to congratulate her, to pray to her, and to thank her.

She's been given more flowers too, along with several small gifts and treats. A few girls Marieke is friends with helped weave the flowers into a crown, which Isla is wearing proudly now.

"I hope they get here soon," Marieke says. "This is the most fun I've ever had at a Guardians' Day festival, and I'm sure Isla misses them!"

"She does." I smile and turn to look through the crowd once more until I spot Isla and Audun. A band started playing music a short while ago, and Isla dragged Audun out into the middle of the street to dance with her. I'm proud to say that I only felt jealous for a few seconds when she chose to dance with him first instead of me.

"I know people have been saying this to you guys all day, but I really am happy for you," Marieke says softly. I probably wouldn't be able to hear her over the loud music if I didn't have enhanced senses. "The four of you have been so...sad and lost, for as long as I can remember. I've never seen you or Audun light up the way you have today. I know Isla didn't come here under the best circumstances, but I'm still glad for it."

Her words are genuine and heartfelt, and hearing her say all of that really means the world to me. Mal feels guilty for making Isla our wife and for making it impossible for her to go back home. I don't, and maybe that makes me selfish. But Isla *belongs* with us, and I'll never regret claiming her.

"Thank you, Marieke."

"Caelan!" Isla screeches. I grin when I see her running toward me with a smile plastered across her face. She's wearing one of the new dresses we bought her, and she looks gorgeous and carefree.

"Is it finally my turn then?" I smirk at her teasingly and shove all of the bags and boxes at Audun when he sidles up behind Isla.

The moment my arms are empty, Isla grabs my hand and pulls me into the crowded street where dozens of people are still dancing. Isla and Audun were the first to dance along to the music, but it certainly caught on quickly.

I let her lead for a few songs. Isla's a very good dancer, and her moves make me more curious to learn about her old life and the world she's from. When the band begins playing folk songs that were popular around the time I first became a Guardian, I grin and hold Isla close as I lead her in the traditional steps of the dances.

She's vibrant and stunning, and I steal more than a few kisses while we're dancing. I keep expecting her to push me away, but she never does. I'm starting to question whether or not Audun and I were stupid to agree to take things slow with her for now. There's so much chemistry between us—more than I've ever felt with any woman in my entire existence—and Isla has shown every sign of accepting us as her husbands in all ways imaginable.

There's a brief moment between songs when Isla wraps her arms around me and rests her cheek against my chest. Her eyes are closed, and there's a peaceful smile on her face. All the noise and people around us fade away as I allow myself to focus every bit of my attention on the beautiful girl in my arms.

Her eyes open slowly, and the look she gives me when she smiles up at me makes my heart stammer in my chest.

"Thank you, Caelan." Her voice is quiet and slightly uncertain like she's not sure if she's saying the words correctly or not. She's heard Audun and I thank numerous people today, so I know that's how she was able to pick up the phrase.

I grin and nod down at her to let her know she's said the words correctly, even though it should be me thanking her. I'd like to be able to tell her how happy she's made me and my brothers, but I'll just have to show her instead.

First, I kiss her nose, and then I lean down again to kiss each of her slightly pink cheeks that are flushed from the cold. I hardly notice the chill anymore, and the main roads of the village have been cleared of snow. Audun and I will have to be more careful to remember that Isla's probably not used to the climate here and shouldn't be outside for hours on end.

The music begins playing again, and I look up to search for Audun and Marieke. There are a few cafes in the village, and Isla could use a break from the cold. Besides, it's well past lunchtime, and I'm sure she's hungry.

My gaze lands on Maalik first, and I perk up in surprise. Finally, he and Reule have made it back. I'm ridiculously excited to tell them about our day with Isla. Mal is already standing with Audun, and he looks pissed off about something as per usual.

Before I'm able to locate him, Isla gasps and exclaims, "Reule!"

I spin around to find the idiot standing a few feet in front of us. He meets my eyes for barely a second before looking down at Isla with a nervous half-smile. He's probably worried she's angry at him for ditching her on our first day after the claiming. Then again, Maalik's probably spent the entire day convincing Reule that Isla's going to be pissed about us claiming her, period.

He has nothing to worry about. The second I loosen my hold on Isla, she launches herself at him and throws her arms around his shoulders. The stunned expression on his face is hilarious enough to distract me from my momentary jealousy.

"Isla," Reule whispers her name and lifts her up, holding her like he's afraid she's going to disappear any moment. "God, I missed you so much!"

He kisses her, and a goofy smile threatens to take over my mouth. My brothers and I have spent so long talking about sharing a wife and wondering what it would be like. The Guardians in the other kingdoms have given us plenty of advice—even when we didn't want to hear it. Experiencing it for ourselves is so different than I'd ever expected. I'm not nearly as jealous as I feared I'd be, and I'm exuberantly happy for Reule, Audun, and Maalik.

As soon as Reule sets Isla down, she grins up at him and points to the flower crown on her head. "Queen of Beasts!"

The look on Reule's face is priceless, and I bark out a laugh. He gives me a questioning glance and I shrug in amusement. "People have been calling her that all day, and she started repeating it. She likes it."

Reule rubs the back of his neck and smiles awkwardly down at our gorgeous little wife. "I figured it would happen at some point. Mal and I didn't expect you guys to make such a scene here in the village today. Janak is planning some sort of big ceremony to reveal that we've chosen a wife. I think this might ruin the surprise factor he was going for."

"Who cares?" I laugh. I grab Isla's hand and quickly lead her and Reule off to the side of the street so people can continue dancing without us being in the way. "He doesn't get to control this, no matter how much he wants to. Did he really think we would keep her a secret?"

Isla stands up on her tiptoes and begins searching through the crowd once we get far enough away from the band. In a hopeful tone, she asks, "Maalik?"

It's cheesy as hell to admit, but my heart melts at seeing her ask after our eldest brother like that. Reule smiles and wraps his arm around her shoulders to lead her over to where he's standing with Audun.

"I'm assuming she's not pissed at him?"

"Of course not." I scoff. "She should be though, for the way you two ran off this morning. What took you so long, anyway?"

Reule makes a face and grunts. "Janak had a million excuses and reasons for having her brought here. I don't think he expected us to be as angry as we were, and he vastly underestimated Mal. Still, he would only admit that Isla came from a Forbidden Realm, but not which one specifically. After we finished our meeting with him, Maalik dragged me to three different temples to try and get information from some of the Elders."

Forbidden Realm? I don't know why that surprises me so much. It makes sense, considering Isla is familiar with magic and vampyres of all things. Still, my heart drops into my stomach when I hear Reule say it so confidently.

"And?" I ask. I'm even curiouser to learn where she's from now, and I want to help find Alistair just as much as my brothers do.

He opens his mouth to answer, but Isla makes a whining

sound and pouts up at us. It's not that we've purposely ignored her, but we forgot she asked about Mal before we started talking.

"Sorry, kitten." Reule gives her a lopsided smile and kisses her pouty lips. "Let's go find him now."

CHAPTER SEVENTEEN
ISLA

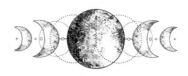

Caelan steals another kiss while we're dancing, and I nearly melt in his arms.

I'm glad he's leading our steps. Audun was fun to dance with, but he wasn't as confident or as dominant as Caelan is. The longer I dance with him, the more butterflies I feel writhe in my stomach. I barely feel the chill in the air anymore. All I feel are his lips against mine and his hands as they slide against my body.

We're not even, like, grinding or sexy dancing at all. But my body doesn't seem to realize that. Every time he spins me or steps close, he kisses me, and I am losing my goddamn mind. Every kiss and light caress from him make me feel dizzy with need.

His lips meet mine again just before the current song ends. I close my eyes and lean against him, wrapping my arms around his waist. He's so strong and muscular and sexy, and he's mine.

Today has been surreal. I've learned so much about my new mates without being able to speak to them or anyone else here. They're obviously famous or royal or *something* based on the reactions they've been getting from everyone. People love them, and they're terrified of them. It's fascinating.

It also makes me feel really fucking cool and powerful every time someone bows to me and gives me a present, the fear and awe obvious in their eyes.

Part of me wonders if I should feel worried or hesitant, especially with how I ended up in this world. But this mate bond I share with the guys makes me feel so secure. Back home, I never could have imagined feeling like this. I always had to worry about surviving, and worry about protecting myself and Alistair. For the first time in my life, I feel like I can just let go and breathe.

The more I open up to the guys, and the closer I feel to them as the day progresses, the more I can physically feel the bond. Rather than being freaked out about it, I feel so fucking lucky and happy. I've known my guys one day, and I already know they'll never let anything bad happen to me.

Aside from the supernatural aspect of my relationship with them, I just really, *really* like them. They're sweet and attentive, and they've been spoiling the crap out of me all day. Audun's holding about a million shopping bags with stuff that's all for me, and they've allowed me to follow any whim or desire I have. Including dancing in the middle of a crowded street in front of random people.

I nuzzle Caelan's chest and look up at him with a shy smile. I hope he likes me too, and not just because we're bound together.

"Děkuji, Caelan." I hope I said the word right. I think it means thank you because I've heard my guys repeat it every time someone approaches me with a gift.

He grins and nods, so I must have said it right. I need to start writing down all the words I learn when we get home so I don't forget them.

Caelan leans down to kiss my nose and both my cheeks, and a goofy smile spreads across my face. So fucking sweet. If

Reule and Maalik were here too, this day would be almost perfect.

The band starts up a new song, but I don't feel like dancing any longer. I turn to search for Audun in the crowd so I can tug Caelan toward him and let him know I'm ready to go home. Before I spot Audun, my eyes land on Reule standing just a few feet behind me. I gasp, his name tumbling from my lips as I drink him in. I've missed him all day. We haven't seen each other or spoken since last night, and a tiny part of me has worried he and Maalik won't feel as affected or excited as I do about our new mate bond.

He gives me a tiny smile, and I leap forward to throw my arms around him. It's the craziest thing ever to feel so strongly about a guy I barely know.

"Isla," he whispers. He says something else, his voice full of relief and affection. My insecurities about his absence fall away as he lifts me into his arms and presses his lips to mine. I don't even mind the beard anymore. I pull him closer, deepening our kiss, telling him without words how much I missed him.

He sets me down, smiling like he's never been happier. I want to gush and tell him all about my day, about all the people I've met and the shops I visited. I want to ask him where he's been. It's so frustrating that I can't say any of the things I want. I'm determined to learn the language here as quickly as possible.

Since I can't say what I really want to, I point to the flower crown on my head that Marieke and some other girls made for me. It's beautiful, and I want to make sure to hang it up to dry once we get home. I've never seen flowers like these.

At the questioning look on Reule's face, I repeat the title the people of this village have given me. "Královna Nestvůr!"

I have no clue what it means. The words sound pretty to me, even though I'm probably saying them wrong. I've also been addressed as Dáma Isla, but the longer title sounds way cooler. I hope it means Princess or Queen, or something equally amazing. I certainly feel like a princess after the way I've been treated by everyone today.

Reule seems taken aback, and his eyes move to Caelan behind me. Caelan laughs and answers Reule's unspoken question, and Reule gives me an adorable lopsided smile. He and Caelan talk back and forth as Caelan takes my hand and leads me to the sidewalk so we're not in the way of everyone still dancing.

I crane my neck to search for Maalik. If Reule's here, he must be too. I want to see him and kiss him and let him know I'm happy to be his mate. I know he was more hesitant than the other guys, and I don't want him to feel any doubt that I'm all in with this relationship.

"Maalik?" I ask. Reule and Caelan are taller than me, so they'll be able to see better than I can.

Reule wraps his arm around my shoulder, but they ignore me and continue their conversation. I try to be patient. I know they probably have a lot to catch up on. They've all been pretty good about not purposely leaving me out of conversations, even though I know it's just as frustrating for them as it is for me that we can't communicate properly.

When a few minutes pass and neither of them acknowledge me or show they're looking for Maalik, I whine and tug on Reule's hand while I pout at him and Caelan.

They chuckle, and Reule mumbles something as he leans down to kiss me. At first, I think he's only appeasing me, but he pulls me along through the crowd until I see Maalik's bright red hair and beard.

Tension unfurls in my stomach, and I breathe out a sigh of relief as his cerulean eyes meet mine. I didn't realize how much I missed him until this moment. Our bond tingles beneath my skin. It's like everything's right now that we're all together again.

Well, mostly right. Once I figure out a way to reach Alistair and see that he's okay, then I'll be fully at ease.

I smile and move to run to him, the same way I ran to Reule. But Maalik's shoulders tense, his eyes sweeping over me dismissively. He turns away like I don't matter to him at all, and he continues speaking to Audun.

Dumbfounded, I go still and stare at him in shock. He's not happy to see me? After everything that happened between us last night and going hours without seeing each other? Tears form in the corners of my eyes at his obvious rejection.

Reule squeezes my shoulders, and Caelan growls. Maalik frowns at him, and Caelan says something angrily as he points at me.

Maalik looks at me again, furrowing his eyebrows. I look away. I don't need to see his disdain. He was so sweet last night after he finally gave in to the moons. I never thought for a second that he would still hold onto his dislike for me after the bond was formed.

I take a deep breath and lean back against Reule, reaching out to grab Caelan's hand at the same time. Today's been a lot of fun, and I've done my best to embrace this new world and everything in it. But it's still fucking scary. At least three out of four of my mates are sweet, loving, and supportive. I know they're doing their best to make me feel happy and comfortable. Even if Maalik never changes his attitude toward me, I'm still lucky.

The guys are talking, but I don't try to keep up since I can't understand them, anyway. I squeeze Caelan's hand until he looks at me. I point at the peak of the closest mountain, hoping he'll understand what I'm asking. "Can we go home, please?"

He snaps at Maalik, baring his teeth, even as he steps closer to kiss the top of my head. Poor Audun is still holding all of my shopping bags with no help from the other guys, and he's biting his lip as he glances back and forth between everyone while the other three guys argue.

I hold my hand up and narrow my eyes, commanding their attention. When four sets of eyes land on me and they go silent, I gesture to our surroundings. "People are still watching us. If you're going to argue, do it at home."

Reule and Caelan glance around us, seeming to realize what I'm trying to say. I don't let myself look at Maalik. I focus on Audun, and he gives me a tiny, crooked smile.

Without warning, Reule scoops me up and cradles me to his chest as he takes large strides down the street toward the mountain I pointed at. He's walking fast enough I'd have to run to catch up, so I'm happy to be carried. I wrap my arms around his neck and settle in for the long trek up the mountain.

People wave and bow at us as we pass. Reule ignores them and stares straight ahead, but I smile and wave at every person I see. If these guys are royalty or something, I don't want the regular old townspeople to think they're mean or we're not getting along.

When we reach the edge of the town, the snow is thick on the ground. I'm even more glad to be carried because it's super difficult to walk in. I don't know how my guys do it so easily. I peek over Reule's shoulder to find the others following behind us. Maalik has taken some of the bags from Audun, but Caelan walks empty-handed with a glum expression on his face.

Instead of staying on the path that leads up to their cabin, Reule darts into the woods to our left. The snow is even thicker here, and there are so many trees that I lose sight of the village and my sense of direction almost immediately. Reule quickens his pace, using his supernatural speed to run until he stops in a small clearing.

He sets me down carefully, calling Caelan's name over his shoulder. Caelan appears in front of me. He gives me a nervous smile and takes several steps backwards, motioning at his body and the space around him.

It takes a few seconds for me to understand, but I stand up straight and smile when I realize he's telling me he's going to shift. I lift my hands to pretend they're claws and make a growling, snarling noise to make sure we're on the same page. I feel silly doing it, but it's still the best way I can think to communicate with them until I learn the language.

Caelan and Audun grin while Reule chuckles. They nod, letting me know I've got it right. I'm so fucking excited. I barely got a good look at Reule last night. I can't wait to see them shift in the daylight.

Maalik steps in front of me, blocking me from the others. He shakes his head and snarls at them. I hear him say no in their language, but it's the only word he says that I know. I narrow my eyes and cross my arms at him. If he doesn't want me to see them shift, then that only makes me want to see them even more.

Rolling his eyes, Caelan steps back a few more feet. Before I know it, he shifts. It's nearly instantaneous. There's a moment where he disappears from sight, and there's a crackling energy in the air that makes my hair stand up. And then he's there in his chimera form. Just as large as Reule the night before, towering over us and taking up almost the entire clearing.

It's different for shifters in my world. Their physical bodies change, and it can be pretty grotesque to watch them shift. Here, it's like a completely different sort of magic controls them. I have to keep reminding myself this realm is nothing like my own, no matter how many things are similar.

Caelan makes a rumbling sound that could be either a growl or a purr, and he lowers his body until he's lying as flat as possible on the ground. His hazel eyes watch me, his ears alert while his long, reptilian tail sways hesitantly behind him. Maalik is straight up panicking. He's still standing in front of me like he's trying to protect me, and his wild gaze darts back and forth between me and Caelan. Reule and Audun stand by, watching me curiously to see how I'm going to react.

I wasn't scared of them last night, and I'm certainly not scared of them now. They're my *mates*. I stand up and shove past Maalik so I can approach Caelan. His throat rumbles as I get closer, so I know for sure he's purring.

His fur isn't as white as Reule's. He has more black marks on his face and the front of his legs, and his fur transitions into shimmery white scales halfway down his chest instead of at his ribcage. His wings, horns, and taloned feet are just like Reule's.

"You're so beautiful," I coo, lifting my hand to pet Caelan's muzzle. The purring gets louder, and a giant black tongue flicks out of his mouth to lick me. I giggle and swat at him playfully.

"Hodná holka." Reule growls, rubbing his hands over my shoulders from behind me. He gently pushes me until we're standing beside Caelan, and he surprises me by picking me up to put me on Caelan's back.

Even though Reule is tall and strong, Caelan's dragon-like body is so large that I have to scramble to climb up his back the rest of the way. I worry that I might hurt him, but his scales are so thick and smooth, like armor. I wonder if he can even feel me.

When I settle behind his head between his shoulder blades, I grin down at the others. Audun and Reule grin back, but Maalik looks like he's on the verge of having a heart attack. I really wish he would chill out. This is probably the coolest thing I've ever done.

Reule shouts something, and at the same moment, Caelan stands until he's in a crouch and flaps his giant, silver wings. I bend forward until I'm practically lying down and grip his fur between my fingers. I trust him not to let me fall, but I'm not going to be careless.

In the time it takes me to blink, Caelan takes off into the air. I grit my teeth to hold in my scream. The last thing I want is for Maalik to fly after us because he thinks I need to be rescued. He might not like me, but it's obvious he feels protective over me. At least that part of the mate bond is working. Even though I trust Caelan, I'm too nervous to sit up or look down. I can't really see much. The sky is white and cloudy. It's also seriously freezing up high like this. I was cold before, but it takes a lot of effort to keep my teeth from chattering. The next time one of them wants to fly me somewhere, I'm bundling up more and bringing a blanket.

Soon enough, Caelan lands and lowers his body to the ground. I sit up slowly, grinning when I see we're right in front of the cabin. It only took us a couple minutes to get here. Way faster than walking all the way back up the mountain.

I scoot sideways and let myself slide backwards down Caelan's front leg. The second my feet touch the ground, Caelan shifts into his human form. He grabs my shoulders and bends down so we're eye level, and he checks me over to make sure I'm not injured.

It's cute to see him so worried, and I'm probably wearing the goofiest smile imaginable. I lean forward to press my lips to his, and he kisses me back without hesitation.

"That was seriously amazing." I smile up at him. "Děkuji."

He laughs, sounding breathless, and pulls me into a hug as he nuzzles the top of my head. He whispers something I wish I could understand, and I hug him back tightly to let him know how I feel.

When he leans down to kiss my cheek, he hisses at the cold of my skin. He lifts me up and carries me toward the cabin, refusing to set me down until he opens the door and walks into the open living room.

"Oh, it got so cold in here!" I lift my hands to blow on my freezing fingers. Audun bought me a pair of gloves earlier, but

I took them off to eat some of the treats people were selling in the village. He shoved them in his pocket when I took them off, and I'm regretting not putting them on before leaving with Caelan.

My strong, blond-haired mate strides across the living room and kneels as he tosses a few logs into the fireplace. He has a small fire going within seconds, though I know it will take a while for it to warm up the whole house.

The flickering flames reflect in Caelan's eyes, making them look more amber than hazel. He grumbles something to himself while he watches the fire, bringing a hand up to rub absentmindedly at the stubble along his jaw. He's so good-looking, I have to bite my lip to keep myself from groaning out loud.

Seriously though, how did I get so lucky? How is a guy as hot as him so fucking sweet? Plus, he's amazing at sex. My eyelids droop as I let myself remember last night. The way his hands, mouth, and tongue felt on me. He's just been teasing me all day with his light touches and stolen kisses.

I sit on my knees in front of him, looking up at him through my eyelashes as I slowly reach out to unbutton his jacket. His pupils dilate when he meets my eyes, and he doesn't move to stop me.

"You've been so good to me all day," I whisper seductively, biting my lip as I finish with the last button. I have no clue how long it will take the others to reach the cabin. I'm not sure why they didn't just shift and follow us. But still, if Caelan and I start something, I'm not going to complain if my other mates walk in and want to join us.

Caelan lets me push his jacket off his shoulders, and I run my hands down his hard, muscular chest. A low rumbling starts in his throat, and I smirk when I realize he's purring for me. Growling, I'm used to, but I can definitely get on board with their purring.

His eyes turn absolutely feral as I continue touching him,

but he doesn't move. I lick my lips and watch his gaze zero in on the action, and I slowly slide my cold hands under the hem of his shirt. He shivers at my touch, still allowing me to touch him however I want to.

When I slip his long-sleeved shirt up over his head, I can't help but ogle his amazing body. The man has abs for days, and the most delicious happy trail. I scratch my nails lightly against his chest, and he finally loses his control.

He wraps one arm around my waist to pull me flush against his chest while his other hand cradles the back of my head, tilting my chin up as his lips crash against mine. His tongue sweeps across my bottom lip, and I gasp into his mouth. His kisses are fantastic, but I am so past the point of being satisfied by just kissing.

I dig my nails into his skin a bit harder and spread my knees apart, mewling happily when Caelan pushes me backwards until he's lying on top of me in front of the fireplace. His lips move to my neck, and his hands wander over my chest and rib cage. My nipples were already hard from the cold, but they're fucking aching at his touch. I arch my back, silently cursing the dress I'm wearing. It's gorgeous, and I was in love with it in the store. But it's long, and the material is thick, and it's going to take forever for Caelan to unbutton the back.

Undeterred, Caelan pushes the hem of my dress up my legs to my hips, and his fingers brush against my thighs, right above the stockings I'm wearing. I lift my hips so it's easier for him to slide my panties off.

"Myslíš to vážně?" Maalik growls from the doorway, interrupting our moment.

Caelan looks up, baring his teeth. I giggle and tilt my head back so I can see the grumpy look on Maalik's face. Even upside down, the frown he's wearing is obvious. I mean, he can join us if he wants. He doesn't need to get so bent out of shape.

Audun and Reule walk in behind him, carrying the rest of

my shopping bags. Reule chuckles when he sees us, and Audun stares at us like a deer in headlights. Caelan sighs in frustration. To my dismay, he sits up and carefully pulls my dress back down.

"Aww, no!" I complain, sticking my bottom lip out in an exaggerated pout. "What kind of rules did you guys stupidly agree to? I mean, you literally gangbanged me last night. Why is fucking me in front of each other suddenly an issue?"

They stare at me blankly, and I roll my eyes hard. I point to the mate mark on my wrist, and then I insert my index finger into my closed fist. That's basically the universal sign for fucking, right? Reule knew what I was talking about when I made the gesture at him before.

Caelan barks out a laugh and grins at Reule as he asks a question. Whatever the question is, Reule nods. He's staring at me like I'm precious, but not like he wants to fuck me right now. I'm starting to get irritated. What's the point of having four crazy-hot shifter mates if they're not going to constantly dick me down?

"Později." Caelan kisses me softly, taking a moment to rub his cheek against mine. It's so cute that I melt in his arms despite my frustration. His eyes light up as he pulls back to grin at me. He points at the guys standing by the door, makes a motion like he's sleeping, and growls while gesturing between himself and me, giving me a heated look.

Oh, I am definitely holding him to that.

Maalik sighs like he's at his wit's end and calls my name, gesturing for me to follow him down the hallway leading to the bedrooms.

I'm a little hesitant to follow him until I see the excited expressions on the other guys' faces. Caelan helps me up, and he keeps his hand on my back as I follow the others down the hallway. Audun reaches for the doorknob of the treasure room at the very end of the hall, but he stops when Maalik pauses outside of his bedroom door and growls.

My grumpy, redheaded mate turns slowly, narrowing his eyes at Caelan and Audun. My cheeks flush when I remember our snuggle session on his bed earlier. Caelan snickers and makes a weird hand gesture. I'm assuming it's basically the same as flipping someone off.

Audun looks a little more bashful, and Reule seems extremely amused. Maalık grunts and says something under his breath, motioning impatiently for someone to open the door of the room at the end of the hall. He's still holding most of my shopping bags.

We walk in once Audun opens the door, though there's not much room for everyone to stand or move around. The room is filled to the brim with boxes and crates. I'm still curious to find out what all these things are for, and I hope I'm about to find out.

The guys set my bags down, and Reule steps in front of me, grasping my hands gently between his. There's a nervous excitement in his eyes, and I smile to encourage him. He pulls my sleeve back enough to reveal the mate mark on my right wrist. He kisses the mark, taps his fingertips gently against it, and gestures to the space around us.

"Tvoje." He says more words, but that's the only one I catch as he repeats it multiple times.

I blink stupidly and look around the room. Is he saying these things are for me?

Caelan walks around to stand beside Reule, and he grins at me as he pulls a folded paper from his pocket. I recognize it as the family tree Runa drew for me to explain Audun's family and my guys' immortality. Caelan turns the paper over, showing me the tally marks he used to mark their age.

He's a hundred-and-freaking-two years old. That would probably be hard for me to wrap my head around if I hadn't known so many ancient supernaturals in my old life. Compared to Madame Deverell and dickface Thaddeus, Caelan and Audun are practically babies. At some point, I'll have to ask about Reule and Maalik. I get the feeling they're fairly close in age. Caelan and Audun are only a few years apart.

Motioning to the crates of beautiful things surrounding us, Caelan taps on the tally marks. Things begin to click. The guy who delivered me in that cage delivered a ton of other gifts too. They must have been collecting these things for a long time. Their whole lives, basically, if that's what Caelan means by pointing to the tally marks.

"For me?" I point to myself, dumbfounded. I recall the word I think they used for mate and point to my mate mark, my eyes widening in disbelief. "For your žena?"

Reule fucking swoons when I say the word, only in a way manlier way. He bites his lip and grins broadly, puffing his chest out proudly as color rises to his cheeks. It's adorable, and it makes me smile even though I'm still shocked about all these presents.

They all look so happy, waiting for my reaction. Well, except Maalik. It's impossible to read his expression. A manic smile forms on my lips as I look around the room eagerly. I barely got a glimpse at some of the items in these crates, but everything I saw was gorgeous. Absolutely fit for a queen.

I can't believe they spent so many years collecting these things, all for their future mate. Butterflies erupt in my stomach. I'm about to throw myself at each of them and lavish them with grateful kisses. I thought they spoiled me shopping today, but this is insane! It will take weeks to go through all these boxes and organize everything.

When I look up, I meet Maalik's eyes first. He's frowning as he watches me, brushing his fingers over his mate mark almost absentmindedly. My eyes widen as I'm struck with a thought. They obviously weren't planning for me specifically. Does that mean they were planning on making someone else their mate? Is that why Maalik is so against our bond? Because he wanted another girl?

The thought breaks my fucking heart. So much I actually lose my breath. I know this was a surprise for all of us—me most of all. But god, I seriously feel so lucky, and I want to make this relationship work. I don't want to think of them being with another girl ever. Even if I could speak to them, I'm not sure I'd have the courage to ask if they were waiting to bond with someone else. If they were, I hope I never meet her.

Maalik's cheeks turn bright red, and I realize I haven't broken eye contact with him. He grunts and nods once.

"Naše žena." He gestures to everything in the room before pointing at me, a sexy growl in his voice as he repeats himself. "Naše žena."

Even though he's been kind of rude and dismissive of me, I can't help but flush proudly at his words. Hearing him call me his mate feels so good, and I feel our bond tingle. I giggle and stroke my fingers against the mark on my wrist, turning to look at all the boxes I get to claim as mine.

"I can't believe it!" I squeal excitedly. "I don't even know where to start. There's so much here."

Thanking them profusely in their language, I throw my arms around Caelan, Reule, and Audun in turn, making sure to give them each a kiss. Maalik tenses up when I turn to him. I was going to kiss him on the cheek, but his reaction hurts my feelings. Guess I'll need to get used to that.

"Can I borrow your sketchpad?" I ask Audun, miming drawing with a pen.

He grins, wasting no time to use his supernatural speed to fetch a notebook and pen for me. It's a new one, rather than the one I used to talk to them before. I thank him and sit down on one of the crates. It's stable enough to hold my weight, and there's no room on the floor.

I spend about a half hour making a rough sketch of a luxury walk-in closet. If this is my room, and these are my things, I want the space to be perfect. I figure I have plenty of time to work on it now that I'm immortal and unemployed. Audun sits beside me and watches while I draw, but the others leave the room.

In my sketch, I draw tons of closet space and drawers along two of the walls of the room, space for a vanity and full-length mirror on another, and a wall specifically for shoes and nothing else. I draw a cushy seating area in the center of the room along with a huge display case for jewelry and accessories. It takes a few pages for me to show everything I want in the room clearly, and I hand it to Audun to see if he thinks it's possible.

He spends a long time looking at the drawing before looking around the room like he's trying to envision it. A slow smile spreads across his face as he nods, filling me with excitement.

"Mal!" he calls.

Not a second later, my brooding mate appears in the door frame with a frown. Reule and Caelan walk up behind him as Audun shoves the sketchbook at Maalik, chattering away while he gestures animatedly around the room.

Maalik squints his eyes at the drawing for several moments before he gives me a puzzled look. He asks a question and makes a motion like he's sleeping. I wave him off. I figure I'll take turns sleeping in each of their beds every night, so it's not really necessary to have my own separate bedroom. A luxury walk-in closet this size is a fucking dream. If I ever decide I need some space from the guys, I'll come in here or make one of them sleep on the couch. I've also been eyeballing that loft in the living room. It doesn't look like it's being used for anything, and I could totally turn it into a little napping area. It would be the perfect space to curl up with a book, but I'm sure it'll be several years before I can enjoy reading a book in their language.

The barest hint of a smile appears on Maalik's face, and he points at the sewing machine I drew.

I grin and rush over to one of the crates I remember seeing filled with bolts of fabric. For years, I secretly dreamed of becoming a fashion designer. Realistically, I never thought it would happen. But with this new life I've been given, I figure I can maybe still chase those dreams. Even if it means just making my own clothes.

Sighing happily, I pull the top bolt of fabric partially from the crate. It's a gorgeous emerald green color, and the texture reminds me of chiffon, except so much lighter and more luxurious. I rub my cheek gently against the fabric, imagining all the garments I could create with this. I'm pretty good at sewing, and I have all the time in the world to get better now.

The guys are still watching me, and Maalik is definitely smiling for real. Probably because I'm making a fool of myself, but I can't help but hope I'll eventually win him over. I make a motion like I'm sewing with a needle and thread, pointing at the sketchbook in his hands. I'm worried he still doesn't get what I'm saying, and I'm thinking of how I can draw the sewing machine to make it more obvious.

But then he leaves the room, taking the sketchbook with him. I furrow my eyebrows in confusion, ready to demand he come back and attempt to have a damn conversation with me. The other guys are all trying their best.

I almost feel bad when he returns carrying a small tool-box. Caelan, Audun, and Reule talk amongst themselves, but Maalik is entirely focused as he pulls out a measuring tape and shoves a few crates aside so he can measure the length of the wall.

Feeling shy but happy, I approach him and watch as he scribbles down the first measurements on a new page in the sketchbook. I bite my lip and smile, reaching out to touch the back of his freckled hand.

He goes still and stares at my hand. He makes the slightest rumbling sound like he's trying super hard not to purr, and I can't decide if it's adorable or just infuriating. Either way, at least it's a step in the right direction.

"Isla," he says quietly, and I meet his beautiful cerulean eyes. He doesn't look away from me when he speaks. "Jsi moje žena a udělám cokoliv, abys byl šťastná."

God, I wish I knew what he was saying. I'm swooning at the sound of his voice and the expression in his eyes, but he could be insulting me for all I know.

It's definitely time for me to start learning this language.

CHAPTER EIGHTEEN
ISLA

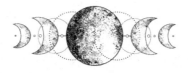

I WAKE UP SNUGGLED BETWEEN TWO HARD, MUSCULAR BODIES.

This time, I don't freak out. I smile and cuddle closer to them, a satisfied smile forming on my lips. I don't bother opening my eyes, even when Reule chuckles and one of them brushes my hair back from my face.

Caelan made good on his promise to me last night. The moment we finished dinner, he threw me over his shoulder, snarled at the other guys, and carried me to his room for the rest of the night. Seeing him get so worked up and territorial was super funny, but also incredibly hot. He spent hours eating me out, fucking me, and pleasuring me in plenty of other creative ways, proving that our chemistry the night before wasn't only because of the full moons.

Eventually, Reule whined outside Caelan's bedroom enough that Caelan asked if I was fine with him joining us. Obviously, I was more than fine with it.

Despite staying up more than half the night, I feel more rested than I have in years. Then again, it could be the middle of the afternoon for all I know. Caelan and Reule murmur quietly to each other while I debate to get up or not. Their voices are so soothing, and they're both being so affectionate.

One of them runs their fingers up and down my arm while the other nuzzles the top of my head every few moments.

I start to drift off to sleep again when I hear a loud banging sound, and my eyes snap open.

"What's that?" I groan, rubbing my eyes.

Tilting my head up to give me a kiss, Caelan growls against my lips. "Mal."

I sit up in the bed with a sigh, taking a moment to appreciate the yummy, shirtless goodness on either side of me. Caelan sits back with his arms behind his head, a roguish grin on his face while he watches me ogle them.

Reule just stares at me like he's in awe. Like he can't believe he's lucky enough to be with me. Maybe I'm projecting a little, because I've always dreamed of having a boyfriend look at me like that.

After stretching my arms above my head, I grudgingly leave the warmth of the bed and grab the first shirt I find on the ground. The dress I was wearing yesterday is gorgeous, but it takes way too long to put on. I slip the shirt over my head, not bothering with underwear, and leave Caelan's room to go to the bathroom before searching out my other two mates.

When I walk into the living room a few minutes later, Caelan's already making something to eat in the kitchen while Reule and Audun sit at the dining room table together. Audun's intensely focused on a sketchpad, his eyebrows furrowed adorably while he draws.

He doesn't even notice me walk into the room. Not until I stand beside him to see what he's working on.

"Isla!" He startles, gasping my name as a joyful smile lights up his face.

Audun pulls me into his lap, hugging me around my waist and kissing my cheek. It makes me giggle like a fucking schoolgirl. Honestly, a small part of me was nervous he might be angry or jealous I left him out by only spending the night with Caelan and Reule.

I lean against him, fully enjoying the affection he's showing me. I nearly forget about his drawing until he taps the page, bringing my attention to it again.

It's a detailed drawing of a ballroom with several couples dancing. It looks like something out of a historical romance movie, and I raise my eyebrows curiously. Audun flips back a page in the sketchbook and shows me another drawing. This one depicts a large dais with four people sitting on thrones. I jerk back when I recognize it as the first place I was taken after Amias bought me and Sadie. Standing off to the side of the thrones, Audun has drawn four men and one woman, all dressed elegantly.

"Is that us?" I ask, pointing at the five standing figures.

He points at Reule in the seat next to us and gestures toward Caelan in the kitchen as he mumbles, "Ano."

Reule scoots closer, giving me a soft smile. He taps his finger against the drawing while he rambles on in his language. Caelan walks over and interrupts him, grinning at me as he gestures at his body and pretends to twirl and curtsy with a skirt.

It's not that hard to guess what they're saying, even if I don't understand all the specifics. That throne room is a real place I've already seen, and they're making it seem like we have to attend some sort of ball or event there. Since they're famous here, and people were so excited to meet and celebrate their new mate, it makes sense there needs to be some sort of official ceremony for the whole thing.

That could be fun. Usually I wouldn't be one for parties or being the center of attention, but I had a blast with Audun and Caelan in the village yesterday. I think part of it is the security and safety I feel with them. Like, I can do anything, and they'll be there to protect me if something goes wrong. The language barrier also helps, as much as it sucks not being able to talk to my guys. I don't have to worry about saying something embarrassing. No one will know the difference.

At the same time, it makes me anxious to think of going back there. I'll most likely have to see Amias again, and the military dude who ordered to have me thrown in a cage and sent here. I might even have to see all the other girls who were brought here. I should probably feel bad, but I haven't spared those girls a thought since I last saw them.

"Isla?" Reule asks, leaning down to kiss the top of my head. He crouches to meet my eyes and tilts his head, his eyes full of concern. It's obvious he's asking me what's wrong.

Grimacing, I point to myself and the thrones in Audun's drawing. "I was there."

Reule's eyes darken, and he glances down at the drawing. He looks nearly as angry as he did when he tore the door off my cage and threatened the monk guy who drove the sled here. I'm positive Reule knows what I'm telling him, and he knows the people responsible for bringing me here.

I don't blame him, and I don't blame the other guys. But I absolutely blame Amias, that military guy, and every other person who let this happen to me. If I ever see that military guy again, I'm going to punch him in his smug face.

The guys talk around me, and I turn in Audun's lap so I'm straddling him. I don't give a shit that I'm not wearing panties. I just wanna be held and comforted. I throw my arms over his shoulders and bury my face in his neck. When he hugs me tightly and his chest reverberates from his soft purring, I sigh happily.

When Caelan sets two plates of breakfast in front of Audun, I move to turn around. Audun grabs my hips to keep me still, and I look at him curiously. He bites his lip, his curls falling slightly into his eyes, and *god*, he's adorable.

He brings a piece of toast to my lips. I debate not taking a bite. I never thought I'd be the kind of girl to let a guy feed her, and part of me wants to cringe away from Audun. But I know he's trying to be sweet. Reule tried to feed me when I first showed up here too, and I wouldn't let him. I wonder if it's a cultural thing. Like, maybe it's special or important for them to feed their mate. How would I know?

I also figure there aren't a ton of ways I can connect with these guys without being able to talk to them. Our relationship is going to be mostly physical for a while, and I should accept any and all affection they want to show me.

Hesitantly taking a bite of the toast, I relax in Audun's arms. He grins and purrs louder when I do, so I think I made the right call. It seriously makes me so happy to make them happy. So far, the pros totally outweigh the cons when it comes to this mate bond.

After breakfast, Reule directs me to go shower, and he swats my butt playfully when I pass him to go down the hallway.

I had no idea what to expect yesterday when I left the house with Audun and Caelan, and I'm even more excited to see what we're doing today. I try to shower quickly, even though normally I'd prefer to spend at least an hour pampering myself. Before I leave the bathroom, I use the lotion Reule gave me on my first night here. I seriously freaking wish I had a hair dryer, or something similar. My hair dries fairly quickly if I towel-dry it next to a fireplace, but it comes out so wavy that way.

Caelan pulls me into his room when I leave the shower, and he gestures for me to choose an outfit from the clothes I acquired yesterday. He seems a little sad, which throws me off. He definitely wasn't like that when I woke up, or even during breakfast.

Since I can't ask him what's wrong, I try to act cute and flirty while I get dressed, and I give him lots of kisses. I have a pretty hard time choosing something to wear. The clothes they bought for me are gorgeous and high-quality. All my outfits consist of skirts or dresses, and after shopping yesterday, I'm fairly certain girls here don't wear pants. It's a little weird to wrap my head around small details about this world like that, but I've always preferred skirts and dresses, anyway.

I decide on a long-sleeved tea-length black dress with intricate red flowers embroidered into the material. It fits my body like a glove, so it almost doesn't matter that it has a high neckline or that my body is covered. Paired with some knitted black tights and thigh-high heeled boots I found stashed in my treasure room yesterday, I look sinfully sexy.

If I had some red lipstick and eyeliner, this look would fucking kill.

After I'm dressed, Caelan helps me pick out a scarf, coat, and some gloves. So, wherever I'm going, I'll definitely be out in the cold for a while. I assume we're going somewhere I can find a gown for the event they were hinting at in the kitchen, and they probably didn't sell anything quite suitable enough in the village we visited yesterday.

Audun and Reule are dressed and waiting by the front door by the time I finish drying my hair and getting myself put together. Audun's wearing his goofy hat again, which almost makes me giggle.

They look excited and call me *krásná* when they see me, which I'm pretty sure means beautiful. Or at least something close. They call me that almost as much as they refer to me by name. When I catch the gloomy expression on Caelan's face, I do a double take and realize he's not dressed warmly enough to go outside like the rest of us.

"You're not going with us?" I step closer to him, pouting up at him.

He strokes my hair and smiles, leaning down to give me a sweet kiss. As sad as he looks, he motions to himself and the house, repeating the word *zůstanu* multiple times. It makes me sad to leave him, but at least we spent a lot of time together yesterday and last night. I'm still excited to spend the day with Audun and Reule.

I'm dying to see Mal too. I wonder what he's doing outside

that made such a loud noise earlier, and I wonder if he's coming with us today. I force myself not to ask after him. He's shown so little interest in me, and I don't want the guys to know how much it hurts my feelings or how desperately I want Maalik to love me.

Caelan gives me another long, lingering kiss, and I walk outside with Audun and Reule. It's a bright, sunny day, and the snow covering the ground is still white and glimmering. I'd like to think I'm getting better at walking in the snow, but I'm still pretty clumsy. Reule chuckles under his breath and grabs my hand as he leads me around to the side of the cabin.

For obvious reasons, I haven't explored the outside of the property nearly as much as the inside. I look around with interest as I walk with the guys to the back of the house. There's a fairly large shed back here, situated right up against the tree line of the forest surrounding the house. There's a lot of noise coming from the shed, like someone is using a buzzsaw.

I bite my lip when I realize the guys brought me out here to see Maalik. I want to see him, but I don't know how to deal when he turns away from me dismissively. I know he finds me attractive, but he hasn't shown me any affection since the night of the full moons, and he hasn't attempted to have a conversation with me the way the others have.

Audun cups his hands around his mouth and calls Maalik's name. The sound from the shed cuts off, and Maalik steps outside.

He does *not* look like he's in the middle of the fucking mountains in wintertime, that's for sure. His sleeves are rolled up on his muscular forearms, and his hair is tousled while a light sheen of sweat glistens against his forehead. As I let my eyes travel over his body, I wonder what he's working on out here. I can easily recall the roughness of his calloused hands on my skin, and I shiver lustfully.

Reule wraps his arm around my shoulders and rubs my arm, probably assuming I'm shivering from the cold.

Maalik approaches us, wiping the back of his hand over his brow. His cheeks redden the moment his eyes meet mine, and he quickly glances away. For a few minutes, he speaks with Audun and Reule. Their tones are friendly, but Maalik's eyebrows furrow like he's frustrated or worried about something. Since I can't understand them, and it drives me crazy to imagine what they might be talking about, I let my mind wander to the point where I practically zone out.

When Reule steps away from me without warning, I startle and turn to look at him in confusion. He gives me a feral grin and strides several paces away before shifting into his chimera beast. His fur, scales, and wings look so pretty against the snow with the sunlight reflecting off him. I desperately want to draw him, though I know I won't be able to do the drawing justice.

Audun pushes me toward Reule gently, so I know we're getting ready to leave. I'm excited to fly somewhere again, but I can't help cringing at how cold I was last time. I dig my feet into the ground to stop Audun and shake my head, gesturing that I'm cold while shivering exaggeratedly.

He frowns and cocks his head, so I point at the house and mime wrapping myself in a blanket. Eventually he grins, kisses the top of my head, and runs around to the front of the house. I hope he understands what I was saying. If not, I'll just go in and get some blankets myself when he comes back.

After Audun leaves, Reule flops onto the ground so he's lying on his side. I giggle and stumble over to him. He's purring so loud the ground is shaking slightly. When I reach him, I stroke the soft fur of his chest and move to scratch his belly. He's so gigantic, it probably doesn't feel like more than a tickle to him.

Still, he rolls so he's more on his back, and I giggle wildly while I try to scratch more of his belly and sides. Even though he's being adorable right now, I can totally understand why the people in the village we visited yesterday might be scared of them. There's no question that their teeth, claws, size, and even their horns and tails can be deadly.

I turn my head and find Maalik standing a couple feet away from me. He's watching me, an intense yet unreadable expression in his eyes. I give him an awkward smile, and he steps closer until he's right in front of me.

Almost like he's enchanted, he reaches his hand up and brushes my hair back from my face. When he speaks to me, his voice comes out deep and growly. "Jsi krásná a milá. Nezasloužíme si tě."

Krásná is the only word he says that I'm somewhat familiar with. Even if the rest of his words weren't a compliment, I still feel myself flush with happiness.

I bite my lip enticingly and give him my best bedroom eyes as I reach my hand out to stroke against his muscular chest. "You're very krásná too, you know."

Maalik's eyes widen and his cheeks turn an impossibly-bright red, practically matching the shade of his hair. Reule snorts loudly and moves to stand up. I shriek and giggle, shielding my face as he shakes the snow out of his fur.

"Isla?" Audun calls as he comes into view from the side of the house. He's carrying an entire stack of blankets, and I grin when he holds them up and asks me another question.

"Dokonalá !" I exclaim, remembering Amias using that word when dealing with Giovanni.

To my surprise and delight, Maalik helps Audun wrap me up in a couple of blankets before picking me up and effortlessly tossing me onto Reule's back. Audun climbs onto his back behind me, and he spends a few moments fussing and wrapping both of us in even more blankets. I relax back against Audun's chest and smile down at Maalik, feeling warm and toasty and like maybe there's hope for me and my burly, redheaded mate after all.

FLYING IS MUCH NICER THIS TIME. MY CHEEKS STILL STING from the cold, and my eyes are watery, but I feel much safer with Audun holding me tightly against his chest. I'm also way more comfortable with all the blankets. I'm able to sit up and look around, which is nice considering we're traveling much farther than we did yesterday.

This world is truly gorgeous. The mountains are breathtaking, and the snow-covered forests and towns below us look like something out of a fairytale. When the landscape starts to become more populated with lots of buildings built closer together, I feel Reule begin to slow down. I nearly gasp when I spot an honest-to-god castle.

Reule descends, heading straight toward the castle. I'm so awestruck that it takes my brain a second to catch up and realize this is where I was brought when I first arrived in this world. The guys warned me I'd be coming back here. I just didn't realize I'd been somewhere so beautiful. Knowing how fucked up the people ruling in this world are kind of diminishes the beauty, which is a real shame.

When we get closer to the ground, Audun tightens his hold on me. We're coming down right in the middle of a courtyard next to the castle, and I grin in wicked delight when I see people below us screaming and scrambling away in fear. Reule lets out a ferocious roar as he lands.

Audun, seemingly unaffected by the spectacle, kisses my cheek and jumps down from Reule's back. He holds his arms out for me with a bright smile on his face, and I jump down and let him catch me. He sets me down, giving me a sweet kiss, and Reule shifts from his beast form and walks over to kiss me too.

It's honestly pretty hilarious to see them being so sweet with me when they purposely tried to scare everyone else. Three monk-guys wearing those ugly brown robes rush over to us while Audun and Reule fuss over me and straighten my clothes.

I watch the robed men suspiciously as they bow low to us and mumble greetings. The guys don't acknowledge them until they're sure I'm comfortable and uninjured after the journey here. Audun looks up first, baring his teeth as he growls quietly. Fuck, that's super hot.

Reule addresses the men cooly, pointing to the pile of blankets at our feet. One of the monk-dudes scrambles and practically falls to his knees in an effort to pick the blankets up.

I'm more confused than ever, but fuck if I'm not swooning over how alpha my guys are acting.

When I give the monk-guys a better look, I realize one of them is Amias. The douche who bought me and Sadie from Giovanni's warehouse. He gives me a shaky smile when our eyes meet and bows again.

"Ahoj, Dáma Isla," he says respectfully.

I wait until he lifts his head again to sneer at him, and give him two middle fingers.

The other two monk-dudes look appalled, and I swear their eyes almost fall out of their skulls. Audun gets this very sexy, very feral grin on his face. A silent promise that he could tear them all apart if he wanted to.

Reule uses his supernatural speed to move behind Amias where he places his hand on the back of the man's neck. Amias makes a terrified, keening sound and tries to get away on instinct, but Reule holds him in place.

Audun and Reule snarl, and I force myself not to react. I'm certainly not going to act like I'm frightened, and I also don't want to let on that I have no idea what's going on. Reule meets my eyes and asks me a question, his pupils dilated so he looks more dangerous and terrifying than I've ever seen him.

To help me understand the question, Audun points at Amias and drags his fingers along his neck, miming slitting his throat. Are they asking if I want them to kill Amias for me?

Is it fucked up that I'm extremely flattered they would even consider doing that?

I raise my chin and look down my nose at Amias. Do I think he should be punished for bringing me here? Maybe. Then again, I know he did it on someone else's orders, and I'm not exactly pissed at the situation I've found myself in. I definitely got lucky. I could have been killed by Giovanni when I continued to piss him off, or I could have been bought by one of those disgusting business men and locked in a sex dungeon god-knows-where.

Still, that doesn't mean it's okay that I was bought and given as a fucking gift to my guys like a possession. My mates are wonderful, but the other people in charge here suck.

Sighing, I shake my head. Amias can go on living. I don't really care about the guy or anything that happens to him, if I'm honest. At least now he'll piss himself in fear every time he sees me, and that could be useful.

Reule lets go of Amias, and he drops to the ground like a sack of potatoes. Without another word to the monk-guys, Audun and Reule each take one of my hands and lead me away.

We don't go into the castle, which surprises me. They lead me the opposite way through the courtyard until we reach a tall, wrought-iron gate. Nobody approaches us or speaks to us, but the gate opens for us immediately.

Outside the gates of the palace, the streets are busy and packed with people. It's totally different from the village we were in yesterday, even though the streets are cobbled and some of the buildings look similar. There's an all-around different vibe, and most people don't even give us a second glance as we pass. The little bit of snow on the ground is all gray and slushy after being stepped on so much. That's what happens when it snows in New York too. I have to say, I already miss the idyllic cabin and the sweet, fairytale village down the mountain from where the guys live.

I'm glad we're only here for the day. I loved New York, but it's really all I ever knew. Where the guys live, isolated up in that cozy cabin in the mountains? It resonates with me in a way my hometown never did.

We stop outside of a building that's smaller and simpler than the others we've passed. It doesn't really look like someone's house, but there aren't any signs indicating it's a store either. While the building is unassuming, the door is large and intricate with a large, brass knocker in the shape of a leopard. Except it has horns too, so I guess it's the type of animal my mates shift into.

A man answers the door with an almost-annoyed expression. He looks like he's in his mid-twenties with short, white-blond hair, dark eyebrows, pretty grey eyes, and thick eyelashes. He's nearly as tall as Reule, and very thin. He looks exactly like the sort of guy Al would be interested in, and I feel a pang of loss and guilt at the reminder of my best friend.

The guy's expression doesn't change when Reule and Audun speak. I wonder if he recognizes them or not. His gaze flits over to me in irritation, and he shrugs his shoulders and sighs as he opens the door wide enough to let us in.

It's definitely a store. Unlike the shops we visited yesterday, there aren't racks of garments lining the walls or shelves set up throughout the store. I can tell immediately this place is high end and exclusive because it reminds me so much of the bridal shop I worked at with Madame Deverell. There are a few designer-esque gowns displayed along the wall as though they're pieces of art, a fancy seating area for clients and customers, and a door leading back to what's probably a storage area and dressing area.

The white-haired guy gestures for us to have a seat, rolling his eyes as he leaves to head to the back room. Audun and Reule take a seat right away, looking extremely uncomfortable. As old as they are, and as famous as they are, you'd think they've been in shops like these to get tuxes or whatever qualifies for fancy menswear here. I decide to walk around the shop and examine the gowns on display.

After taking a closer look at three gowns, I purse my lips. The designs are okay. Kind of stuffy. But the tailoring is killer, and the fabrics used are seriously to die for. If I can just guide this designer in the right direction, hopefully my dress will come out amazing.

Reule says something loud enough that I think he might be talking to me. I turn my head to find him and Audun watching me with amused smiles. Reule repeats himself, and the comment or question is definitely directed at me. Before we can start our usual game of charades to decipher what he's trying to tell me, the back door opens and the white-haired guy reappears with an older, elegant woman.

She's tall and thin with gorgeous ebony hair pulled back in a chignon. She's also wearing makeup! The first I've seen on anyone since coming to this world, and I seriously want to faint in relief. Granted, her eye makeup is way too heavy, but she's given me hope that I'll be able to get my hands on some eyeliner at the very least.

Her reaction to seeing Reule and Audun is much different than the reception from the other guy. She laughs like a schoolgirl, bowing low to them while she flutters her eyelashes and fusses over them. She's talking a mile a minute at them and hasn't even spared me a single glance.

Audun and Reule are back to looking uncomfortable. Reule smiles stiffly and says a few words while Audun points at me wordlessly. She glances at me over her shoulder, frowns, and turns away to keep talking with the guys.

I widen my eyes in disbelief and put a hand on my hip. I'm the fucking client here, technically. If she wants my business, she should be kissing my ass rather than theirs. Even if they're the ones paying for it. That was, like, the number one rule at Madame's shop. The bride-slash-client always comes first.

Reule growls low in his throat and walks over to me, gesturing at me while he says something in a slightly-harsh tone to the older woman. He introduces me as his žena and tells me her name is Bela. With a tight smile, Bela leads us to one of the gowns on the wall I already inspected. Once again, she gives all of her attention to my mates and not to me. First of all, the dress she's trying to sell them on is so not for me. And second, I'm getting really sick and tired of being ignored.

I wave my hand in her face and clear my throat loudly. When she turns to look at me in surprise, I stand up straight and raise my chin, gesturing to myself like the queen I fucking am. "*I* am the Královna Nestvůr." I point to the dress, making sure it's clear on my face that I don't like it. "And this dress is not happening. It looks like high fashion for the Amish."

She looks offended, but I don't really care. The guy who let us into the shop walks over to intervene. For the first time, he doesn't look bored. There's a wicked smile on his face when he looks at me, and he says something in a condescending tone to Bela.

Whatever he says to her, she doesn't look happy. But she sighs and turns away, heading back through the office door. As soon as she's gone, the white-haired guy grins at me and taps his chest. "Dushan."

I nod in acknowledgement and tell him my name in return. He's quick to understand that I don't know the language, so he mimes drawing something and points to the door Bela disappeared behind. "Něco nového."

It only takes her a few minutes to return, and she's much less pleasant this time. She sits on one of the fancy round settees and beckons for me to join her. Audun, Reule, and Dushan all stand over us and watch as she begins to sketch.

She obviously has some talent in design, and her drawing is good. But just like the gowns on display, it's all wrong for me. It's got a high neckline, long, puffy sleeves, and a fucking princess-style skirt. I nearly gag when I see her add ruffles. "Ne." I cut her off, shaking my head exasperatedly.

I stand up and run my hands down my sides, hoping she gets the hint that I'd like something form-fitting. I have an incredible body, and it's worth showing off. Especially for a big event like this where the guys get to introduce me as their forever-mate? I want to look hot!

Dushan chuckles under his breath and snatches the sketchbook out of Bela's hands. She squawks at him, but he ignores her. His eyebrows knit together in concentration while he draws, and a few minutes later, he hands the sketchbook to me.

"Ooh!" I gasp in delight. I love it! He's drawn a floorlength gown with long sleeves and a high neck as well, but the dress is form fitting all the way down to my thighs where the material flares out into an elegant, modern-day mermaid-style skirt with a train to flow behind me when I walk. The gown is also backless, which is stunning.

The only issue I have is with the sleeves. I point to the sleeves for Dushan and then show him my mate rune on my wrist. I don't want to ruin the look, but I want to show off the mark for this ceremony.

Dushan nods and rubs his chin. After a moment of quiet contemplation, he stands and takes my hand to lead me through to the back rooms. Audun and Reule snarl behind us, but Dushan only chuckles and motions for them to follow us.

We pass by an office, which I expected, and a large work room with several tables and a few sewing machines. The machines look a little older than what I'm used to, but it's still a relief to see they're relatively the same. The guys definitely knew what I was asking for when I drew one in my sketch of my dream walk-in closet.

When we walk through another door, I swear I nearly

scream. It's an entire room of fabrics, all organized by color, and they're all positively gorgeous.

I clutch my chest and make heart-eyes at the beauty surrounding me. "Is this heaven?"

The men laugh at my enthusiasm, and Dushan leads me to a section of lace and sheer fabrics. He points out a few that would work with the gown so I can keep the long sleeves and still show off my mate mark. I pick out three that I like and move across the room to the white fabrics.

The guys are basically my husbands now, right? I know this ceremony isn't necessarily a wedding, but when else am I going to get a chance to have my own custom designer wedding gown? Besides, due to whatever mystery heritage I got stuck with from my birth parents who abandoned me outside a fire station when I was two days old, white looks amazing against my skin tone.

CHAPTER NINETEEN
REULE

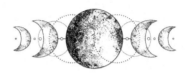

AUDUN FIDGETS AT MY SIDE WHILE WE WATCH ISLA GUSH OVER the fabrics in the back room of the dress shop. I know he feels as prickly as I do. At least it seems Isla's in good hands now that Bela's assistant has taken over.

I was about a half second away from taking Isla somewhere else before Dushan wrestled the sketchbook out of Bela's hands and took control. He was grating on my nerves when we first came in, but Isla seems to like him.

"How is she the most sought-after designer in Briya right now?" Audun whispers, leaning closer to me without taking his eyes off Isla.

Bela whips her head in our direction and frowns. I really don't care that she overheard him. I hold eye contact with her, letting my beast show in my eyes as I bare my teeth. She looks away, her entire frame trembling in fear.

Janak assured Mal and me this was *the* place to get a dress made for Isla. He said all the women of nobility fight over appointments and first say of this god-awful woman's designs. I've never been here before, but I was not impressed by any of the gowns on display.

Audun looked almost as relieved as I felt when we realized Isla wasn't impressed by them either.

If that weren't bad enough, the dressmaker, Bela, started kissing our asses the moment she saw us, reeking of insincerity, greed, and fear. The idiot woman barely glanced at Isla. Whoever set up this appointment must have informed her Isla doesn't speak our language, but that's absolutely no reason for her to be dismissive of our wife. If I know Isla at all after these past few days, she won't sit idly by and let people walk all over her. No matter what the situation is.

Dushan laughs at a gesture Isla makes, and I smile at the happy expression on her face. It amazes me that she can be so carefree after all she's been through. The language barrier doesn't seem to deter her when it comes to anything. She's so intelligent. She takes in every tiny detail around her and watches people's facial expressions and reactions in order to figure out the context of what she's missing verbally. She's also picked up so many small words and phrases in such a short time, and I noticed she started writing out a list of words in one of the drawing pads Audun gave her last night.

I have no doubt she'll be fluent in Briyan in no time.

"Guardians, sirs." Dushan clears his throat, bowing his head in respect to us for the first time since we walked in. "I need to measure Lady Isla, and the measurements will be most accurate if she undresses. I understand completely if this makes you uncomfortable, but I swear to be entirely professional."

Audun and I glance at one another. It makes me slightly uneasy to have anyone outside of our family see our wife in a state of undress, but the dressmaker's assistant hasn't given her any leering glances. Audun shrugs, and I sigh as I turn to glare sternly at Dushan.

"So long as Isla feels comfortable and allows it, we won't bite your head off."

He nods and spins around to grab a measuring tape off a

nearby table. When Isla sees it, she reaches her hands up to the back of her neck to begin unbuttoning her dress.

A snort of disbelief leaves my throat, and Audun smacks his forehead as he groans in dismay.

"I swear, she'll get undressed anywhere," Audun says forlornly. When he meets my questioning gaze, he grimaces. "She did this in literally every shop we took her to yesterday. Every time she sees a measuring tape, she just…"

He trails off, waving his hands wildly at Isla as she continues to struggle with her buttons. I laugh and step forward to help her.

Isla brushes her hair to the side and gives me a salacious little smile over her shoulder. I growl in approval and lean down to kiss her neck before I move to unbutton her dress.

"Maybe it's normal where she's from," I say to Audun.

Of the four of us, Audun still clings to the old-fashioned, conservative views that are the most typical in Briya. I don't think he really cares very much about her modesty, but seeing Isla undress in public clearly embarrasses him. I grin when Isla shimmies fully out of her dress, leaving her only in her undergarments and stockings. She's so beautiful.

The more I think about it though, the more convinced I am. Isla's never acted shy around me or my brothers. She was so forward from the very first night I spent with her. I assumed she'd been forced to wear that scrap of red fabric she showed up at our house in, but maybe I was wrong. Maybe that was what she was wearing before she ended up in that demon's clutches.

"Caelan said the same thing." Audun laughs, though he still seems slightly embarrassed.

Isla puts her hand on her hip and poses as she turns to wink and blow a kiss at Audun. He grins, and I bark out another laugh.

Dushan smiles as he walks over to take Isla's measurements. "Wherever she's from, they obviously have good taste there."

I hum noncommittally. We still haven't been able to figure out exactly which realm she's from. Every Elder Mal and I spoke with yesterday after we left King Janak feigned ignorance. We managed to get a couple of them to give us restricted texts and a few more maps, but I haven't had a chance to look through everything yet. Maalik was furious, and I was too worried about getting home to Isla to keep my mind focused on our task.

Coming back to the capital with Isla today has me kicking myself. I'm angry all over again, and I'm itching to storm out of here and confront Amias. Isla didn't recognize the other Elders, but she certainly recognized him. And she despises the man. When Mal and I briefly spoke to Elder Amias yesterday, he mentioned speaking directly to Isla's demon captor. Amias even said Isla punched him. Why didn't I stop to think about this before?

If Amias was there to take Isla from the demon holding her captive, he obviously knows what realm she's from. For the first time, I can't help wondering if he hurt her. Isla can't explicitly tell us what he did to her, but her reaction to seeing him this morning after knowing she's punched him? That doesn't bode well for the Head Elder.

"She's still *my* client, you know." Bela sniffs, snapping me back to the present. She glowers at Isla and Dushan while he continues to take her measurements. "You won't be making commission on this."

Dushan rolls his eyes. "Like I'm surprised. I do ninety-percent of your work, anyway. At least this time I'll actually enjoy myself."

Well, I don't like the sound of that. Anyone Isla seems to like is good in my books, and I don't want to pay this woman when she's not contributing anything.

Audun growls and bares his teeth, capturing everyone's

attention. "We'll pay Bela for the fabric Isla's chosen, and then we'll commission Dushan privately to design and make the gown."

I grin in approval. Audun rarely speaks up if Mal, Cael, or I are around. Outside of work, he rarely shows this dominant side of himself. It's nice to see Isla bringing it out in him.

"He is my assistant," Bela squawks. She's certainly not kissing our asses now. "I won't allow it!"

My brother and I share a look. He raises his eyebrows, and I shrug. I don't really want to look for a new dressmaker when we only have so much time with Isla before we're forced to go back to our duties as Guardians. But I will if we have to. Isla is apparently fairly high maintenance when it comes to clothing, and she deserves the best.

"Dushan, are you very attached to this job?" Audun asks.

The man in question raises an eyebrow curiously. Isla's standing beside him, still mostly undressed with her hands on her hips, looking sinfully delicious. She's watching the conversation between everyone with keen interest. I would give almost anything to be able to speak with her, and to know what's going through her head.

"Well, yes. But only because this is the only position I could find in this industry. It's not exactly a masculine profession, according to society."

Audun nods. "We're looking for someone to work with Isla exclusively to design and make all her clothes. Not just for special events, but for everyday wear too. As you can see, Isla is very passionate about her clothing. So, we want someone who understands that and who can work well with her despite the language barrier."

"Really?" Dushan's face lights up. He turns to grin at Isla. "I would be honored."

The owner of the shop continues to squawk and argue until we settle on a price to shut her up and sell us the fabric.

It's way too high an amount in my opinion, but it's not like we don't have the money to spare.

As Guardians, we're paid enough that we could live like royalty, which some of the Guardians in other kingdoms do. My brothers and I used to live more extravagantly when we were young, but now we prefer our solitude in the mountains and a simpler life all around. Our work is bloody, dirty, cold, and cruel more often than not, and it's nice to have a quiet and peaceful place to retreat to. Having Isla at home waiting for us to return will make coming home that much more wonderful and worthwhile.

While Audun settles our debt with the dress shop owner, I watch Isla and let my mind wander again. She's perfect for us. She makes it so easy to forget the injustice of her situation every time she smiles at me or my brothers, but I can't let myself forget. As much as I love her, as lucky as we are to have her, she shouldn't have been brought to our world.

Growling under my breath, I lean close to Audun. "Do you have things under control here?"

He meets my eyes, his gaze darkening as he nods. He knows what I'm thinking, and I'm glad he's taken charge of this situation so I can focus. I walk over to Isla and lean down to kiss her before quickly helping her back into her dress. I spend a few moments longer than necessary buttoning the dress, and then I stroke my hand over her soft, wavy hair.

"I'll be back soon, kitten. Be good for Audun." I know she doesn't know all the words I've said, but I'm determined to always try and speak to her as if she could.

She furrows her eyebrows, obviously picking up on my tone. I hate that I don't have a better way to explain things. I only hope she's not angry at me for abandoning her, even if it's only for a short time.

After kissing her one last time, I spin around and leave the shop to make my way back to the castle.

THE FIRST SERVANTS I FIND WHEN I RE-ENTER THE COURTYARD flinch and lower their eyes. I look them over quickly before dismissing them. They're only groundskeepers, so I highly doubt they'll know where I can find Elder Amias.

I walk through the courtyard with my head held high, for once not letting it bother me when people cower as I pass. I've always hated that the people of Briya see us as monsters, even while they love and respect us. Today, I could really not care less.

Before I make it to the doors leading into the Great Room of the castle, two young Elders approach me. They look barely old enough to have finished their schooling, and they're careful not to make direct eye contact with me.

"Guardian Reule," one of them addresses me, bowing his head. "Is there something we can help you with? We were under the impression you were here in the city with your mate for a shopping trip."

Clasping my hands behind my back as I take a typical military stance, letting authority exude from my person, I frown at the Elders. Letting a growl enter my voice, I say, "I'm looking for Elder Amias."

The other Elder, the one who hasn't spoken yet, looks up in surprise. He flinches when our gazes meet, but he nods quickly. "Yes, Guardian Reule. I'll bring him to you."

I tell him to meet me in the war room and head there to wait without another word. The only person here who has more authority than I do is King Janak, and even he can't intervene if I decide to take action against Amias for harming my wife. Not unless he wants to break laws that have been in place as long as Guardians have protected this world.

I pass a few servants and maids on my way, but the castle is fairly quiet today. I know it will be different in a few weeks when preparations for our ceremony begin. My brothers and I have waited longer than any Guardians before us to claim a wife, and it seems our entire realm wants to celebrate. The Royals and Guardians from several other kingdoms have already sent word they'll be attending the ceremony. Everyone is curious and excited, and probably relieved, to meet Isla.

The war room is empty when I reach it, but I wonder if Janak will bother to track me down here. I have no doubt he's already been told about the way Audun and I arrived in the city less than an hour ago.

There are maps covering the walls, pins stuck in the areas we have armies stationed in each realm. I've been to every one of these places, having spent years helping to eradicate these realms of their demon population. On the large table taking up most of the space in the room is a map of the realm we're currently working in. Briya and the kingdom of Želová have been working with the human government there to wipe out the dark creatures and magic nestled throughout their realm.

I've become numb to my job for the most part after almost a century. It used to bring me pleasure to kill demons, back when I was young and excited to live a new life away from my abusive family. I felt important. After a few years, I finally started to feel guilty. To feel like a monster.

These days, I mostly feel nothing. Demons are evil, and they deserve to be killed. It's that simple. Other creatures like vampyres and wytches are evil too, but we normally offer them the choice to leave these realms willingly. We only kill them if they refuse or if they harm innocents.

Looking over the map laid out on the table brings a sharp pain to my chest. I don't want to go back to work. I don't want to leave Isla, and I definitely never want her to know how much of a monster I truly am. If she knew how many creatures I've murdered in my lifetime, no matter how evil they may be, what would she think of me? Would she be relieved to know there are less demons in existence because of me and my brothers?

The door opens behind me, and I turn around to see Elder Amias step into the room. He bows and closes the door behind him. The scent of his fear is strong, and I notice his hands trembling even as he attempts to show a brave face.

"Guardian Reule." He walks further into the room hesitantly, pausing a few feet in front of me. "I didn't expect you back at the castle so soon. How can I help you?"

My lips curl back from my teeth as I look him over critically. His black eye is still healing from where Isla punched him. Why didn't I question him more thoroughly yesterday? I'm a moron for assuming his innocence in her situation.

I clasp my hands behind my back and stare him down, keeping my voice even despite my beast demanding I tear him to shreds. "Why did my wife react that way to seeing you, Amias?"

He meets my eyes for only a second, and he takes a shuddering breath as he struggles to find his words. An hour ago, Audun and I threatened to snap his neck for Isla's honor. And now I've called him here to speak with me in private. He should be scared.

"King Janak and I told you yesterday. She was very frightened when I took her from the demon's place."

His voice wavers, and I let a snarl escape my throat.

"Tell me again. Every detail." When he doesn't answer right away, I step closer and growl until he meets my eyes. "If you don't tell me what happened to my wife from the moment you first saw her to the moment she ended up on my doorstep, I'll kill you for harming her. It's well within my rights, as you know."

"I—I swear, Guardian Reule. I never touched her, never harmed her! I would never!"

"It's her word against yours, and her actions thus far have shown otherwise." Maybe he never physically hurt her, but he did something to make her react in anger at seeing him again. Was he the one who shoved her into that cage? My mind races with the possibilities of how that scenario might have played out.

He takes a terrified, gasping breath when I take another step closer, and words spill from his mouth.

"Five of us were sent to her realm, all to different cities. We've been watching the realm in secret, always checking to see if the threat from demons and darker creatures has grown out of control. Demons like the one selling Isla, well, it's not uncommon to find others like him selling magical creatures illegally. Wealthy humans in Isla's realm see them as trophies to own. Isla and another human girl were being sold alongside dozens of magical creatures. There were some there even I was unfamiliar with."

My eyes widen at this revelation. I've always considered all dark creatures bad where humans, mages, Elders, and Guardians are *good*. There's us, and there's them. To hear that a demon would sell his own kind is just...abysmal and mind-boggling. How did Isla get involved? How did she find herself there?

Amias continues. "I told the demon I was interested in buying a human girl, and he informed me he had two. He gave me very little information about them, just that Isla was brought to his facility by a vampyre, and the other girl was sold to him by a wytch after she was unable to pay a debt she owed. He warned me Isla was violent, that she'd killed one of his human guards in an attempt to escape. He also said she refused to eat, so his human guards held her down and forced the food down her throat."

"Humans?" I suck in a sharp breath. My chest feels tight, and my ears are ringing. *Humans* did that to Isla? To my beautiful, brave little kitten? The things she was forced to endure, not only by dark, evil creatures...but by her own kind?

I need to learn where she came from so I can go back there and kill every person and creature that dared to harm her. My original mission might have been finding her brother,

Alistair, but now I know I'll never rest until these disgusting people and creatures are nothing but dust and bones.

"Yes, Guardian Reule," Amias says sadly. "Lady Isla's home realm is corrupted. It's one of the few realms where demons and dark creatures are permitted to live among humans. They have governments in place to protect humans, to keep them safe. But their magic is dark and it leaks out, polluting the minds and souls of every living creature in the realm, regardless of their knowledge of the supernatural world."

Swallowing back a growl, I turn away so I have a moment to think before I hear any more. My poor, sweet Isla. I know it's wrong, but part of me feels glad she was taken from such a terrible realm. She'll be safe here, and she'll be happy with us. She'll never have to kill or fight to protect herself again. It breaks my heart to know she ever had to do such a thing. Killing so many creatures has made me feel like a monster in the past, and she never deserves to feel that way. I wish I could talk with her, hear her thoughts and know her feelings. I wish I could tell her how brave she is, how radiant she is, and how lucky we are to have her with us.

"What happened then?" I ask, keeping my back turned from him.

Amias swallows audibly. "He let her out of her cage at my request. The other human girl with her was crying, but Lady Isla argued with her demon captor. When she stood in front of me, head held high and fire in her eyes despite being wounded and covered in blood, I knew right away she would be the perfect mate for Briya's Guardians."

He sounds proud, but I'm riddled with guilt. "This other girl she was sold with. She's here in the castle?"

"Yes." When I finally turn around to face him once more, I'm glad to see he's still smart enough to keep his eyes lowered submissively. "Her name is Sadie. Lady Isla did not seem very fond of her, to be quite honest."

I snort, hating myself for smiling at a time like this. Isla is so feisty, so unafraid to be herself and show her feelings no matter what. I wonder what she was like before she came here. Did she have a job? What were her dreams for the future? The more I learn about her, the more questions I seem to have.

"Lady Isla hit me when I reached out to comfort her, and that's why the demon put shackles on her. I was afraid to touch her or remove them myself until I brought her and Sadie through the portal. Prince Ilari was already upset about the state the other girls were in when I arrived, but he was furious when he saw Isla. King Janak did not allow any of us to remove them, or to clean her up or tend her injuries. She was barely in the castle ten minutes before she was placed in the sleigh and sent to your home."

Janak already gave me and Mal his half-assed reason for letting things happen that way. While I can see his point of view, I'm still beyond angry. Mal is too. I've never seen my eldest brother this way. He's just as infatuated with Isla as the rest of us, but he's trying so hard to keep his distance out of guilt.

Even if we discover her home realm, she'll never be able to go back to her old life. Not without us. We've bound her to us for the rest of our immortal lives. She needs to be in close proximity to one of us at all times. Any prolonged separation will kill us all.

The Guardians of Briya before us died within weeks after their wife killed herself. The same thing would happen to us if Isla left this realm or if she were killed. So, I can fully understand Mal's guilt.

"What realm is she from?" I ask gruffly. She can't go back to her old life, but we can at least help her find closure. Help reunite her with Alistair.

"Please, Guardian Reule," Amias begs. "I'm not permitted to—"

I cut him off with a snarl and use my unnatural speed to bring myself face to face with him in a flash. He gasps in fear, and I pin him to the wall at his back by his throat.

"I didn't ask what you were or weren't permitted to do. I asked for the name of my wife's home realm. If you don't tell me, I have absolutely no qualms about killing you, Amias. Your status means nothing. You purchased my wife and treated her like an animal, preened about her qualities like she's a trophy to have won for your kingdom, and you refuse to admit to the injustice of it all."

His face turns an ugly shade of purple before he finally gives in, choking out the name of the realm on a gasping breath.

I'M ONLY MILDLY SATISFIED WHEN I LEAVE THE CASTLE grounds to go looking for Isla and Audun. Maalik will be glad to hear the information I've learned, and it gives us a better chance of figuring out our next step. I can't get over my guilt and self-loathing though. Not only for Isla's sake, but for being forced to prove I'm the monster everyone knows me to be.

Amias deserved punishment for his part in Isla's suffering, but it still doesn't bring me any pleasure to harm an Elder. They're supposed to be good. They're supposed to protect our kingdom and our people with their knowledge and light magic.

I head toward the main street of the city where most of the best shops are located. Audun wanted to take Isla to pick out paints after her dress appointment. When I get closer, I track them by their scent. I'm surprised to find Isla and Audun sitting outside a bustling café with Dushan.

Her eyes find mine before the others do, and she stands up with a bright smile on her face. "Reule!"

A grin takes over my face, and my heart feels as though it

might burst from happiness at seeing her. The mark on my wrist tingles pleasantly as I open my arms, and she runs to me and allows me to lift her up against my chest.

She kisses me, and I purr in elated surprise. My dark thoughts evaporate until I only have room to feel love and happiness at being able to call this woman my wife.

"You weren't gone nearly as long as I thought you'd be," Audun says when I set Isla down.

She grabs my hand and leads me to their table. Instead of taking the empty seat across from hers, I sit beside Audun and pull Isla into my lap. She relaxes against me as I wrap my arms around her waist and rest my chin on her shoulder.

"I got the information we were after," I say vaguely, glancing across the table at the dressmaker's assistant. Well, former assistant, I suppose. "What are you all doing? I thought you were going to look at paint."

"We will," Audun says. "Isla wanted to shop for some beauty products, and Dushan made some suggestions. We decided to stop for an early lunch while we discuss the details of his contract."

Before I can ask, Isla leans forward and reaches into a shopping bag near my feet. She pulls out a large, round light stone and babbles excitedly. I raise my eyebrows in confusion, doing my best to understand her.

"It's to dry her hair after bathing," Dushan chuckles. "Guardian Audun told me you're not very familiar with some of the more modern trends for women. I helped Lady Isla choose some makeup too."

I turn my head to take a closer look at my wife. I feel stupid for not noticing right away, but she has done something to her eyes to make her lashes longer and thicker. Her lips are a vibrant red color too, making them look even more inviting than usual.

"Very beautiful." I growl and brush my thumb over her bottom lip. She bites my finger playfully, her tongue darting out. My cock hardens, and I quickly look away from Isla before I do something insane like claim her right here on this table.

Audun snorts, and Dushan grins wickedly at me. He doesn't seem offended at our public display of affection. Maybe public affection isn't as frowned upon here as it used to be, but I know it's still a bit scandalous for us considering Isla has four husbands. Relationships like ours are not socially acceptable for anyone other than Guardians.

Isla's been very accepting of our relationship from the beginning, even before she met Audun, Caelan, and Maalik. Not for the first time, I wonder if this sort of relationship is normal in her realm.

A waitress walks out of the café and sets three steaming mugs of tea on our table. She bows politely and takes my order, promising to bring some baked goods out for Isla to sample. While it's cold outside, there are enough light stones floating above us to keep the seating area outside the café warm and toasty.

Dushan and Audun quickly catch me up. Dushan has an apartment here in the city where he'd like to continue living, and he agrees to make a trip up the mountain to see Isla once a month for work. He says he can send fabric samples and sketches between visits for Isla to approve or reject, and he'll take care to look over the materials we already have at home when he comes to deliver her ceremony gown in a few weeks.

The younger man seems completely taken with Isla, but not in a way that worries me. I feel relief at the idea of Isla making more connections here, of making friends. If she has other people besides my brothers and me in this realm to talk to, maybe she'll feel better about being here. Maybe she'll feel more at home.

The four of us talk and laugh amicably while we sip our tea and eat our treats. We teach Isla the Briyan words for things she points out, and I swear I melt over her endearing little accent.

I'm having a surprising amount of fun, and I'm distracted enough that I don't notice Prince Ilari approach us until he's standing right beside our table.

"Oh, Ilari! Hello." Audun greets the young prince first, flashing a genuine smile.

Prince Ilari smiles awkwardly, his eyes flickering back and forth between me, Audun, and Isla. She sits up and stares at him, obviously recognizing him. It's rare for me to see him out of uniform these days. He's wearing black trousers, a thick black coat, and a black hat and scarf.

"Good morning. I mean, afternoon." He says, appearing more flustered by the second. "I—I saw you sitting here and wanted to properly introduce myself to Lady Isla. And apologize as well."

I look down at Isla, waiting to see if she's going to flip Ilari off the way she did Amias. When she smiles instead and tells him hello, I feel equal parts relieved and angry. Amias may have painted a clearer picture of his first meeting with Isla for me, but I'm not convinced he didn't leave some details out. Ilari was there the night Isla was brought here too, and she clearly doesn't have any ill feelings toward him.

"This is Ilari," I say to Isla, gesturing to the prince.

"Ilari," she repeats his name, and he smiles nervously at her.

Even though his station is technically above ours as he's the heir to the throne of Briya, he bends down on one knee and takes Isla's hand in his, pressing his forehead to the backs of her fingers.

"Lady Isla, it's an honor and a pleasure to formally meet your acquaintance. I sincerely apologize for our first meeting, and I hope you eventually feel at home here in our kingdom." He lifts his head and smiles at her bashfully. "I, uh, I know she doesn't know the language yet, but I still thought…"

Isla giggles and pulls her hand away to pat the top of his head. I have no idea if she realizes he's royalty or not, but the action still makes me snort in amusement.

"I think she forgives you, Ilari. Trust me when I say you'd know if she was still angry." I shake my head, trying not to dwell on thoughts of Elder Amias. I gesture to Dushan to introduce him. "This is Dushan, Isla's new dressmaker. We were just discussing the upcoming ceremony to officially introduce Isla as our wife."

Ilari stands, brushing his hands off as he nods respectfully at Dushan. "Good to meet you, sir."

Dushan bites his lip, bows his head slightly, and looks up at Ilari through his eyelashes. "It's a pleasure to meet you as well, your Highness."

The prince's cheeks redden. I bite my tongue to keep myself from laughing, and Audun coughs into his elbow. No wonder Dushan and Isla get along so well. They apparently share the same skill set in flirtation.

Giggles burst from Isla's mouth, and she wiggles her eyebrows at Dushan when she catches his eye. His grin widens, and Ilari only looks more flustered now than when he first approached us.

"You're welcome to join us," Audun says to the prince.

Ilari looks at the empty chair beside Dushan longingly, clears his throat, and shakes his head. "No, thank you. I should get back to the castle. But I'm looking forward to seeing you all again in a few weeks."

He bids us farewell, and we watch as he walks away down the busy street. The moment he's out of sight, Isla grins like the cat who got the cream. She brings both her pointer fingers together in a lewd gesture, saying the men's names in a sing-song tone.

"Dushan? Ilari?" She wiggles her eyebrows suggestively while she does it, and I bark out a laugh. She made the same damned gesture when she asked me if Audun, Caelan, and Maalik were my lovers.

Audun widens his eyes in horror and clamps his hands over hers. "For Briya's sake, Isla. We're in *public!*"

That only makes me laugh harder, and I'm happy to see Dushan seems amused too. He grins at Isla and tells us, "I don't care if she never learns Briyan. I think I want to be her best friend."

CHAPTER TWENTY
ISLA

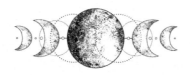

"Vstávej, kotě."

Someone brushes their fingers through my hair. Reule is the only one who calls me *kotě*, but I'm, like, ninety-nine percent sure I went to bed with Audun last night. I guess that really doesn't mean much. Reule and Caelan have snuck into bed with me every night the past week, no matter whose room I've decided to sleep in. I groan sleepily and grab the hand of whoever's touching me.

"Just come back to bed, Reule. It's cold, and I want to snuggle."

I reach behind me to pull Audun closer only to discover I'm in bed alone. My eyes pop open in surprise, and I sit up. It's still dark out, the only light coming from the embers burning in the fireplace. I have to blink several times before my eyes adjust, and I find Reule, Caelan, and Audun standing beside the bed.

"What are you guys doing?" I ask, my stomach twisting. I don't know why, but I have a horrible feeling.

Caelan steps forward and cups my face in his hands, leaning down to kiss me softly. He doesn't say a word. He just wraps the comforter around me and pulls me up, leading me out of the bedroom. I grip the blanket tighter and look between each of the guys frantically.

They never wake me up like this. Everyone is tense, and it's still fucking dark outside. Why are we awake at this hour, anyway? Did something bad happen? Caelan holds me close, and Reule and Audun keep darting glances at me over their shoulders until we make it to the living room.

The fire is brighter in here, and the lights in their weird lamps are on, so it's much easier to see. My eyes nearly bug out of my head when I realize the guys are dressed. And they're wearing fucking military uniforms. The same ones I saw in the photos Reule showed me days ago. It's also the same uniform Ilari and that older military guy were wearing when I first arrived in this realm.

"What's this?" I gesture angrily to Caelan's uniform. I've never hated this stupid language barrier more. "What the fuck is happening? Where's Maalik?"

My red-haired mate may be distant from me, but he's still the leader of this family. He'll help me understand what's happening even if I won't like it.

"Kotě, prosím." Reule whines, stepping close and pulling me into a tight hug.

Caelan and Audun surround me too, and the three of them kiss all over my face and the top of my head. Tears prick at the corner of my eyes. It doesn't feel like they're just being sweet. It feels like they're saying goodbye.

"Musíme jít do práce," Audun whispers.

I sniffle and meet his eyes. "I don't know what that means."

If they're leaving me, where is Maalik? He might not have wanted me to be his stupid mate, but I am. Before I can call out for him again, someone clears their throat. I turn my head to see Maalik standing a few feet away, holding a steaming mug of tea in his hands. He's fully dressed too, but just in his regular clothes. Not a uniform like the rest of my guys.

He grumbles something to the others, and Reule shakes his head solemnly. Mal sighs and sets the mug down on a side table beside the sofa, and he walks over to stand in front of me.

"Isla," he says gruffly. He rubs his hand through his hair, seeming to struggle with what to say next. He gestures between me and him, his eyes full of guilt. "Zůstaneme."

When he keeps gesturing between us, and pointing to the floor, my shoulders relax. He's staying with me, so at least I won't be alone. I take a shaky breath and turn to face my other mates. Caelan meets my eyes first, and he looks fucking miserable.

"When will you be back?" I ask pitifully, pointing at the clock they have hanging above the fireplace. I had no idea what it was until a couple days ago. It doesn't look like a clock, and I still have no clue how to read it. There are all these weird lines and constellations that may or may not be decorations, and I'm pretty sure it runs on some kind of magic. There aren't even any symbols that look like numbers. Audun and Reule spent a long time explaining its purpose to me when I asked about it.

Caelan flinches and shakes his head. From his reaction, I'm pretty sure he knows what I'm asking. He just doesn't want to answer.

"Tři dny," Audun whispers, holding up three fingers.

Three days!? I've been doing my best to learn their language all week, and I've probably been driving them crazy with the flashcards I made that I carry around the house with me constantly. I'm getting better with basics, and I thought I had numbers one through ten down. But there's no way I understood Audun correctly, right?

Audun furrows his eyebrows and rushes over to the kitchen table where I left my flash cards and notebooks. He flips through them for a moment and looks up at me again sadly. "Tři *day*? Tři day a Caelan se vrátí."

They've been trying to learn English too, which has been really sweet. It's getting both easier and more frustrating to talk to them every day I'm here. The more I learn about them and this place, the more questions I have. And the more I like them.

Audun's words catch up to my brain and I gasp. Does he mean only Caelan is coming back in three days!? "What? Ne!"

They spend a few more minutes pantomiming to help me understand that Audun, Caelan, and Reule are leaving, and Caelan will come back in three days. Three days after that, Audun will return, and then Reule. I'll always have one of them with me, but it will be almost two weeks before I have them all home again. By the time I fully understand, the sun is beginning to peek through the windows, and I'm about a second from bawling my eyes out.

I guess I should have expected them to go back to their regular everyday life at some point. They've spent the last week I've been in Briya here at home with me. Other than our trips to the village down the mountain and to the bigger city near the castle, we haven't left the cabin. I've been getting to know them, painting with Audun, learning their language, working on my closet, and fucking Audun, Reule, and Caelan damn near constantly. But I knew they were important in this realm. They must have jobs and other obligations aside from babying me.

But still. I didn't realize I'd be saying goodbye so soon, and for such a long time. What about the wedding-slash-mate-ceremony thing at the castle? Is that not happening? I figured Dushan was still working on my dress. Can't my guys wait to go back to work until after that, at least?

It's obvious they don't want to leave me either, and I force myself to keep my tears at bay. I don't want them to feel worse about it or make it harder for them. I kiss them all about a million times, hoping I can tell them without words how much I'll miss them.

All too soon, they pull away and shuffle out the front door. Maalik keeps his hand on my shoulder as we walk out behind them, but he stops me on the front porch when the others march into the front yard. They call goodbye to me again, but I stay silent as I watch them with watery eyes. It's taking everything in me not to break down. If Maalik's gentle hand wasn't touching my shoulder, keeping me grounded, I think I might actually collapse from the pain of having to say goodbye to my mates.

Caelan, Audun, and Reule shift, shake their gorgeous, silver feathers out, and leap swiftly into the air. I lose sight of them within seconds, and my heart shatters into a million pieces.

A sobbing gasp finally escapes my throat, and I feel myself falling. Maalik catches me against his broad chest and holds me up, shushing me and whispering words that sound comforting. I turn so I can lean against him, gripping his shirt between my fingers while I cry into his shoulder.

He strokes his hands through my hair and down my back, whispering the same words over and over again. When I manage to calm down enough to look up at him, still sniffling pitifully, he frowns and pulls away a bit.

Of all the guys, I'm the least comfortable with Mal. He's fucking beautiful, and I want to know him better. Every time I look at him, I can't help remembering the way his hands felt on me when we had sex during the three full moons. I know he cares about me to an extent. He's kind and polite, and he's been working almost nonstop to build my dream closet.

But he never seeks me out, never talks to me unless I approach him first or end up alone with him. He never sits next to me at dinner, never shows me affection, and he seems so uncomfortable whenever I try to talk to him.

I blink up at him, whimpering quietly when he pulls even further away. He grunts and turns away, walking back into the house. My throat closes up in shock as I stare after him. Before

I can break down again at the thought of him leaving me totally alone, he comes back with a steaming mug in his hands. The same one he had before that he set down in the living room.

He presses the mug into my hands and mumbles, "Pro tebe."

"Oh," I say stupidly. The mug is warm in my hands, and I bring it closer to my lips for a sip. I go still when the scent hits me, and I widen my eyes in momentary excitement. "Is this hot chocolate?"

One of the biggest disappointments I've experienced since ending up here in Briya is realizing they don't have coffee. The guys drink a lot of tea, which isn't necessarily bad. The food here is good too, and mostly familiar to me. But not having coffee has been a secret sore spot I've kept to myself.

Taking a sip of the drink in my hands, I literally moan out loud when I taste the hot chocolate. This almost makes up for the fact there's no coffee to be found in this realm.

Maalik's mouth twitches in a hesitant smile, and he wraps me more securely in the blankets I took from Audun's bed. It's still mostly dark outside, the sun just starting to peek over the tops of the trees. Mal leads me down to the first step of the porch, and we sit down together. He even puts his arm around me when I snuggle close to his side. I'd rather sit in his lap, but I don't want to freak him out too much.

Even though it's freezing outside, there's something nice and peaceful about sitting here like this with a fluffy blanket, hot chocolate, and my hunky red-headed mate. The slowly rising sun brings out Maalik's freckles and the fiery color of his hair, and I dart side glances at him as I sip my drink.

Did he volunteer to stay home with me first? Or is their weird, rotating schedule something out of their control? It drives me crazy that I still don't know anything. All I can do is guess at what's being said and happening around me. Until

I'm totally fluent in Briyan, I'm going to stay in the dark about so much.

Seeing the guys wearing military uniforms has only given me a million more questions, and my mind is racing. Are they going to war? What if they get hurt? What if they don't come back? They told me they're immortal, but that doesn't mean they can't be killed. What will happen to me if something happens to them?

I'm so caught up in my thoughts that I'm startled when Maalik stands up. The sun has fully risen in the sky, and I blink up at him in worry and confusion. Sitting with him distracted me for a little while, but not nearly enough.

He holds his hand out to me without a word, and I let him pull me up and back into the house. He looks nervous too, instead of just worried.

Clearing his throat, he points to the kitchen and the hallway leading into the bedrooms while he grunts something under his breath. It takes me a moment, since I'm still shocked from the others' departure, but I'm pretty sure he's asking if I want food or if I want to go back to bed.

Biting my lip and pulling my blankets tighter around me, I point down the hallway. "I think I just want to sleep a little longer."

Maalik nods and follows me to Audun's room. He walks over to stoke the fire and add a few new logs to get the room warm and toasty again. I make myself comfortable in the bed while I watch him, pushing the pillows closer together and straightening the blankets while keeping myself cocooned.

When the fire's successfully going again, Mal turns to me in the bed. I bite my lip and give him a shy smile, patting the spot next to me. I definitely want some quiet time to think, which is why I decided to come back to bed. But Maalik *is* quiet, and I won't pass up an opportunity to snuggle with him.

His pupils dilate and he stares at the spot I'm patting longingly. Before I can celebrate that I'm finally winning him over, he shakes his head and makes a pained grimace.

"Ne, nemůžu," he says. He rubs a hand over the back of his neck, not bothering to make eye contact with me. He points out the window, gesturing outside where he disappears to his workshop most days, and stumbles out of the room away from me as quickly as he can.

I sigh sadly, tears pricking at my eyes again. That settles it. Maalik definitely didn't choose to stay here with me like this. He was being sweet to me when the others first left, but now that I'm calm, he doesn't want to spend time with me at all if he can help it.

Pulling the blankets up over my head, I close my eyes and release a shaky breath. Maybe some more sleep will give me a clearer head and make me feel better.

A FEW HOURS LATER, I KICK MY BLANKETS OFF WITH A HUFF. I've been dozing on and off fitfully since Reule, Caelan, and Audun left.

This is the first time I've been alone since the day I was brought here on that sled. I mean, yeah, the guys give me privacy when I go to the bathroom or when I need a moment to myself. But one of them is always nearby, always watching over me, always distracting me.

I can hear Maalik outside periodically, so I know he's not far. So, I'm not technically alone. But it's still the longest amount of time I've truly had to myself.

And I don't like it at all.

I scrub my hands over my eyes and groan. It's too quiet, and I have way too much time to think right now. The past week, I've been trying to distract myself from my situation by throwing myself into my new life, getting to know the guys, finding small tasks to do like helping to clean or work on organizing the things in my new closet. I've barely let myself think about Alistair the past few days.

Thinking of him breaks my heart. I'm still determined to figure out what happened to him, and part of me still trusts the guys will help me too. It's just, where do I even start? How do I even begin to find him or figure out where I am? Until I can actually converse with these guys, I can't tell them specifics about myself, Al, my old life, or how I ended up here. I don't know what sort of magic or resources they have.

But how long will that take? Briyan is a complicated language. I'm lucky I've even picked up as much as I have so far. Realistically, it could be months or even years until I'm able to say all the things I need to say so the guys can help me. And Alistair's never gone more than a few weeks without getting himself into trouble.

If he doesn't have anyone looking after him, what's going to happen to him? I left him enough money that he should be fine financially for a while. But what if he gambles it all away? It wouldn't be the first time. What if he hires someone to help find me, and he ends up signing away his life—or worse—in a contract? What if Thaddeus is holding him captive or did something horrible to him like he did to me, just because Al wouldn't get back together with him?

Alistair's powers are getting stronger too, and I shudder to imagine what he might do by mistake out of anger and fear at losing me. How many innocent people might he accidentally kill? How many supernaturals will he piss off? I've protected him in the past to the best of my abilities, but who will help him now?

Horrible memories flash through my mind and threaten to swallow me up. Blood, screaming, dark alleys, the laughter of cruel men, rough hands, fire, death. All the things Alistair and I have been through together. It's never mattered that he constantly gets himself into trouble and frequently drags me into it. I would protect him from anything.

It feels silly to cling to the hope that Lord Rian and the witch, Matthieu, might take care of Al. But it's the only hope I have. If they really are Al's mates, they'll help him, right? Mate bonds are strong and sacred for any creature. And Lord Rian seemed so sure that night at his party.

He seemed pretty sure *I* could be his mate too. And look where I am now. It's too confusing and gut-wrenching to let myself think about that too hard, so I shove the idea away and swallow the lump in my throat.

There's a loud crash outside, and I tilt my face toward the window. It's not like I can see anything from here, but it's a good reminder that I'm not alone. Maalik, Reule, Audun, and Caelan are good men, and they've taken good care of me so far.

Lying here feeling sorry for myself, worrying about Alistair and my mates, isn't doing anyone any good. I need to just keep moving forward. Keep learning everything I can about my mates, this world, and their language. And is it really so bad if I enjoy myself in the process?

I decide to get up and shower so I can join Maalik outside. Maybe he doesn't want me for a mate, or maybe he's shy, for whatever reason. But we're not going to get closer unless I force him to endure my presence. Besides, I've realized way too quickly that being left alone is the last thing I want. I dress in multiple layers along with a scarf, hat, and gloves since I'm sure I'll be outside for a while.

Before I lace up my boots and leave the cabin, I decide to grab a quick snack. When I walk into the kitchen, I grin like an idiot when I see a plate of muffins sitting on the counter. I have no idea which of the guys made them. Caelan does nearly all the cooking, and it's possible he made these early this morning.

When I touch them, they're soft and still the tiniest bit warm. Which means they're fresh and they haven't been cooling for that long. Butterflies erupt in my stomach at the realization Maalik probably snuck back inside while I was sleeping and made them for me.

I snatch two of the muffins, shove my feet into my boots, and walk outside with renewed determination.

Despite the fresh snow on the ground, it's sunny and not as cold as I expected. Or maybe I'm just getting used to the climate up here. It's getting easier to walk in the snow too, and I only stumble once before I make it to the back of the cabin where the shed and Maalik's workshop is.

There are nervous butterflies in my stomach as I take a step into the outdoor workshop. Maalik is nowhere to be seen, and I can't help widening my eyes in awe. It's bigger than it looks on the outside, and there are so many tools organized neatly around the space. I bite my lip against a grin when I see hand-crafted shelves and drawers set off to the side.

I knew Maalik was working on building my closet, but I haven't seen anything he's made yet. Audun painted a mural of constellations on the ceiling to match the ones in their bedrooms at my request, and Caelan helped me paint the walls a dark, shimmery blue. With good lighting and white accents, it's going to be fucking gorgeous.

Setting the muffins down on the closest workbench, I step closer and carefully run my fingers over the shelves. They're so intricately detailed. I can't believe Maalik made these himself. For me.

"Isla?"

I jump at his voice and spin around to find Maalik standing in the doorway. His hair is messy and his sleeves are rolled up, and the butterflies I've had since coming out here multiply by about a million.

"Hey." I smile, tapping my fingers gently against one of the wooden shelves. "Did you make these for me?"

He walks closer, rubbing the back of his neck as his cheeks redden. He places his hand beside mine and glances at me sideways. "Líbí se ti to?"

Maalik looks so nervous, and this is so incredibly sweet. I think maybe I've been wrong all this time about his feelings for me. I thought he was against having me as a mate, but maybe he's just scared and inexperienced with relationships. The night of the full moons kind of made us all crazy, so I guess I can understand him not being as forward now as he was then. Especially when even then he tried so hard to keep control of himself.

I step closer so we're only a couple inches apart, and I watch in delight as his Adam's apple bobs. Before I can psych myself out or feel self-conscious, I stand up on my tip toes and brush my lips against his. Sparks shoot down my arms, making my mate runes tingle.

"Děkuji." I giggle, stepping away slightly.

His face is still red, but he looks pleased. There's the barest hint of a smile on his lips as he watches me walk to the other side of the room to grab the muffins I left on the table. I join him by the shelves again and offer him one.

We eat them together, never taking our eyes off each other. It's a strange sort of intimacy I've never experienced. The guys love feeding me. While it's totally not my favorite thing, I like making them happy. Maalik has the same pleased look on his face watching me eat that the others get when they feed me. I figure it must be a sort of pride thing for them. Providing and caring for their woman. Some of the customs in this realm seem old-fashioned, and I have to remind myself that the guys *are* old. Even if they don't look like it.

I brush my fingers off on my coat when I finish and grin at Mal. I don't know how to ask what he was working on before I came outside, but I point to myself and say the Briyan word for help. I've learned that one well enough after bugging the guys to let me help them with things around the house incessantly the past few days.

Maalik furrows his eyebrows and raises his hands to adjust my scarf. He growls under his breath and mumbles, "Je zima."

Cold. I silently high-five myself for remembering that one too without having to check my notebook. Maybe I'm getting the hang of this language thing quicker than I give myself credit for. Instead of answering or trying to explain that I don't want to be alone in the house, I stick my bottom lip out in a pout and give Maalik puppy-dog eyes.

He grunts again, but I can tell he's giving in. He turns to walk outside, looking over his shoulder to make sure I'm following him. I'm filled with nervous energy now that spending the day with him is actually happening. He's normally so quiet, reserved, and oftentimes seems grumpy. What's he going to be like after hanging out for a few hours?

All I really know about him is that he's the oldest of the guys, and he's their alpha, if they use titles like that. Like Reule and me, he didn't have a family, though I don't know any specific details about his childhood. I also know he's hard-working, and he's obviously good with his hands.

I trip in the snow behind him when I follow him into the dense forest surrounding the property. Maalik grunts when I stand up and grabs my hand, keeping me close and walking at a slower pace for my sake. I haven't been into the woods like this yet. And if we're following a path, well, I can't see it.

We stop when we reach a small clearing where there are two fallen trees and a large axe lying between them. I grin at the thought of Mal out here chopping down trees like a sexy, muscly lumberjack. Maalik gestures for me to sit on one of the tree stumps before picking up his axe and moving to a new tree. He seems a bit awkward at first, like having me watch him makes him nervous. But soon enough, he gets into a routine.

At first, it's kind of hot watching him. His muscles flex deliciously as he works. He's so strong that it takes hardly any time at all for the first tree to fall, and he moves the fallen tree effortlessly with his bare hands to line it up against the others he already cut before I came out here.

Eventually, I start to feel bored. I fight back a yawn and glance around the clearing, looking for any distraction. Maalik notices my fidgeting almost right away. Which is surprising, since I assumed he was focused entirely on his task. He asks me to stay put and rushes away back through the woods the way we came.

He's back in just a few minutes, and he hands me a cute little wicker basket. When I raise my eyebrows at him, he takes my hand and leads me a little way into the woods. He surprises me again by crouching and pointing out tiny blue berries growing on a bush. They're covered in frost, but Maalik picks them carefully and places them in the basket.

I pick a few too, and Maalik grunts like he's pleased with me. Before I can continue, he pulls me away and points out another bush. This one has bright red berries growing on it, and they're much easier to see in the snow. He shakes his head as he points to them and grumbles the word *špatný*.

I grin, giving him a thumbs up to let him know I understand not to pick those ones. I seriously adore him for giving me a task to do that will keep me occupied and out of his way without making me feel silly. It helps that he'll be nearby too, and I don't have to worry about getting lost in these woods. I know he'll come find me within seconds if I call for help.

Before he can disappear to go back to the clearing to chop down trees, I surprise him with another soft kiss on his lips. Maalik kisses me back this time, hesitantly wrapping his arms around my waist. His kisses are sweet and gentle, and *god*, I'm fucking melting. Way too soon, he pulls away, kissing my forehead as he lets his arms drop.

I watch him walk away and wait until I hear the *thunk* of his axe before going in search of more of the blue berries. I pop one in my mouth to taste it, but it's frozen and a bit tart. Still, I'm sure Caelan will be able to make something tasty with them. Hell, maybe even Mal will be able to. I'm still surprised by how delicious those muffins were.

Berry picking is fun and peaceful, and I find myself laughing quietly to myself as I search them out. Living in New York my whole life, I never thought I'd find myself doing something like this. Living this kind of life. Alistair would laugh his ass off if he could see me.

What would he think of my situation? I'm living in a secluded cabin in the mountains with four hot men who spoil me every chance they can, and I get to spend my free time drawing, painting, and picking berries. It's so provincial and so vastly different from my old life, but I can't deny how happy it makes me. If I had the chance to go back home, I'm not sure I'd want to. To see Al, yeah, of course. But to my old apartment and my job with Madame Deverell? I don't think so.

Alistair would hate it here. It's too quiet, and he's always loved the atmosphere of living in the city so much more than I ever did. If we found each other again, could I convince him to move here, anyway? He could have a cabin next to ours, and we'd be able to see each other every day. If he's with Rian and Matthieu like I hope he is, maybe he can bring them too.

A long time later, a twig snaps, jarring me from my daydreams and silly fantasies for the future. I look up, expecting to find Mal checking on me. Instead, there's a large, white animal standing a few yards in front of me.

I say animal in a vague sense because I have no idea what it is. It's the size of a fucking wolf, but it looks like a rabbit. Sort of. It's got fluffy white fur, four long, gangly legs, long, rabbit-like ears, a fluffy tail with a little poof at the end, and crazy long whiskers.

Remaining completely still and silent, I keep my eyes on it and hope it'll leave without a fuss. To my dismay, it takes a step closer to me, and I scream Maalik's name as loud as I can.

The animal doesn't go running off. Not even when Mal crashes into the woods behind me. The animal sits there stupidly, staring at me with its big, black eyes. I point it out to

Mal, which shouldn't even be necessary considering how big the damn thing is.

Maalik huffs out a laugh and grins at me like I'm ridiculous. He says something, probably explaining the animal won't hurt me. I smack him for laughing at me, but that only makes him smile wider.

The fluffy forest rabbit thing steps closer, looking clumsy on its four long legs. If Maalik thinks it's safe, then I have no doubt it is. But also, the thing clearly has shit survival instincts if it's not afraid of Mal. It has to smell that he's a predator, right?

When it gets close enough to touch, Maalik reaches out with zero hesitation to stroke the thing's ears. I do the same, and it doesn't look at us. It's much more interested in my nearly full basket of berries, and I squawk out a laugh when its fuzzy black tongue darts out to steal a few.

Maalik shoos it away with a warning snarl after it eats a few berries, and it gallops away into the forest.

Maybe I should feel embarrassed, but I don't. I just feel happy and lucky. I miss Alistair. I miss Reule, Audun, and Caelan too, and I hope they stay safe until they can come back home to me. But I'm glad for this time with Maalik. I'm glad for the warmth and love and security he and the other guys have provided for me.

"Je ti zima?" he asks, brushing the back of his hand over my cheek.

I grin at him and shake my head, stepping close enough that our noses touch when I tilt my face up. "You can warm me up, can't you?"

He might not understand exactly what I've said, but heat pools in my lower belly when his pupils dilate. This time, he doesn't wait for me to kiss him first. He brings his hand up to the back of my head and presses our lips together in a searing kiss. I gasp into his mouth and pull him closer, satisfied when his other arm wraps around my waist.

His hands and lips feel so good, and I seriously want to lick and kiss every single freckle on this man's body. I shiver at the thought of finally feeling him inside of me again, and I almost drop my basket of berries and lie down on the snow-covered ground right then and there. I'm so hot for him right now I'm not even sure I'd feel the cold.

Maalik pulls away, making me whine. He grumbles something about it being cold, and I roll my eyes at him. He snorts and gives me a lopsided grin. Like a gentleman, instead of the beast I really want right now, he takes my hand and leads me back through the woods. It takes longer than I thought it would to reach Maalik's workshop. I didn't realize I'd wandered so far.

"Jdi dovnitř." He points to the cabin.

Assuming he's telling me to go inside, since he's so worried about me being cold, I smile and beckon him to come with me. "Come with me, please? *Prosím?*"

He furrows his eyebrows and points to the workshop and the trees he chopped down that he's dragged here from the woods.

I'm suddenly filled with irrational anger. He'd seriously rather stay out here and work than come inside with me? He'd rather carve wood than *fuck me?* Seriously? Before I really think it through, I throw down my basket of berries, pick up a horribly-formed snowball, and launch it at his head.

The snowball hits him in the chest instead, and he stares down at his coat in shock. When his eyes snap up to meet mine, I squeal and turn to run away.

He catches me right away, of course. He asks me a question, laughing incredulously, so I know he's probably teasing me. As embarrassed as I am at my actions, I love seeing him this way. I wish he'd let his guard down more and just relax around me.

I playfully bite his hand to make him let go of me, and half-heartedly run a few feet away, picking up another handful of snow to toss at him. He barks out a laugh and watches me crouch in the snow to make another snowball.

To my delight, he follows my lead and bends down to make his own snowball. I screech in laughter when he throws it at me, even though I know he totally could have thrown it harder. Before I know it, we're both running around the yard, laughing and playing in the snow. Maalik lets me win our impromptu snowball fight. He could easily outrun me or hit me with dozens of snowballs, but he doesn't.

I can't remember a time I was able to just play or be so free and open with anyone other than Alistair.

When I stop for a break, shivering from the wet and cold while trying to catch my breath, Maalik picks me up to carry me inside. I don't fight him this time. He leaves me alone in the cabin for a minute, and I breathe a sigh of relief when he promptly returns with the basket of berries I left out in the snow.

The fire's nearly burned out in the fireplace, but I get it going again within a few minutes. When I turn to look at Maalik, I find him watching me with a warm smile.

"Come here," I purr flirtatiously, using my pointer finger to beckon him closer.

He growls quietly but follows my command, kneeling beside me in front of the fireplace. His eyes are a bit feral, and I can tell he's trying to hold himself back again. Keeping my eyes on his, I raise my hands to slowly unbutton his coat. He takes a shuddering breath and lets me take it off him, but he doesn't move to touch me. So, I unbutton my own coat and shrug it off of my shoulders.

"Isla," Maalik whispers my name like it's a prayer on his lips. He gulps and takes my hand between his, brushing his calloused fingers over my knuckles. He takes a deep breath and begins rambling. It's more than I've ever heard him speak at once, and I can't follow a single word. But I can read guilt in his tone.

It reminds me of Reule that first morning here, when I woke up in bed beside him and he rejected my advances. Is Maalik really afraid he's taking advantage of me? Is that why he's always so distant and hesitant?

"Shh." I press my fingers to his lips, cutting him off. I give him a bright, genuine smile, twining our fingers together and lifting our hands between us. I stroke my finger over his mate rune, feeling tingles on my own wrist when I do so. "We're mates now. I'm yours, and you're mine. No matter how we ended up together."

He stares at me for a long moment, and pulls my sleeve up enough to see the matching mate rune on my wrist. He kisses the mark, and a quiet moan escapes my lips. Who would have thought something so innocent could feel so good?

And just like that, his hands and lips are everywhere as he kisses me like his life depends on it. And I am so fucking here for it. I help him undress while shimmying out of my own clothes, feeling desperate and feverish every time his skin touches mine.

"Krásná," he groans. He kisses down my jaw and throat until he reaches my breasts, and I arch against him.

He takes his time with me, unlike our first night with the full moons when we were all so rushed and wild. He kisses every inch of my skin, leaving soft little love bites along the way and leaving me squirming with need. His beard is even fuller than Reule's, and the way it scratches at the insides of my thighs while he continues to tease and torture me with his worshipping mouth has me fucking panting.

"Please," I beg. I say it in English and Briyan over and over, curling my fingers roughly in his hair.

Maalik chuckles and finally lowers his mouth to my aching, wet pussy. Having him eat me out only ends up being more torturous. He licks me slowly and thoroughly like he has all the time in the world to savor me. I twist my fingers in his hair more desperately and thrust my hips to find more friction against my clit, but he just laughs and uses one of his hands to pin my hips down while he continues his slow ministrations.

My orgasm totally blindsides me, and I moan loudly as I cum and writhe underneath Mal. He growls in satisfaction and slides two fingers into my core, finger fucking me relentlessly while he sucks on my clit before I've even finished coming down from my first orgasm.

"Oh, god!" I cry, another orgasm racking through my body.

He does this several more times. Alternating between soft and slow, and then fast and rough, I lose track of how many times I cum. My body feels like jello, and he hasn't even fucked me yet. It takes a ton of willpower, but I manage to shove him away.

I push him onto his back and crawl on top of him, letting my legs fall open on either side of his hips. His hard cock brushes against my ass, and he grins up at me with a feral smile. As badly as I want to map out the constellation of freckles across his chest and stomach, he's left me too desperate to have him inside of me. I'll have to torture him another time.

We both groan as I sink down onto his cock. Maalik grips my hips, almost hard enough to leave bruises, and I ride him until I reach another blissful orgasm. Mal snarls and digs his nails into my skin, lifting me up and down onto his cock hard and fast until he cums inside of me.

I collapse onto his chest, and he holds me tightly while we catch our breath. It's almost too hot now, sitting beside the fire, but I'm way too exhausted to move further away.

Maalik turns so we're on our sides facing each other, and he kisses me softly. I can still taste myself on him, but I'm so sated and happy that I don't care.

"Miluji tě," he whispers.

He looks mortified the moment the words leave his mouth, which makes me grin. He must have said something pretty sappy and embarrassing to react that way. Instead of letting him pull away out of nervousness or guilt or something else ridiculous, I curl against him and hum in content.

There's a tiny white scar on his chest, and I lean forward to kiss it as I look up to meet his eyes. I'm so happy and relieved that he's finally opening up around me, and finally accepting the bond between us.

I give him a playful, sexy smile. "We have a lot to catch up on over the next few days together."

CHAPTER TWENTY-ONE
MAALIK

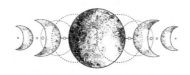

I HEAR CAELAN APPROACHING LONG BEFORE HE ENTERS THE house.

Dread curls in my stomach as I pull Isla closer to my chest and nuzzle against her soft hair. She hums and subconsciously rubs her cheek against me. Even in her sleep, she's so open and affectionate. It only proves what I've known since day one. My brothers and I don't deserve her.

The front door opens and closes quietly. My heart hammers so loudly in my chest that I almost don't hear Cael's footsteps through the cabin. I squeeze my eyes shut just before he enters my bedroom, praying for a few more moments alone with our wife. I know it makes me a hypocrite, but I'm not ready to leave her.

"Well, well," Caelan whispers with a chuckle. "Isn't this cozy?"

I sigh and open my eyes to give him a disgruntled look. He grins at me before focusing his gaze on Isla with a soft expression. If I'm this hesitant to leave her, I can only imagine how excited he is to see her again. I stare down at her, debating whether I should wake her or not.

"Seriously, Mal." Cael steps closer, sitting on the edge of

the bed. "This is great. We all hoped you would finally pull your head out of your ass when it comes to being with her."

Swallowing the lump in my throat, I force myself to pull away from Isla. "You were right."

I still feel some guilt for making Isla's place here permanent, but I can't deny how wonderful it's been to finally drop my guard and give in to my desires. I love being around her. I love seeing her reactions to everything, love showing and teaching her new things, love the attention she gives me and my brothers, and I love feeling useful and spoiling her. I love how just being around her makes me feel young and carefree again. Mostly, I just love *her*.

"Wake up, beautiful." Caelan reaches forward to brush his fingers over Isla's cheek.

Her nose twitches, and she blinks her eyes open sleepily as she mumbles something unintelligible. She sits up with a gasp when she realizes we're not alone. "Caelan?"

"Did you miss me?" he asks teasingly, a lovesick grin spreading across his face.

Isla launches herself into his lap, wrapping her arms and legs around him. She peppers his face with kisses, laughing and crying the whole time. We may not be able to understand the words she's saying, but her emotions are obvious. My heart swells with happiness for her and my brother as I witness their sweet reunion.

"God, I missed you." Caelan groans before he claims her mouth. When he pulls away, he laughs breathlessly. "I love you so much, Isla."

His words cause a sharp pain to form in my chest momentarily. I force myself to look away from them while I attempt to shove aside my feelings of jealousy. It's completely unfair of me. I slipped and told Isla I loved her multiple times these past few days, and I was already aware that Caelan and Reule felt that way about Isla. I have no idea if she's guessed what the words mean. She's intelligent and observant, so I wouldn't put it past her.

One of my greatest fears of having a wife is that she'll prefer my brothers over me. Isla's made it clear she likes me and takes our bond seriously, but I still worry she won't miss me as much as she's missed Caelan after I leave.

Deciding to give them some privacy, I move to stand up from the bed. I need to shower and get ready, anyway. I'm sure Janak is waiting for me. If I can throw myself into work and keep busy, maybe the time away from Isla will go by faster and easier.

"Maalik?" Isla grabs my arm, staring up at me with wide, panic-stricken eyes. It's awful of me, but her reaction brings me relief. As excited as she is to see Caelan again, she still doesn't want me to leave.

"I'll be back, love." The pet name slips out accidentally, and my face warms in embarrassment. If Isla could understand even a few of the things I've admitted to her in the heat of the moment, she'd probably tease me relentlessly. I'm sure Cael would tease me too if he wasn't so distracted.

Isla whines and grips my arm tighter, making me smile. "I promise I'm not leaving yet. I'm going to shower."

She lets me go hesitantly at the word *shower*, which I know she's familiar with. I kiss the top of her head and scurry to the bathroom quickly before I change my mind and crawl back into bed with her and Caelan. I haven't shared her in bed with my brothers since the night of the claiming, but I know Isla's open to it. Before they had to go back to their duties a few days ago, my brothers shared her bed together almost every night. I'm curious about what it will be like without the influence of the Beast's Moon.

Caelan says something to make Isla laugh, and I close myself into the bathroom with a forlorn sigh. It's going to be torture to leave her. To miss out on a single second I could be spending with her instead.

As much as it aggravates me to think it, Janak might have been right about the necessity of us having a wife. Never have I been so motivated to complete my duties quickly so I can come back home again.

That doesn't mean I'm okay with the way she was treated or brought here, and I'm not sure I'll ever stop feeling guilty for claiming her without giving her a true choice in the matter. I already planned on doing my best to remedy the situation and keep my promise to help Isla reunite with her family. After spending these past few days alone with her, I'm more determined than ever.

Reule learned the name of Isla's home realm by threatening Elder Amias several days ago. And I plan on confronting Janak today. If he won't take the necessary steps to send someone to find Isla's family, I'll demand I be given access to a portal so my brothers and I can find him ourselves. Whatever it takes.

Thinking through my plan and the conversation I expect to have with Janak helps me focus. When I come out of the shower, I hear Isla moaning from Caelan's bedroom. I lose my resolve for half a second and pause in the hallway before forcing myself to go to my room. Isla and Caelan deserve to have this moment to themselves after his absence. I just have to get through the next nine days and bring good news about Alistair home to Isla.

At least Cael took her to his bed instead of using mine. I'm not sure it really matters anymore, but I'm left with less distractions while I pull on my uniform.

By the time I finish and step back into the hallway, Isla and Caelan's love making has grown louder. My eyes glaze over lustfully, and I have to grit my teeth and force myself to walk to the kitchen. Part of me wants to leave now while they're distracted. I don't want to see the heartbroken expression on Isla's face when I walk away from her. It was hard enough watching her break down when the others left a few days ago. But I know my sweet Isla will be furious if I do that to her. It's better to suck it up and wait so I can give her a proper goodbye.

I consider making breakfast while I wait. But my stomach is too unsettled to eat, and I'm sure Caelan probably plans on making some elaborate meal for Isla. He's always loved to cook, and I know it's a big point of pride for him to take care of our wife that way.

To waste time, I pace around the kitchen and living room while tidying a few things. I light a fire so Cael won't have to worry about it for at least a few hours. I'm so focused on my task—and trying not to think about leaving Isla—that I don't hear Caelan walk into the room until he's right behind me.

"Thanks, brother." I spin around to find him smiling at me. He's out of his uniform now, only wearing a pair of sleeping pants. He looks happy and relaxed. More so than he's looked in decades. Between my brothers, he's been the most disheartened and burdened by the work our kingdom asks of us. Isla being here has already done so much good for him.

"You're welcome," I mumble. I'm not sure if he's thanking me for lighting the fire or for giving him privacy with Isla, but it doesn't matter. I glance over his shoulder with my eyebrows furrowed. "Where is she?"

"Just using the bathroom." He smooths a hand through his hair and grins wider. "Anything I should know about that I missed the past few days?"

I shrug, smiling despite myself as I think over the past three days. "We made some progress on her closet, and I showed her the woods around the house. She's been cleaning the cabin and picking berries while I work, and she's been studying her Briyan every night. Oh, and there's a moon rabbit hanging around the woods nearby. I tried to explain to Isla that it won't hurt her, but I don't think she likes it much."

Calean snickers and shakes his head. The clumsy animals are supposed to signify good luck in our kingdom, but I've always found them annoying. They're harmless enough, and predatory animals avoid them. Having one follow Isla around in the forest does make me feel more at ease about letting her go off on her own. Not that I would ever let anything happen to her, regardless.

Isla comes in while we're talking, and she walks straight into my arms with a pout. She stares up at me with her pretty amber eyes and whines. "Maalik, stay."

She's getting so much better at learning our language, and she has the most adorable accent. I lean down to give her a kiss, smiling sadly against her soft lips. When I pull away, I rest my forehead against hers and cup her face between my hands.

"I have to go, Isla. I'm so sorry." I close my eyes and take a deep breath, reminding myself of my goal to bring her good news. "You'll be safe here at home, and you'll have fun with Caelan."

Before I can step away from her, she stands on her tiptoes to kiss me again. I hug her close and whisper how much I'm going to miss her, and how I'll be thinking of her every moment I'm gone.

"The time will go by fast, Mal. You'll be back here in no time," Caelan says. He pulls Isla back against his chest and smiles warmly at me. "We can probably talk Janak into giving us some more time off together, especially with the ceremony happening soon."

He makes a good point, and I make a mental note to bring the subject up with Janak later today.

With a heavy heart and a hell of a lot of determination to do right by my wife and brothers, I leave Caelan and Isla at home and make my way to the castle.

SERVANTS AND ELDERS SCRAMBLE TO HIDE WHEN I FLY OVER the courtyard of the castle. I huff in annoyance even though their reaction this time is my fault. I may have scared them purposely when I landed in the courtyard last week when I came to confront Janak about Isla, but the people of Briya should know my brothers and I would never do anything to hurt them. We exist to protect them.

I land in Queen Zhanna's gardens like I usually do. There's a large platform hidden from public view here specifically made for us to arrive and depart in our beast forms. The gardens are on the opposite side of the castle from the throne room and Janak's offices, so it's a bit of a walk.

Every person I pass averts their eyes as they greet me. I keep my head held high to show my authority. Their fear doesn't bother me the way it does my brothers. I've been an outcast my whole life, even long before I became a Guardian. I was raised in an orphanage here in the city and joined the military before I was old enough to grow a beard. Nobody truly cared about me until I shifted into my Beast the first time.

Reule, Audun, and Caelan were the first people to ever fully accept me after we all became Guardians. They've always been my family. I may have considered Janak a friend before his scheming and meddling, but there will always be an imbalance of power between us.

Now that Isla is part of our small family, I intend to make her feel happy, comfortable, and secure for all of eternity. Hopefully someday she'll be fluent enough in Briyan for me to tell her just how much her acceptance of me and my brothers means to me.

I turn a corner and nearly bump into Prince Ilari. He grins when he recognizes me and says, "Good morning, Maalik. I was actually just on my way to the gardens to meet you."

Which means Janak is definitely waiting for me. I don't particularly want Ilari around when his father and I discuss Isla, but it's his right as the heir to the throne. Someday he'll be my king, and it's better for him to learn the intricacies of our kingdom and our work in other realms sooner rather than later.

We make small talk on our way to his father's office. He asks after Isla, admitting he ran into her with Audun and Reule when they brought her to the city for her first dress fitting. I like Ilari. He's always been a good kid, and he's growing into a good man.

Ilari stops talking mid-sentence and goes stiff beside me. I look up to see his twin sister turn into the hallway with two ladies-in-waiting behind her. I look at Ilari curiously and ask, "Is there a problem?"

He shakes his head and clears his throat, keeping his voice low. "One of the girls Ozara is training to be her lady-in-waiting came here with Isla. Most of the others were given jobs in the kitchen, so I don't see them as often. I know it's not their fault, but I feel uncomfortable around them. I just wish there was a way to send them home safely."

My eyes widen with interest, and I pay closer attention to the girls as they approach with Ozara. The princess smiles when she sees us, stopping in front of us with her hands clasped in front of her. "Good morning. Are you two off to see Father?"

"Yes, we are." I say politely. Ozara is wearing a dress, which is unusual for her. She's always been quite rebellious, dressing in boys' clothing and smarting off to her parents. I suspect she's trying to appease Janak since he finally agreed to take some of her militaristic ideas into consideration.

"Have you met Sadie?" Ozara gestures to the petite blonde behind her. "She was held captive by the same demon as Isla."

Sadie jolts in shock at hearing her name, meeting my eyes for a split second. She's rather plain-looking with straight, white-blonde hair and blue eyes, and she looks barely older than the prince and princess—still practically a child. I'm hit with the horrifying thought that Janak easily could have sent Sadie to us instead of Isla, or any of the other girls he 'rescued' for that matter. The thought of bonding with any other woman makes me sick.

What were the chances of Isla being captured by the same demon as Sadie and brought here by our Elders just before the Beast's Full Moon? And then chosen by Janak among several other girls? My thoughts are spinning with the idea that maybe Isla was meant to be with us all along. I quickly shake the idea off—it's nothing more than a coincidence, and I still owe it to Isla to find her family for her.

"I didn't realize Isla's situation was common knowledge," I say carefully. Ozara mentioned the demon so casually in front of her other lady-in-waiting, I can't help but be a bit surprised. I was sure Janak would want to keep the details of the girls' rescue from their realm a secret.

"Oh, yes." Ozara smiles wickedly. "Rumors have been spreading all over the city. People are even more excited to see their new Queen of Beasts after knowing she escaped the clutches of a filthy demon. The story of her killing demons with her shoe as a weapon even has women petitioning to join the military. Lady Isla is so inspiring."

My mouth twitches while I try not to smile. It's abundantly clear Ozara has been the one spreading the rumors and using them to her advantage. "Yes, it appears she is."

"Well, we really should be going," Ilari says with a tight smile.

"Of course." Ozara bows her head, a tiny smirk forming on her lips. Sadie and the other lady-in-waiting curtsy to us, and Ozara meets my gaze before they walk away. "I'm sure Sadie would love to talk to Isla if you or your brothers would like to bring her to visit. Otherwise, we'll see you at the ceremony in a few weeks."

The women take their leave, and Ilari grimaces at me as we begin making our way to Janak's office once more. "My father is livid with her. Everyone is talking about the dangers of Isla's home realm and the way she and the other girls were brought here."

It doesn't change anything for me, my brothers, or Isla, but it is amusing to realize the chaos Ozara has created. I'm sure my brothers will appreciate hearing about it.

We're quiet the rest of the way, and I try to gather my thoughts. Ozara and Sadie were a distraction, but right now I need to focus on what I'm going to say to Janak. Someone needs to go to her home realm to find Alistair. Everything else can wait, but that can't.

There are a few guards outside of Janak's office. That's not entirely unusual, but it still puts me on edge. Ilari shoots me a concerned glance when one of the guards holds the door open for us, and we walk in to find Janak speaking to two Elders in hushed tones.

They go quiet, and Janak meets my eyes with a fierce expression. Keeping my curiosity and apprehension at bay, I nod my head and greet him cordially. "King Janak."

"Hello, my friend." His voice doesn't give anything away. He dismisses the Elders, leaving Janak, Ilari, and me alone in private. Janak stares at us for a long moment before gesturing to the seats in front of his desk. "Have a seat. There's something I need to discuss with both of you."

I feel even more on edge, but I'm good at hiding my emotions. I take a seat beside Ilari, declining when Janak offers me a drink. Ilari declines too, rubbing his hands over his pants anxiously. It's easy to scent his nervousness and Janak's anger. I wait patiently to hear what Janak has to say.

My King and old friend paces before stopping in front of me. "Are you still determined to return to Isla's home realm to track down her supposed brother?"

Feeling prickly, I meet his gaze head on and barely hold back a growl. "Of course."

He turns his eyes to his son. "And are you still convinced

I'm wrong about dark creatures? That maybe they're not all so bad? That the girls we rescued from their demon captors might be better off if we send them back to that poisonous realm they used to call home?"

Ilari's face flushes, and I blink in shock. I had no idea he had such an opinion. The fact that all demons are evil, and that other dark creatures like wytches and vampyres are just as bad, has been ingrained in my mind since I was a boy. The entire reason for Guardians' existence is to track down demons in order to eliminate the threat they pose. Briya and the other kingdoms in our realm have been safe from such darkness for centuries, and now we work to bring salvation to other realms in need.

"Well, I think it's a matter of perspective," Ilari says cautiously. "I'm sure demons and dark creatures see us as the evil ones, right? What if we're both wrong?"

Janak looks disgusted at the sheer idea. "Please believe me when I say I feel absolutely no pleasure at proving you wrong."

"What does this have to do with finding Isla's brother?" I ask. While Ilari's certainly given me something to think about, I've never insinuated I believe demons to be good. All I want is to find Alistair and bring him here, and maybe some of Isla's old belongings, so she'll be happy and have her family with her as long as she can. I can't make him immortal, but it still might bring her some peace of mind for a few years.

"Everything," Janak says angrily. "I know I broke your trust by going behind your back to find you a mate, and I hated putting that distance between us. To prove I had every intention of making things right and attempting to remedy the situation, I sent Elder Amias back to confront the demon who sold Isla to him. I hoped he'd be able to bring back some information about where she came from so we could track down her brother and any other family."

I'm filled with a mixture of surprise and guilt. Honestly, I didn't expect Janak to keep his word. Maybe I should have trusted him more. Deep down, I know he had good intentions by forcing us to claim a wife, even if I don't agree with the way he did it.

"What happened?" I ask. Obviously, something went wrong.

Janak pulls a light stone out of his pocket and holds it up for us to see. "The Elders used their magic to capture a moment. Instead of a photograph, we're able to see an entire scene play out with sound as well as images. Elder Amias captured his last moments alive in Isla's home realm."

I lean forward, resting my elbows on my knees. Without another word, Janak waves the light stone in the air in front of us. A transparent screen appears, along with a scene that looks like a photograph. It quickly becomes evident we're watching the scene from Amias's perspective.

"Yes, of course I remember the girls you bought. I believe I still have their records if you want to follow me to my office," a man says. He's tall and broad with dark hair, and his face is covered in gruesome scars. I jerk back in my seat slightly when I realize he's a demon—the one who sold Isla to Amias.

Amias follows him through a dim hallway with low ceilings until he stops in front of a metal door. The demon pushes some buttons on the door before opening it, allowing Amias to enter in front of him. I can hear the Elder's shaky breaths, making his unease obvious.

Three men are waiting in the dingy room that looks more like a cell than an office. Amias goes still. "What—"

His words are cut off by the demon closing the door behind him, and he stares at the three men as he holds his hands up defensively. He says something to the strange men in a foreign language. Some of the words sound similar to Isla's, so I assume it's the language she speaks. When Amias begins breathing more heavily, the demon turns to him and speaks in Briyan.

"These are the mates of one of the girls you bought. It seems there was some sort of mistake, so hopefully we can work something out. I wouldn't have sold her if I'd known."

Mates? The word makes me jerk in my seat again. He can't possibly mean Isla, can he? And there's no way *mate* means the same thing in their realm, right?

The demon continues speaking, switching back over to the language that sounds like Isla's. Demons have the power to speak and understand any language, making it that much easier to deceive people. Two of the men speak back and forth with him, never taking their eyes off Amias. The third approaches the Elder with a feral look in his eyes.

He asks something in a low voice, pinning Amias to the wall. Amias lets out a muffled cry, and the demon looks up from his interrogation with the other two men. He says something to the man threatening Amias, appearing agitated.

"Where is Isla?" the man pinning Amias to the wall asks again. I watch with absolute shock and horror as his irises and the whites of his eyes turn black, grotesque horns emerge from the top of his head, and his nails transform into claws as the skin on his hands and forearms darkens. He's a demon too.

I've met plenty of demons in my life. They have the most terrible scent, and the sight of them always makes my beast feel tense. In my experience, only the most dangerous and powerful demons can drop their glamours as seamlessly as this one. I growl low in my throat, curling my hand into a fist while I watch the demon scum on the screen ask about my wife. Why would he be looking for her?

Amias mumbles prayers to himself instead of answering, and the demon makes a horrible sound somewhere between a hiss and an animalistic snarl. "What did you do with her? I know you took her, you sick fuck!"

"Careful, Alistair." One of the other men approaches, placing his hand on the demon's shoulder as he glares at Amias. He's tall and pale with fiery-red hair, and he speaks

Briyan with a thick accent. "Don't hurt him before he tells us what we want to hear."

Alistair? No. No, this can't be right. Alistair must be a common name in Isla's realm. There's no way *her* Alistair is a demon.

"If you've hurt Isla, I swear—"

The Alistair demon's threat is cut off by Amias's terrified voice. "Isla is safe from your evil. You'll never see her again!"

Amias lifts a light stone from his pocket and shoves it at the red-haired man. The man crumples to the ground in pain, proving he's not human either. Alistair shouts something in another language, fury lighting his demonic, black eyes. A horrifying scream tears from Amias's throat, and I watch his hand on screen disintegrate into ash. His scream cuts off abruptly, and the light stone is left floating in the air on its own.

"No!" Alistair blinks, his eyes appearing human once more. He stares at the floor in horror, shaking his head back and forth. He babbles wildly in their other language, and I curl my hands into fists as I desperately try to decipher his words.

The other man leaves the first demon and runs over, wrapping his arm around Alistair. He whispers something soothingly in the same language Isla uses, and then the scene before me disappears.

I stand up in outrage, speaking without thinking. "Is that it? Is that all he witnessed?"

"Unfortunately, yes." Janak sneers. "The magic our Elders used stopped working shortly after Amias was killed."

"Why would that demon be looking for Isla?" Ilari asks, reminding me of his presence.

Swallowing the lump in my throat, I rest my hands on top of my head and pace the small space of Janak's office. My thoughts are reeling, and I have no idea how to make sense of everything I just witnessed. Those creatures were looking for

Isla, and they seemed to care for her. The word *mate* was used too. None of it makes any sense at all.

"That demon scum who murdered our Head Elder, reducing him to nothing more than ash, is Isla's supposed brother. He's the one Maalik and Reule asked me to search for. I checked with my sources, and Alistair isn't a common name in their realm. Do you know what could have happened if we'd brought him here without realizing his true nature? Your mate is luckier than I ever realized. I'm no longer sorry for bringing her or those other girls here, no matter what you have to say about it, Maalik."

I look up and meet Janak's fuming gaze. I understand he's angry that he lost an Elder today, but we all know the risks of traveling to different realms and working with dark creatures. Amias will be known as a hero among his fellow Elders.

As for the potential risk of bringing Alistair to Briya? It's a lot for me to wrap my head around. How can I reconcile the fact that my wife considers a demon to be her family or her friend? How many dark creatures was she connected to in her old life? How am I going to explain everything to my brothers?

Most importantly, how am I going to face Isla after this? I wanted to bring her good news. What if she still insists on going home to find Alistair?

Unless I break my promise to her, I'll be forced to break the oath I made to my kingdom the day I became a Guardian.

ACKNOWLEDGMENTS

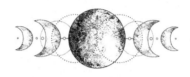

Wow. I can't believe I'm already writing another of these so soon! Of Moons and Monsters is my fourth published book, and my second of this year already. As much as I love my other books, this one is extra special to me.

I started working on Isla's story last April. I was still working at my old, miserable job then where I was considered an "essential employee" in the middle of the pandemic. I was constantly stressed, having panic attacks almost daily, and I couldn't focus on any of my other writing projects (which were only a hobby at that time). Something compelled me to set all of my other interests aside to work on *this* story instead, and Isla's world began to come to life. I can see my growth as a writer in this book more than anything else I've written so far, and this book also helps me remember that I can persevere and get through anything.

Of course, this book would still be nothing without the support of my closest family and friends.

Thank you to my husband, David. Even though you lost your shit and found it absolutely hilarious when you realized I named a fae character Rian. The teasing has been relentless.

Thank you to Kelly, always. I'm sad I can't just shout

down the hallway to inform you I have a new chapter written anymore, but you'll still always get the first peek at new Isla updates in the future.

Thank you, Taryn. My co-captain, best friend, and editor. For always making me a better writer and for loving Maalik so much. Not sure I'll ever be able to top Chapter 9 by your standards, but I promise to try! Also, I'm really sorry about Chapter 11, you little trooper.

Thank you to Savannah, for making my life so much easier and for being the best PA in the universe. My releases have been so much smoother and so much more successful since I hired you. Thank you to Verča, Bonnie, and Kika from the bottom of my heart for your help with the Czech translations in this book. And a special thank you to Seneca, Danielle, and Rachael for making me feel like I always have friends to reach out to about anything on a daily basis.

And most of all, thank you to my readers who continue to support me and show their love for my characters. You guys are one hundred percent the reason I'm able to keep writing and publishing.

ABOUT THE AUTHOR

Willow Hadley is a self-published author who primarily writes reverse harem romance. She lives in North Carolina with her husband, their doggo, and two demon-familiars (aka cats). She started writing in early 2018, and she joined the Wattpad Stars program in 2019. She loves character driven stories and fluffy books that give you a warm, fuzzy feeling. She's also obsessed with Disney movies, and her favorite candy is licorice.

Of Moons and Monsters is her fourth published book.

Join her reader's group to keep updated on new releases!

facebook.com/groups/willowhadleyreaders

f facebook.com/willowhadleybooks

o instagram.com/willowhadleybooks

g goodreads.com/willowee

p pinterest.com/xwillowee

ALSO BY WILLOW HADLEY

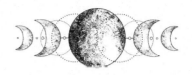

Cricket (Cricket Kendall #1)

Wildflower (Cricket Kendall #2)

Smile Like You Mean It (Charlotte Reynolds #1)

Of Dreams and Demons (Of Moons and Monsters #2)

RELEASE DATE TBD

Made in the USA
Columbia, SC
10 July 2021